D1121257

# THE VALANCOURT BOOK OF
# WORLD HORROR STORIES

## VOLUME TWO

*Edited by*
James D. Jenkins & Ryan Cagle

*featuring stories by*

Viola Cadruvi
Roberto Causo
Bora Chung
Dare Segun Falowo
Mélanie Fazi
Stephan Friedman
Ana María Fuster Lavín
Anton Grasso
Wojciech Gunia
Indrek Hargla
Konstantinos Kellis

Luciano Lamberti
Jayaprakash Satyamurthy
Steinar Bragi
Braulio Tavares
Yavor Tsanev
Yasumi Tsuhara
Gary Victor
Teddy Vork
Val Votrin
Zhang Yueran

VALANCOURT BOOKS
Richmond, Virginia
MMXXII

*The Valancourt Book of World Horror Stories, Volume Two*
First published February 2022

All stories copyright by their respective authors.
This compilation copyright © 2022 by Valancourt Books, LLC
All translations copyright © 2022 by their respective translators.
The Acknowledgments pages on pp. 11-12 constitute an extension of
this copyright page.

Published by Valancourt Books, Richmond, Virginia
http://www.valancourtbooks.com

ISBN 978-1-954321-06-9 (limited hardcover)
ISBN 978-1-954321-07-6 (trade paperback)

Also available as an electronic book.

Set in Bembo Book MT

This book was translated with financial support from:

 **ICELANDIC LITERATURE CENTER**

# CONTENTS

# Editors' Foreword

WHEN WE PUBLISHED THE FIRST VOLUME of *The Valan-court Book of World Horror Stories* in 2020, we opti-mistically subtitled it 'Volume One'. We say 'optimistically' because at the time we didn't know whether there would be a Volume Two. After all, for the previous fifteen years, Valancourt Books had published exclusively old British and American books. A volume of contemporary, foreign-language horror stories was something we had never done before – nor had anyone else, for that matter – and we didn't know how it would be received. In the end, the response was phenomenal, both from readers and reviewers. The book earned glowing reviews in *Publishers Weekly*, *Library Journal*, the *Washington Post* and elsewhere, received nominations for the World Fantasy Award and Shirley Jackson Award, and has already been adopted as a textbook at several American universities. Given the book's reception, it quickly became obvious that we would have to do a follow-up volume and continue the important work of discovering the world's best horror fiction and making it available for an English-speaking audience.

We knew from the beginning, though, that we didn't want Volume Two to be just a repeat of the first book. Most of the authors in Volume One have other excellent tales we could have published, or we could easily have found enough great stories from Spain, Mexico, Italy, Sweden, and other countries featured in the first book to fill a whole second tome. But we wanted Volume Two to be something entirely new – new authors, new countries, new types of stories.

Because we didn't initially know whether there would be a second book, we held nothing back in the first volume – we included every great story we could find, over 400 pages of them. Which made for an excellent anthology, but it also meant we would be starting Volume Two entirely from scratch. In the foreword to the previous volume, we explained why most of the stories in that book were written in languages we could read, like Spanish and French, for example, and we discussed the challenges of finding stories in languages we couldn't read, like Japanese. It looked at first as though the second volume was going to pose an insurmountable difficulty: if we planned to exclude all the countries featured in the first book and focus on stories written in languages like Polish, Chinese, and Korean, how on earth were we going to find them?

But as we began putting the book together, an odd thing happened. Our research would uncover a writer whose work sounded promising, and we would reach out to them, explaining our interest in their work but our inability to read their language. In a surprising number of cases it turned out that an author had previously commissioned an English translation of one of their stories and it had simply languished in a drawer because they hadn't been able to find a publisher for it. It's agonizing enough to think about a story as good as Wojciech Gunia's 'The War' remaining unknown to readers worldwide because the text exists only in Polish, but imagine there being an English translation just waiting for someone willing to take the time to seek it out and publish it. In other cases, where a translation wasn't available, several authors prepared a draft translation themselves or had an English-speaking friend help, which enabled us to read and evaluate many texts we otherwise would not have had access to. In contrast to the first volume, in which we wound up translating seventeen of the stories ourselves, this time we received a lot of help from a number of truly excellent translators. Some of them, like Larissa Kyzer, Anton Hur, Jeremy Tiang, and Maya Vinokour, have already won awards and widespread recognition for their work, while some others are making their debut here; all of them are of outstanding quality.

The stories published in this book come from twenty countries on five continents and were originally published in a total of sixteen different languages. They run the gamut from psychological horror to body horror to weird fiction to folk horror and everything in between. It's a rich and varied collection that should have something to please almost any taste. And if there was any question after the first book that horror is truly a universal phenomenon, this book should put all such doubts to rest.

JAMES D. JENKINS & RYAN CAGLE
Valancourt Books
July 2021

JAMES D. JENKINS and RYAN CAGLE founded Valancourt Books in 2004 and since that time have republished over 500 lost and neglected texts, primarily in the fields of Gothic, supernatural, and horror literature, with an aim to making these books available in affordable editions for modern readers. They are also the co-editors of the four volumes of the acclaimed *The Valancourt Book of Horror Stories* series and the two volumes of *The Valancourt Book of World Horror Stories*. James holds a BA in French and an MA in Romance Languages and Literatures and also studied Dutch and Italian at university; he has since learned over a dozen more languages and took advantage of his language studies in translating a number of the stories for this volume.

# Acknowledgments

First and foremost, we would like to thank all the talented authors who submitted stories for our consideration. It was a pleasure reading all of them and a difficult task choosing which we had room to include. Grateful thanks are also due to the translators, all of whom did outstanding work and made our jobs so much easier for this second volume.

Even more than the first volume, this book was truly a collaborative effort, and we'd like to acknowledge the following people, without whose help this volume would not have been possible: Nicky Harman at Paper Republic for her help with Chinese horror; Hildur Knútsdóttir for recommending Steinar Bragi's story; Jakub Kozłowski for recommending Wojciech Gunia's work; Edward Lipsett for his help with Japanese horror; Joseph Camilleri for kindly translating several of Anton Grasso's stories for us to review; Ángel Isián for his kind help with Puerto Rican horror; Gord Sellar, Soyeon Jeong, and Charles La Shure for their information and recommendations as to Korean horror; Rico Valär for pointing us to Viola Cadruvi's work and for his helpful comments on our translation; Luis Pérez Ochando for his useful feedback on the Spanish translations; Bernardo Miller-Villera for fielding some Portuguese translation questions; and Jette Holst for recommending Teddy Vork's story.

Yavor Tsanev

# The Recording of the Will

*Bulgarian horror began in earnest in the 1990s and is going strong today, with a fairly bustling horror scene, considering the country's small size. Much of the horror publishing activity centers on the group known as Horror Writers Club Lazarus, which has published a number of anthologies, including the one in which this tale first appeared. Among prominent writers of Bulgarian horror, we might cite Alex Popov, Elena Pavlova, Ivan Atanasov, the late Adrian Lazarovsky (who translated a lot of foreign horror, including Lovecraft and King, to Bulgarian), and the author of our opening story, YAVOR TSANEV. Tsanev, a native of Ruse (the birthplace of another Valancourt horror author, Michael Arlen), is a prolific and award-winning writer of horror and also a publisher and editor. This story is from 2016 and makes its first English appearance here.*

THE WHOLE TOWN KNEW that the old moneylender was an evil man. And not just because of his activities; popular opinion wasn't based solely on the fact that everyone had had dealings with him or that at some point everyone had owed him money. Wickedness radiated from him with a particular shadowy aura, as if dark powers nested in his silhouette and were always present.

There was an inexplicable sharpness to his gaze that made people look away, their minds filled with confusion and the uncomfortable feeling that something inside them was being bared, groped, and soiled by his staring eyes. His voice was harsh and the timbre especially disagreeable and viscous – like meat that had spent a while outside in the heat and was not yet worm-riddled, but you could already imagine the worms.

He stood slightly hunched over, which made his arms look overly long, as if there was no point in running away because they could always catch you. When people had to talk to him, usually because of money, they did so quickly and with their heads bowed, agreeing to his terms so they could flee far away from him as fast as possible.

Sometimes he would pause in the middle of a sentence and lift up his chin, his nostrils flaring to inhale the nervousness, anxiety, and fear that he himself was causing. At these moments he looked like a passionate smoker holding the smoke in his mouth and enjoying it. But the smoke was the crumpled-up soul of some unfortunate wretch, trying to save itself.

Of course, no one dared to show the feelings this sinister person aroused in them. But they couldn't hide them either.

That's why, when the moneylender's servant boy informed the notary of his master's request to be visited at home today, the notary shivered, and a vague unease began to work its way through his otherwise dignified bearing.

The boy was dressed in nice clothes so as not to embarrass his master, but he looked ill-treated as always. He stood with his hand outstretched, and the notary felt sorry for him, even though he would have liked to send him away. An envelope trembled slightly in the boy's fingers.

The notary considered for a moment what it must be like to spend all day around a man like the moneylender, to serve him. The thought made him shudder, so he got up to accept the letter and find out the reason for this visit.

He tore open the envelope and took out a small folded sheet. He unfolded the rustling paper and his lips began moving automatically as he read:

*Dear Mr. Notary,*

*Please come urgently to record my last will and testament. The state of my health does not allow me to visit you.*

At the bottom was the moneylender's signature, which the notary knew well. The town was small. Most documents he worked with contained it.

He read the short note a second time and grunted involuntarily. He was not keen on making this visit. He glanced over the top of the paper at the boy. Then he decided it would be best to get it over with quickly, so he started putting on his coat.

When they stepped out into the street, the notary took out his pocket watch and checked the time, as was his habit. Then he strode off with a sure step, while the moneylender's servant boy maintained an acceptable distance, discreetly following a step or two behind him.

It was a gorgeous day. There were people bustling around the merchants' stalls, crossing the street, or standing in the sunshine in front of their houses. The sun shone bountifully, enriching the colors of everything.

A shame to have such an unpleasant chore come up on such a lovely day, thought the notary, and at that moment it dawned on him that if this was urgent and his 'state of health does not allow', then maybe there was a real chance that the town could soon be rid of the moneylender's presence.

He was startled for a moment. That was not a good thought. In no way was it righteous. But if this person's presence was a punishment from God, then wasn't it possible that the term of punishment was over, and their unknown sins had been redeemed? Why couldn't the dark shadow be lifted, so that life could be more peaceful and wholesome?

He stopped abruptly and the boy caught up with him.

'Tell me . . .' the notary began uncertainly, still confused by the thoughts raging in his head, but he quickly realized there was no reason for him to feel uncomfortable in front of the servant, who was just a kid. 'What's wrong with your master?'

'He's been lying in bed for three days, he says he sees the end coming,' the boy hurriedly replied, mechanically straightening his clothes as if he might be yelled at for doing something wrong at any moment.

The notary bent down and looked at him inquisitively.

The boy blinked a few times, as though he were to blame for the news he'd just given.

'The cook says he's really on his deathbed this time – he won't eat anything . . .' he added, as if there was a chance he would be accused of spreading rumors otherwise.

The notary didn't move, for the simple reason that he didn't want to accidentally break the spell. Could they really be freed of this grim person's presence so unexpectedly? The thought was not a good one, but how it lightened the heart . . .

Then the embarrassed boy said something that made the notary's heart beat fast and hard, almost like applause:

'I already went to the priest, but he refused to give him the last rites . . .'

When they entered the house, and afterwards too, as they climbed the sagging and creaking wooden stairs to the second floor, the notary couldn't help recalling a whole lot of unpleasant and revolting actions by which the money-lender had become a fixture in the town's mind. From petty, everyday cruelties, which were commonplace, to inexplicably harsh and completely inhuman acts.

For example, when cats started chasing each other on spring nights, making noise around yards, fences, and roofs, he would shoot them from his windows and send his domestics the next morning to gather and discard the bodies. The death of his last servant was suspicious, as was that of his neighbor, with whom he'd had a brief argument because the neighbor was convinced he had poisoned his dog. But that was nothing compared to how he seemed to take a perverse pleasure in feeling that people were dependent on him and watching them tremble while he considered a new interest fee to burden them with. To a spectator, it might have looked like a scene between a raging vampire and his victim. The notary had had the chance to be present at such moments, having been asked by various townspeople for assistance. The poor souls, they had hoped he could help them . . .

He would never forget the pregnant woman begging for an extension on her loan, and how the moneylender's knitted eyebrows jumped when he stood up, as if ready to pounce on her, while his shadow stretched grotesquely, forming monstrous shapes on the wall. But even more monstrous were his words, hissed in a voice that might have come from the dregs of a shaken bottle of malice:

'Be glad I'm not asking for double the interest, since I'm giving it to both of you!'

A moment later the notary grasped what he had said, and everything inside him bristled, his whole being lost its foothold, became a disgusted bird that wanted to fly off, to get away at once and never return to this obscene place that was so full of a shadowy evil.

He shuddered at the memory even now, and that coincided with the creaking of the hinges as the door opened. The servant stepped aside to let him pass. The notary hesitated for a moment to try to regain some of his dignity. Then he stepped over the threshold and the room swallowed him.

The curtains were drawn, and even though there was enough light, the feeling he got was of a den of shadows, and his uncertainty was replaced by a vague anxiety. If until now his thoughts had wavered, now he had only one desire – to finish all this and get back to fresh air as soon as possible. A peculiar and inexplicable sense of dread floated in the air here, clutching him and squeezing harder and harder the closer he stepped to the sick man's bed.

The moneylender turned his head and fixed his gaze on the newcomer. His eyes gleamed slightly in the twilight, but his face remained expressionless, frozen in that permanently unpleasant countenance of his which people found so disconcerting, repulsive, and frightening. The notary felt a desire to rush to the windows and throw the curtains open, as if that could banish the charged message of doom hovering in the room.

Then the sick man spoke:

'Come closer, Mr. Notary, I won't eat you . . . ha-ha . . .'

The words sounded as if they meant just the opposite. Nonetheless, taking a deep breath, the notary came closer and even sat down on a chair by the bed, obeying a gesture from his host. His next gesture was to the servant, who stood by the door in silence, awaiting instructions. And it plainly told him to leave them alone.

The notary stared at the closed door for a second or two with the feeling that his escape route was being cut off. Then he pulled himself together and turned his attention to the moneylender. The sick man had already taken out a sheaf of papers from somewhere. Had he been keeping them under the covers until then?

Their eyes met, but that uncomfortable feeling, like something digging around in his soul, made the notary look away and shift his glance to the documents. He was here on business, and that should protect him. He wasn't here to think about the repulsive person before him, but to do his job. As quickly as possible.

'I know you don't like me, Mr. Notary . . .' drawled out the sick man, and this time his tone revealed distant pain. Nothing like this had ever happened before – or was it a trick?

The visitor remained motionless, trying, at least outwardly, not to show his surprise at the unexpected change. Within him, though, his previous thoughts mingled again – the fact that the moneylender really was on his deathbed, and that this was good news for the town, along with the deep conviction that such a wish was not righteous. As soon as he left he might have to go to the priest and confess.

'You're not saying anything,' the same sickly voice interrupted his thoughts. 'But it isn't necessary. Everyone hates me, I know . . .'

The notary really didn't want to say anything. He was starting to think it might be possible for even the wickedest person to change before departing this world. Was that what was happening at this very moment?

'Who knows how I look from the outside,' the moneylender continued after a short pause. 'I know very well that everyone hates me. Not only that – they fear me . . .'

He raised himself up, and his shadow stretched its tentacles along the opposite wall. He picked up the triple candlestick, which stood meekly on the nightstand, and brought it closer so that the light of the pale flames illuminated the papers in his hand. But it also illuminated his face, at which the notary barely refrained from gasping – this man was truly a goner. Either the netherworld had already left its mark on him, or else it was a most incredible trick of the light.

'Perhaps you are the only one able to remain yourself to some extent, Mr. Notary – ' he coughed, 'in my presence, I mean . . . ha-ha . . .'

Melted wax poured from one of the candles, rolling down its length before dripping onto the moneylender's hand. He paid no attention to it. He handed the pile of papers to the notary and announced:

'I plan to leave everything to you . . . everything . . .'

Time has the ability not to think about us, just as we sometimes forget about it. This forms the illusion of a bubble of timelessness, within which we float between walls of oblivion. Then suddenly it bursts and we stand there stunned, not knowing how long has passed, painfully marked by the loss of this unknown interval.

Were we breathing? Were we existing? Where were we? What happened? Did the cruel dimension stretch or fly by us?

The notary could not say how much time had passed. His mind refused to accept what was happening and hit a dead end searching for a reason for the unexpected wish. Was he being ridiculed? To what end? What had he done to deserve all this? And of course there was what the servant said, that the priest had refused to come . . . No, this was not one of the moneylender's twisted jokes . . . But why? And how could he turn his will away from himself? How do you refuse a dying man's wish, even a man like this one?

He was about to speak when he realized that his mouth was already half-open and terribly dry. Who knows how long he had been sitting like that. See, the candle had dripped a few more times and was beginning to accumulate in twisted shapes on the sick man's hand.

'You heard right,' the moneylender's feeble voice stretched towards him. 'Write down that I leave everything to you!'

'But I . . .' the notary tried to object.

The moneylender raised his hand and interrupted:

'Let me tell you something while I still can . . .' The flames at the tips of the candles flickered as he moved the candlestick aside. His shadow started dancing on the wall again as if alive. 'Listen to me. I have never told anyone this, but you will inherit everything because that is my will. And inheriting everything, you'll find out anyway.'

An unpleasant, wheezing cough filled the silence in the room. The notary was unable to find the right words in the short interval before the moneylender continued speaking. He was still stunned by what he had heard.

'You are a strong man, but just like the others, when you are around me you feel confusion and hostility, mixed with a vague fear, which fills you and even paralyzes you. See, even now you do not want to be here, and yet you stay, while deep inside you wish for something else. You think that by overcoming your desire to flee as far as possible from this room, you are showing strength of character; you do not want to admit to yourself that in fact you have no choice. I will tell you: I have never given anyone a choice, that is the truth. Still, you are a little stronger than the others. That's why I chose you. Someone must inherit everything. I wouldn't leave the city just like that.'

The notary flinched at the final words. What did they mean? It was clear from his feeble voice that the man lying before him was dying, but was he starting to speak incoherently as he plunged towards his end?

'People are strange creatures, Mr. Notary. They put themselves at the center of the world and think they rule it. They imagine that their experiences are the most important, the most significant . . . They do not realize that they are just the moving conductors of far more powerful forces. Each of you walks the earth and thinks he has free will, that the future depends on his actions. Even my servant believes he can put aside some money and have a different life someday. They try to reason, to fight their daily battles, and they don't see life's big picture. They imagine that money makes the world go round, and they see nothing else. They think I have power because I have money . . . and yet the whole time they clearly feel that I control them in a different way. But no, they will never admit this. They will live within the illusion.'

The moneylender raised himself up again and smiled, but the smile transformed into an ominous grimace that made the notary involuntarily shudder once more. Something inhuman and predatory showed for a moment underneath the familiar disagreeable expression.

'Now, I tell you to record my will – and you will do it, even though you don't want to. Because, my dear Mr. Notary, despite being stronger, you too are wrong about the structure of the world and existence. Just like everyone else, you believe that man has free will, and that his shadow follows him. He moves, and it is attached to him. What a huge mistake, Mr. Notary . . . ha-ha . . . what a huge mistake . . .'

The notary's hand began moving over the paper on its own, writing words that no one had dictated. If some part of him had remained calm so far, now everything turned upside down, a storm raged in his soul, a demonic tempest that threatened to throw his mind overboard.

'Now do you understand what I'm talking about? Are you starting to comprehend the words of this dying senile man?' The ominous grimace grew even sharper. 'There are shadows that people throw and which they drag after them, but there are also other shadows – shadows that move people. You are just shells, a necessary part of existence, but you are not existence! You don't even suspect or understand what leads you, what exactly you are a manifestation of . . .'

The notary watched as his hand wrote letter after letter – in his own handwriting but without his consent. With difficulty, he shifted his gaze from the tip of the pen to the moneylender's sunken face. He felt totally lost trying to figure out what was going on. It was like he was scattered around the corners of the room, and as he wrote the will, somewhere deep inside he was battling for the last stronghold in the kingdom of his own will. A stronghold that was irrevocably collapsing.

The moneylender moved the candlestick between them, and the shadows began playing over the walls again. Something alive and demonic was making his shadow twist, as if it were about to wrench itself from the surface and take on a life of its own.

'I bequeath everything to you,' the dying man repeated in a trailing voice. 'Everything to you . . . Now it will all be clear to you . . . I am so tired . . . I want to rest . . . this shadow that drives me has chosen you, and now I bequeath it to you . . . yes . . . everything to you . . .'

With a crazed look, the notary followed the shadow as it tore itself from the wall, separated and became completely independent, with no connection to the lifeless body that had fallen back onto the bed. Greedily it slid and crawled the insignificant distance to his own shadow to fuse painfully with it.

*Oh, noooooo . . .*

What was left of his soul screamed piercingly and flew away on the wings of its own scream. His body writhed for a moment, trying to survive the pain and take on the shape of its new shadow.

Gradually, the whole city discovered that the notary was also an evil man. It seemed that until now he had only been pretending and impersonating someone else. Some mentioned under their breath, while looking around furtively, the connection between the moneylender's death and the notary's inheritance. There was no way it was a coincidence. There were even rumors he might have falsified the contents of the documents in his favor. Why had the hated man suddenly decided to leave everything to him of all people?

Wickedness radiated from him with a particular shadowy aura, as if dark powers nested in his silhouette and were always present. There was an inexplicable sharpness to his gaze that made people look away, their minds filled with confusion and the uncomfortable feeling that something inside them was being bared, groped, and soiled by his staring eyes. His voice was harsh and the timbre especially disagreeable and viscous – like meat that had spent a while outside in the heat and was not yet worm-riddled, but you could already imagine the worms.

The rumors also linked the death of the old priest to the grim figure who paced around the town like it was his own domain, but that wasn't the only thing which made people lower their heads and eyes. It was as if an invisible evil power were moving his body, issuing from his eyes and stupefying everyone around him. It was impossible not to obey him. Even his shadow seemed somehow . . . sinister.

The new priest had been living there for almost a year, had gotten to know the people, and had met the notary several times. In his presence he felt his faith seriously shaken, as if some unseen demonic evil loomed, freezing everything in the vicinity. His mind would be filled with anxiety and dismay, and for a long time after these meetings he couldn't compose himself or recover his peace of mind. He had heard what people were saying, and as much as he didn't want to listen to innuendo, deep down he harbored a view of the notary as an unholy and evil man. He was therefore more than astounded when the notary's servant – a tired and visibly hard-driven boy – brought a letter, which read:

*Please come urgently, my health has suddenly taken a turn for the worse and I cannot visit you myself. I want to bequeath everything I have to the church. Everything.*

A little later, as he strode towards the notary's home, the priest's soul rejoiced – it was lighter, winged, and convinced that if it was possible for even this wicked man to repent, albeit at the end of his days, then everything in the town might get better.

The day was gorgeous.

The air – fresh and full of life.

The sun shone bountifully, enriching the colors of everything.

The priest felt like singing, while his shadow followed silently at his heels.

*Translated from the Bulgarian by Roberta Basarbolieva*

# Gary Victor

# Lucky Night

*American horror writers have been using Haitian themes in their work for decades, from curses to voodoo dolls to zombies. But what would a voodoo-themed story look like if written by a Haitian author? GARY VICTOR is an award-winning journalist, playwright, and novelist who is one of Haiti's leading literary figures and one of the most widely read authors on his native island. His foray into horror fiction,* Treize nouvelles vaudou *[Thirteen Voodoo Tales], features a baker's dozen macabre stories, many of them with a darkly humorous or satirical bent. In some of the tales, like 'Lucky Night', ambitious but talentless opportunists use voodoo to try to attain wealth or a high position in the Haitian government, usually with unforeseen consequences.*

THE BÓKÓ HAD BEEN EXPLICIT. *A beggar in the vicinity of a cemetery, on the night of a dark moon!* The senatorial candidate Kerou had gone home appalled. It wasn't that he doubted Ti Pat's abilities. Quite the contrary! If he'd survived in politics this long, climbing the ladder from the lowly post of assistant mayor in a remote Haitian village to become a member of the Chamber of Deputies and now run for a senatorial seat, it was thanks to him. The man had never begrudged either his help or his advice. Kerou still remembered the morning when someone had left some powder in his office at the Chamber of Deputies and he had gotten it on his hand. A poison, which should have struck him down in less than forty-eight hours. Everyone would have thought it was just a bad fever. Ti Pat had saved him in the nick of time.

But now things were getting serious. Ti Pat had made it clear that this was the only way of attracting the forces that would propel him into a Senate seat without a fight. Kerou quivered with pleasure at the idea of winning the election. Women would be at his feet. He'd have his pick of the ones he wanted. People would come to ask his help for all sorts of things. He would trade his vote for well-stuffed envelopes or five- or six-figure checks – preferably in American dollars. He and his family would be free from want in this fucking country that he couldn't care less about, even if he made a point of speaking in the name of the people during his public appearances.

*A beggar in the vicinity of a cemetery on the night of a dark moon!* The senatorial candidate wondered if he'd be capable of it. 'No risk of catching anything,' the sorcerer had reassured him. 'But you must give this beggar a night of total pleasure. Then, under the dark moon, you'll get the luck you need.' Kerou adored women. Beautiful, plump. He liked women who used perfume; he hated body odor. In his way, he was an aesthete. That's why he was so worried. Would he be able to go all the way with this ritual, which others besides him had managed without any qualms? 'You can't fool the devil,' warned the sorcerer, noticing his reluctance. 'You have to sleep with the beggar. If you don't manage it, the *pwen-chance* won't work. Forget about the Senate.'

Forget about the Senate! Out of the question! Kerou rebelled internally. He gave his faithful chauffeur the job of reserving a suite at a chic and discreet hotel. He wasn't going to falter so close to his goal. He waited feverishly for midnight to strike. Midnight, the hour of those who have sold themselves to the Evil One, the time for every sort of debauchery! He took some money from the box hidden under his bed, then went to join Carl, the driver, who was waiting for him in the jeep with the engine already started, since the senatorial candidate always demanded that the vehicle's interior be well cooled. Carl, simultaneously his chauffeur, his bodyguard, and his confidant, was up to speed on all his activities.

'To the cemetery,' Kerou barked at the driver.

Carl set off without a word. They passed through the deserted town, plunged in darkness, a town murdered by that wave of unrest brought about by the populism of Marx's new disciples and liberation theology. Carl drove quickly, a loaded Glock in his lap. He had sworn to defend the man he already called Senator, at the risk of his life if necessary. He had good reason. The survival of Carl, his wife, his seven children, and his mistresses depended on Kerou's continued political success. As Carl often said, Kerou *se nèg ki sèvi*. The main political platform in Haiti, the one that allowed you to keep trustworthy men by your side, was as simple as that: *Byen sèvi*. That meant serving those close to you well by letting them help themselves freely to the country's coffers.

'We're there,' Carl announced. 'Always keep your gun within reach, Senator. The Devil is on our side, but thugs know neither God nor Devil.' Sometimes Carl could turn into a philosopher.

Kerou got out of the jeep and made his way towards the cemetery entrance in the darkness. A night watchman, understanding quickly, for he was used to this sort of practice, only asked Kerou for a toll. Five hundred gourdes. Kerou paid without hesitation.

'The path to the left,' the watchman advised.

Kerou gave an approving nod. He walked slowly, aware that his political future depended on this historic moment. He took the indicated path. He immediately noticed the bodies stretched out on the ground, most of them swaddled in piles of stinking rags. Some of the beggars weren't asleep yet. A few of them were talking around a large pot of soup simmering over a wood fire. Kerou's arrival in that slum immediately stirred up interest.

'I'm the one who gives you the best chance!' shouted a toothless old woman with pestilential breath who came up and clung to him.

Horrified, Kerou pushed her away. A thin, one-armed man with a scarred face came over to offer his services. Kerou made him understand that it was a woman he wanted. The man walked away, shouting a volley of insults at him. Hungry eyes peered at Kerou in the night. He was luck passing by, the luck that the spirits allowed to come to them that night. Kerou walked the whole length of the path without making up his mind. Despite Ti Pat's warnings, he didn't feel brave enough to go through with the ritual. It wasn't that he was incapable of going to bed with wretchedness. He often paid wretched girls for a moment of pleasure. Yet those girls could cover up their misery with cheap perfume, a decent pair of jeans, a simple blouse . . . But here, nothing. It was misery in its purest state. The ultimate physical degradation. The odor of sweat, piss, and shit. His cell phone rang. It was Carl.

'Well, Senator, found one?'

'Not yet,' Kerou almost groaned.

'You have to be fast. We can't stay here long.'

Kerou was on the verge of tears. Even if he took the least decrepit, the least nauseating of these wretches, he'd never manage to get it up. Ti Pat had been categorical. For the *pwen-chance* to work, he had to drink the cup down to the dregs. Kerou took a deep breath. He would find a solution. A half bottle of rum. He'd send Carl to get two or three Viagra tablets. He didn't usually need it, but in this particular case, it would certainly help. He had a sort of epiphany, telling himself that he, Kerou, hadn't yet reached the depths of Haitian madness. From what he'd heard, very few men or women had experienced this sort of reluctance when carrying out this ritual. 'The end justifies the means,' Kerou told himself. 'Just go for it. There's no other choice. It's either that or forget about the senate seat. The other candidates will stop at nothing.'

Kerou was getting ready to walk back up the lane when he saw a human form sitting two or three yards away from him in the grass in front of a tomb. He went closer to see.

'Is tonight my lucky night?' a voice whispered.

Kerou leaned in to see better. It was another beggar. But she had a young face. A pretty face. Kerou was able to recognize quality merchandise immediately.

'Get up,' he ordered.

The beggar stood up. As if by accident, the sheet covering her opened halfway, granting a glimpse of a beautiful body.

'My God, thank you,' Kerou exclaimed to himself. 'She can't be more than fifteen or sixteen.'

He advanced and took her hand.

'Come with me.'

She let herself be led without protesting. Walking along the lane, Kerou and the young beggar girl endured a storm of insults. Kerou, very happy, gave the watchman another five hundred gourdes, stressing that he was the candidate Kerou and that he wanted his vote. Carl, as soon as he saw his boss, rushed to get out and open the door for him.

'To the hotel, quickly,' said Kerou.

Carl started the car and sped off. A room was waiting for the future senator in a hotel somewhere in Pacot, a rich neighborhood close to downtown. Everything had been arranged for this evening. Dinner, drinks, perfume. It was essential that the beggar perceive this evening as her lucky night. It was only on this condition that the spirits would give Kerou the luck he needed.

'What's your name?' Kerou asked the beggar.

'Mercila,' she replied, staring at him questioningly.

'You're going to have a lovely night,' Kerou told her. 'You'll remember it your whole life.'

'It's my lucky night,' the girl agreed with a shy smile.

Kerou squeezed her hand. It was cold. She must be scared.

'It's the first time you've been lucky like this?'

'Yes,' she said, lowering her eyes.

It certainly wasn't the first time she'd gotten laid, the senatorial candidate told himself. The streets were a jungle. Children, forced into begging at an early age, knew all about sex.

'Here we are,' Carl announced.

The chauffeur drove the jeep into a deserted parking lot. A hotel watchman apprised of their arrival came to greet them.

'We've reserved the best suite for you, Senator,' he said. 'Kindly follow me.'

Carl stayed in the jeep. He was happy, everything had gone well. He put in a CD of his favorite orchestra and turned the volume up loud enough so that he could really enjoy the music. His boss had been fortunate to stumble on a beggar who was young, beautiful, and didn't smell bad. He chalked it up to the candidate's lucky star ... The boss was a lucky guy, Carl exulted. Finding a young and pretty beggar like that, whose body was still firm, was an extremely rare thing. Suddenly he was surprised by that thought. Extremely rare? It had never happened before! Everyone who went to pick up a wretched beggar from a church or graveyard always hoped to stumble upon someone who would make the ritual less of a chore. Kerou, his boss, was the first to have had that good fortune.

Carl imagined what was happening up there in the suite. Kerou was going inside with the girl. Her eyes would open wide when she saw how magnificent the room was. On the large table in the sitting room there was a meal waiting that would delight even the most finicky gourmet. Mushroom rice with shrimp, chicken with onions, fried pork, fried plantains, fish stew, yams, potatoes. There was fruit too. Grapes, bananas, mangoes, apples, sapodillas, caimitos. An impressive choice of desserts was offered: sweet potato pie, eleven different flavors of ice cream, cassava bread pudding, rice pudding, coconut milk. It was like offering a meal to the *lwa*. The girl would eat until she got a stomachache, Carl thought. Then the boss would bathe her in the large marble tub. That was more luck for the beggar, to be scrubbed, washed, and massaged by such an important man. Then the spirits would scrub and wash all of Kerou's impurities away. Once the girl was clean, the boss would carry her onto the bed, apply perfume to her whole body. Then would come the second part of the ritual. Sleeping with the beggar. It wasn't a matter of rushing to penetrate her and ejaculate. The beggar had to be given as much attention as possible. Kiss her, play with her tongue, her saliva, explore all the smallest details of her body, give her the maximum pleasure before the final act. Intercourse! That thought gave the driver an erection. He imagined the girl's warm body against his. He unzipped his pants and grabbed his penis to pleasure himself. Now it wasn't the boss making love to the beautiful young beggar, it was him, Carl. He bellowed when his solitary work reached a climax, soiling the windshield with a powerful jet of sperm.

When the driver recovered from this moment of madness, he immediately had a bad feeling. He feverishly put his clothes in order, cleaned the windshield with kleenex, then switched off the music. He checked the time on his watch. Already three a.m. The boss should be getting the beggar back to the cemetery now. The old zealots would be getting ready for the first morning mass. He stuck his head out the window. From where he was sitting Carl could see the blinds of his boss's suite. He was proud of himself for having thought of everything. As the boss's bodyguard he left nothing to chance. The lights were on. The boss didn't like making love in the dark. That eased the sudden fear that had taken hold of him.

Then Carl heard an explosion. He saw the windowpanes shatter. A fireball spiraled into the sky before disappearing behind a cover of clouds. No one had said anything to him about shooting off fireworks. He rushed to get out of the jeep, his Glock in his hand. The night watchman, uneasy, came to meet him.

'I saw a fireball. What was it?'

'We have to go and see what's happening,' said Carl.

They raced up the stairs and knocked at the door of the senatorial candidate's suite.

'Senator!' called Carl. 'Senator!'

No one answered.

'Senator!' Carl insisted. 'Senator . . .'

A cold sweat was now pumping from the driver's every pore.

'Open the door,' he ordered the guard.

The latter was trembling so badly that it took him two tries to get the door open. Carl went in, gun in hand, ready to open fire.

'Senator!' he called again.

The meal was on the table, untouched. Carl went towards the bedroom. The glass door leading to it was wide open. The breeze rushing in through the broken window made the curtains flutter. The bedclothes were disheveled, of course, but there was no one in the room.

'Do you smell something?' Carl asked.

The watchman sniffed.

'Yes. It stinks in here. Smells like a corpse.'

'Shit!' Carl shouted, struck by an idea.

'What's wrong?' asked the watchman.

'No time to explain.'

Carl rushed down the stairs, retrieved the jeep, and drove towards the cemetery at breakneck speed. He made it there in less than ten minutes. He leapt out of the jeep, not bothering to close the door. The night watchman didn't want to let him in, but Carl put the barrel of his Glock to his temple and relieved him of his rifle.

'Take me where the beggars are. Quick.'

The guard obeyed without a word. He understood that Carl wouldn't hesitate to shoot if he resisted. Something must have gone wrong tonight. Five minutes earlier, before this madman showed up, a fireball had flown over the cemetery. He led Carl towards the lane where the beggars usually slept. He was surprised to see them all gathered around a tomb that was set to be demolished soon, since for the past fifty years there'd been no sign of the family who owned it. Carl went on, pushing the guard in front of him. The crowd of beggars made way for them to pass. The guard let out a cry. Carl's heart skipped a beat. On a tombstone was lying, naked, the senatorial candidate Kerou, clutching a skeleton with yellowed bones. They couldn't tear the semi-conscious candidate away from the skeleton's furious embrace. Carl had to go wake up a junk dealer at a nearby shop to rent a saw.

The candidate awoke in a Port-au-Prince hospital three days later. He had lost his mind, but in a country where madness is the norm, no one really ever noticed. He was elected to the Senate and quickly occupied an important government post. However, his colleagues in Parliament found it bizarre and unsettling that he always kept a saw in his briefcase, a saw he brandished every time anyone dared to contradict him during a legislative session.

*Translated from the French by James D. Jenkins*

# Zhang Yueran

# Whitebone Harp

*Not much contemporary Chinese horror fiction has made it to American shores, though there are some promising signs that this situation may be changing: one novel by China's best-selling horror author, Cai Jun, has recently appeared in English, as has a volume of Chinese Lovecraftian horror by the pseudonymous 'Oobmab'. Chinese folklore is rich with ghosts and monsters, and the Chinese lunar calendar even features an entire 'Ghost Month', when the ghosts of ancestors return from the underworld to move among the living and must be appeased with offerings of food. One prominent author who incorporates elements of horror, ghosts, and the supernatural into her work is* ZHANG YUERAN *(b. 1982). Regarded as one of China's most influential young writers, she has published four novels and two story collections and has won numerous awards. 'Whitebone Harp' is from her book* Ten Loves *(2013), a collection of tales that all take love as their theme, though they deal with it in disturbing and bizarre ways that often incorporate elements of the weird or fantastic.*

I

SHE CAREFULLY REMOVES THE COLLARBONE from her left shoulder and gives it to her husband. There is a crisp snapping sound as the bone separates from its neighbor. She feels the sharp wind entering this new hole, eddying through her body like a whirlpool. Shivering, she sprawls against the cold wall.

Her husband's eyes gleam as he studies this bright bone. Nimbly, he takes it from her. Of course, he doesn't forget to thank her, pressing his enchanting lips to Whitebone's forehead. A chill is spreading over her face, but her cheeks are still peony pink. He kisses her frantically, whispering endlessly how grateful he is, how much he loves her.

2

Whitebone Spirit now sleeps under three quilts. With so many bones pulled out of her, her body is all holes. The early autumn wind shouldn't be so cold. She trembles with it, a kite about to take off.

Her husband makes musical instruments. Previously, he made flutes and pipes. Right now he is working on a harp, which has so far incorporated thirty-seven of her bones, far more than any previous instrument. The frame is made from the stronger bones of arm and shoulder, with some softer ones like ribs thrown in for flexibility. This is his best work so far. The carving has already taken three times as long as he'd planned. She spends many nights propped up in bed, watching him raise his shimmering knife, carving her bones until they gleam like ivory. His little fingernail is an inch long. He traces it across the harp, and notes rise into the air, like water droplets, entrancing. He throws open the windows and birds flock inside. The notes hit the ceiling and shatter, broken droplets that the birds swoop on before scattering. The house is quiet again. Her husband's face is flushed, he is lost in the crystalline sound. Only after a long time does he rush to the bed to cradle his limp wife, stroking her few remaining bones with infinite tenderness, his voice trembling as he says, Darling, you're the best, you'll always be the best.

The Whitebone Spirit lives for this moment. She adores her husband's stolid red face, the moment he flings the windows open and birds crash into his chest, how he stumbles like a child to her bedside and pours a waterfall of caresses over her. Of course, she loves the music too, water droplets and birds. Some nights her body feels like an old clock, moving more slowly than real time, allowing great gusts of wind to pierce her. Her white skirt fills with wind and billows like a sail.

3

Whitebone Spirit feels sad that her right collarbone is next. She loved those collarbones. You could see them poking out of her white dress, shining faintly through her pinkish skin, the color of azaleas. That first summer – the instrument-maker watching her steadily, as if possessed, following her . . .

Whitebone weeps as she tugs at the bone. Now she will be unable to wear her silver necklace – and sure enough, the instant the bone leaves her, it slips off, sliding right inside her. Her whole body is filled with the sound of tinkling metal. Worse, the pendant is a sharp-edged rhombus, sure to slice her insides to bloody ribbons. Her husband gave her this necklace, placing it around her neck so gently, the metal gently tapping her collarbone, ding ding. Her husband was enchanted. That was autumn.

Seeing Whitebone cry, her husband hastily says, Darling, don't be sad, so what if you lose all your bones? I'll love you forever. You're the best. Lift your head – look at our achievement.

Behind him are many priceless instruments. Like oversized furniture, they dominate the house. Did they really come from her body? How could they look so huge now?

4

When the harp is three bones short of completion, White-bone grows depressed. She has calculated that by the time the instrument is finished, she will have used up all her bones. This satisfies her; she doesn't mind sacrificing her bones, even though she can no longer raise her head, and spends much of the day slumped on the wide bed. Her husband bought her a wooden frame to help her move. It makes her look like a clumsy marionette. But then – what does it matter? She is happy to spend the whole day simply waiting for night. Night brings her red-faced husband, his footsteps, his embrace, the notes rising to the sky. This is enough for her.

Still, she cannot help but worry about her situation. She's always been a skinny girl, and without her bones, her body is so light, growing lighter by the day. Will she start drift-ing like a kite? Winter is coming, and the north wind here is fierce.

She is always worried about being blown away. When her husband hugs her, she finds herself thinking he is not holding her tightly enough, that she will slip away from between his arms. When they make love, she fears being whisked away from under his thrusting body. Each night, as he opens the windows to let the birds in, she makes sure she is safely tucked into bed. She uses four quilts now, needing their weight to feel secure. One night, she dreams of her husband endlessly making love to her, all day and night, his heavy body pinning her down. What security, what joy! Her face is red when she wakes up. But this isn't possible. What should she do?

I might as well die, she decides. A gust of wind just then makes her body quiver, and the sharp pendant inside her gashes open yet another wound. Whitebone thinks, If the wind blew me away, I might never see my husband again, not even to say goodbye. The thought is unbearable.

## 5

When her husband has removed the final bone, Whitebone Spirit begins to plan her own death, weeping helplessly. Her body is now so limp she does not even have the energy to run at a wall, or jump from a high place.

The rhombus-shaped pendant is an inadequate tool. Her heart is covered in scabs, too tough for it to penetrate. But a weapon of some kind would be good, she thinks, and scans her surroundings. Her husband's carving knife — but no, he brings it everywhere with him. What else?

Then she sees it: the harp. Right at its center is an especially sharp bone. Every time he adds to the instrument, her husband sharpens it a little more. At the moment it has a soft cover on it — he kept cutting his hand on it, but didn't seem to mind. It is the brightest point of the instrument. When he strokes it, his face gleams brighter than when he touches her.

This is just a loan, she tells herself. Whitebone believes that when she hands her bones to her husband, they belong to him completely. But she will allow herself, just this once, to borrow it. When she is dead, her husband can retrieve it and place it back into the harp, and the instrument will be complete again.

It is now winter. When her husband leaves early the next morning, Whitebone watches him go with wide eyes. I'll only need it for a short while, she thinks. Please don't be angry.

6

Such an exquisite bone. She holds it in her hand for a long time, playing with it, before plunging it into her body. Blood rushes out, the bone a white sail bobbing on a red ocean. Her flimsy body is nailed to the bed. All the light in the room is absorbed by the gleaming bone. Flocks of birds cover the entire window, drawn to the magical beam.

But there is always something to regret. Whitebone never considered that by the time her husband drew the deadly weapon from her, it would no longer be stark white. The piercing bone is now mottled a grisly red. It has no place in the flawless purity of the instrument. Not even a sparrow would be drawn to this ugly bone. Whitebone's husband rubs sadly at the once-precious object. He tries all kinds of polishes and remedies, but it merely grows darker, like an elephant's tusk dipped in poison. He is heartbroken. Finally, he fashions it into a narrow memorial plaque, and places it on Whitebone Spirit's grave.

*Translated from the Chinese by Jeremy Tiang*

# Wojciech Gunia

# The War

*For decades, Polish horror and weird fiction have been dominated by the works of Stefan Grabiński (1887-1936), a volume of whose stories is forthcoming from Valancourt. But in recent years a new generation of talented Polish horror authors, including Jakub Bielawski, Anna Maria Wybraniec, and our next author, WOJCIECH GUNIA, has begun to emerge, and it's only a matter of time before their excellent work is discovered and made available to English-speaking audiences. Gunia (b. 1983) is considered one of the most influential contemporary horror authors in Poland. His debut collection, from which the following tale is taken, appeared in 2014 and he has published four more volumes since. He has also translated the works of Thomas Ligotti into Polish and cites Ligotti and Kafka as two of his major literary influences. Horror fiction can do many things – it can entertain us, it can frighten us, but it can also make us think. And the implications of this story lingered in our thoughts longer than perhaps any other in the book.*

I RECALL THAT ON THE NIGHT BEFORE, the sky was exceptionally clear for that time of year, and I could count the stars. Huge clusters of tiny points, dense in some spots, in others submersed into the black of the nightly firmament. I stood gazing at it, breathing cold air and wondering what other constellations could be thought up, what stellar configurations created and recorded. If the horoscopes had been otherwise, and we had drawn different maps of the sky, would our lives have turned out any differently as well?

I went to sleep, only to be awakened in the middle of the night by the pounding rain washing in sheets down the windows of our flat.

The next day, the war broke out.

At first there was nothing to indicate that any kind of conflict had erupted, except perhaps for subtle signs which imparted to the day a cold, gray aura of vague disquiet, cut through – especially at that magical time just before dawn – by the harsh light of street lamps settling into the layer of moisture coating the walls and the sidewalks. The bus, carrying inhabitants of our district to work, spewed up fountains of filthy water from under its wheels, splattering sidewalks and courtyards. We rode in silence, lulled by the monotony of the ride and the stale, stuffy air. Everything looked as it always did: gray, tired faces, headlights of passing cars reflected in their pupils. Walking toward my office, I picked up a newspaper from the invariably silent street vendor at a kiosk on the corner.

The front page announced in large print: 'Steel Producers Fixed Prices', while the article itself told the inside story of some economic scandal. An expert gave his opinion, someone offered a comment. Then, details about the World Championship of some sport. Just at the bottom, in a small column, as though shamefully, secretly, appeared the heading 'The War Is Now', not followed by any text. Nowhere in the whole paper was there anything about this mysterious conflict, and when I asked the street vendor about it, he responded by turning and leaving with his bundle of papers, which were beginning to get wet by the fat raindrops of an approaching storm.

No one was yet in the office at that early hour. I remember how cold my hands were. I turned the radio on to hear the news, but the announcer's words were broken up by static interference. Only after a few minutes did I hear anything connected to that press announcement:

*We . . . rrupt the newsc . . . in order to deliver a . . . ecial report from the Comman . . . ief of the ar . . . d forces.*

*Fellow Citize . . .*

*Our country is on the verge of an atta . . . A complicated political and . . . onomic situatio . . . in our region has spiraled out of . . . ntrol and we find ourselves now confron . . . by a terrible threat. Times of fear and misery are coming, but our collective stren . . . will allow us to prevail, and safeguard a home for our ch . . . dren. But now, we are in a state of war.*

With that the message ended, and the announcer moved on to other news from the country and the world. Traces of a historic settlement were discovered. Someone won a huge lottery jackpot. There was a car accident. A vaccine had been developed for a particular illness. A well-known actress revealed a secret romance. One of the popular and admired sports clubs declared bankruptcy.

Gradually my coworkers trickled in. They sat behind the old desks strewn with piles of papers, some important, some utterly trivial – shopping lists, one-off notes. In the high, cramped room a fluorescent light buzzed, its dim glow imparting a leaden-blue tint to the gray of the day. The dado paneling on the walls gleamed. 'Did you hear about the war?' some asked, but no one was able to tell exactly what was going on, and no one knew enough about the situation to give an informed opinion. 'They say it's really bad,' they whispered. 'They'll probably reach an agreement quickly, that's how it always is,' others responded. 'We heard that their armies are headed toward the city,' the inquirers rejoined in a dramatic whisper, as though revealing some secret, but they couldn't say where they had heard this, and which armies were meant. 'Apparently all this started a long time ago, but it was kept under wraps,' someone else said, but he too didn't know exactly what had started, nor who had kept it under wraps. We remained in a state of nervous tension which only increased the more we learned or asked about the outbreak of the war. We listened to further statements on the radio, but there was nothing more besides the brief proclamation broadcast earlier in the day. Outside the windows, the streetcars rode at the same tempo, and the cars spewed up the same torrents of sludge. The cold air of the rainy day carried the same scent as usual, and our disquiet only grew.

In the evening, in our dated apartment on the top floor of the housing block, my family and I gathered in the kitchen, exchanging news in hushed whispers and knowing glances. 'They're supposed to come from the north.' 'They're extremely brutal.' 'Apparently, a number of ours have fallen.' 'There are spies among us.' Someone had heard about someone, who allegedly saw with his own eyes a column of our soldiers gathering at the gates of the city.

The next day, nothing happened. The same newspaper, along with the others on the rack, only repeated 'The War is Now', adding incidentally that the national authorities had implemented a state of emergency. But there were no patrols in the streets, no word of any curfew. The radio, too, repeated the same message as the day before, precisely at the same time. We listened impatiently, numb with anticipation. Finally we heard alarm bells and ran to the window, only to watch an ambulance flit past us. 'It's started, there go the first victims,' someone muttered behind me, but no one ventured a response.

The first signs of war only became apparent after several days, at a time when the ground, soaked to capacity by the perpetual rain, exuded decay and endless rising clouds of milky-gray mist. While out on some errands, I noticed a group of soldiers outside a manufacturing plant – commandos, in battle formation. They were strategizing, preparing for an assault on the building. People passed on all sides, paying very little attention to the soldiers. They only appeared to be wearing identical uniforms; anyone who looked more closely could tell that each was wearing an outfit of a different set, and the accessories didn't match up. One wielded a real rifle, but his companion tasked with covering his back held what looked like a homemade firearm. Another had a helmet that looked like a standard colander covered in black canvas. Even so, their behavior suggested the utmost professionalism, and I did not doubt for a second that these were career soldiers.

When I got home, I told my father about all of this. He only nodded, saying nothing. Only later in the evening did I hear him whispering to my mother: 'We have to think about stocking up for hard times, because we don't know what will happen.' She agreed and recounted that she had also come upon soldiers that day, forcing their way through the market towards her tram car. Once on board, they hastily reloaded their weapons and discussed their situation, getting off a few stops later and disappearing into one of the housing blocks. I asked her if she remembered what they were talking about. She said that she recalled something about 'retaking a critical strategic point'. I brought out a map, but the building she indicated was an ordinary old tenement house inhabited, like most of the district, by elderly people. My mother said that the soldiers went inside, and though she watched the building for a while, she didn't hear any shots or explosions. I turned on the television, but found no newscasts; the stations were airing replays of films and serials, or paid programming. Before going to bed, I looked out the window. It seemed to me that a group of people was moving in the thick shadows across the street, creeping in the cold light of the moon piercing through the clouds, but I soon lost sight of them, not even sure that I had actually seen anything at all.

The next few days passed in much the same way. Somewhere people would flit by wearing uniforms, organized in battle formation, running along the streets, only to disappear with a shout into some alley or tenement house gate. They could be seen in outlying subdivisions, sometimes surrounding a house. It was also rumored that their leadership had set up barracks in some private apartments scattered throughout the large housing blocks of the city. Sometimes a division of soldiers entered a bar or restaurant. The soldiers would order food, wait in silence, eat, pay the bill and then leave – supposedly on an important operation. At some point, new information appeared in the press: 'Enemy Forces Drawing Nearer', but in the next edition of the paper, this was retracted.

One day, as I was coming home from work, I heard strange noises coming from the basement. Someone was whispering; there was a sound of knocking, and something like a radio out of tune. I went down the stairs in the dark, noticing faint light from a bulb at the end of the corridor. The radio static intensified, as did the whispering. Suddenly I felt something sharp press up against my back. I turned to find a boy of about ten sticking a rusty old bayonet into my jacket.

'What are you doing here?' I asked.

'Password,' he spat.

'I don't know any password, I live in this building. On the top floor,' I said as mildly as I could. The boy was underfed and dirty.

'We're fighting here. This is the secret headquarters of the communications division,' said the boy, pulling from his belt what looked to be a pistol. 'On behalf of the armed forces of our country, I will have to check your identification. Please hand over your documents,' he repeated, in a tone that did not allow for protest. I pulled out my wallet along with a chocolate bar. The kid verified the information I'd given him and, having confirmed that I did in fact live in the building, immediately relaxed his demeanor. I gave him the chocolate. He broke off a piece, ate it with gusto, then wrapped up the rest and ran into the basement, nearly shouting, 'I've got chocolate.' I followed him. In one of the basement rooms, beside a pile of abandoned, unused crates, lay some flimsy, dirty sleeping bags with a group of haggard boys sitting on them. Close by, on a small table, was a radio communication station. The broken device buzzed and crackled. The boys looked at me with their wide, sad eyes.

'We haven't been able to leave here for a few days. It's a very difficult situation. They're keeping us in check. For weeks, we've been waiting for some very important orders,' one after the other said, in low voices. They quickly devoured the chocolate, eating it with wild abandon. I went upstairs to fetch them some soup that my mother and sister had made the day before, but when I came back, there was no one in the basement. Only the flimsy, dirty sleeping bags and the silver chocolate wrapper.

The days wore on in tedious monotony, and we grew more and more accustomed to the war. Sometimes information reached us that someone we knew, or more often, a friend of someone we knew, had died. Digging into the details would reveal, however, that the person hadn't necessarily died, just disappeared. Further questioning, corroboration of all accounts, opinions and scrupulous inquiries would then prove in fact that the person had not even disappeared but left on their own, sometimes even years earlier. Cases of real disappearances did exist, of course, but never involving anyone we knew personally. Without doubt, a significant change in the life of the city was the deployment of street patrols – finally the soldiers were plainly noticeable. They didn't sneak around, hiding in doorways and courtyards, but rather conducted official patrols. While they didn't carry out identity checks, their tense attitudes showed that they always maintained the utmost alertness. I saw one such patrol in front of the grocery store. They were gathered around a flowerbed in the middle of which grew an old rowan tree. At times they would sit on the low wall around the tree, then get up after a while, adjust their weapons and resume their duties. I was watching them when suddenly an old lady bumped into me as she made her way down the street. She was carrying a fresh loaf of bread and some water bottles toward a group of homeless people who, lately emerged from one of the alleys, had stopped at a nearby bus stop. The lady turned to me and said indignantly:

'Who are you looking at like that? Those are veterans, just returned from the front. Heroes deserve respect, not the sort of look you're giving them. They risked their necks for you. Some gave their lives. They're still a long way from home. They've been through so much ... what horror! What heroism!'

Finishing this monologue, she headed toward the bus stop, humming a famous soldiers' song. The men gladly accepted the bread and water, but their faces – overgrown and grimy – expressed more embarrassment than pride.

That same day, the first in a long while without so much as a drop of rain, a sniper set himself up on the roof of our building. The first to notice him was my sister as she came home one morning from the hospital where she worked as a nurse. He lay right beside our window. He must have gotten there by passing through our apartment, but later claimed that he had come from the other side, up the fire stairs. He had spent several hours lying there looking through his rifle scope when my sister offered him some dinner. He readily accepted and joined us at the table, then returned to his post.

I went and sat at the window, asking him questions, trying to find out more about the war.

'They haven't said anything about this yet officially, to avoid causing a panic . . . and really I shouldn't even be talking to you, since it's against the rules . . . but I personally think that such things should be known, so . . . well, the enemy is close, real close, and has been for a while. If you want to come out here, I'll show you. Just look through these binoculars out at the hills, across the whole valley, right at the forest line, you'll see them. Or at the meadow to the east, oh, you can see there very clearly. The whole armored company there, waiting. My commanders want to know when they attack, and they will certainly attack.'

'What are our chances?' I asked.

'Zero. It's going to be a slaughter. They'll wipe us out, just like the other towns.'

Carefully I hoisted myself over the windowsill and went out onto the steep roof, climbing over the filthy tiles which had long been slowly and inexorably crumbling, and which my father had been wanting to replace for years but could not get the approval of the administration to do so. I lay down beside the sniper, clad in a Ghillie suit (which he had not taken off during supper). He gave me the binoculars and told me to look east. At first I didn't see anything, but then made out indistinct reflections, flashes of light among the distant trees.

'That's their snipers. We keep each other in our sights, but no one's fired yet.'

At last I saw what the sniper was talking about. In the clearing, just before a thicket of trees, a group of tanks idled. They sat motionless: massive, angular, greenish-gray. For the first time, I had obtained tangible proof that there really was a war going on. The immensity of the machines, spread across the entire hillside, frightened me.

'They are far more powerful than us. They've acquired everything with no trouble, and no one has dared to defy them. But no one's talking about this. You won't read about it. You won't see anything about it. If you turn on the TV, you'll see doctored recordings from other cities. You'll hear accounts recorded in the studio, news reports written on their orders. If you telephone another city, you'll hear the familiar voice of a friend, but this will be a recording done beforehand – you can tell this by the strange repetition of neutral phrases. It's all lies; they've taken over virtually our entire country. We defend ourselves now as one of the last towns left.'

My legs trembling, I made my way down to the apartment, leaving the sniper behind without a word. Though I didn't tell my family anything of what I'd heard, nor of what I'd witnessed, a heavy silence had crept over us, pregnant with indescribable fear, weighted down by the darkness like clouds gathering before a storm. All the way till evening, not a single word passed among us. Only during a sleepless night did I hear my mother crying softly in her bedroom, and my father whispering, trying to comfort her, but I couldn't quite hear what he was saying. Some time later a change occurred, and my father began spending more and more time in his room. He would slip by close to the walls, looking around intently, stopping when his ears picked up a suspicious sound. He would disappear for days at a time, shut up in his room and only allowing entry to my mother, who had to knock in a particular way.

The sniper continued to come every day, just after sunrise. He'd knock at the door, pass through the hallway and the kitchen, and then assume his position on the roof. In the afternoon we would invite him in for dinner. After the meal, he'd return to his duties. I'm pretty sure he would nod off at times, resting after the abundance of food, as I could hear a gentle snoring. But this could have been illusory. Sometimes we'd chat about various things. When the sun set, the sniper would come down from the roof, bid farewell and leave, still fully clad in his gear. Even though I'd look out at the street, I never saw him leave the building. Once I decided to follow him; it turned out that he went downstairs, took off his uniform (revealing a gray suit beneath) and locked it away, along with his rifle, in a box stuffed in the sand. He took from the box a leather dressing-case, fixed his disheveled hair, and went on his way. After that, I always watched him: in a suit and tie, he would cross the street, get into a modest but well-maintained car and drive off. One time he left the building and went to a nearby shop, coming out with several large bags full of items which he carefully packed into his small car.

Occasionally I went with him to the roof and watched the tanks lying in wait on the hills around the city. Over time the sniper became friendly with us, and I had the impression he was becoming even closer with my sister, but I kept these thoughts and observations to myself.

The image of an army threatening our city with growing menace and capacity for destruction began to affect my mental state. Sometimes I would dream that I'm sitting on the roof at nightfall and watching the distant trees, when suddenly I hear a tremendous sound. After a moment I see, like mountains looming over the horizon, immense waves of black mud which crash down upon our defenseless city with terrible and paralyzing force. A rush of mud smashes into our house, shaking it at the foundations, and I fall out into the interior courtyard, falling, falling, until just when I'm about to smash into the filthy old concrete I wake up screaming, drenched in sweat, weak and disoriented.

During one of those nights, when the black ocean tossed me from sleep and prevented me from closing my eyes again, I heard, absorbing the sounds that permeate the quiet of a frightened city, a crunching noise coming from my parents' bedroom. The moon, distant and cold, poured its light through the windows, saturating everything in the pale glow of this surprisingly chilly night. Unable to stand this faintly audible sound, intensifying amid the silence to a multilayered stream of monotonous, rhythmic noise, I got up. The floor was frigid, its tiles like slabs of ice freezing to my feet. I felt that if I were to step more forcefully, I would plunge into a dark lake around which grew the forms of walls, furniture and clocks. I pressed my ear to the old door separating my parents from the rest of the house. The cracked paint scratched my ear, and through the worn wood I could hear grunting and snorting.

'Is everything all right?' I asked in a low voice. The noises stopped, scared by my presence. On the other side, I sensed someone holding their breath. 'It's me,' I said. No answer. I pressed the door handle as gently as I could. To my surprise, it yielded with a loud creaking of the hinges, ungreased in years. The bedroom was completely dark. The wider I opened the door, the more icy light began to trickle in. An ever-widening pillar of light rolled across the old carpet. In the corner, something was curled up, some soft, curved form squatting under the overhanging shelves and clocks, behind the armchairs. I noticed that my father's side of the bed was empty. My mother was sleeping, covers pulled up over her face. The comforter rose and fell in a steady rhythm. The form in the corner hunched over even more. 'Dad?' I whispered, taking another step onto the rough old carpet. The shape collapsed upon itself, trying to reign in and flatten its protuberances to form an inconspicuous ball. 'Dad?'

As I approached, my father lifted his haggard face; it took me a moment to realize that he was naked and shivering from the cold. His lips were dirty with fragments of something, crumbling off onto his sunken, wrinkled chest.

'What happened, Dad?' I asked softly, trying not to wake my mother.

'I'm sorry, there's no more,' he stammered.

'No more what?'

'That was the last of our reserves,' he said, revealing an old tin of canned meat in his trembling hands. He wiped its interior with his fingers and licked them. 'There's nothing at all left. I'm sorry. I was so terribly hungry,' he whispered, tears streaming down his furrowed cheeks. 'Hunger is such an unimaginable force,' he said.

I leaned toward him. He shielded himself, as though expecting a blow. 'Come on, dad,' I whispered, as gently as I could muster. 'Don't be scared.'

He looked at me with suspicion.

'You haven't come out in a long time. Let me show you something.'

He stood up, looking like a living corpse. Is that how I remembered him? I guided him toward the door. Obediently he followed, one step at a time, and when I turned my head to make sure he was coming, he abruptly stopped and averted his eyes. I took him to the kitchen and opened the refrigerator. His face was illuminated by the glow of the open fridge, as well as a strange look of profound happiness.

'Where did this all come from?' he whispered, looking at me.

'Eat something,' I said.

'Can I?' he asked, and I nodded. He started pulling things out of the fridge, wanting a bit of everything. 'I didn't think that I'd ever fill myself up again,' he said after a while, his mouth full. 'This is such incredible luck,' he added, swallowing, consuming with increasing rapacity, his eyes aglow with satisfaction. Pieces of food were crumbling out of his mouth, which he tried to catch and cram back in. His head, perched atop a long, slim neck, moved back and forth like a bird pecking for crumbs. I didn't betray the embarrassment I felt at this humiliating scene; I only smiled at him genially. In time my father, having succumbed to his own gluttony, stopped paying any attention to me and celebrated his ritual of devourment; or, one might say, his food orgy following a long fast. I backed out of the kitchen and returned to my room. The next morning, I found my father sleeping by the fridge. He steadfastly refused to go to his bed. Over the next few days, he stood guard in the kitchen like a dog, suspiciously eyeing anyone who came near the fridge to retrieve something, and smiling widely at those who only put something into it.

At work we remained quiet — no one had found out anything new (I didn't repeat the ominous news I'd learned from the sniper, feeling bound to keep it secret). Only the accountant admitted that he had wanted to leave the city, but he learned that the buses and trains were temporarily not running. He would have left by car, but his vehicle had broken down a few weeks earlier, and so he gave up. No one else I knew had tried to leave the city.

'Leave the city' — this idea stuck in my head. 'It might be your only means of survival,' I told myself. Take the family, flee, travel far away. Head south. There — so it was rumored — peace reigned. The tanks still stood in ominous silence, and the sniper scopes shone like the eyes of predatory animals lying in wait. The soldiers were carrying out their operations, and our sniper — who, incidentally, no longer hid his feelings for my sister — remained on guard.

I started to wonder which way we might flee. Unfortunately, as the sniper claimed, we were surrounded. Though no one would say so out loud, the city was waiting in passive expectation for the ultimate strike, the final maneuver of our enemies. We were tired, and although the rhythms of life continued, behind the well-oiled and familiar ticking of the cogs, one could detect the buzzing and scraping suggesting that the materials were wearing out, the parts exhausting their lifespan, their moment of capitulation growing ever nearer. We all dreamed about our impending doom, and the days – quiet, and growing shorter – had the bitter taste and color of rust.

One day, fed up from another bad dream (can there be anything worse than alternately falling asleep and waking up, each time being left to one's fate in the same nightmare?), I decided to do something, anything. Our sniper had already taken up his position. I asked him to lend me his binoculars – he typically used his rifle scope, which was more powerful. One time he let me hold the weapon. It seemed surprisingly light, as though made of plastic, but I didn't pester him with potentially stupid questions about it. The sniper hesitated for a second, but my sister, who had just brought him biscuits and tea, managed to convince him. I took the binoculars, packed some bread in my shoulder bag and left the house.

The city was drowning in the cold morning fog, cut through now and then by headlights of people rushing to work. The roar of horns and engines, the clatter of cars and trams – and in the midst of it all, not a single human voice. We all stayed silent, suffering our weariness and fear in mute resignation. Here and there soldiers could be seen, at this time of day profoundly groggy. Either they were returning from some exhausting operation, or – having been violently awakened – just on their way out to one. I got on the bus whose last stop was by the forest adjacent to the city limits. I wondered what our soldiers would say when I encountered them. 'At worst they'll make me turn around, and I'll say that I had gotten lost. Either way, I've got a connection, the sniper will vouch for me,' I thought, consoling myself. On the other hand, I didn't know what to do if I were to come across the invaders. I promised myself that I would just be as careful as I could.

Several people rode till the end of the line. I lost sight of them right after leaving the bus. I took a map of the region from my bag and checked the route once again; I had decided to explore a small path leading away from a minor hiking trail. I knew that I had to avoid open spaces – enemy snipers were definitely watching. I walked onward and very soon was absorbed by the forest.

The morning was pleasantly chilly, the sun just break-ing through the dense trees and the mist enveloping them, lending a softness to the shapes and sharpening colors. Birds were singing. The tall dark spruces rustled, and occasionally I heard sounds from the underbrush. I walked along slowly, my coat allowing me to blend in with the surroundings. The air smelled of winter and, indeed, once I had gone higher I saw in the hollows small islands of snow which must have recently fallen. Every now and then I stopped to listen. All signs indicated that there was not a soul around. I tried to tread quietly, avoiding stepping on any small branches. There was a rather steep approach before me, which caused me to stop halfway in order to calm my pounding heart. The ground was covered in damp clay. Roots, forming natural steps, were slippery, and glistened in spots where the sun pierced through the treetops closing over me like a Gothic vault. Drops of dew settling on the mosses, ferns, and cobwebs scattered the light, shimmering iridescently in the darkness. There was silence all around, broken by my heavy breathing. Stopping to rest, I noticed a small bird sitting on a stone nearby. It stared at me, every once in a while opening its black beak. It had a beautiful color – black, opalescing in the faint light with a kind of dark blue. Its eyes were shining. It stared for a moment, then flew off and disappeared into the thickly overhanging branches. I continued on, feeling as though I was heating up despite the cold temperature. My back was sticky and wet with sweat. The rustling of trees, chirping of birds and my own breath sounded each with its own rhythm, but coherently, in harmony with the surroundings. In such moments, it can seem like there is no better place for one's life to end than in the forest. If only a person could attune himself to its tempo of life, if he could calm his heart, regulate its beating, then merely dying amid such conditions would give to his passing the authentic sublimity that flows from the beauty of the natural. Entering the forest, to become a part of it; first its tempo, by the rhythm of one's final heartbeats, and then, its material.

The vegetation thickened, and the path I had taken away from the trail gradually disappeared into the undergrowth. I found myself repeatedly having to bend back branches concealing the way. I was angry with myself, feeling that I was being obscenely loud, drawing attention to myself, and that someone would hear me, see me, and decide to stop me – perhaps with violence. But nothing like that happened. It was only when the shrubbery began to close in around me so tightly that I felt as if I were in a cramped cage, or a sack of fine mesh, that I spotted a small clearing. I bent down, straining my vision. Something shone in the distance. Immediately I recognized it as the reflection of a rifle scope.

Terrified, I clung to the thickly-strewn leaves and branches, breathing in their scent. I continued to watch the gleam of the scope. I lay there, inwardly cursing my own recklessness. I waited for the moment of execution when the sniper who had targeted me, finally satisfied that it was a person he was aiming at, satiated by his own power and my fear, would pull the trigger – then the tension freezing my body into motionlessness would disperse, liberated in a splattering of blood. I was completely paralyzed by fear, pressing my limbs into the cold, moist ground, as if they were one more set of roots sucking up juices and pulling them upward, toward the cold. I regretted my expedition, a foolish idea with no chance of changing my situation in any way. Where would I escape to with my family? Rumors of peace in the south could very well be lies, stories told to disorient, to incapacitate with the false hope that there was still a chance for something to happen, that things were still normal somewhere, that life retained its joyful, vital pulse, and sunlight warmed smiling faces. Perhaps feeding us with longings was the well-planned desire of the enemy: lying in wait for us, its hand raised to deliver the final blow, yet still allowing us to believe that we might go on living, that it might still be worthwhile to be afraid, to be cautious, to conspiratorially devise ways of making existence bright and beautiful, and to persist in these imaginings in a passive stasis, sneakily, saying nothing to anyone. I had lost that hope, waiting now only for the last glimmer before succumbing to the darkness and silence. In the end I plunged into it, enveloped in fear, incapacitated by fatigue and cold. I sank into it, certain that I would cease to exist, accepting this prospect of nonexistence, perhaps even delighting in it in a strange, barely perceptible way, feeling the remainder of my awareness eager to rest within it.

But after a while, I opened my eyes.

Nothing had happened. I was still lying there, afraid to look in the direction of the scope, though I raised my head meekly. The lens still reflected the light, but it did not move. I got up slowly, hunched over like a thief eluding the watchful gaze of the guards. Nothing. The sniper could not have been farther than twenty or thirty yards from me. He had to see me, as close and loud as I was. Why didn't he shoot? I took two steps toward the reflection – still nothing. The light didn't move. Slowly, step by step, breath by breath, I approached it, beginning to feel suspicious. Every now and then I stopped, making sure that my heart was still beating, that my head was whole. I crept quietly through the underbrush like mist. Finally I got to within a few yards. There was still no reaction. The flash had come from a cluster of bushes next to a big old tree. Now almost certain that nothing would happen to me, I went up to it and spread the branches aside. Hanging there was a small mirror, strung on an old shoelace.

I began to laugh hysterically, but it was a fake sort of laughter – I felt like one obliged to be amused, as though the victim of a clever and cruel joke, in the face of which laughter is the only thing to avoid stark humiliation. I tore off the glass and pocketed it. In a nearby clearing, I could make out some shapes. I ran toward them, heedless of my own safety. The silence gave it all away. Tanks sat in the clearing, from one edge of the forest to the other, all the way up to the top of the hill. I went up to one of them and reached out my frigid hand; its armor yielded to my touch. The tank turned out to be a mock-up, a thin wooden skeleton with canvas stretched over it.

I went up to each armored vehicle in turn and examined its construction. They were entirely fake – even the tangibility of their forms had an element of deception in it. Each one in and of itself was a sham, and together they made up one giant falsehood, a fragment of that terrifying meta-lie, the purest mockery, whose echo sounds throughout every day, every year, spat from a mouth twisted into a crooked smile of indescribable loathing. It was starting to get dark.

I looked toward the city, which rested in a sea of mist, gray and tired, its lights like the flames of cigarettes smoked by condemned men in a mass grave just before execution. An execution, however, never to take place, postponed to eternity, like the final collapse into a black hole after crossing an event horizon. I fell to my knees, tore at the grass with my hands. It was wet and cold; soft, plump clods of earth clung to my fingers, lodged under my nails, like a body pressing itself into a set of sweaty bedsheets in the morning, along with the full burden of its just-forgotten, or sometimes still-pulsating dreams. I wanted to weep, so I did.

I don't know when I finally stood up again. I strolled about in a somnambulistic trance amid this false spectacle of power, among the cheap decorations imitating tools of destruction. I was the only actor on the miserable stage of this worthless performance. No one was maintaining these props. I went to one of the trees where something was glimmering, reflecting the sun's dwindling rays – a cat's eye fitted into the vestibule of night. Another mirror. There were no snipers in the forest. No soldiers. Just birds, rustling trees, first snowfall, wind.

I had been going in circles for a while before I noticed the shelter clinging to the forest wall – probably to provide tourists protection from the rain. I sat down, feeling a need to rest, waves of exhaustion coursing down to my muscle fibers. Inside the shelter was twilight and gloom, the narrow window cut from the rough-hewn boards admitting little light. It contained two benches and a table set in the hard dirt of the ground. I sat down heavily and rested my face in my hand. The air was brisk and smelled of livestock. I noticed a large chest up against the wall and went over to it. It wasn't locked, so I lifted the heavy lid, its rusty hinges squealing. It was too dark for me to make out what was inside. Inspecting the interior, I felt something cold and metallic, as well as a soft material, some kind of fabric. I took these things out and raised them to the fading light coming in from the low entrance. A uniform and a rifle. The garment appeared to be about my size. I wanted to burst out laughing. I put my discovery on the table and, despite the cold, took my clothes off. Steam was rising off my body, and the feeling of cold coupled with my exhaustion suffused me with a sense of blissful relief – as if my physical body, this ragdoll structure, weighed down towards the earth after a lifetime of soaking up the grime of sadness and uncertainty, were floating up to the roof of the shelter. There was no longer any place for such grime. The uniform fit perfectly. I also found in the chest an old helmet and military boots.

Late at night, when I was heading back down towards the city, my path illuminated by a flashlight, I already knew what I had to do, what my orders were. It was all completely clear to me now, frightfully apparent. The war would always be. It never ends, even during periods of ceasefire, even when our days are not regulated and put on hold by police curfews, even if planes are not dropping bombs, and bodies are not lying in the streets.

The media had lied about its having broken out. It has to lie; that's its role. The war had not broken out just then – in truth, it had never ended. It began long ago, beyond the range of the clock hand, outside the frames of calendars. It is a form of play, and like all play has its beginnings in the darkness of the absolutely serious, the despair of the world, whose skeleton has been crammed into the grim framework of the dialectic of hope and fear. Later, everything exploded in a riot of color, fireworks bursting, effusions of blood and the spontaneous laughter of those toward whom victory tips its scales. Laughter is the key to winning the war; those who laugh are the victors. It requires just a modicum of courage to discern, within the ubiquitous silence, that faint chuckle, and a bit of willpower to join in with it. And so I laughed, taking hold of my weapon, adjusting my helmet, evening out my steps.

*Translated from the Polish by Anthony Sciscione*

# Braulio Tavares

# Screamer

*Brazil has a very long tradition of writing horror stories, a tradition recently rediscovered and explored in the anthology* As Melhores Histórias Brasileiras de Horror [The Best Brazilian Horror Stories] *(2018), which collects tales spanning 1870 to the present day – including our next story.* BRAULIO TAVARES *is a central figure in contemporary Brazilian speculative fiction, not only as an award-winning author but also as a scholar, translator, and anthologist. In 2014 he published* Sete Monstros Brasileiros [Seven Brazilian Monsters], *a volume of tales inspired by Brazilian mythology and stories he had heard during the course of his life. With its blend of cultures – Portuguese colonists, enslaved African people, and indigenous groups – Brazil developed a rich folklore tradition, explored by Tavares in his horror tales. The story of the* bradador *(literally 'screamer'), a corpse haunted by guilt at its misdeeds in life, is one Tavares heard in his youth and has adapted here to a chilling modern-day folk horror story.*

I WORKED FOR AN AUDITING FIRM in Rio de Janeiro and had to travel to Miraceli, in Minas Gerais, to go over some reports with the board of directors of a factory that had hired us. My meeting would be at eight a.m., so I'd have to go by car the evening before and spend the night there. It was a three-hour trip from Rio. I drove at a leisurely speed; the late-afternoon sky was blue and gold, and the road ran between green hills that looked like a Windows desktop background.

Miraceli was a small, pleasant woodland town with a little stream running through a cement canal in its center. There were a lot of trees, a lovely park with mandala-shaped flowerbeds. The hotel was on a little hill. I parked, got out with my suitcase, and handed the keys to a porter, who took the car to a parking lot.

I filled out the registration form at the front desk using a ballpoint pen hanging from a rather frayed cord.

'Here from Rio?' asked the receptionist, a balding man with bright eyes.

'Uh-huh,' I responded as I wrote.

'Will you be staying for a while?'

'Just for the night,' I said. 'I go back tomorrow afternoon. Checkout is at noon?'

'Yes, but if you want to stay a little longer, we won't charge for another day.'

'Maybe just for a bath before I go.'

The room key was chained to a star-shaped piece of soapstone. The room was small, but the bed was good. I put my suitcase on the counter and stretched to relax my back muscles. The ceiling had a light fixture that branched out into three metal arms with three frosted glass bulbs. Then I went to the window. You could see the ascent of the street, some homes, a motorcycle shop. In the opposite direction, downhill, there was a newsstand on the corner and then a stretch of the tree-lined canal.

I lay in bed for a while, reviewing the reports for the following day, planning how the meeting would go and sipping a soft drink from the minibar. I napped for a few minutes. When I opened my eyes, it had gotten dark and the chilly night air of Minas was coming in through the window. I washed my face, put on a light jacket, and went out.

I like to leave a hotel (no matter what city or country), turn to the left, and go exploring. I enjoy getting to know a new city by going alone, on foot, looking at the shapes of the houses, the people's clothes, the stones on the ground. As I walked, I passed a strip of park filled with soapstone sculptures, benches with parallel wooden planks supported on rusty frames. There wasn't much foot traffic; there were more people stopped than going. What I mean is, there were people buying things in the shops, drinking in the little bars, etc., but I was the only one walking.

I climbed a hill, curious about an old church, and stopped at a restaurant, more for its terrace – since from up high you got a good view of the city spread out in the valley below – than out of hunger. A menu came; I asked for a beer and some bean soup and promised to order dinner shortly. I sat watching the city lights scattered throughout that dark ravine, each little light a house, each house a story. 'What a thing the world is,' I thought, 'so many interesting people, so many things to do, and here I am, auditing cost spreadsheets for other people's businesses.'

I was daydreaming over my second beer when the waitress returned. She was a tall girl, pretty, with curly hair pulled back in an enormous bun of whose existence she seemed unaware and a pair of mischievous brown eyes.

'If you'd like to order something, sir, you'd better do it now because the kitchen's about to close.'

'Already?' I asked. I looked at my watch. 'But it's not even ten . . .'

'Yes, it's because we close early here today.'

She gave me an apologetic smile so charming that I wound up smiling back and forgot to ask, 'Why *today*?' In the end I ordered a simple dish of beans and sausage called *feijão tropeiro*, which was delicious and went down quickly. As they were lowering the restaurant's sliding door, I paid and returned along the streets which, according to my unerring mental GPS, would bring me back to the hotel. When I picked up the room key, I said good night to the bald man, but he only gave me a nod and didn't say anything.

A brief aside here. There are people who don't like sleeping in hotels. I love it. Why? I don't know. Hotels give me a sensation of power, of wealth. I talked about this once with a therapist I had when I was in my twenties and kind of messed up. I told her, 'I want to be rich, but being rich doesn't mean owning a house; it's being able to go into any hotel knowing that I can pay to have that room, that bed, that bathroom, all to myself for a day. The only thing better would be if I could say that waitress is mine too. I'm paying? Then I'm entitled to everything. That's what being rich is for me, not owning a house in Praia Grande or wherever. Having to worry, paying bills, property taxes. Being rich,' I said nervously, pacing back and forth as she made a gesture indicating I should speak more softly, 'isn't having things. It's buying what we want, the moment we want it.'

I think that's what I was thinking about when I piled up the pillows on the bed, leaned back, and switched on the TV to find out what was going on. I only took off my shoes. My sweatshirt was still in the suitcase, but I didn't have any intention of going to sleep yet. I was enjoying the pleasant drowsiness of the meal, the silent night, the delicious cool air, that room which until several hours earlier I didn't know even existed and which was now mine for a few hours. I lay there watching a newscast with the TV on mute. Crowds of silent people were running through the streets, tear gas bombs exploding noiselessly. Beer commercials. Goals from soccer teams I didn't recognize. Car commercials.

I must have fallen asleep, but before dozing off I switched off the TV, or else I'd set the timer without noticing. I woke up with my neck a little uncomfortable from the position I was in. The room was dark. The TV was off, and the only light in the room was coming from the window, whose curtain was open. I was lying sort of crooked in bed, my neck hurt a little, and that's what woke me up.

That's a lie. When I started to get settled, I realized that what had woken me was the noise.

What was that noise? It was a kind of howl, the wailing of a dog or a wolf, a gloomy sound that started as a low groan and then gradually got louder and sharper until it rose above the houses, spread out on the breeze, came in through the window, and kept expanding until it filled my room completely. A howl of unbearable sadness, and it was a human voice.

There were three or four howls in five or six minutes, and after that the voice went silent. I got up, half stumbling, and went to the window – I don't know if I wanted to close it or to try and listen to that silence outside, so reassuring but so uncertain. I leaned out, took a deep breath, and only then did I really look at the houses across the street from the hotel. There were two houses together, semi-detached, mirror reflections of each other; both were closed up, overgrown with weeds, the walls crumbling. When I saw them, I instantly thought that the sound had come from there.

It hadn't, because at that very moment it could be heard in the distance, coming now from over the rooftops, and it was the same voice as before, but not that endless wailing; instead they were rapid, piercing, desperate cries, like someone protesting against an intense and repeated pain. I gripped the windowsill, looked one way, then the other, and all I could see in the moonlight was a horizon of red-tiled roofs and satellite dishes.

How long did it go on? A few minutes, a few hours? Time was irrelevant. But what was it? I took a couple of steps back into the room. Someone was being tortured, physically tortured, not more than three blocks away. Weren't there police in the streets? And the bald man at reception, wasn't he going to do anything? The terrified pain of those screams troubled me; if someone was going through that, then there was no way I was safe either.

As I took the first sip of sparkling water, cleansing and refreshing my parched mouth, the screams started again. Or rather, a third series began, with the same voice, but now in a different situation – out of place and improbable coming after the others, since now it didn't indicate physical pain but a deadly sadness, a killing misery. Imagine someone who has just received the worst news imaginable and who needs to unburden himself on the world. And it was a man's voice, the same as before, a voice like mine, the voice of someone of my age, of my strength.

I went to the window and waited for it to end.

That lasted, in hindsight, about two or three hours. Maybe more, maybe less; it doesn't matter because I didn't have the nerve to call the front desk and complain, and I couldn't figure out if I was scared, if I felt pity for someone who was suffering so much, if I was unsettled because no one was doing anything, if I was angry because of my meeting at eight . . .

At some point it all stopped. I remember looking at the clock and thinking: 'Forty minutes now, everything seems fine,' because until then there hadn't been a single pause in that chorus of tortures.

Finally my cell phone's alarm went off at seven and I got out of bed like I always do, whether I'm well or ill, sleepy or wide awake, alive or dead. I have to earn a living. And I do. Because when the alarm goes off, I get up, without complaining.

I went down to breakfast, my legs weak and about to give way, and my eyes burning with sleep. There was no one in the restaurant. Just an employee who was bringing in thermoses and distributing them at the end of a long counter covered in a green tablecloth placed diagonally over a white one, along with little wicker baskets containing rolls, the local cheese bread called *pão de queijo*, slices of cake, croissants.

I helped myself to juice, papaya, coffee, toast with jelly, and cheese bread. I changed clothes, got the car, and arrived at 8:10 for the meeting. Which was chaos. I have a rather confused idea of what they explained to me, the numbers on the spreadsheets they used for comparison, the standards we agreed on and signed with a view to the next assessment. The boss, a certain Dr. Benjamin, answered all my questions, showed me a stack of papers, he was very nice. He kept saying: 'Mind you . . . this number here, obviously, doesn't need to be taken into account . . .'

I think they were satisfied, which reassured me, because I was sleepless, disoriented. The whole time during the discussions, screams kept recurring to mind from that incredible repertoire that had kept me up all night. A random image came to me, for no reason at all, of standing there at breakfast with a little plate in my hand, seeing the counter filled with wedges of sliced papaya, twenty, thirty wedges of papaya, for nobody, nobody except me.

It was already 2:30 p.m. when, after making the necessary changes, saving everything on a flash drive, signing papers and all the rest, I refused their insistent invitations to have lunch at a steakhouse, got my car, and went back to the hotel. For some reason I thought I would be safe there. This time there was a fat, meticulous blond woman at the reception desk, who double-checked all my information before handing me the key. She asked if I was feeling all right and I said yes, thank you.

All that was left was to finish packing and go down to pay the bill, but I remembered that, for some reason, I could stay a little longer. The next thing I knew, I found myself half reclining, propped up against the pillows, in the exact position in which I had fallen asleep the night before. Why did I lie down like that, dressed, with my shoes on? What was the hurry? It was as if the screams were going to start again just because I had gotten in bed.

They didn't start again, but I began to hear something else. It was a rhythmic beat, percussion, not from instruments, but from all sorts of objects, forming a kind of cadence, 'tan-dandantandan . . .', which made me think of the evenings before Carnival, clowns and masked revelers in the streets, a chorus of boys beating cans and whistling.

That's what I was hearing now, and without even going to the window I rushed down the stairs, not waiting for the bloody elevator – after all, I was only on the third floor – and came to the street. It was three o'clock, but there was already an oblique golden light of late afternoon; the sun set earlier there because of the mountains all around. I walked towards the drumming and realized it was coming from the same direction as the screams of the night before. The avenue bordering the canal was deserted, but the noise got closer and closer, until a wall to my right gave way to a wide open space the size of an entire block, with whitewashed walls topped with a forest of crosses, as though they were antennas. It was a cemetery, and the drumming was coming from there.

I entered, passing the lanes, the chapels, the low trees that provided shade. I saw a group of people gathered at a distance. The chorus had seemed to be made up only of children and youths, but, coming closer, I saw there were a large number of adults and elderly people clapping their hands too, there were even some spinning those reco-recos that have a little handle and are made to turn with a movement of the wrist.

I saw some of them wielded rattles; others were beating on small drums. They were all singing, disorganized, but with the visible practice of an ancient custom, a barbarous hymn whose lyrics I didn't understand, though I was able to discern something archaic-sounding in the syllables.

I stopped beside a woman with a scarf tied round her hair, who was clapping her hands.

'What's going on?' I asked her.

She turned around, excited, but without paying much attention to me, and said:

'Screamer! Screamer! We're finding the Screamer!'

Or at least that's what I understood. She took two steps forward, euphoric, singing and clapping with redoubled energy, like she was getting revenge for some very ancient mishap.

I looked around. Behind the cemetery there rose a new apartment building, eight stories high, rather tall for the local topography. On many of the balconies there were people waving their arms, holding white handkerchiefs.

I glanced around. I kept going. I pushed my way through the crowd, which was unfazed by my intrusion and opened up for me to pass.

A man was speaking in front of a recently dug grave, yet it didn't seem to be a burial but rather an exhumation, because I immediately saw four muscular men tightening ropes and pulling a heavy horizontal object slowly upwards, a rectangular thing that poured dirt and dripped mud.

They maneuvered the combination of ropes with long practice and dropped the teetering, dilapidated coffin onto the ground. The man went on talking, one of those biblical chants that we only know are in Portuguese because of the words, but whose phrases don't make the slightest sense. The coffin was worm-eaten, almost breaking apart.

The man, who was wearing an old gray suit (if I looked closer, I was sure I would see it had all been mended, patched together), raised his arms, calling for silence. And didn't the drumming stop?

'*Old friends, brethren. Morinfante tenebras, peroperia manis-signo cardenoso,*' he said. Or something like that. '*Beatudinous moment of the souls, moment of the sublime sign.*'

'Amen,' they all said, with long practice.

'*We have cried, we have suffered, we have delivered up our blood to God, but no more.*'

'But no more,' they echoed.

'*How long shalt thou suffer, shalt thou endure with us, Screamer, how long shalt thou adumbrate thy calvary?*'

'Thy calvary.'

Was that really what I heard? I don't know, that's what it sounded like just then. I remember I staggered and recoiled, not wanting to see up close what would emerge from that coffin they were starting to uncover, prying it open with crowbars and tools.

'Who is it?' I asked a skinny boy with a large Adam's apple, who was looking over the others' shoulders.

'It's the Screamer,' he explained. 'He killed his mother for money.'

At the same time, on my other side, a half-distracted girl put her hand on my arm, unaware of the words the boy had spoken, and said:

'He let a child die of hunger and was punished.'

I heard cracking there in front of me, the sound of wood splintering, and a collective 'ooooh' from the crowd. I glanced to the side. A little old woman with very neat white hair and pretty clothes, all very tidy, had her eyes fixed on me as if she had been staring at me for quite a while, and when my gaze finally crossed hers, she said to me:

'It's the Screamer.' She paused. 'He screams, we listen.'

I looked away. The men were removing the planks with their hands (one of them protected his hands with a dirty rag). And from there inside a creature was rising up. What was it? I imagined that I was going to see someone emerge wrapped in a white shroud covered in stains, or else a shiny, bare skeleton. It wasn't. It was a man, who might well have been nude, since I didn't see a trace of cloth on him, but his torso was shriveled and dark like cured meat, his arms and legs mere bones covered in crispy, dried skin. He stood up, fumbling around like someone getting to his feet after being thrown from a car in a crash.

The white-haired woman stood beside me. She looked at me sympathetically.

'Many people can't sleep at night, hearing his suffering,' she said.

'Who did this to him?' I asked.

'Why, he did it himself. He burned down a house full of people.'

And then the pounding from earlier started up again spontaneously, tandandan-tandan . . . And everyone stepped back and made way as the thing got to its feet. Without fear. Just letting it pass. The false corpse, showing almost no sign of being aware of anyone's presence, started to walk, faltering, wavering, but determined, and yet absent-minded, like a drunk who wakes up in a ditch and thinks he has to get home.

The thing staggered in my direction. His eyes were like those of a fish, intact, lacking only an expression. His skull looked like it had snakeskin stretched taut over it; his face was tanned and scaly. As he advanced, the crowd made way before him and closed in at his sides, accompanying his stumbling steps, whose route never changed.

And the chorus all around was now a low tone, almost respectful, almost reverent, and was saying:

'Screamer . . . Screamer . . . Screamer . . .'

He came up to me! He stopped, almost touching me, and – I'm not crazy – I felt, I saw, the movements of his chest, the effort he was making, I saw him breathing. On that afternoon, that real, normal afternoon, that monster came up to me, while the crowd beat on beer cans and plastic drums. He stopped in front of me, and everyone clapped, shouting in chorus, 'Screamer . . . Screamer . . .' as if they expected us to have some kind of duel or confrontation. He looked at me with those glassy eyes and reached out his hand. He made a sign to say 'Come!' and I went.

Around me the voices shouted.

'He whored out his little girl! He's the Screamer!'

'He poured alcohol on an old man and set him on fire! He's the Screamer!'

He walked back to the rotten, disassembled coffin. Then the crowd started throwing rocks. The rocks hit him and he felt nothing. I walked behind him, following him, deafened by that drumming, 'tandandan-tandan . . .', which didn't stop, and an anguish, a mortal unease was growing in my chest, making it hard to breathe. We arrived at the grave. I looked at the rotten, disassembled planks. Screamer! The preacher's voice was heard once more.

*'We have circumscribed our posterity. We have ministrated the nemiserias.'*

'Amen!' Voices from all directions.

*'Let us lapidate the guilty, and the penitent!'* he shouted.

The stones began to fall again. And with them the insults.

'Torturer of the helpless!'

'Abductor of virgins!'

I fell into the pile of dirt beside the grave, trying to protect myself from the stones, which struck me from all sides but didn't cause me any pain, even the heavy ones that knocked me down into the mud again.

'He chained up a dog and slit its throat!'

And the stones were aimed just as accurately as the insults, knocking me over; I got up each time only to be toppled again.

The face of Dr. Benjamin appeared then in the midst of the crowd, and only at that moment did I realize how cruel a face it was, the face of someone who doesn't back down from getting what he wants. He had a piece of brick in his hand and, lifting it up, he said with scorn:

'He sold himself for money.'

The stones rained down, and I took shelter once more in my coffin's muddy planks, handfuls of mud hitting my face as I raised my withered arms, pulling the planks back over me, suffering for having woken up once more, enduring all of that again without knowing when it would end, without knowing when another piece of me would be gathered up, punished, and buried. Ah! I wish I were buried in the silence and shadows forever, forever.

*Translated from the Portuguese by James D. Jenkins*

# Yasumi Tsuhara

# The Old Wound and the Sun

*Japan is no stranger to horror: ghost stories in Japanese (known as* kaidan *or* kwaidan) *date back centuries and were introduced to English readers with a 1904 volume by Lafcadio Hearn. In modern times horror has been very popular in Japanese culture, not only in prose fiction but also in forms like film and manga. Readers of this book are no doubt familiar with Japanese horror cinema, from classics like* Godzilla *to more contemporary hits like* Ring, The Grudge, *and* Dark Water. *And you might find Japanese horror works on the shelf at your local bookstore, including Koji Suzuki's* Ring *series, Otsuichi's* Goth, *or manga by Junji Ito. But we're told there isn't much of a market in Japan for short horror fiction, so we're glad we were able to find this weird little gem by* YASUMI TSUHARA *to feature here. Tsuhara (b. 1964) is a popular and award-winning author who has been translated into several languages and who writes in a number of genres, including horror. This tale, in which the narrator's frank storytelling style contrasts with the bizarre nature of what he has to tell, first appeared in a 2008 collection and makes its first English appearance here.*

I S IT MY TURN? Gee, you're really putting me on the spot here. I've got no anecdotes like you guys. Besides, all you've told me so far are rehashed stories of books you've read, right? Don't get me wrong. I'm not saying there's something wrong with that. Those kinds of books are my cup of tea, too, so I've read quite a few. But once alcohol addles my ancient brain, I have trouble remembering what they're about. Even if I manage to recall the beginning, I've got no idea how it ends. I've got them all mixed up.

All right then. Let me tell you a true story, courtesy of a friend of mine. He's a graphic designer around my age. I promised him I wouldn't tell a soul, but none of you will have anything to do with him, so I'll keep him anonymous. His story concerns a couple who died at the same time. But it's not murder-suicide. In a nutshell, the woman killed the man, but he took her with him without knowing. But the whole thing is bizarre, otherworldly, and disturbing. When I first heard the story, it gave me chills.

The woman had worked for my graphic designer friend's company for fifteen years. She herself dabbled in graphic design. From the get-go, they mixed business with pleasure. She was his secretary by day, mistress by night. It was a run-of-the-mill affair. The man who died worked for a publisher and frequented my friend's company. He was a twenty-something kid. She – let's call her 'Saori'. And him, 'Goro'. Saori fell for him for a simple reason. Goro was from Ishigakijima, an island west of Okinawa Archipelago. She left a note in which she said she had the hots for him at first sight, even though he lacked the exotic looks one expects from someone from a tropical island. She was in the habit of chronicling the sordid details of her private life. Even though she was past her prime, she was quite attractive. That's what my friend told me. Everyone in her family inexplicably died young and left her with no relatives to speak of. One of her few memories of her family concerned the early days she had spent in a rented vacation house on Ishigakijima. Back then, her family was prosperous and intact. Fires of desire kindled in her when she learned that Goro was born and bred on the island, as she described in her journal. We can only imagine why he reciprocated Saori's advances, despite an age difference of more than ten years. Perhaps he didn't dislike her, but I don't know how serious he was. For all I know, he might have been seeing other women.

Goro visited Saori at her home on weekends when my friend went back to his family. When Monday came, she put away Goro's belongings and clothes in a suitcase. Once she became intimate with him, he repeatedly disappointed her. For instance, he lacked ambition. He was cheerful and even-tempered, but he lacked the drive to improve his lot in life. He was utterly disinterested in acquiring power, wealth, or knowledge. He was content to maintain the status quo. The past seemed to haunt him. Saori suspected that he had been involved in some crime back home. An old knife wound ran from his navel across his abdomen to his side under his ribs. Although the color of his wound had faded, it was surely deep.

'I got into a fight long ago,' Goro said.

He often moaned in his sleep and kept her awake at night. On one of these occasions she turned on the bedside lamp to find Goro groaning, drenched in sweat.

'What did you dream about?' she asked him after she shook him awake.

'Nothing,' he said, never giving her a straight answer.

After they made love, she went to bed naked. She woke up to his moans in the middle of the night. When she reached to turn on the light, she realized that the room was dimly lit. Yet no lights were on. Saori rubbed her eyes. A ray of light seeped from under the cotton blanket wrapped around their bodies. She flipped over the blanket and saw his abdomen shining. His old wound was open, oozing light. Goro still groaned. Saori moved her face close to his wound. It shone as blue as the sky. She peeked into the narrow gap. The sun shone. She let out a cry and shook him. When he woke, the room went dark suddenly.

A few weeks later, she woke up again to Goro's groans. She pulled the blanket off him and rolled up his pajama top. His wound shone again. She peeked inside. Thin clouds floated through the tropical sky. The sun glared. Saori touched the wound and put her hand inside. Goro let out a loud groan, but remained asleep. Her fingertips felt the sun's heat. She pushed her fingers forward and groped to feel the boundary of the two worlds. Goro's abdomen was empty except for a thin layer of skin. His skin felt grainy like sand on her fingers. The scent of the sea tickled her nostrils. She woke him up.

'You were talking in your sleep,' she lied, caressing his now sealed wound. 'You dream about the island, the beach.'

Goro turned pale, but he said nothing.

The following weekend, he visited Saori again.

'Can you keep a secret?' he asked.

'Yes, I promise.'

'I killed someone long ago,' he began. 'I was fifteen. Just for the hell of it, I slipped into a middle-aged woman's home. She lived alone. It's not that I wanted money. I wanted to sleep with her. She ran into the kitchen and brandished a kitchen knife. I pushed her down and sat astride her. I expected her to calm down, but she didn't. She attacked me with the knife and slashed my stomach. My vision went blank, but I didn't pass out. She fled outside. I followed. I stumbled through the field, toward the beach. She still held the knife. I picked up an edging stone, caught up with her, and struck her with the stone. She fell down. I struck her again and again, feeling as if I were in a recurrent dream. She stopped moving. I wiggled out of the torn, bloody T-shirt, removed her blouse, and put it on. I dragged her body to the sea and laid it face down. I sneaked into my home, splashed shochu over the wound, and sewed it with cotton thread. I crawled onto my futon and writhed in pain. I told my folks I had a cold. While I lay on my futon for days, the wound became infected. A fever seized me, and I drifted into unconsciousness.

'When the fever was gone, I raised my head and looked around,' he continued. 'I found myself on a hospital bed. A bandage was wrapped around my stomach. When I removed it, I saw the wound was neatly sewn up with small stitches. I thought I was busted, but nothing happened. A few days later I was discharged from the hospital.

' "You've got nothing to worry about," the doctor repeatedly told me. My parents might have bribed him.'

His confession convinced Saori that he was trapped in his hometown in his dream. After all those years, his guilty consciousness still chained him to the beach of Ishigakijima. While dreaming, he went back to the scene of the crime. I don't think what Saori saw was a mere hallucination, but it wasn't something anyone else could see either.

My friend knew about the lovebirds all along. But he kept quiet. It's his philosophy. Take an old coat, for instance. Even if a button goes missing or the sleeve becomes frayed, he's not the type of guy who mends it every time. He keeps wearing one coat until he gets tired of it and decides to buy a new one. He discards the old one. That's the kind of man he is.

Yeah, you got me. It's me all right. I mean, this really happened to me.

It was high time I dumped Saori. One weekend I went to her apartment building late at night. I shot her a text from the street below her home: 'I'm here.' I wanted to catch the lovers in the act and break up with her once and for all. I lit a cigarette and took several puffs before I got on the elevator. I pressed the chimes, but nobody answered. I opened the door with a spare key and stepped inside. When I switched on the lights in the bedroom, I found two naked bodies lying on the blood-soaked bed. My knees buckled at the sight. Saori had her head stuck in Goro's abdomen. Both were dead. I later learned what she intended to do. She tried to escape to Ishigakijima.

With her head buried in his body, Goro's face was distorted with agony. I never imagined a human head would fit in somebody's stomach. I calmed myself, approached the bed, and touched Saori's shoulder. Her body rolled listlessly. She had no head, as if she had been guillotined. I let out a cry. But a closer look revealed that Goro had no visible hole in his stomach. Where did her head go? I combed through the apartment, but to no avail. Instead, I found her journal and put it away in my coat. Then I called the police. They would find out about our affair. No matter. If I didn't cooperate with the investigation, they would suspect me. A few officers arrived and took me in for questioning. I was reunited with the headless Saori once more. They wanted me to identify her. Since she had no relatives, I was the only one they could ask.

The following morning they let me go. I went home. While I was reading Saori's journal in my study, the phone rang. It was the police. A woman on the line sounded like Saori and gave me a startle.

'We'll send someone to pick you up,' she said. 'We want you to come to Ishigakijima with us.'

'Why on earth?' I asked.

'We need you to identify something.'

'What?' I asked. 'What do you want me to do?'

'We found Saori's . . . on the beach.'

'What did you find?' I wanted her to be more specific.

'You'll see,' she said. No matter what I asked, that was all I could get out of her. Each time I phrased my question in a slightly different manner, but she parroted, 'You'll see.'

*Translated from the Japanese by Toshiya Kamei*

# Anton Grasso

# The Ant

*Likening a horror author to Stephen King is commonplace, even when the two are entirely dissimilar. But in at least a couple of respects, the comparison is apt when it comes to* ANTON GRASSO. *Both men published their first horror book in 1974, both have gone on to be extremely prolific (Grasso has published over 50 books and more than 1000 horror stories), and both have become household names in their respective countries. Just as King is a byword for horror here, so is Grasso in Malta – during a Maltese Parliament debate a few years ago, for example, a lawmaker denounced sanitary conditions at a hospital as 'like something out of a Grasso story', a reference he must have expected everyone in the chamber to understand. And yet, shockingly, in his nearly fifty-year career, none of Grasso's work has ever been published outside Malta. Given the quantity of his output, it is unsurprising that Grasso's work covers a wide range of styles, ranging from more subtle ghost stories and Gothic or folk horror to tales of extreme violence, body horror, and gore. In our opinion, Grasso is arguably at his best in his subtler tales, but because we had already accepted a number of more subdued tales for this book, we chose to present one of his more overtly horrific stories, a delicious* conte cruel *that would not have been out of place in one of the classic British* Pan Book of Horror Stories *volumes.*

I T WAS STRANGE – very strange and curious – that Annie should receive that cake from Francis 'with best wishes'. She couldn't stomach it. Laurence wasn't at home at the time; he was at a meeting with another publisher about some new contract. When she heard the doorbell, she wondered who it could be.

She opened the door and was greeted by a man she had never seen before, standing next to a delivery van, holding something round, quite large, wrapped in colorful paper with a flowery pattern.

'Are you Mrs. Annie?'

'Yes?' she replied quizzically, noticing that he seemed unsure what to say next.

'This is for you, ma'am.'

'For me?'

'I've been going round in circles all morning, trying to find out where you live. I knocked at a couple of other doors before finding you.'

'I'm not sure what you're driving at . . .' she ventured, haltingly.

'Well, the sender told me to ask for an "Annie", without giving me your surname. You're "living with another man", he said.'

'What do you mean?' she asked, confused.

'Why don't you just read the card, ma'am?' he suggested.

She reached for the note stuck to the top of the gift and recognized the handwriting as soon as she set eyes on it. After having spent seven years living with Francis Morris, how could she not? Incidentally, he was still her husband . . .

'*To my dearest Annie, with best wishes from Francis.*'

'Are you sure . . . it's for me?'

'Ma'am, don't do that to me! You've read the note! Whoever sent it to you wanted to make sure he got the right person. Special instructions they were too: *"give it to her and to no one else"*.'

'And why should you give it to anyone else?' she asked, puzzled.

'Because you're living with Laurence Potter ... the author, right? Isn't he the one who writes adventure books for children? My daughter, it so happens ...'

'Yes, he's the one,' she cut him short, irritated.

'My daughter just got one of his books for her birthday. She liked it, you know! She's nagging me to buy her his latest.'

'What were you saying?' she resumed. 'That I'm living with Laurence Potter ... and so what?'

'You're not married to him, are you?'

'That's none of your business!' she cried, flustered.

The man was somewhat taken aback. 'Hey, hey, lady, no need to get angry with me! Why should I care? I never thought of getting married myself, and look at me with two kids! But for the sender it seemed to be a big deal. "*No mistakes*", he kept insisting. And that's why I've wasted the whole morning – I was looking for an Annie Potter, but your surname is still his. But now, it seems, I've finally got the right address.'

A gift from Francis, she wondered, her ex-husband? This was the man she left after she got fed up with him and his ways, when she understood that she didn't and wouldn't ever love him. Her life had become boring and he had done nothing to change that. She had realized early on that he wasn't the man for her, but Annie was the type of person who needed a partner by her side, and she wasn't ready to leave him until she knew she had found herself a better companion.

Francis had taken it very badly. He loved her. He couldn't understand what he had done wrong, why she was leaving him. The truth was that he had a hard-headed, hard-driven streak, and was often more interested in his weird experiments on his collection of live and embalmed insects than in her. Perhaps he did not give Annie the attention she yearned for, but that did not mean that she was not his woman, his wife.

His dismay grew when he learned that Annie had left him for Laurence Potter, a mediocre writer of children's books and sentimental, tear-jerking chick-lit. Of course, Potter was successful. Kids and women are easily fooled, right? But that didn't make him a proper writer. Surely not a man worthy of Francis's wife.

And now Francis was sending her a gift?

'What is this?' she asked.

The delivery man was becoming visibly uncomfortable. He had thought he would just leave the gift with her and make his way back. And yet here he was, his arms outstretched, standing on the curb, sweating in the hot midday sun. But Annie lived with a writer, and writers are all a tad eccentric, he thought. It doesn't take long for their oddness to rub off . . .

'I thought you would want to open it, ma'am,' he said. 'But since you're asking, it's a lovely cake. One of the best we've ever baked.'

A cake? Annie was perplexed. From Francis Morris? With best wishes? But why? Because it was a year to the day she had left him for Laurence Potter, a scribbler of no worth? Francis knew she had always been a fan of Potter, even though his books were trash . . . Francis envied the man. But now here was Francis sending an anniversary cake for her to share with his rival. Evidently some sort of game, but what? If she hadn't seen the delivery van with her own eyes, if she hadn't been told the wrapped gift was a cake, she would have suspected it was a bomb. Because if Francis still thought of her as his wife, and she was sure of that, why would he send her a gift to remind her of their separation? Francis was no fool, that she knew. He wasn't loved, he was considered a recluse, never wanting to share his esoteric knowledge. But he was, in his own way, a genius.

With a shiver, she suddenly remembered a particular day when he had shown her an exotic butterfly flying around in a jar.

'Annie, look at it closely!'

'It's lovely,' she said, with no particular enthusiasm. It was really colorful, but it pained her to see it crashing against the sides of the jar, as if conscious that its freedom was being taken away.

'I will make it grow.'

'Under the microscope, you mean? You're going to study it?'

Francis broke into a sneer. 'You never understand what I tell you, do you?' he whispered softly, as if to himself. 'Evidently, our minds do not think alike. Don't you think I've had enough of just pushing insects around under a lens? I will grow this butterfly to three times its size. All it will take is some powder on its wings and in two days this butterfly will not just look bigger, it will actually grow.'

'How can that be?' she asked uneasily, amazed at these words.

She looked at Francis in disbelief. This was new to her. Her husband had never done anything of the sort. Could a man play God?

'Just wait and see,' he cried. He left the room with a sardonic smile on his face, confident that he would succeed. The sad sight of that trapped butterfly kept flitting before her eyes.

'Come here, Annie!' he called two days later.

A scream escaped her. The butterfly had grown to nearly the size of the jar.

'How did you do that?' she stammered.

He laughed scornfully. 'Zeal and ambition. That's all a man needs to succeed,' he told her. 'One drives the other.'

The gigantic butterfly lived on for four days and then he

found it dead in the jar and promptly added it to his grim collection.

She'd had enough of that man and his eccentric experiments. Nothing could convince her to keep on sharing her life with him. His behavior horrified her. She had once admired his ambition, but now could only see him as a madman who had lost all sense of direction in life. And she could not find a man more different from Francis Morris than Laurence Potter.

They had been meeting secretly for a few weeks before she decided to leave Francis. She hardly expected her husband to cry, but he did. He never guessed that she would leave him. He felt that lately she had been different, as if dissatisfied with him (although aren't women always like that?) but he never expected that she would just pack her bags and leave, as if this were a decision of no consequence.

'If you've made up your mind,' he sobbed, petulant, 'I will not keep you here against your will.'

'The decision has been made, Francis,' she said haughtily. 'You have your experiments. They are more important to you than anything else. You're not cut out for married life, and it's too late for me to try to change you.'

'You're right,' he admitted. Better be honest, he thought. In any case, she seemed determined to leave. 'I can't change. If you're not happy with my way of life, I guess that you're better off leaving me. Even though you know full well that you're breaking my heart. I love you, Annie.'

She had prepared two suitcases with her clothes. 'Keep everything else,' she said, with an air of triumph. 'I don't need anything of yours.'

This surely meant that she had met another man. He knew that she disliked living alone – but her words, her attitude only confirmed his suspicions.

'Who are you leaving me for?' he asked.

'Is it important for you to know?!'

'Why not? You're still my wife. As your husband, I at least have the right to know who is taking you away from me.'

'You will know soon enough,' she retorted with a touch of arrogance. 'Nothing will make me change my mind now.'

She left, a suitcase in each hand, without a tear, without a kiss, without a farewell, and – he was sure – without any sense of guilt or pity. Just as if he had been a stranger to her all along.

It did not take him long to learn who Annie's new partner was. Frankly, one hardly needed Francis Morris's acumen to discover that. He had followed her several times and had spotted them getting into the hack writer's car, coming out of his house, eating at restaurants or queuing at the theatre. He saw them, just as the entire world did. Everyone knew she had abandoned him for that worthless wordsmith, whose popularity owed more to his good looks than to his nonexistent talent.

Annie was vain and would surely be basking in her partner's fame. Francis was of a different stamp. He never sought popularity. His experiments could easily have brought him notoriety, but he preferred not to share them with anyone; he would rather enjoy them in silence – his and, sometimes, hers. How could he ever impress such a woman? A woman who wasn't interested in knowledge, science, study, research, but only sought to be popular and liked? Poor Annie, what an absolute fool she was. But she was still beautiful, and he still loved her. She had destroyed him.

Now, to remind her of that tragic day of separation, here was Francis sending her a cake. Could one trust such an uncharacteristic gesture? Of course not, she thought. There was some trick behind this, some mystery she hadn't yet unraveled. Francis loved secrets more than surprises. Wild thoughts raced through her mind. Perhaps the cake would explode as soon as she touched it. Or else it was poisoned. But then she willed these fears away. Francis was crafty and afraid of trouble. He would never plant a bomb in a cake. It could go off and kill other people apart from her or, if not, he could end up being reported to the police. As for poisoning the cake ... the confectioners would be investigated, their employees laid off ... surely Francis would not want to be sued for that? Well, she could easily just refuse the cake. Yes, refuse it then and there ... and wait for the delivery man's crestfallen and confused look. She couldn't do that ... Besides, she was curious now. Francis still knew how to grab her attention when he wanted to ...

'Look, why don't you join me? Wouldn't you like to taste it?' she suddenly asked the man.

He looked at her in disbelief. 'Don't tempt me, ma'am!'

'Why not?'

'Because if I could, I wouldn't just try this cake, I would keep it all for myself! This cake was specially commissioned, my boss spent hours on it. Believe me, it's his masterpiece!'

'Precisely. Come in, try it, and let me know what you think.'

'Are you serious?' He looked at her suspiciously. This had never happened to him in all his years of cake deliveries.

'Yes, of course.'

She didn't seem to be joking, and so he made his way in, placing the cake on the dining table. He asked her for a knife and a plate, and she watched him take off the wrapping and cut a slice. It didn't explode after all. She laughed. They were still alive.

The man placed the slice on the plate and tasted it, eyes bright, his mouth widening into a good-natured grin. 'I've never tasted the like, ma'am, I swear. You have no idea what you're missing. Have a bite, and once you start, you won't stop!'

As she smiled at his childlike enthusiasm, she felt her fears melting away. 'Tea? Coffee?' she offered.

'I'll have a cuppa, if you don't mind. Without sugar, ma'am. This cake is sweet enough!'

She was calmer now and her mind clearer. Francis was not plotting any revenge against her. If anything, it was Laurence who was his rival, Laurence who had taken her away from him. But if he tried to kill Laurence, he would put her in danger as well and Francis wouldn't want that. Francis was always very meticulous in his experiments. He was careful about risks. This was no different. So what Francis must have wanted was to impress her, to get her back, to try to convince her that he still loved her, that he held no rancor. On the contrary, Francis would use that unexpected gift as proof that his love was still true. Admittedly, this behavior was hardly normal, but had Francis ever acted normally?

She had a long kiss reserved for Laurence when he arrived.

'My new book is out in three months' time,' he proudly declared. 'They accepted it.' He kissed her back.

'Laur!'

'Tell me.'

Her eyes glistened in a strange manner. In a year of living with her he had grown used to her moods and he could sense that something had happened.

'You'll never believe me . . .'

'What's up?'

'Come to the dining room.'

When he saw the cake, Laurence was as perplexed as she had initially been. He read the greetings traced in colored icing and the handwritten note. He didn't know him personally but when he saw the name – Francis – he realized that this could have only come from her ex-husband.

'Exactly!' she confirmed.

'But it can't be!' he felt like telling her. Instead he asked, 'Have you tasted it?'

'Not yet. But I asked the delivery man to try it. To be honest, I was afraid of two things: a bomb or poison, but the man told me that he had never tasted a cake as good as this. Let's have a piece. He didn't die, and we won't either!'

That night, over a sumptuous dinner, a bottle of wine and another of fine champagne, they had two occasions to celebrate: their first year together and Laurence's new book, his third one for children. They had made love before leaving home, but on their return their desire for each other was unquenched, as urgent as when they first met.

Annie woke up with a start in the middle of the night. Laurence was asleep. She was happy. It had been the best year of her life. How had she managed to put up with Francis for seven years? What a difference between the two men! One a recluse, obsessed with his experiments, an introvert who rarely spoke, the other popular, affable, sociable, with a lively sense of humor, and most importantly, proud of being in the company of a beautiful woman. As if to resume their celebrations she went down to the dining room. She couldn't resist having another slice of cake.

Suddenly she felt a sting. As she pulled her arm back, she noticed a red spot, like the prick of a pin. Then she froze, staring at a black creature crawling towards the cake. It was a giant ant, with pincers resembling a scorpion's, and small, black, bulging eyes.

A cold shiver went down her spine.

She had never seen such an ant, not even in Francis's exotic collections. She couldn't help recalling the experiment with the butterfly. This was an unnaturally large ant, just like that butterfly. She did not know how he had done it. But here was the ant, very much alive, and it had stung her. She looked again at the palm of her hand. Was she still dreaming?

She felt dizzy. How did he manage to smuggle that ant in the cake? The monstrous insect crawled on the colored icing.

As if struck by lightning, she started to scream. 'Laur . . . Laurence . . . come quick . . .'

Startled out of his sleep, the man sat up in bed, switched on the light, and saw Annie trembling in front of him.

'What happened?'

'There's a monstrous ant in Francis's cake – it bit me.' She twisted her arm and showed it to him.

'What's got into you, love? An ant? A monster . . . ? What bit you?'

She tried to calm down, realizing that she was so tense that she was not even making sense.

'I woke up . . . I went downstairs . . . I wanted another piece of cake. As I was going to cut a slice I felt a sting. I pulled my arm back and noticed the ant crawling on the palm of my hand. I brushed it away and it fell on the cake.'

'Is an ant in our house such a big deal?' he asked, half smiling.

'But it came out of Francis's cake . . .'

'So, it was one of his dead ants?'

'No, a live one.'

'How can that be? A live ant hidden in a cake?'

'Don't ask me how. I know that Francis is obsessed with strange experiments on insects. I can't explain how he does it. But whatever he puts his mind to, he manages to do.' She continued, increasingly agitated, 'He put the ant in the cake, and the ant is still alive. It bit me Laur . . .'

'OK, love. Let's go downstairs and find this damned ant.'

The lights were on in the dining room, but there was no sign of the ant. The cake was still there, half eaten, its sugary greeting destroyed.

No ants in sight.

Annie turned the cake around, turned it upside down,

hacked what remained of it into pieces. Then, panicking, she crouched and started looking feverishly under the table and the furniture.

'Come on, Annie. You must have been dreaming.'

'For fuck's sake Laur,' she burst out, eyes red and tears streaming down her face. 'Don't tell me I dreamt a giant ant coming out of the cake, that I dreamt I saw it on the palm of my hand, that I dreamt it bit me. I never dream. You're the writer – I don't invent stories.' She hurt him without wanting to.

'Ok, fine, so where is it now? Disappeared? Spirited away?' he added sarcastically.

She started to look for the ant again, desperate to be believed.

'I don't know,' she said, giving up. 'But I know it bit me. I'm not imagining things.'

'Show me.'

'Here.' She put up the palm of her hand.

'Where?' he asked again.

Now not even the prick could be seen. 'But it can't be . . .' she whined.

'Tell me where it bit you, Annie?'

'Here,' she told him, hysterically jabbing at her palm with her finger, 'there was a red prick here, where it stung me.'

'So where is it now?'

'I don't know, I don't know,' she sobbed in despair. 'I feel as if I'm going crazy! I know I saw it, it was unlike anything I've seen before. But now it's disappeared. It's disappeared and its bite as well . . .'

He didn't believe her; there was no sign that what she was telling him was true, but he felt he should humor her. After all he knew that lying was not in Annie's nature; she had no idea how to dissimulate. She really seemed shaken, afraid, frustrated, desperate to show him proof of her nightmarish experience.

'Come, love, let's go back to sleep,' he whispered, putting his arms around her appeasingly.

'I don't want you to think I'm a liar, Laur,' she wept. 'Why can't we find the ant now? I'm sure I saw it. After all, why should I invent such a thing? What did I stand to gain? I realize now. Francis is a cunning man. I'm the woman he loves, and you took me away from him. No husband would send a gift to the house of his rival.'

She had a point, Laurence thought. If he were in Francis's place, he surely wouldn't send a cake to his estranged wife and her lover. But why did she realize that only now? Why did this dawn on her in the middle of the night, when imagination works its dark magic even on the most unimpressionable of minds? They had both eaten the cake, and the delivery man as well, so why was she now so afraid of it?

'Let's throw the cake away, Laur,' she begged.

'All right.'

She shoved it into a plastic bag, walked to the trash can, pressed the foot lever to push open its lid, and dumped the cake in the can, slamming the lid shut.

They went back to bed, but the rest of the night was very different from the hours they had spent together before. As he drifted back to sleep, he could hear her muffling her sobs in her pillow.

'Don't cry, my love. If you're in pain, we'll go to the doctor, first thing tomorrow.'

'It's not hurting.'

'So forget all about this and go to sleep. The cake is gone, as if it never existed.'

'I'm sure of what I told you, Laur. I swear I didn't invent anything.'

'I have no doubt about that.'

'I know you don't believe me . . .'

'I do believe you, Annie,' he said, slipping his arm behind her back. 'To be honest, yes, at first I thought you might have been dreaming. But now I know you're telling me the truth. You're right. Why should you make up such an incident?'

'I was terrified. I froze when I spotted it. I could feel it crawling. It bit me, Laur, it bit me. I know that. You think I'm a liar . . .'

'You're not, Annie. I believe you.'

'Are you sure?' She turned to face him.

'Yes.' She kissed him on the cheek.

'It's not hurting you, is it?'

'No. I felt a prick at the time, but now everything's fine. You make me forget everything. After all – perhaps – ' she began, sniffling and struggling to find the right words, contradicting herself, 'perhaps it's true that my mind played tricks on me when I was downstairs all alone. I remembered one of Francis's ghastly experiments. I've often mentioned how he would spend his time.'

'Yes.'

'Once, using some sort of powder, he managed to grow a butterfly to three times its size. It's unbelievable, but I saw the poor insect both before and after his treatment. Francis is crazy. No one in his right mind would take pleasure in such unnatural experiments. But he lived for them.'

'And I live for you,' he said, brushing his lips against hers.

'And for your writing,' she said.

'You come first.'

'I know,' she said tearfully, 'but don't abandon your books for me. I'm so proud of you.'

'I will keep writing,' he promised. 'But you're more important to me.'

'You're the best thing that ever happened to me,' she said,

snuggling up to him. 'Perhaps it's true I imagined everything. Let's sleep now, Laur.'

When she opened her eyes the next morning, there was no sign of any insect bite. The day after was a happy one, and so were the next few days. Not only did she feel no pain, but the memory of the awful incident was wearing off as well. Yes, that night of celebration had a nasty shock reserved for her. But now, without the pain, without the sting on the palm of her hand, without the cake, with the memory receding, life was back to normal.

A few days before the launch of Laurence's new book, Annie was in the bathroom and noticed that her navel was changing shape, as if it were being pulled down, growing narrower and slowly closing. Using two fingers, she delicately touched the upper and lower part of her belly button. And then, like a pregnant woman at a doctor's office, she gingerly pressed at her abdomen, first to the right and then to the left of her navel. She felt a stab of pain.

She told Laurence as soon as he was back home.

'Let me see,' he asked.

'Careful . . .'

'Does it hurt?'

'Yes, when you touch it.'

'But it's perfectly normal to feel some pain if you press your abdomen,' Laurence said to calm her down, knowing full well that he wasn't touching her hard enough to cause any pain.

'Well, it never happened to me. Or else I never noticed,' she replied.

'But what did you feel?'

'When I was in the shower, I noticed that my navel had an unusual look.'

'We'll go to the doctor tomorrow.'

'No,' she replied hurriedly, shaking her head. 'No need to

make a big deal out of this. Let's wait for a few days. Maybe it will pass.'

'If you feel any pain, let me know.'

'All right, fine.'

She didn't raise the subject again. He tried to convince himself that this meant she had got over it, even though when they were in bed together he would notice that her navel had not returned to its usual shape. He would also catch Annie worriedly looking at her navel, touching and observing it. Her belly was really changing. Strangely, it brought to her mind a bird's nest clogged with hay and grass. Sometimes she felt spasms of pain. She never told Laurence, but lately she often felt a pull on her insides, as if her belly were sore, and she would need to sit down until it passed. On occasion, the pain felt like that of the ant bite of that fateful night when she had gone down to the dining room. An electric pain, a sudden hurt. She would close her eyes, bite her lip, and slowly breathe in and out, her hand massaging her belly. Sometimes, she would feel her insides churning, or an unsettling numbing sensation – pins and needles fanning out across her abdomen. Horrific images haunted her imagination.

She went to a doctor on her own. She didn't want Laurence with her. Lately she had been feeling self-conscious in his presence. At night, in the dark, her swollen belly wasn't that obvious, but in the light of day there was no mistaking the bump underneath her navel.

'There seems to be a cyst which is pulling at the skin,' the doctor told her.

Annie caught her breath. 'Is is serious?' she asked.

'I hope not.'

'But what is it? Where is it coming from?'

'I'll give you an appointment for a scan. We won't know before then.' He leafed through a register open in front of him. 'How long have you been in pain?'

'Three, four weeks? Not all the time. But in the past days, I've felt it more often.'

'What?'

'The pain . . . sometimes it's a throbbing soreness. Sometimes it feels like pin pricks.'

'You should have seen a doctor before.'

'I thought the pain would just go away. The swelling as well. It's ugly. It's bothering me now.'

The scans did not reveal anything. But in the following days, the pain became more insistent, and the cyst – or whatever it was – started to grow at an alarming rate. The doctor decided to admit her to hospital with urgency.

Four doctors congregated in the operating theater, behind a milky-white curtain, under the unforgiving glare of two spotlights. One of them put a surgical scalpel to her body. As the folds of skin parted under the touch of the blade, three curious pairs of eyes peered towards a gelatinous sac attached to her navel. Before the surgeon could rip the sac open – perhaps because of the heat coming from the bright lights, or because whatever swarmed in it had reached maturity – it burst open. Before the shocked and terrified doctors, an infernal procession of ants snaked its way out of the woman's body. Ants the color of obsidian, waving pincers like a scorpion's, crawling and twisting – weird, hairy, strong and very much alive – the most monstrous species of ant ever beheld by human eye.

For the launch of his third book, Laurence Potter wore a black tie.

*Translated from the Maltese by Joseph Camilleri*

Val Votrin

# The Regensburg Festival

*Though Russian-language literature is perhaps not often associated
with horror fiction, a certain undercurrent of horror does run through
many of its classic works, from Mikhail Bulgakov's* The Master and
Margarita *to tales by writers as diverse as Nikolai Gogol, Daniil
Kharms, and Ludmilla Petrushevskaya. In many cases, the horror
is inextricably linked to a sense of the absurd, and the absurdity not
infrequently has to do with government or bureaucracy. 'The Regensburg Festival' has a distinctive 'Russian' flavor to it, and one feels it
would not be out of place in an anthology of classic tales by Russian
literary masters. And yet, though he writes in Russian and has been
nominated for literary prizes in Russia, labeling* VAL VOTRIN *a
'Russian' author for the purposes of this book is a little tricky. He was
born in Tashkent, in present-day Uzbekistan, moved to Belgium (of
which he is a national) in 2000, resided for many years in the United
Kingdom, and now lives in the Netherlands. Regardless of where
exactly we place him geographically, however, there's no question that
this story deserves a place among the best in the volume and will be one
that readers will no doubt want to return to and read again.*

A T THE BEGINNING of November, fog descended on
Regensburg. This happened every year – a few days
before the city filled with festival participants and guests,
fog would begin to rise from the river. It floated in on the
current in enormous white piles, which, steaming, adhered
to the riverbanks and slowly disintegrated, shrouding the

surroundings in thick, heavy drapery. This impenetrable veil muffled every sound, and city residents would joke that nature itself was rebelling against the noise of the festival, plugging its ears with fog as if with cotton. On the day of the festival's grand opening, the city was entirely shrouded in a mist barely pierced by the flicker of streetlamps and the odd car headlight. For two weeks, festival and fog would jointly reign over the city.

The Regensburg Festival was the best-known international festival of the choral arts. Long before the onset of festivities, musical groups would begin arriving in the city, and the enormous ancient cathedral of St. Peter, as well as innumerable other chapels around town, would transform into rehearsal spaces. Unofficially, the festival began at this moment – and then, when the grand opening was announced in early November, any city building with even minimal acoustic potential was transformed into a concert hall. Choral singing became endemic to Regensburg. Singing emanated from the most unexpected places – issuing from the windows of the old Town Hall, thundering in unison inside the mall, echoing resoundingly through underground parking garages, or, muffled by fog, suddenly ringing out in the middle of the street. And of course, people sang in countless bars and basement pubs. People everywhere felt the sudden and irresistible urge to grab each other's hands, and, rocking back and forth, commence singing as one – so strong was the festival's energy, its imperious force.

That year, Worton and the festival arrived in town together. Worton came in secret, riding in on the first morning train. Stealthily, he made his way through the narrow streets of the old town center toward his long-abandoned apartment, the keys to which he still retained. Worton was a tall, very thin man with a gloomy, exhausted face and a disheveled mane of white hair. He crept slowly through the thick fog along unrecognizable streets. He was tormented by dark premonitions. This was the third time he had come unbidden to the festival. His presence here was so undesirable that the festival guards were warned ahead of time about his stubborn attempts to penetrate the city. In past years, they had recognized him by his photo, stopped him somewhere just outside the center and politely escorted him beyond the boundary of Regensburg Township. On one occasion, he tried to return, but the ever-vigilant festival guards quickly apprehended him on the street, across from a little pub with a signboard in the shape of a smoking, smirking carp. He remembered the place well. Now he was weaving through crooked little side streets, keeping his distance from the main pedestrian thoroughfares, finding his way with difficulty in the dense, yellowish mist.

Here, in the old town center, the fog's dominion was especially palpable: in something like three days it had managed to build out an entirely new city for itself – spectral, distorted to unrecognizability, labyrinthine. Where a dead end had been before, there was suddenly a street; where previously it had been possible to walk straight through, a dank stone wall had sprung up. Fog had painted over the writing on the street signs, and now they were indistinguishable. Soon Worton realized he was lost. He paused and took a look around. All he could discern in the muddied-milk shroud enveloping everything from top to bottom was a lamppost and a segment of wall with a boarded-up window. Worton took several steps forward, hoping to find a house number, but the wall just continued into an invisible dimension – he couldn't even locate the door. He turned the corner, firmly resolved to examine the street sign – and collided face to face with a man in a militarized black uniform with silver patches sewn to the front. One hand held a twisted-handle staff topped with a treble clef. It was a festival guardsman.

After colliding with Worton, he apologized automatically, then peered suspiciously into his face.

He blurted out, 'Herr Worton?' and took Worton firmly by the arm.

Worton did not struggle, but only gave a silent nod.

Without saying a word, the guardsman began leading him through the impenetrable fog. Worton followed obediently, trying to walk in step. They walked in an indeterminate direction through narrow medieval streets where ancient houses emerged suddenly from foggy nonexistence, only to return there in the next moment. The guardsman spoke into his walkie-talkie, keeping a firm grip on Worton, and soon they were joined by two more guards. Two more men emerged from the nearest side street, and by the time they arrived at Town Hall, Worton was surrounded by a crowd of guards, silent and serious, no fewer than a dozen in number.

The old Town Hall stood in the fog, looking like an enormous hill. Worton was ushered up several long, desolate flights of stairs to see the Burgermeister. His spacious office, furnished in dark wood, was hung with portraits of frowning old men in frock coats with beribboned lapels – previous Burgermeisters. Among them was a portrait of the current one: in it, the Burgermeister, a man far from senescence, was depicted as an old man with a petulantly protruding lower lip and a dully glinting monocle in his left eye.

When the guards led Worton into his office, the Burgermeister raised his head and stared silently from behind his bulky desk. He was a thick-set, baldish man with a sour expression. A tray set in front of him held an elegant porcelain coffeepot, and the room, dark and comfortless, was filled with the wonderful smell of freshly brewed coffee.

Worton knew him all too well, knew his unpleasant character, his tendency to suddenly fly off the handle and start screeching, his fanatical love for choral singing – strange even for Regensburg and entirely incredible in a man so completely lacking an ear for music. At the time of the Burgermeister's election, Regensburg paradoxically had no city choir, with residents stubbornly insisting on singing in pubs and on the street. And so the Burgermeister became obsessed with the idea of creating a choir the whole world would hear about, a choir befitting a city hosting the most famous choral festival. By decree, he first established a medics' choir, then a bakers' choir, a barkeeps' choir, and, finally, a choir of museum workers, because the Burgermeister thought, for some reason, that a person's creative tendencies flourish precisely in the professional realm. Yet none of these choral collectives found success – the medics wanted not to sing, but to operate, the bakers were blasphemously off-pitch, the barkeeps, fresh off their night shifts, fell asleep standing up, while the museum workers had scarcely more talent for song than their exhibition pieces – stone slabs from the Museum of Mineralogy. Only Worton's choir had offered the Burgermeister a measure of success. Now he gazed silently at Worton. Finally, dismissing the guard with a nod, he spoke:

'Herr Worton! I didn't expect to see you in town. You came uninvited, I presume?'

Worton said:

'Please – give me back my choir!'

He intended the words to sound firm and decisive, but what came out was pleading.

The Burgermeister smirked slightly and nodded several times.

'When I was informed of your arrival,' he said in a querulous high tenor, 'I very nearly ordered you driven from the city, like last time. But then I thought – what for? Let him come. Let him come and submit an official petition for consideration of his request. We know the law,' he added with satisfaction.

'I read the order,' said Worton. 'Your signature was on it.'

'What order?' the Burgermeister asked quickly.

'The order transferring the choir to a different director.'

'I only ratified the city council's decision. You know perfectly well that our decisions are collective.'

Worton spoke again:

'Herr Burgermeister, I was removed from the position of choir director and banished from the city. This was done in accordance with your order. I was given no clarification and instructed to leave the city limits within three days. Twice I attempted to get a hearing with you in order to obtain official clarification of the reasons for my dismissal, but was twice sent away with insufficient explanation. Then I sent you a written request, but it, too, received no response.'

'Official responses are accorded only to citizens,' shrugged the Burgermeister, who had spent the meantime apathetically examining the pattern on his coffeepot.

'I understand,' said Worton. 'I'm not a citizen here. I'm a foreigner. But I've done a great deal for the city. I created a choir that is recognized as one of the best children's vocal groups in the world. Our concerts fill entire arenas, Herr Burgermeister. And I daresay it wasn't just any choir, but a vocal collective composed of orphans. I took talented children from the orphanages, where they had been languishing . . .'

'Please,' said the Burgermeister, wrinkling his nose and gesturing in protest.

'I repeat — languishing!' Worton said again, raising his voice. 'I became their father. I provided a roof over their heads, food, an opportunity to study and develop. Whereas in your orphanages . . .'

'Enough!' the Burgermeister screeched, trilling. 'Those are our children! They belong to the city! They are its citizens and must serve it!'

'Will you force them to labor in workhouses?' Worton inquired.

'No!' the Burgermeister shrieked and banged his palm on the table, which made the lid on the coffeepot clink. 'Their talent! They must serve the city with their talent, here and now! Not gallivant around the world on endless tours!'

'But they're singers,' said Worton quietly, once the Burgermeister had calmed down a little. 'Their presence is hotly desired everywhere – across the ocean and even in Siberia. Our schedule was booked for the next two years.'

'That's of no concern to me,' said the Burgermeister. 'Let those who wish to see them come here. The choir has been granted a dedicated concert hall and provided with every comfort. Plus, we can replenish the budget at the tourists' expense.'

'But where do the children live?' Worton inquired, his voice still low.

'Live?' repeated the Burgermeister, hesitating slightly. 'For now, they had to be placed back in care. In the future we'll consider a dedicated residential complex . . .'

'So you returned them to the orphanages?' interrupted Worton, growing pale.

'Well, yes,' said the Burgermeister. 'We don't have hotel space for them, after all. For now, we have placed them in orphanages. Temporarily, I assure you. Their living and other conditions are strictly monitored, and there have been no complaints on the children's part.'

'Herr Burgermeister,' said Worton, clasping his hands together. He was near tears. 'I ask you for one thing – let me see them. I want to see my children, make sure that all is well with them. If, as you say, they want for nothing and the housing difficulties are only temporary, if they are content – I will withdraw all objections. I will make my peace, Herr Burgermeister. But I beg you – let me see them!'

The Burgermeister shook his head.

'Unfortunately, I do not have that authority, Herr Worton. The choir is within the city council's purview, and only the council can allow you, as former choir director, to see the children. The next council meeting is tomorrow. You may attend and state your request. For my part, I will be glad to execute any decision the council renders.'

Worton was silent, thinking over the Burgermeister's words.

'Does this mean I am permitted to remain in the city until the council makes its decision?' he asked.

'Naturally,' said the Burgermeister, nodding benevolently.

'In that case, I will come to the council meeting tomorrow,' Worton solemnly declared.

After leaving Town Hall, he hurried home. On the way, he ran into groups of singing citizens who blocked the street in their vocal frenzy, and had to squeeze and push his way through the caterwauling crowd. In one spot, where several side streets intersected to form a small square, Worton stopped: it seemed to him that this was a different square, one located nearer to his house. But then he noticed several murky figures at the square's center and realized his error.

These stone figures had once been street performers. At one time, the composer Friedrich Burgmüller, who lived nearby, was so incensed by their off-key singing that he uttered a curse – turning the poor wretches instantly to stone. For nearly two hundred years they stood in the center of the square, bespattered with pigeon excrement to the point of unrecognizability – the superstitious residents dared not transport them elsewhere, fearing that the curse of Burgmüller would fall upon their heads, too. It is known that Burgmüller himself was powerfully frightened by the consequences of his wrathful words and never scolded anyone again. Many pressed him to reveal the enigmatic incantation, but the hapless composer took his secret to the grave.

In the middle of the nineteenth century, Richard Wagner took an interest in Burgmüller's spell, burning as he did with the desire to turn his hostile critics – Eduard Hanslick first and foremost – into stone. In 1865, Wagner traveled to Regensburg for three days in order to repeat Burgmüller's experiment. For three days the famous composer chased Regensburg's itinerant musicians, cursing them in the vilest terms and calling all the thunder and lightning of the heavens onto their heads. During this time, two street violinists kicked the bucket, three singers were struck with boils, and one organ grinder was swallowed up by the earth – and yet, in the end, Wagner failed to turn anyone to stone. Enraged and dispirited, he departed Regensburg.

Worton heard this story on something like his first day in Regensburg. That same day, he set out to see the stone singers for himself. He was shocked by their small height. Was it really the case that, as scientists assert, people used to be shorter in those times? Or had the poor singers been children? He could have taught them to sing. This was his talent – thanks to his efforts, and within an incredibly short time, even the deaf hatched an ear for music, and even the mute erupted in song. 'Worton could make stone sing,' they used to say. Yes, he could teach these poor devils to sing. How many times had he passed through this square named after the hapless composer-magician – Bergmüller-Platz.

He knew the way from here. Worton's apartment was on the third floor of a modern five-story house crammed between two ancient buildings – their pediments, darkened with age, were embellished with elaborate stone coats-of-arms. Two years ago, Worton had been ejected from this house in such a way that he had scarcely had the time to pack up the bare necessities. All this time he waited in fear for news that someone else had moved into his apartment. But his friends in the city – who still numbered quite a few – related that the apartment was as empty as ever and that none of Worton's belongings had been touched.

Trembling, he entered the shadowy lobby and took the stairs up to the third floor. Passing by the mailboxes, he noticed that his own box was filled to the brim with yellowing advertisement flyers and letters, but felt no desire to scoop out or sort the pile – Worton was suddenly exhausted and wanted to lie down. Opening the door with his key, he paused on the threshold for a moment and then immediately proceeded to the bedroom. Half-light reigned in the apartment; the curtains were drawn. The air was filled with that special, dusty smell of the unlived-in space. Worton lay down on his bed in all his clothes, without taking off his shoes. He fell asleep almost at once.

Awakening after many hours, he lay there for a minute, confused about where he was. The half-light had long since become darkness, and silence oppressed his ears. Worton drew his palm over the covers; the feel of the familiar ribbed fabric calmed him. He was finally home. Standing up, not without effort, he made his way to the bathroom and splashed his face with water. Then he walked through the rooms and opened the curtains. Outside, evening had already fallen; across the way, the yellowish light of a street lamp barely shone through the mist.

Worton had slept almost five hours, but one look at that light – and he felt inexorably pulled into sleep again. He had a sickly feeling, like at the beginning of a serious illness. These, evidently, were the consequences of the nervous tension he'd been under in the week before he left for Regensburg. Though he had not eaten all day, Worton did not feel hungry. A vast fatigue weighed on his shoulders, but Worton had the wherewithal to descend the stairs and go outside. He had to eat something and find some way to fill up the rest of the day.

As it mixed with the nighttime gloom, the fog transformed into a damp, ashy mist with special light-blocking properties. Worton wandered almost by feel through this wettish darkness, where faint splotches of streetlamp light floated and disappeared like drowned suns. Somewhere around here, he recalled, was a cozy tavern where he used to have dinner fairly often. But after turning yet another corner, Worton realized he'd lost his way. The surrounding houses, barely visible in the misty obscurity, were completely unknown to him. The end of the alley – or was it a narrow street? – was drowned in a darkness so impenetrable, it was difficult even to imagine that it too contained houses where people lived. Hoping to make out something, anything, Worton turned to go the other way – and noticed a flickering light far off in the distance. Like a swimmer paddling through the murk toward a blinking lighthouse, he hurried toward the yellow spot, and soon it expanded, emerged from the fog, and acquired the contours of a paper lantern glowing above a Chinese food stand. Worton approached and stopped in front of the window, examining the arrayed trays of meat, fish, shrimp, vegetables. The bright lantern bathed all this penny splendor in an unnaturally thick, fog-tinged light, as if in yellow milk. The fish was yellow, and so were the vegetables, and so was the greasy face of the Chinese peddler. Take one step back – and the stand would be enveloped in strands of fog and become spectral. One step forward – and it would be transformed into a large, blurry patch of light.

Worton chose a dish of meat and bean sprouts served in a cardboard container, and sat down on a stone bench to eat. Tasting his meal, he noted that the food had a vaguely swampy, even putrescent flavor, and realized this was the flavor of fog. The sensation was disgusting, and he quickly threw the container into the trash. He had to get back, and fast – he was shivering all over, and the taste of fog had permeated his mouth. Trying to breathe in as little as possible, he started in a random direction, through an unknown square – he heard snatches of cheerful singing and saw embracing figures briefly surface, then vanish back into the fog – and suddenly walked up to something dark and enormous, something that disappeared up into the whitish, misty yonder.

It was the Regensburg Cathedral. Worton had approached it from a side street and now found himself in a dense crowd. The Cathedral Square was full of people and saturated with market-day ebullience. All around, singing voices, little bursts of laughter, snatches of conversation could be heard. At the same time, the people themselves were barely visible – dark, blurry figures would surface suddenly and immediately disappear back into the fog. Worton received several hard shoves followed by immediate apologies – and then he, too, ran into someone and excused himself automatically. A few more collisions with invisible people, and then he was right next to the cathedral. The dark pediment on the side of the building was suddenly right above him, and in the swirling air it was even possible to discern some of the sculptures embellishing it. Worton paused and craned his neck, looking up.

He knew this cathedral and all its sculptures very well – the famous Judensau, the smiling angel, the innumerable saints, apostles, prophets populating its walls and chapels. Dozens of stone gargoyles – monkeys, boars, dogs, gryphons – gazed at him from above, their maws yawning in soundless screams. These mute mouths looked crazy in a city seized with choral fever.

And suddenly, looking at these frozen figures, Worton realized something he had only dimly guessed before. These hideous beasts also wanted to sing! They'd wanted to sing for many centuries now, but could not. They had been able to, once – but then they'd been turned to stone. And yet they love to sing, he understood that clearly now. They have terrible voices, but they love to sing. 'All right,' he thought dispassionately. 'Now I know what to do tomorrow if they don't let me see the children.'

He was still standing there, looking up in an effort to make out the statues on the cathedral wall, when the fog near the cathedral gates was suddenly illuminated and voices rang out. Worton realized that another concert had come to a close. He took a few steps in the direction of the bright patch of light and found himself in the very heart of the audience, now on its way out of the cathedral. Obviously depressed, the people spoke to each other in quiet tones, discussing the concert. Worton could hear only bits and pieces, but had already caught the familiar name, and immediately, without thinking about it, dashed toward the cathedral doors. Desperately peering over the tops of heads, he could see the nave, bathed in light, and the blinding blaze of chandeliers. But it would be impossible to push his way inside – a dense crowd was exiting the church, while festival guards stood motionless on either side of the entrance. Worton turned, dived back into the dark fog, and broke into a run along the cathedral wall, making his way to a side door he knew, which he had once used to enter the rehearsal space. But this door, too, was guarded by silent black figures. Worton paused nearby, despondent. He wanted to rush at them, to push, to beg, to curse. But instead he simply shifted his weight from one foot to the other and cast beseeching glances at the stained-glass windows, which were lit from within.

His children were behind those stained-glass windows. He understood from what he had heard that a choir – his choir – had just finished a performance that had attracted a record number of listeners – and these listeners were clearly disappointed with the boys' singing. Worton was not surprised at this circumstance; he hadn't expected anything different from the new choir director, who had been appointed from above. Much more painful for him was that he, Worton, the cast-out director, could not even see his children. Wringing his hands and sobbing, Worton turned away and dashed back into the darkness.

Not knowing where he went, barely suppressing his weeping, he ran down dimly lit streets plunged into impenetrable fog. Intersections and turns rose up abruptly before him, and he changed direction automatically, consumed with bitter thoughts. He had very nearly forced himself to accept that he would see the children only in the distant future, if at all. And all of a sudden he'd had the chance to see them at once, out of the corner of his eye, at least. A spectral, sly chance that winked and immediately disappeared – and the anguish and despair that now gripped Worton were simply unbearable.

Suddenly, the alley he was walking down gave way to a wide, well-lit street. Even the all-consuming fog could not obscure the houses here, and their festive façades, decorated with statues and busts and beautified with tasteful lighting, were clearly visible. Worton paused in confusion, not knowing which way to go. But before he could figure out his location, he was illuminated by a headlight from the left. Out of the fog, quietly rumbling, floated a dark blue bus – the kind normally used to transport tourists into the city. The bus braked softly in front of Worton, the front door slid open, and he saw that the driver's seat was occupied by a black-uniformed festival guard.

'Good evening, Herr Worton!' came the polite greeting.

Worton didn't answer, eyeing the bus warily.

'If you're lost, I can give you a ride,' the driver offered.

'What, have you been following me?' asked Worton.

'Absolutely not,' the driver smiled. 'I saw you and stopped. I thought you looked lost.'

'I decided to take a walk, that's all,' Worton replied.

'Don't you remember me?' the driver asked suddenly. 'We've met before. You know, when you came here last ... and we apprehended you. I was the one who did the paperwork ... remember?'

'There were a lot of you that time. A whole lot,' Worton said slowly.

The man behind the wheel leaned toward Worton. He wasn't smiling any longer.

'What are you doing here?' he asked abruptly. 'You're alone, no one can help you. But there is another option. We are aware of your constrained circumstances. Take a seat, we'll discuss everything on the way.'

Worton looked at him uncomprehendingly.

'What's wrong with you!' the driver said, already annoyed. 'I can take you wherever you want. To the train station, for instance. We'll pay all your return travel costs. You can also set any conditions for the payout of compensation. Understand?'

'So you weren't just passing by, after all!' Worton blurted.

The driver winked, which was so vile that Worton took a step back.

The driver noticed this.

'So you won't go?' he asked with unfeigned sorrow.

Worton shook his head, resigned to fate, expecting armed guards to appear from within the bus and shove him inside.

But nothing happened. The driver pressed a button and the door rustled shut. The bus revved quietly and vanished into the fog.

Worton was alone again. His fear and irritation gave way to joy, as though he had just won his first battle. The wistful pain that had driven him here was also gone. He felt an influx of energy. The fog seemed to sense the change in his internal state and thinned, growing weaker; the false streets, built up to misdirect Worton, disappeared. Worton quickly found his way home.

The apartment was filled with the wettish smell of fog, which was seeping in through the partly opened window. Worton closed it, turning the handle with a firm crunch, as if crushing vermin. Then he paused in the center of the room, lost in thought. He did not feel tired at all and had no desire to sleep. Entering the living room, Worton walked up to a bookshelf and took out a volume by José Escarsega, his favorite. He sat down in an armchair and opened the book to a random page, and the very first poem his gaze fell upon was the famous 'Song', which Escarsega had written before he'd even turned eighteen:

> A copper mouth above lets forth its knell:
> The singing of the belltower bell.
> Stentorian tone ascending to the sky:
> Metallic tongue could not be clearer, aye.
> Its words possess the clarity of truth:
> A blow would make you cry out, too.
> And when your turn arrives to sing,
> Like copper, you will learn to ring.

Worton froze, his lips moving soundlessly: he was repeating the lines of the poem. Leaping from the chair, he began pacing back and forth. The gaping mouths of the cathedral statues and the Burgermeister's smirking face flashed before his eyes. Worton stopped in the center of the room and slowly said aloud:

'I struck them, and they rang out too strongly. Someone had to plug up his ears.'

He froze again and stood there for several moments, as though struck dumb by this thought — then, a sudden fatigue rolled over him like a wave, toppling him into the chair. Worton fell asleep.

He slept so soundly that he didn't hear the doorbell ring. It rang long and persistently, however, and eventually the trills roused him. Massaging a semblance of feeling back into his creaky waist, Worton dragged himself to the door and opened it. His visitors looked wary. One of them Worton recognized as the driver of the bus from earlier – except now he looked stern and somewhat irritated.

'Herr Worton, they're waiting for you in the Town Hall,' he said stiffly.

Worton suddenly remembered.

'Oh my God!' he mumbled. 'Please forgive me! Yesterday was a difficult day . . . I dozed off.'

'It would behoove you to hurry,' interrupted the second guard, a short, stocky man of warlike appearance. 'The council is already in session.'

Worton apologized again, dashed into the bathroom, made a hasty toilet, and left the building in the company of the guards.

Now he couldn't have recognized the streets even had he wanted to. Overnight, the fog had thickened to an almost viscous consistency. It invaded the eyes and nose like thick, humid, bitter smoke. The guards didn't notice and marched along, faces full of solemn dignity and staves upraised, whereas Worton walked with a handkerchief pressed awkwardly to his face. But his ears remained open, registering the astounding silence all around – Regensburg, a city where the music never stopped, had now fallen silent, as though it had been gagged.

Just as before, the enormous knoll of Town Hall surfaced in front of them with no warning. Their faces still solemn, the guards conveyed Worton through an inconspicuous door on the side of the building, walked him up to the second floor and there, in front of a pair of large white-and-gold doors, bade him wait with a gesture. Their movements synchronized, the guards took turns opening just one of the doors and peering inside. Then, they opened both halves wide, turned to Worton, and invited him in with identical ceremonious gestures.

He entered through the doors and found himself in a large, silent chamber. Worton took a couple of steps and stopped, because the clatter of his heels on the polished parquet floor sounded deafening. The chamber's walls were festooned with enormous paintings depicting various battle scenes. On one wall, strapping, mustachioed grenadiers were charging forward, bayonets bristling. On another, a naval battle raged between two sailing fleets, filling the frame with cannon smoke. In a third painting hung directly across from the doors, some Bavarian monarch, astride a white steed, was leading his impressive army to besiege a fortress that looked more like a molehill.

Beneath that painting stood a table, behind which sat the members of the city council.

The Burgermeister sat tall in the center of the group. Usually glum and unfriendly, today he was beaming. When Worton entered the room, the Burgermeister had just leaned toward his neighbor on the right, a balding, unremarkable man in very thick glasses, and was speaking to him cheerfully. The other man was nodding, his eyes sloshing comically around behind thick lenses like a bluish liquid in a hermetically sealed vessel. Also nodding was the Burgermeister's left-hand neighbor, a haughty gentleman in an expensive blue suit. The fourth chair on the right stood empty.

Worton cleared his throat. The Burgermeister turned toward him with obvious reluctance, his face instantly assuming a bored expression.

'Oh, Herr Worton!' he said in an official tone. 'We've been waiting for you for quite a while now. We'd just about decided you'd gotten lost in the fog.'

He opened his mouth and exhaled: 'Ha! Ha!' – this was laughter. No one joined in; the other councilmembers sat motionless at his sides.

'All right, shall we?' said the Burgermeister and began examining his papers. 'Present at the council meeting are Joachim Stackensteiner, Municipal Minister of Theater (the haughty gentleman inclined his head), Josef Opitz, head of the Office for Youth Affairs, and I, Gerhardt Vogt, Burgermeister. Another councilmember is set to arrive any minute. Now then, today we will hear the case of Herr Worton. Herr Worton, known to everyone here, expressed a wish to attend this meeting in order to state . . . well, you already know what Herr Worton intends to state. Now then, Herr Worton: we're listening.'

Worton was too agitated to speak. He managed to shift his weight from one foot to the other, but failed to produce any words – something was caught in his throat. A minute as never-ending as eternity had to pass before he could squeeze out the now-habitual words:

'Give me back my children!' And in the cavernous space, the words sounded like a whisper.

The Burgermeister wrinkled his nose, Opitz trained his lenses on Worton, and the Minister of Theater snorted loudly.

'My choir,' Worton fairly exhaled.

The Burgermeister cleared his throat, but Opitz was the one who spoke.

'We understand your feelings, Herr Worton,' he said in a quiet, soulful voice. 'Your achievements in creating the choir are indisputable. Not only did you manage to recognize gifted children – you were able to nurture their talent, unite them into an artistic collective, and bring that children's choir to worldwide success. We greatly value your contributions to the prevention of orphandom and to the city's reputation in the international arena. However, there have been some problems, let's just say that.'

'Yes, there have been some problems,' repeated the Burgermeister weightily and with obvious pleasure and fell silent, awaiting Worton's answer.

'Herr Opitz!' began the flustered Worton. 'I am glad we can finally talk face to face; previously, I was able to speak only to your subordinates. As you know, I took the children out of orphanages, where they had been placed by the Office for Youth Affairs, torn from their parents for minor infractions reported by neighbors and other ill-wishers. At the time, I was in the process of assembling my choir. By happy coincidence, I learned that several orphanages held musically gifted children, and I went to see for myself. Then it turned out that there were talented children at other orphanages, too. I submitted a request to your office to "temporarily excise" the children, as you call it. My private sponsors provided us with a dormitory, complete with amenities and a service staff, so that I was able to prove to you that the children would be housed under excellent conditions and receive the necessary education. We signed a long-term partnership agreement with the city administration, according to which the city budget would receive the majority of . . .'

The Burgermeister exclaimed in protest, and Opitz quickly spoke:

'Everything was exactly as you describe, Herr Worton. The children's living conditions and the quality of their education were indeed excellent, as the results of our inspections show. But allow us to remind you that the partnership agreement also stipulated another, quite important, obligation on your part. You were not to allow any contact between children and parents. You must agree, Herr Worton,' he added with a quiet smile, 'that from that moment you took upon yourself the obligations of a parent with respect to these unfortunate children, whose real parents had proven themselves incapable of meeting their responsibilities. But what did we find during one surprise inspection – whose results, incidentally, are fully documented? We discovered that not only did you not prevent contact between children and parents, but that you actually encouraged it! Moreover, it turned out that you regularly released the children to the custody of their families – in some cases, we found evidence of stays of two days or more! This is not only a violation of the terms of the agreement, Herr Worton – it's a violation of the law!'

'If it's a violation of the law, why did you not report me to the courts?' asked Worton.

Instead of answering, the councilmembers conferred in a whisper; only the Burgermeister spoke at any length, while the others just nodded and made monosyllabic replies.

'We also received information from the Agency for Integration,' said the Burgermeister, assuming a dignified air. 'You are well aware that the law requires you to complete an intensive language course shortly after registering at your place of residence. Yet according to the Agency for Integration, you consistently ignored this requirement. What do you say to that?'

'I attended integration courses for the first six months of my residency here,' said Worton, surprised. 'There is a certificate attesting to this fact; it says that I completed the required course in its entirety. Until now, no one has notified me of any problems.'

The councilmembers held a second lengthy conference, from time to time casting wary glances in his direction. Worton realized that they were coming to the most important point.

Now the Minister of Theater took the floor. 'Herr Worton,' he said, clearing his throat impressively, 'our joint efforts – I mean the efforts of the inspectors of the Authority for the Guardianship and Administration of Cultural Affairs – uncovered a more serious violation. You are doubtless aware of these matters, Herr Worton, because we officially admonished you numerous times.'

'I have my guesses,' said Worton, somewhat provocatively.

'At issue are your ... er ... artistic views,' said Stackensteiner, wrinkling his nose. 'Your theories. I was present at several choir rehearsals. Do you recall what you told the children? The hero needs a choir! The choir helps him resist the conditions of his existence!'

'By "hero", Herr Worton no doubt meant himself,' offered Opitz with a quiet laugh.

'A hero!' the Minister repeated derisively. 'We are all aware of your irrepressible thirst for fame, Herr Worton, your aspirations, your poorly concealed ambition. And you were not ashamed to share with the children – our children! – these depraved words about yourself! You used the children for your own personal goals!'

Worton could feel the last bits of his patience evaporating with every word. But still he kept himself together. And when the Minister of Theater, having made his accusatory exclamation, leaned back, satisfied, in his chair, Worton spoke, emphasizing every word:

'I did indeed say those words to the children, Herr Stackensteiner. And then to you, when you tried to steer me straight. But as you just remarked – correctly – I have my own views. Thanks to these views I have created and released into the world several artistic collectives composed of children who had been deprived of opportunities. And I must acknowledge these children as heroes. They were deprived of everything – their parents, their home, their childhood – and yet they sing. They are true artists. You can take everything away from them, but not their gift. Because it is in the nature of the artist to resist his circumstances. But this is very difficult to do alone, which is why singers must often unite. That is what we call a "choir". Their voices are not drowned out in the choir – no, here each singer develops his own theme, each one creates. Sooner or later the artist must leave the choir in order to create as an individual. But he does so when he feels strong enough to set himself against the entire world. The choir helped him accomplish this. A choir is a gathering of heroes. That, Herr Stackensteiner, is what I told your children.'

His words were followed by deathly silence. Finally, the Burgermeister took the floor.

'Herr Worton,' he said reproachfully, 'you should have taken greater care to familiarize yourself with the terms of the agreement. All that you say here has nothing to do with its main purpose. We signed an agreement with you as a talented musical pedagogue, because we needed a choir. Do you understand? A choir, not a bunch of individual person-alities. Believe me,' he added sarcastically, 'I should know what I'm talking about, because I also created vocal collec-tives, more than once. A choir is a choir. And there's no need to fill our heads with your theoretical derivations. People unite into a choir precisely in order to sing. For instance, as you exit Town Hall to the right, you'll find Fat Peter's Bar – and every night, a choir gathers there. A very well-known choir in the city. And how they sing – especially when they get a few beers in them!'

Everyone at the table had a friendly chuckle.

'So just don't, Herr Worton,' said the Burgermeister, wrinkling his nose again. 'And especially when it comes to children. These are tender, easily wounded souls we're talking about, and you're all, "Individuality! The Artist!" They'll understand all of that on their own, when they're older. They're clever children. Look how well they sing, in spite of all your preposterous ideas. It's not a bad vocal collective, not a bad one at all, Herr Worton. And we wanted it to stay that way, before you ruined it completely ... Aha, here comes our Herr Dunkle!'

A young man strode confidently into the room, dark-haired and fairly plump, wearing a white dress shirt with the top few buttons unbuttoned and a fashionable black blazer, a little tight on his thick frame. The newly arrived man let his dark eyes linger on Worton for a moment, then proceeded to his chair at the table. He sat down in the fullness of dignity, spreading his knees wide and crossing his arms over his chest.

'Yes, yes,' said the Burgermeister, examining him with a soft smile. 'This is our Lothar Dunkle, director of the boys' choir. Your former choir, Herr Worton,' he added with vengeful finality.

Dunkle and Worton exchanged glances. Worton gave a curt nod. Dunkle did not respond.

'Tell us about your collective, Herr Dunkle,' the Burgermeister offered effulgently, then turned to Worton: 'Now Herr Dunkle will recount his achievements ...'

'It's a little early to speak of achievements, Herr Burgermeister,' interrupted Dunkle, somewhat unceremoniously. 'As you are aware, I have not yet been in charge of the choir for a full year. As for the choir itself ... Surely you will not deny that the group I inherited is far from easy. To be more precise, I've never encountered such stubborn boys before.'

'Improperly raised by their parents?' Opitz prompted softly.

'I wouldn't know anything about that,' Dunkle cut him off. 'But their aesthetic upbringing has definitely been improper.'

He gave Worton a hostile look and continued:

'And the issue isn't their repertoire. The issue is their worldview. You may laugh, but the problem is their view of art. These children talk about themselves as though they'd already earned their place as artists! Their thinking is ... well, I don't know, but in any case, not in any way acceptable at their age.'

'And what would be acceptable at their age?' asked Worton.

'I wouldn't know,' Dunkle answered superciliously. He continued, his arms still crossed: 'I'm not a child psychologist. What I do know for sure is that it's very difficult to remake these children, because they've been inculcated with incorrect views on art. Each of them is too individualistic. Together, they don't form a choir, a united collective; each of them strives to distinguish himself, if you can understand what I mean. A choir should be a singular voice, obedient to the director. There cannot be any other opinions in a choir.'

'Are you saying they don't sing in unison?' asked the Burgermeister with concern.

'No, that's not it,' replied Dunkle irritably. 'It's just that they have their own views of what they do. You see? To make them sing anything at all, you first have to convince them, prove the significance of this or that artistic act. You can't persuade them to do anything for the good of the city. To sing in church on a holiday, for example, or in the square on Regensburg Day.'

He stared daggers at Worton, who had erupted in a short, mirthless laugh. The councilmembers exchanged glances.

'But what do they want to sing?' Stackensteiner inquired timidly.

'The same stuff as before,' replied Dunkle with a moue of disgust. 'Mozart, Bach, and various lesser-known Baroque composers.'

'And what, in your opinion, is the problem with these composers?' Worton asked.

Dunkle gave him a sidelong glance.

'There's no problem,' he growled. 'It's just that, when you listen to them, you quickly forget your roots.'

Worton thought he had misheard, and asked in astonishment, 'What?'

'Your roots, Herr Worton!' Dunkle repeated forcefully. 'Your choir had become too international, whereas children must develop their patriotic feeling. That is why I expanded the repertoire to include German folk songs.'

Worton broke into astonished laughter.

'I don't see what's so funny,' said the Burgermeister, pursing his lips. 'By the way, this is your fault, Herr Worton. You left us an ungovernable choir.'

Worton shook his head.

'No, Herr Burgermeister. The boys are entirely governable, if I correctly understand what you mean by that. It's just that they spent a lot of time in my company. And my views on art are well known. I'll say it again – their truth is demonstrated by the worldwide success my collective has enjoyed. And I'm delighted that my boys are continuing to develop these views. Tell me, Herr Dunkle, was it really German folk songs the choir performed at the cathedral? I was there and saw the audience as it dispersed. It's been a very long time since I've seen such disappointed faces.'

Dunkle turned beet red and did not reply. The Burgermeister hastened to his defense:

'What can I say, Herr Dunkle inherited a difficult situation. Not that we're in a hurry. The most important thing is the result.'

'The result is already in evidence,' Worton remarked. 'My advice to you, Herr Dunkle, is to assemble a different choir. You won't get anywhere with this one.'

Dunkle had already opened his mouth to object, but here Opitz entered the conversation.

'Let's return to the question under discussion,' he said quietly, his glasses glinting. 'Herr Worton, tell us – if you were permitted to return to the position of choir director, would you find the courage within yourself not to repeat your mistakes?'

'I don't understand, Herr Opitz,' Worton replied.

'The courage, Herr Worton,' Opitz said again, patiently. 'I was speaking of the courage not to repeat . . .'

'I know what courage is, Herr Opitz. But I don't understand in what my mistakes consist.'

Opitz shook his head regretfully:

'I see. Here we've spent a whole hour explaining your errors to you, and yet you refuse to understand and accept them.'

'Yes, indeed,' the Burgermeister chimed in sadly. 'Of course, the council will confer some more, and, naturally, you'll receive our decision in writing . . . but if we're honest, Herr Worton . . . I don't think that, in the current situation, you should count on a renewal of the agreement.'

Silence fell over the group. Worton observed the men sitting at the table. The Burgermeister, looking sour, leafed through his papers, while Opitz shook his head, crestfallen. The Minister of Theater's eyes roved over the paintings; Dunkle, resting his chin on his chest, examined his impressive knees. And, when the Burgermeister made to speak again, Worton cut him off:

'Gentlemen, I think everything was clear to you from the very beginning. Naturally, I will impatiently await your written verdict. Yet I have just heard the verbal decision, and see no reason to hope that you will meet me halfway and fulfill my request.' He paused, then continued, emphasizing every word: 'Today I shall quit Regensburg. But before I do so, I will assemble a new choir. Your city is rich in musical talents, and I will certainly be able to find new singers here and now, before I leave. And when that happens, you will hear about it.'

He spun around and strode out, his resolute footfalls echoing thunderously through the enormous chamber. For a moment, he felt tempted to look back and see what impression his words had left on the councilmembers. But he suppressed this desire. Too important was the task ahead of him – he had to conserve his strength.

The guards met him at the door. Apparently, they had not yet received clear orders regarding his person, so they simply walked alongside Worton – two in front, and two behind. They descended the stairs. At the exit, the guards in front of him blocked the doors, and Worton was forced to stop. One of the guards spent a long time phoning someone, but awaited an answer in vain – in the end, he slowly placed the receiver down on the base and gazed sorrowfully at Worton. And Worton, realizing he was free, circumvented the confused defenders of law and order and left Town Hall.

The street was filled with impenetrable whitish mist. Even the ground underfoot was invisible. Yet Worton was possessed by a strange certainty – he felt that this dim shroud was no obstacle. It was as though an inner eye had opened inside him, and now he could see the traps of the treacherously narrow streets, the dead ends – and was able to avoid them in time. His legs carried him of their own volition along a familiar route, to Burgmüller-Platz.

Only once did he pause, as though tripping over something. A doubt had crept up on him, and for a second the feeling of confidence in his own strength deserted him. But he shook his head and banished the momentary weakness. He was overwhelmed with fury, fury and love. And, as he came to Burgmüller-Platz, he knew what to do.

The stone singers were concealed in the fog, like everything else around, but Worton found them quickly. Four hideous humanoid forms covered in layers of pigeon excrement, ossified with age, loomed in front of him. Worton gazed at them, stroking every curve and every protrusion with his eye. A colossal power lurks within unfulfilled wishes. And the force of song can be truly gigantic. It can topple centuries-old towers and raise the dead. What monstrous power, then, must lie within an unquenched thirst for singing! All he had to do was liberate this power, awaken it. And Worton, approaching the nearest statue, struck at it with a short, sharp word:

'Sing!'

At first, nothing happened – the statue simply continued standing there. But then it uttered a creak and moved. Shifting its stone arms, it gathered enough momentum to tear its feet from the pavement and stepped to one side. Here it froze again, as though lost in thought. It seemed as if it needed to get used to its new condition before it could obey Worton's command. It already looked different: a face with almost human contours was emerging, while on the body, outlines of what looked like clothing had appeared. After standing still for a minute or so, the statue turned around and jerkily approached its stone brothers. Here it emitted a strange and terrifying sound – as if a stone crusher was clearing its throat. It sounded more like a call than the beginning of a song, and Worton realized that the statue was inviting the others to sing along with it, that it wanted them all to sing together. He found it both terrifying and joyous to observe this awakening of stone. The newly living statue awkwardly touched the stone shoulder of one of its brothers with a short-fingered paw, then turned helplessly to Worton. He understood, filled his lungs with air, and addressed all three with a command that rang out louder than before:

'Sing!'

It was as though they'd waited two hundred years to obey – jerking to life, they raised their arms, trying to clean themselves of decades' worth of bird droppings. Their stone eyes examined their neighbors, their lips moved, but not a single sound yet escaped their gullets. Worton waited. The statues, as though performing some sort of ritual, at first spread far apart – Worton lost sight of them in the fog – and then, gaining speed, leaving behind trails of dry, whitish droppings, trash, and dust, converged again. They had all undergone a metamorphosis. These were not the faceless stone monsters from before – no, they had acquired human features. Their stone eyes came alive and rotated in their sockets; their mouths opened and closed to reveal teeth and flicking tongues. Worton thought for a moment that they were about to join hands and dance. But suddenly, as if remembering his orders, they formed a line, opened their mouths, and began to sing.

Never, not once during his long life, had Worton heard such monstrous sounds. The statues forgot themselves as they sang, their eyes closed, and not even the fog could shield passing listeners from the horrifying roar – all around, windows opened and people exclaimed in surprise. Worton listened closely, feeling satisfied. These nightmarish sounds were music to his ears. Finally, when the boulder-like voices became unbearable, he clapped his hands and shouted:

'Enough!'

They fell silent – not all at once, but each in his turn. He could hear them shifting their weight from one stony foot to the other as they awaited his next order. And then Worton commanded:

'Follow me!'

Now he was walking through the city as though there had never been even a hint of fog. Stepping lightly and with confidence, he turned every corner required, and behind him came the four statues, thundering and stomping loudly. The few people they encountered reacted in different ways: one woman fell into a quick and soundless faint, a man behind the wheel of a sports car turned rapidly onto a pedestrian-only lane, while two festival guards patrolling the street dissolved instantaneously in the thick fog.

Worton led the stone singers to the cathedral. The statues sauntered slowly along, but Worton didn't hurry them – the last thing he wanted was for them to crumble. The cathedral's silhouette floated majestically toward them out of the fog. Soon, they emerged from the last narrow street to approach it in earnest. The statues' footfalls should have rung out especially clearly on the cobblestones of the cathedral square, but the fog successfully dampened these noises, transforming them into a muffled echo of someone's distant stride.

Worton led his charges up to one of the cathedral walls, the same one he'd been looking at the other day. He thought he saw, in the eyes of the gargoyles populating the wall, a flash of something like hope. And once again, a momentary doubt gripped him – he felt afraid of deceiving these stone beasties, who had dreamed of singing for so many centuries. For an entire minute, or perhaps even two, he struggled internally, suppressing listlessness and uncertainty. But when he looked up at the wall again, he realized the moment had come. And, holding his arms aloft, Worton shouted up to all those mutely open-mouthed monkeys, boars, and curs:

'Sing!'

What followed this command was difficult to describe. Only the stone angels and prophets continued to hold their silence. All the other sculptures erupted in unimaginable howls. They had, of course, always wanted to sing, but when they got the chance, they weren't prepared to do so.

Their animal essence took the upper hand – the monkeys screeched, the gryphons roared, the boars oinked, the dogs broke into hysterical barking, but all of this noise was drowned out by the unhinged shrieking of the Judensau, the brood swine. And to top it all off, the stone street singers now joined in. Forming a circle, the four of them raised a howl, and the cathedral answered with the redoubled, unnatural wailing of hobgoblins desperately yearning to scream free.

But Worton raised his arms in an imperious gesture, and hundreds of stone eyes trained themselves on him from on high. The nightmarish yowling on the cathedral walls grew somewhat quieter. The dogs sniffed at him, wagging their tails, the pigs squealed happily, as though expecting food, the gryphons flapped their wings. Then, without turning around, he waved at his four statues, and they began to roar out something resembling 'Silent Night', so that his ears began to ache. Be it some other time, he might have stopped them, but today Worton smirked contentedly – and signaled to the cathedral. The stone gargoyles promptly obeyed his will, and – each after his own manner – began to growl, roar, bleat out 'Silent Night'. Worton conducted, lost in the moment, each new upswing of his arms calling forth further waves of screams that crested and broke on the walls of the surrounding houses.

It was then that Town Hall heard that Worton had assembled his new choir.

He was filled with an unexpected feeling of joy. So this, it turned out, was what he had desired – to liberate walled-up sound, to hear with his own ears the song of the silence-tortured gargoyle. Worton was starting to understand their language – the language of stone brutes mounted as terrifying scarecrows on the cathedral walls. They sang a song of fury – it was the only one they knew.

Hanging in the air in front of Worton, it seemed, were

hundreds of barely visible strands of fog, and each one of these was a voice. He stretched his hands out as far as he could, wrapped masses of the damp, slippery strands around them, and gave a short, sharp jerk, making the cathedral shake in a paroxysm of inhuman screeching. The gargoyles wailed ecstatically, closing their eyes and gaping their maws. When the shrieking had quieted down somewhat, Worton pricked up his ears.

A reciprocal howl came from somewhere far away – but those were just the emergency sirens. Festival visitors were fleeing the cathedral gone mad, locals abandoning their homes in a panic. With his newfound inner eye, Worton could see the police cars and ambulances rushing nonsensically around the city. And everywhere people ran, stumbling, trying to save themselves from the sonic onslaught.

But still he could not see his children.

So he gathered up even more strands from the air, clasping a thick bunch in each hand, and pulled with all his might. The stone gullets now produced a second, even more powerful and lengthy scream that caused the roofs of several houses on the edge of the square to collapse. And then the screaming ceased, with only a single stone dog, forgetting itself, still baying raucously in one of the galleries. But soon it, too, fell silent, and now the continuous honking of car horns, the faraway howling of sirens, and the hum of helicopters could be clearly heard. The streets were jammed with cars, all filled with frightened, fleeing citydwellers.

But his children were not among them.

Worton could feel fatigue rolling over him. But it was too early to give up. He had still not accomplished anything. The city wasn't conceding; it had no desire to give up the children.

He glanced at the cathedral walls. Baring their teeth, thousands of stone beasts come alive were gazing down at him – snuffling, yelping, and whining. They were waiting for his signal. They had acknowledged his authority as conductor – or no, it was more like they had acknowledged him as leader of the pack. In one of the niches, he suddenly saw the four singers – it was incomprehensible how and when they had managed to climb the façade. As they looked down on him from above, their hideous mugs, piebald with pigeon droppings, broke into grins of satisfaction. He involuntarily smiled back. A choir like this one, of course, was the perfect place for those masters of song.

He was filled with a feeling of languid desperation and raised his clenched fists in the air. Let them sing. Enough senseless screaming! Are you a choir or not? So sing, then! Sing!!!

And sing they did. He had no idea what they'd want to perform until they began belting out the 'Ode to Joy'. He burst out laughing and couldn't stop. It was the most nightmarish performance he'd ever heard in his life, but the monsters knew the words perfectly and sang with enormous pleasure.

Worton could feel his strength ebbing away. His ears were ringing; he had gone nearly deaf and was on the point of losing consciousness, as if shell-shocked. He was at the epicenter of a nightmarish sonic whirlwind – a transcendently hellish shrieking filled the air, and even the fog, it seemed, had thinned out and begun floating away in tatters under this ungodly assault. The shrieking made it impossible to think, to move, to live – the whole world had transformed into one infinitely long, unimaginably loud scream. And when the stone monsters faltered for one glorious second, Worton had just enough time to fully realize that he couldn't take much more. He managed to look around and see the depopulated city through the fog – empty streets, abandoned houses. The city authorities had evacuated the residents with speed and coordination, as during any emergency. But nowhere on those streets could he see his children. His children were nowhere to be seen.

Suddenly the beasts fell silent, looking down on their master with satisfaction, waiting to sing again just as soon as he said the word. Worton thought, in the silence that followed, that he had gone deaf, and shut his eyes tight in despair. But something forced him to shake himself and prick up his ears. It took several more minutes before he got used to the silence and gradually became convinced that his ears weren't playing tricks on him.

Yes, there could be no mistake – the city was capitulating. And Worton, relieved, commanded the waiting gargoyles:

'That's plenty! Enough!'

And he didn't look at them again as they slowly froze in their contorted poses, mouths agape with suffering. He was gazing into the fog, his face breaking into a happy smile.

He could hear a swelling sound – the patter of hurrying, running, impatiently jumping children's feet.

*Translated from the Russian by Maya Vinokour*

# Bora Chung

# Mask

*In recent years, several South Korean novels have caught American horror readers' interest, including Han Kang's* The Vegetarian *and Hye-Young Pyun's* The Hole, *and Netflix is currently teeming with Korean horror movies and television shows. But although the genre is quite popular in South Korea — especially in the summer, when the chills induced by horror books and films are used to combat the heat — very little Korean horror fiction has been translated and published for an American audience. The recent publication of* BORA CHUNG'S *much-anticipated debut collection in English,* Cursed Bunny, *in July 2021 may be the first step towards changing that. The following tale, which opens with a married couple hearing strange noises in their Seoul apartment and then takes a number of unexpected twists and turns en route to its macabre conclusion, was first published in Korean in an online magazine in 2012 and makes its first English appearance here.*

o

A TAXI STANDS AT THE INTERSECTION. It's not quite in the middle of it, but much of its bulk sits on the crosswalk as if it got stuck in the middle of outrunning a red light. Now it's bothering the cars making right turns. The drivers in the passing cars, of course, honk and swear at the taxi for single-handedly creating a traffic jam.

Despite the honking, the taxi does not move. There's no

one inside. The motor is running and the hazard lights blink. There's no sign of a driver.

Time passes, but the driver doesn't return.

I

It began with a noise. At night, and from the ceiling. A swishing, as if someone was sweeping the floor upstairs. *Seuk seuk seuk*. Sometimes, scratching. *Ggik ggik ggik*. Rarely, footsteps. *Bbiguk bbiguk. Koong koong koong*.

Upstairs was the roof. There was no way someone would go up there in the middle of the night to sweep the floor.

The married couple, therefore, tried to ignore it. They had never lived in a 'unit house' before, those five-floor multi-household buildings so common in this city. Everyone said they were not well insulated against sound compared to apartment buildings. Noise coming from next door would sound like it was coming from the ceiling. Not that next door sweeping the floor in the middle of the night wouldn't be strange, either. But that was their business. A little sweeping noise was all right. It wasn't like the whine of a vacuum cleaner. And there would always be noise in multi-residential housing. Neighbors had to make room for each other.

The sounds grew louder. *KOONG KOONG KOONG. KWANG KWANG KWANG. KKEEEEEEEEEEEEEK seuksak seuksak BBIGUDOK BBAGAK*.

They asked next door. Their neighbor had no idea about any noise. When asked if he did any cleaning at night, he bristled. He had to go to work at dawn, how could he have time to do anything at night except sleep? He'd be the first to complain about such a noise if he heard it. He didn't seem to be lying.

They waited for the night. When the sounds began, they

listened carefully. It wasn't next door. It wasn't the wall. It was clearly coming from the ceiling.

In the morning, they tried to go up to the rooftop. But their way was blocked. The steel door was locked, a chain wrapped around the door handles.

They called the landlord. He claimed they never used the roof. That it was always locked. There was no way someone would go up there at night and sweep it. The couple suggested children might go up there at night to play, but the landlord was doubtful. When the wife raised her voice, saying she was finding it hard to sleep at night, the landlord reluctantly agreed to go up there and take a look.

It did not seem like he took a look. The mysterious sounds continued.

They called the landlord again. This time, the husband demanded they go up to the roof right that minute. He shouted that he was determined to rub the landlord's face in the noise so he wouldn't weasel himself out of doing something about it. The landlord finally began to take it seriously. He said now was not a good time, but he would send maintenance staff to look into it.

The maintenance staff came in the middle of the night. Such staff were usually old men, but their doorbell was pressed by a young boy. He was overly pale, and the strands of hair coming out from under the brim of his cap were not black but a translucent brown. At the sight of the husband, the boy's face blanched and froze in fear.

'Y-y-you h-heard a noise from the r-r-roof?'

The husband gave the boy a once-over. Had he even graduated high school? How on Earth was he working this job? Was he the landlord's grandson?

'Let's go,' the husband spat out. Not the friendliest tone, but the boy looked grateful he was being spoken to in the polite form, and turned to lead the way.

Up the stairs, he put a key into the lock and tried to turn it. Rusted shut. He struggled with the lock before taking the key out and putting it in again, this time managing to turn it.

The husband watched the boy straining to open the door. It would not budge, despite his exertions. On the back of the boy's right hand pulling at one of the handles, the husband noticed a star tattoo between his thumb and forefinger.

That's when the rusty door opened with a loud and reluctant groan.

The night outside was dark. As the husband tried to step in front of the boy, he was cautioned, 'W-w-watch your f-f-feet.'

Not answering, the husband pushed the door open wider and took a step outside. The hinges screamed.

'Oh, wait, there – ' The boy flashed the path before him with a flashlight instead of finishing his sentence.

The moment he saw what was illuminated, the husband understood why the landlord had been doubtful about playing children. It wasn't a rooftop up there but a roof, just like what the boy had said. There was a narrow path leading to the ventilation shaft on the other end, but the rest of it was a tiled roof. Only someone unsound would go up there and sweep it. There were no lights whatsoever on the roof. One misstep, and it would be death by five stories.

The fight went out of the husband.

'T-t-tomorrow when the s-s-sun comes up, I'll t-t-take another look,' the boy mumbled behind him. 'Th-there might be a c-c-cat on the r-r-roof.'

A plea for them to go back down. Not that there was anything else to look at up there.

The boy turned. Just when the husband was about to follow him, he stopped. He called for the boy again.

'Give me the flashlight.'

'What?' The boy was already halfway down the stairs.

'The flashlight. Give it to me.' He held out his hand.

The boy hesitated. 'Um –'

'It'll only be a minute.' He bounded down the stairs and took it from him.

'B-b-but . . .'

The husband ignored him and went back, throwing open the steel doors. He shined the light on the roof.

Across the roof, in front of the ventilation shaft, there was a person. The flashlight showed their outline. A skirt fluttering in the night wind, long black hair flying.

The husband took a step forward. He was about to call out to her but stopped himself. It was dark, and there were no railings; he didn't want to surprise her.

It was a mystery why he did not think it was strange a woman was standing by herself on the roof of this building. He raised the beam a bit. The woman's outline was a clear black, but her face and other features were obscured. Despite the flashlight, she was pitch black as if lit from behind, which in itself was strange, but the thought that it was strange did not occur at all in the husband's mind.

Perhaps because the woman was that kind of woman.

Lit up by the flashlight, the woman turned to look at him. Or she at least moved as if she had. The husband wondered one more time whether calling out to her was unsafe. That's when she started walking toward him.

Her steps were slow and careful. The long skirt and flying hair had made him assume she was a young woman. But the manner of her walk and the sharpening outlines of her form made him think she might be very old.

She painstakingly made her way across the roof. Thinking he would do his best to talk her down, the husband waited patiently. Which was why when the woman was almost right in front of him, he stretched out his hand.

The woman vanished.

The husband was taken aback. He shined the flashlight everywhere around him. She was well and truly gone.

Fear seized him at the thought that she had fallen. He dragged the stammering boy down the steps and out of the building, but there was no sign of her body anywhere.

The wife, tired of waiting, came out and found him staring into space in the backlot of the building. When he explained what had happened, she looked skeptical. The husband had expected the boy to corroborate his story. And the wife had expected to hear a more reasonable one.

But the boy, looking very uncomfortable, could only mumble a few incomprehensible words. He cut the couple off, stammering quickly that it was late and he could come back tomorrow, grabbed the flashlight from the husband's hand, and left.

2

The woman came into the house.

After the roof inspection, there were no longer any noises from the ceiling. The couple was happy. And in a week, the wife saw a black stain on the edge of a wall in the master bedroom. It was right under the edge, where there was almost always a shadow, which was how the stain had evaded detection.

It was therefore impossible to tell when it had first appeared. The wife crouched down and stared at it. Not a liquid stain, more like . . . black powder. She wiped at it with a rag. It spread and faded a little. She wiped harder. The stain faded into almost nothing, and the wife had to be satisfied with that.

But it came back. There it was a few days later, a little darker, and a little more spread out. It did seem to get fainter with more wiping, but it wasn't easy wiping away at the edge, and her own shadow falling on the spot made it hard for her to see what she was working on. She didn't realize the stain had spread as widely as she had wiped.

The next day, the spot was back, enlarged and as dark as ever. Wiping it was only effective for a moment. It spread the more she wiped it, and even grew darker.

And the nightly ceiling noises returned.

The wife was the one who heard the noise. The husband had to go out at night for work. She lay in bed alone, her eyes closed, listening to the old sweeping, swishing sounds.

This time, the sound was much fainter. If she hadn't been in her room alone, the wife wouldn't have noticed it. But the bedroom was quiet, and there is a period in the night where even the faintest sounds can be heard. And that's why she heard this one.

It sounded as if a very small broom was sweeping the floor. She became convinced there was an insect in the room. Turning on the lights, she searched everywhere for it but she found nothing. The next day, she bought some bug spray and sprayed every corner of the room.

The noise never disappeared completely. It grew neither quieter nor louder. Because it wasn't loud enough to disturb her sleep, she decided to ignore it.

Which was why she never thought to connect the stain on the wall and the noises at night with the burnt smell that permeated the room.

The husband had switched to the night shift. He drove all night and came home in the mornings to sleep during the day. The neighborhood during the day was sometimes quieter than at night. Adults went to work, the children went to school, and it was only the old people and home-makers who remained. A peddler's truck might drive by announcing its wares or a group of old friends might gather to while away the time, but there was a brief period before that when the alleys were silent. The sun would be too bright for the husband to sleep, which was why he'd draw the curtains. Then the light and all the colors in the room would come down an octave.

In the dimness of the room, the stain at the edge of the wall stood up and came toward the husband.

He had thought it was a young woman when he first saw it on the roof. And an old woman when it came walking toward him. Seeing it climb onto the bed, it looked like a little girl. Light, small, quick. *Swish.*

They say the first hit is the strongest. Those who've done illicit drugs can never forget that first hit, searching for it over and over until they have lost their fortune, family, job, and everything else, eventually overdosing. It's the same with gambling addicts who can never forget their first win and eventually lose everything they have. Like one's first love lasting all of one's life, which is only a bit weaker but the same in principle. Whatever the stimulus, the sensation of dopamine flooding the brain goes beyond anything else a human being can experience. There are very few who have experienced that initial first hit who can consciously deny the experience after. To spend one's life pursuing that rush, to give one's life for it, to die for it, is perhaps our natural, human response.

The husband was caught that way. Before he could determine what it was, a young girl or an old hag, a human being or a ghost, the woman had already swished up to the bed and mounted him. There was no one at home to disturb them. His wife was at work and the children were in school and kindergarten. Until the curtain-filtered sunlight moved from one side of the room to the other and disappeared, the black stain ruled over the husband.

Those who go their whole lives without facing uncontrollable pleasure are as lucky as those who never experience uncontrollable pain.

When the wife returned home in the evening, she found her husband lying in bed with his eyes wide open. He didn't respond to her voice. She touched him. Only then did he blink as if coming out of a dream and turn to his wife's face. The wife made dinner but the husband did not eat. All he did was silently, weakly struggle to put on his clothing and go to work.

All through the night, the husband wandered in a haze. It was sheer luck there were no serious accidents or anyone dying, but who knows if that was luck or misfortune, considering what happened later. He finished his work earlier than usual and came home at dawn, waking up his wife. Not even answering her greeting or showering, he shed his clothes and climbed into bed, pale and with unfocused eyes. His wife asked if he was sick; he didn't answer. Thinking some sleep would restore him, she left him alone.

After the wife and children each left the house to go about their business, he managed to sleep for a couple of hours. And when the quiet time arrived with the sun shining into the house, the woman came alive once more from the black stain on the edge of the wall.

3

Who this woman was, and why she came to him, the husband didn't know. Not that he wasn't curious, but there was almost no opportunity for him to ask, and even when he managed to, the woman did not answer.

The husband was unable to do anything else.

The reason why addicts, no matter what their addiction, still make an effort to maintain their jobs is because they need money to keep feeding their addictions. Drug addicts need money to buy drugs, alcoholics to buy alcohol, and gambling addicts to spend on gambling.

The husband needed nothing. All he had to do was lie still on the bed and his addiction would come to him.

The state of addiction means everyone else in the addict's life simply falls away. The addict focuses only on the object of his addiction.

And that was why the husband always lay in bed.

Partly, it was because he was no longer able to work. It was too much to hope that he could drive in his dreamy state and not have accidents or hurt anyone. The husband caused an accident. Thankfully, no one was hurt. But it was a very stupid accident; he was taking one of his company's taxis out of the garage when he rear-ended another taxi. But he had ignored it and tried to maneuver his taxi out of the parking lot, forwarding and reversing and jostling his cab against the others, scratching and denting them. The other drivers shouted at him and the company employees came running out of their offices at the commotion. By the time he was dragged out of his cab, through a series of unsightly exertions by the people around him, it was clear the husband was in no state to drive. His eyes were unfocused and there were bags under them, and he was drooling through his slightly open lips. He responded to his name but his motions were noticeably slow, and no matter what question he was asked, he remained completely silent.

Someone called his wife. Shocked, she came running to the company, and taking one look at her husband, brought him to the hospital. He never did manage to get any help there. After some time staring up at the ER ceiling, the husband suddenly insisted he be taken home. They were yet to see a doctor, which was why the wife suggested they wait just a little bit more. But the husband began to scream that he wanted to go home and flew into a rage. The wife had no choice but to comply.

At home, the husband went straight to bed. He shouted at his wife to leave. Worried for him, she had wanted to cook him something to eat, or give him something warm to drink. But no matter what she offered, he only grew louder and angrier at her. Until eventually she gave up trying to care for him and went back to work. And as soon as he was left alone, the woman from the black stain appeared once more.

This was how the husband came to be always lying on the bed. And because he was always there, but the children were in school and needed clothes and food, the wife had to keep working. She had to keep working for longer hours.

When the children came home from school and kindergarten, the husband would push them out of the house. At first he would give them cash and cajole them into leaving. But eventually he ran out of money, leading him to push them out by force. One day, he changed the combination on their front door lock, and the children were unable to come home.

Banished, the children wandered the alleys until they grew hungry and went to where their mother was working. The wife brought the children home. The husband did not open the door. The wife pressed the doorbell, shouted for him, and called him on his phone, but there was no response. At first she was angry, but then she grew frightened by the prospect that he might be seriously ill or even dead. She called the landlord. Because he did not pick up his phone, she called a locksmith. The bald, potbellied locksmith took his sweet time coming and was full of complaints when he did arrive. In any case, the door was opened and the wife entered the house.

The husband lay on the bed. Away from normal life, his time with the woman of the black stain had left him skinny as a rake. The outlines of his bones and tendons were clear through his skin, his face was gaunt, and his eyes seemed to have increased threefold in size. The husband had trained those large, unfocused eyes on a corner of the room.

The wife tried to take the husband to the hospital. But the moment she attempted to pull him from the bed, the husband thrashed and cursed. She was too weak to fight him. There was no one around she could ask for assistance; she had no choice but to give up.

Left alone, the husband was docile as he lay on the bed. But he did not want to eat, did not answer when talked to. All he did was lie in bed with his eyes open and stare at a certain corner of the room. The wife tried to determine what exactly it was he stared at for so long, but she couldn't see anything.

After she fed the children and put them to bed, she tried once more to talk to her husband. But all she got was more of the same: silent staring at the wall. Desperate, the woman gripped her husband's bony hand and burst into tears. The husband slowly extracted his hand from her grasp. That was the only movement she saw him make that evening.

The wife cried herself to sleep, exhausted. She woke when she heard his panting and moaning. Still half-asleep, she turned her head and saw a reddish form was wrapped around her husband. The husband was naked, and the panting and moaning was a different sound from what she was expecting.

Realizing what was happening, she gave an involuntary scream. She sprang out of bed and ran to the door. Before her hand hit the light switch, she turned around toward the bed – it was less than a second.

The reddish form was standing by the foot of the bed. In the dark room, it was the color of half-transparent blood. It was pointing at something. And it spoke.

*Get me out.*

Whispered in her ear, a low, slightly hoarse voice. She heard it clear as day.

When the lights came on, the form was gone.

The wife didn't realize this, but the stain on the edge of the wall was also gone. And the strange woman never returned.

## 4

After the woman had disappeared, the husband still lay in bed for a while, waiting.

There is no way to explain with certainty why human beings persist in their self-destructive behaviors. A psychologist tried with the following experiment. They installed a small lever in a rat cage. When that lever was pressed, the rat received a shock. Not enough to kill it, but enough to make it suffer. The cage was large enough for it to roam without touching the lever, and there was also plenty of water and food.

After the rat had eaten its fill, it started to explore the cage. It pressed the lever accidentally. The shock hurt the rat, which squeaked – as expected, it avoided the lever from then on.

The cage was in all respects a comfortable environment. But that was all. There were no companions, no mate to copulate with, no toys to play with, nothing special to do. All the rat had was food, water, and the emptiness.

After a certain amount of time, the rat started going up to the lever and pressing it on its own.

Rather than peaceful boredom, the rat had found the occasional suffering to be much more interesting.

Human beings are not, fundamentally, that different from rats.

There is another experiment, conducted in another context, but similar to this one. A rat was given a cage, once again, with plenty to eat and drink. This time, they put in a mate and some toys. And also a lever. This time, the lever dispensed heroin.

Once the rats tasted it, they stopped doing everything else. Copulating, playing, even eating or drinking; they stopped doing everything that is normal for a living creature. All they did was press the lever again and again, for more and more heroin. Soon enough, they died of malnutrition and overdosing.

The husband's situation was closer to the second experiment.

But sometimes even rats in an experiment are better off than people.

It was hard to make a living as a taxi driver. In times of economic downturn such as the one they were facing, people were reluctant to take cabs. The price of gas went up but the fares stayed the same. Private cabs might be a little better off, but company-employed taxi drivers had a hard time meeting their quotas. Sometimes, they had to fill their quotas with their own money, something that had been going on for a while with the husband.

Their previous landlord had also raised their rent, which was why they had moved from a large apartment complex to the smaller building. But just because the building was older and smaller, it didn't mean rent was cheaper. With the end of their tenancy approaching, they hadn't been able to find a place in the Seoul metropolitan area in their price range, which was why they had taken the desperate option of paying a lower deposit and a higher rent.

Now that their rent was higher but the husband's pay was the same, they struggled to make ends meet despite having moved to the smaller place. The wife began working at a nearby coffee shop. She had worked hard the past ten years raising the children and taking care of the house, but there were almost no jobs for a housewife with no certified skills or licenses. Thankfully, the café owner was a married woman with children of similar age with whom she hit it off from the beginning, and she managed to negotiate good hours, but her pay, the wife felt, was too low. But there was nothing she could do about that. The owner consoled her saying she would give her a raise when she gained more experience, but the wife didn't really believe her.

The children grew. Which meant their expenses would mount. The wife wondered if she should quit the café job and find work at a restaurant instead. The pay would be higher, but the hours, no matter what restaurant, would be too long. The children were simply too little for that.

They were doomed to a future of moving to continuously smaller homes and working longer and longer hours until their bodies broke down, a future where nothing improved no matter how hard they struggled. Neither the wife nor the husband was unaware, on some level at least, that this was their fate when they moved to the unit house on the outskirts of the city.

And this new home had turned out to be a trap. Someone had put them in a cage, one where a lever had been installed. The husband had inadvertently pressed the lever one day. And he had fallen into the trap. They had no idea how easy it was for a plain and ordinary life to shatter in an instant.

But of course, in her situation, the wife was not at leisure to consider such a broad view.

Once she had witnessed the bloody form and heard the low voice whispering in her ear, the wife was of course filled with terror. Having had no previous interest in, or knowledge of, such things, she went to a place she had glimpsed in her neighborhood, a place that had a sign for a Buddhist temple but was understood by everyone as not, strictly, having anything to do with Buddhism. As soon as she entered this temple that wasn't really a temple, the person inside, who wore a monk's robes but was not really a monk, suddenly opened her eyes wide and screamed at her to leave. The wife tried to explain her plight, but the fake monk jumped to her feet and forcefully pushed the wife out the door. The fake monk's sole piece of advice before she slammed the steel door on her was that something venomous had stuck to her and she must move houses as soon as possible.

The wife visited one more similar place of business and called a couple of hotlines, but finally came to the conclusion that the first place was the most legitimate. The other specialists she contacted would listen to her whole story (the ones on the phone charged her by the minute for the call) and would suggest remedies ranging from a couple of hundred thousand won to several million. Talismans, shaman rituals, ancestral rites, prayer, 'care' – they had several words for it, but the conclusion was always money.

She had no such money, of course. In despair, she went back to the first temple. This time, the fake monk didn't even open the door for her. The wife pressed her ear to the door and as much as she could make out what was being screamed at her, she should 'for the sake of her children immediately leave that house'.

The wife returned home. She stared at her husband lying in bed. He was almost skin and bone, he refused to eat, work, or go to the hospital. He never met her gaze nor paid the children any attention when they came to his side. The only thing he waited for was the unknown red thing that came from the stain on the wall. If he were only, at least, having an affair with a real woman, it would have been much less frightening, the wife thought. She began to seriously consider the screamed-out advice of the fake monk.

And so she packed her bags and took her children to her mother's.

After his family and the woman in the stain were gone, the house became truly his own.

The husband lay there in the bed of the empty house, alone.

5

He lay like that for several more days. And then, he crawled out of it on his own.

There are two choices a person in the husband's situation can make. Whether that situation is one of addiction, pleasure, boredom, pain, despair, falling into a trap, or an awareness or unawareness of walking into one's own grave – whatever it may be, when one disregards the specifics, there are only two remaining courses of action: to work towards going back to the state of freedom before one's addiction, or to work towards perpetuating the state of addiction. This is the point where an individual's fundamental strength and humanity are put to the test.

The husband unhesitatingly chose addiction.

Unhesitatingly.

It had begun as a trap, but he had been given a choice. And he chose. Therefore, we have no real choice but to admit that what follows next was largely of his own making.

Perhaps humans are congenitally weak. Perhaps the husband merely did what any ordinary person – not a particularly bad person, but not a particularly great one, either – would have done, had they gone through the same travails.

By what right can one person truly judge another?

Since the disappearance of the woman of the black stain, the husband had experienced a truly rare level of hunger and thirst. Once he had replenished himself, he quickly went searching for what he craved.

Of course, the woman was long gone from his house. He tried rubbing the spot on the wall, tried shouting for her, but she did not appear. He thought perhaps he should go up to the roof, like the time he had first seen her. But the steel doors were locked, of course, which is why he called the landlord.

As before, the landlord, irritation in his voice, said there was nothing up there anyway, and furthermore, it was dangerous to go up there. As the husband raised his voice, the landlord once more said, annoyed, that he would send a person. The husband, before hanging up, asked him to send the same boy as before.

'Boy? What boy?'

'That boy, the one who looks like he just got out of high school. Pale face, stuttering –'

'I've never sent such a boy.'

'No, he was here, he wore a cap, brown hair, severe stutter –'

'A pale face, brown hair, and a stutter?'

'Yes. A very young man.'

'So what did this boy say to you? Did he say who he was?'

'He said he was maintenance staff.'

The landlord quickly replied, 'What staff? This isn't an apartment. There's no superintendent office.'

The husband felt his voice was caught in his throat.

'So this maintenance staff,' said the landlord. 'What did he say to you? Did he come into the house?'

'No, nothing like that.' The landlord's voice was so serious that the husband's grew small. 'He opened the door, so we went up to the roof –'

'*He opened the door?*' The landlord was frantic. 'That boy? He opened it? How could he? *How?*'

'He . . . had a key.'

'A key!' It was more of a scream than a question. 'What key! A key to the steel doors?'

'Y-yes, and the lock to the chain –'

'*The chain?!*' The landlord, with seemingly great effort, lowered his voice. 'Listen to me. I'm going to call the police. Stealing keys, going in and out of the building . . . I'm calling the police, so when they come, I want you to talk to them. Give them a description, and that, what is it, the stuttering thing, and . . . *who is this bastard?*'

The landlord slammed down the phone.

The husband went outside. He went up the stairs. He stood in front of the steel door.

The thick chain was wrapped around the handles, as always. The husband meekly pulled at the chains. The chain did not, of course, budge. The lock on the chain was as big as an adult man's fist.

Standing in front of the steel doors, the man looked at his phone. The boy who had claimed to work as maintenance staff had obviously not left a business card or a number. There was no way of knowing at this point who he was. The man touched the handles of the door and stood there for a long time.

## 6

The husband waited for the woman.

He didn't wait for his wife. Or his children. He waited for the woman of the black stain.

He asked his neighbors about her, but no one gave him a good answer. Never mind giving him an answer, they treated him like he was crazy. It was pointless asking the landlord, who was too preoccupied with the prospect of an intruder on his property.

The police did come. But after a short conversation, the investigation fizzled out. There just wasn't any way to get further details on the boy. What the husband knew was all they could discover.

But the husband was still addicted. He couldn't give up. Because he couldn't get what he needed from his neighbors or landlord, he began wandering around the neighborhood, finding nothing.

At a nearby general store, he happened to ask the old woman at the cash register if she knew anything about the roof of the unit house. That's when an old man, standing behind the husband and holding a bottle of soju and some shrimp crackers, butted into the conversation.

'Someone died on that roof.'

'What?' said the husband, turning around.

The old man didn't look at him directly, and it was obvious he was trying to sound casual. 'Someone died on that roof. It used to be a tenement house that was about to fall apart, they razed it to build a unit house and found a body there.'

The husband's ears perked up at the mention of 'body'.

'Do you know who it was? Who had died?'

The old man looked pleased that someone was finally paying him some attention. 'I don't know, some woman. She was burnt beyond recognition. The police came and everything, it was a mess.'

Some woman.

*The* woman.

'When was this?'

'Was it five or six years ago?'

The supermarket woman interjected, 'What are you talking about? It was almost ten years ago.'

'Really?' said the old man as he gently put down the soju and shrimp crackers on the counter. Without a word, the husband paid for that as well. He sat the old man down at an outdoor table with a parasol and tried to get more information from him, but he just repeated the same story over and over again. They ripped down the tenement house, they were going to build a unit house with one more floor, a body was discovered, it was a burned body, a woman, it was a mess, such a mess.

The husband brought home the snacks he was eating for his dinner. Munching, he searched the Internet, using words like 'murder' and 'burned corpse' and the name of his neighborhood, but there were no notable articles. He put in the name of the unit house with the term 'tenement house,' but there still weren't any relevant hits.

It was an old incident. Since he didn't know the exact date or details, he was unable to refine his search. Perhaps he had misheard the woman at the general store and the old man. There were too many unknowns. The only thing keeping him going was the obsession of an addict.

Which was how he input a countless number of terms and combinations into the search and ended up with a hit.

It was a tiny article in a local paper. Some tenement house – with a completely different name from the unit house – in the same neighborhood, where a woman's body was found on the roof during construction. It was discovered wrapped in white plastic and tape, with the face and various parts of the body burned in places. The construction worker who discovered it had initially thought it was building material. He called the police, who got some fingerprints and determined the body was the daughter of one of the tenants, and they put the prime suspect, who was the woman's boyfriend, on the wanted list.

That was all. Whether they found the boyfriend, whether he had really killed her, why he had killed her, or who the real criminal was – none of that information was available. It was already an old incident, and articles from the same period were only full of soccer news.

7

The man went to the edge of the wall where the woman's stain had been. He crouched down next to it.

'Come to me,' he said to the wall. 'Come to me. I'll avenge you. I'll release you. I'll be by your side.'

There was no answer.

The black stain did not return. The wall remained the same.

The woman did not return, either.

8

The husband went back to work.

Not because he wanted things to go back to normal. It was because he needed to keep the house so the woman could return to him. And that meant he needed to pay rent. Therefore, he needed money.

The only work he knew how to do was driving. But he'd been fired from his last company, and he couldn't go back. Elsewhere, his bad reputation preceded him, or they weren't hiring because of the recession, or the terms were terrible.

The husband was not in a position to choose. He was willing to do anything as long as he could make rent. He said yes to whatever work he could find.

The work hours were long and the customers were few. The husband spent most of his time in the driver's seat of a car. When he went home, he spent hours crouched in front of the edge of the wall and fell asleep there. When he woke up, he went back to making the rent and would return to the wall and beg for the woman to come back.

His wife called several times. He avoided her. Either he didn't answer, or he mumbled a few words before hanging up.

Everything valuable he had worked hard to build, he destroyed. And he had no awareness of what was valuable or what he was destroying. The husband thought only of the woman. To know who she was and how she died, and where she was now, and ultimately to experience her once more – that was the only thing he wanted.

At the end of the year, the number of drunk passengers increased. The ones who vomited in the cab were the worst. They rambled, or they rambled on the phone, or screamed at him from the moment they got in until the moment they got out, or sang songs that might as well have been screams.

And, of course, there were also the strange passengers.

A man got in the cab alone. He did not smell of drink. This reassured the husband somewhat.

The man, who looked to be in his forties, spoke his destination and was quiet for a while. Which was a relief, as the husband hadn't felt like making small talk either. He drove on in silence.

Then the man suddenly opened his mouth. 'A friend I know.'

'. . . Excuse me?'

The man spoke again, in a patient tone. 'A friend I know is in a bit of a bind. He's involved in something bad.'

'Oh . . .'

A vague answer to a vague story.

The man continued. 'He said to me, "If only I could change my face at will. The most recognizable thing about a person is their face, so if I could change my face when I needed to, I could walk the streets in broad daylight and live like everybody else . . ."'

'I see.' A ridiculous story, thought the husband. He remembered a foreign movie he had seen long ago. About a law enforcement officer who changes his face to infiltrate a criminal organization.

'You know, like in that movie? The one from a while back.' It was as if the man had read the husband's mind. 'Something about changing his face with someone else. That's what my friend suggested. It's probably easier to change your face with someone else's instead of changing your own face. If you could do that, it would be really convenient.'

'That's true.'

If whoever this was could no longer show his face on the street in daytime hours, he really must be in a bind. Well, if he's still sitting around wishing science fiction movies were true instead of doing something about it, maybe he deserved his misery.

The man in the back seat continued, 'But you would need a face to switch with, in that case. Don't you agree? So I asked him, where would you find a face like that?'

'And what did he say?' said the husband, humoring him. The taxi eased to a stop at a red light. A left turn here and they were at the man's destination.

The man seated behind him said in a gentle voice, 'My friend said, his girlfriend was very good with people, and she could get whomever he wanted to change his face with.'

The light turned green. Not having a chance to answer, the husband turned left and entered an alley.

'Let me off there at the sign.' As he took out his wallet he said, 'It felt so strange listening to him say that. Because his girlfriend is why he got into that bind in the first place.'

'Oh.'

The husband stopped at the sign. The man paid in cash. As he handed him the money, the husband noticed a tiny star tattoo between the man's thumb and forefinger. But before he could ask anything, even before he could open his mouth, the man slammed the door behind him without taking his change, and disappeared.

For a long while, this memory of the star tattoo lingered

like an afterimage. But he couldn't quite put his finger on what it was that bothered him.

## 9

A week passed, and then another week, and then another . . .

The man's life was the same. The only difference was that he and his wife were nearing divorce. She called him again, had him listen to the children's voices, and carefully suggested he leave the unit house and join them. The man began shouting at her, but the wife already knew his answer. Was he still living with *it*, he was going to die because of *it*, she shouted back. The husband roared that he was the one who would die, she should mind her own business, and he would never leave the house. He hung up. That was their final conversation.

But the husband was not living with *it*. The woman in the black stain did not come back. He was losing hope every day.

And then, he saw her.

It was a large intersection. At night. The husband had let his passenger off and was headed back downtown. Just when the light turned green and he was about to drive on, he turned his head to the right.

There, the light was simply too bright. He saw a convenience store between a bank and a bakery. The hour was late, the bank was long closed. So was the bakery. Between the two dark storefronts, the convenience store shone so brightly it was almost unearthly.

The man saw the woman in the black stain standing there inside the glass front of the convenience store.

Her head was bowed a little. Slowly she raised her hand and pointed to a place behind the cashier.

The husband followed the direction of the woman's hand, spellbound. The cashier had a pale face and brown hair – the boy.

He stopped the car. There was no time to find a proper parking spot. He didn't even turn off the engine. He was in such a rush that it was a miracle he turned on the hazard lights at all. Leaving his taxi behind, the husband ran toward the convenience store where the woman from the black stain and the pale boy with the brown hair were inside.

10

The taxi at the intersection was left there for quite a while. The reason it took so long for someone to report it was probably because despite its being a traffic nuisance, it wasn't completely blocking the street. It was also late at night, and there wasn't so much traffic to begin with that far from downtown Seoul.

Finally, a passerby became suspicious of the abandoned taxi and reported it. A tow-truck arrived. It hitched the front of the taxi on its hook and took it away.

The tow-truck did not go far when its driver began noticing that all the cars behind him were honking their horns and flashing their brights. There was a thick, sticky liquid flowing out of the trunk of the taxi.

Terrified, the tow-truck driver called the police.

11

The husband was found dead, his body crammed inside the trunk.

When it was first opened, a large amount of blood gushed outside. The body had its back to the opening and was rolled into a ball. Half of it was submerged in blood, but it was wearing its clothes and there were no noticeable wounds at first glance.

But when they took the body out of the trunk, they found it had no face. The skin was missing, leaving just the bones of the skull, as if it had been a mask that had been peeled off.

The culprit was not easily found.

The woman never returned to the unit house. She stayed at her parents' place even after her husband's death. She ended up finding some other place for herself and her children to live. She never had anything to do with the unit house ever again.

Nothing more is known about the woman in the black stain or the pale-faced boy.

Or perhaps, nothing more could ever be known.

*Translated from the Korean by Anton Hur*

# Steinar Bragi

# The Bell

*Icelandic horror fiction is a relatively new phenomenon; in fact,*
STEINAR BRAGI *(b. 1975) can almost be said to have invented it in*
*2009 with the following tale. This story was recommended to us by an*
*Icelandic writer who had read it a decade earlier when it was first pub-*
*lished in a literary magazine, and it had stuck with her all that time —*
*just another example of how powerful good horror fiction can be. One*
*Icelandic critic has likened 'The Bell' to the films of David Lynch and*
*David Cronenberg while calling it 'by far the best horror story that's*
*been written in Icelandic'. Steinar is one of the leading writers in his*
*native country, best known for his poetry and literary fiction. Unlike*
*many authors in this book, he is not entirely new to American readers:*
*his novel* The Ice Lands, *about four young people from Reykjavik*
*whose car breaks down in the creepiest and most remote spot on the*
*island, was published in the U.S. in 2016 and is well worth seeking*
*out — it's one of the more atmospheric horror novels we've come across*
*recently. The following story's title in Icelandic literally translates to*
*a particular part of a bell, the 'clapper'. Those who remember 1980s*
*television commercials will understand why we've taken the liberty of*
*altering it slightly.*

I

THERE ONCE WAS A SMALL VILLAGE called Requim. The
village was on one of the World's End Islands that Kliny
wrote of and, like most hamlets on those isles, had been built

above a rocky shoreline. Thus was the sea forever purling in the villagers' dreams and The Quivering permeated anything of matter made, provoking nausea in all and sundry. Though not in the locals, poor sods, who undoubtedly grew accustomed to it, and there were but few newcomers to speak of following The Great Devastation. Actually, no stranger had set foot on the island for two or three hundred years. That is, not until those events unfolded that will henceforth be told.

In the middle of the village there was a church surrounded by a small cobblestone square. People would gather there to chat about this and that, and it was also home to a market six days a week where the villagers sold their wares. Not so long before, a tower had been added at the back of the church, and in it there hung a giant bell made from a hunk of bronze that was found in one of the mines. The bell was rung for weddings, funerals, and mass every Sunday – all the goings-on in this otherwise sleepy community that eked out its day-to-day beyond the church walls.

One night, shortly after midnight, it happened that the bell began to ring, rapidly and erratically, for close to a minute before falling silent once again. This aroused, as you might well expect, no little curiosity in the village, and so the priest and a few of the church's most wakeful neighbors gathered in the square and gazed up at the window in the tower without catching sight of anything particularly noteworthy. After conferring about what the best course of action would be, they proceeded, single-file, into the church – some of them, admittedly, quite shaken, their knees doughy and trembling.

The sexton, by far the brawniest of the group, was the first up the tower stairs. There he saw five or six of the most emaciated stray dogs he'd ever set eyes on – little more than ribs, teeth, and bulging eyes. They were crowded under the bell and snapping at something that was dangling from it.

When the dogs became aware of the people, they darted howling to the walls, but the attention of those now huddled in the doorway was directed at what was hanging upside down from the bell: a baby, one that appeared to be dead. On the floor below the child was an ever-growing pool of blood, which had started to darken in some places and had been smeared across the floor by the dogs' paws. But most horrifying to those present was the child's bulging belly, which seemed on the verge of bursting and expelling its entrails onto the floor, and the face – if you could call it that – which, being closest to the floor and therefore the mongrels' jaws, had been clawed at and eaten away. There was nothing left but a blood-white skull; lips and tongue had been devoured and so, too, the eyes, which were not but black holes.

*The dogs*, thought the sexton, and his first reaction was one of nearly overpowering hatred and disgust. Not only had they consumed the child's face, one of them had even managed to shimmy up and hang from it while gnawing into its belly. Perhaps it was that assault that had started the bell ringing.

The sexton took a few steps into the chamber and then stopped again. What was the babe doing there? How did it come to be there? He stood there frozen, unable to drag his eyes from the child and the bell, so grotesque was the sight; its face was like a grinning mask. Those assembled in the doorway behind him didn't do anything either, or at least, not right away. They all just stood there, frozen and gaping. Suddenly, the child was wracked with a cramp, its back arching and swinging upwards – almost as if it were doing so intentionally. One hand looked to be groping for the rope that was wound around its feet, the same rope the clapper hung from, *as if it wanted to free itself*. Convulsing thus, the babe's head struck the bell with a single, resounding clang that sent such a profound terror through the sexton that his whole body went numb.

And then it was over. After its final spasm, the child seemed, finally, to die. A slow shudder passed through it and then it went still, this young life vanishing, unequivocally and ineffably, back from whence it came.

The priest was the first to get his bearings. He strode past the sexton and over to the child, made the sign of the cross over it and then commanded the people to leave the church. It was then that the village constable and the doctor shambled in.

The constable immediately commenced his investigation, cordoning off the church and handling the scene, from the very beginning, as though a crime had been committed. Anyone could see, after all, that the child could not have gotten *itself* into such a situation. After closer inspection, it was discovered that the bell clapper was nowhere in evidence, while the rope, on the other hand – that is, the rope that the clapper ought to be hanging from – wended into the child's rectum. After some palpating of its abdomen, it was determined that the clapper – however this had come to pass – was *inside the child*.

The investigation downstairs in the church revealed that the timber wall next to the altar had recently cracked and this was where the dogs had slunk inside, lured by the smell. Then again, truth be told, there was a very strong odor in the bell tower as well – one that, as those present agreed, was not unlike what you'd smell after lightning struck.

At long last, the child was cut down from the bell and carried, with the clapper, back to the doctor's house, where he immediately commenced with the postmortem. In the process, he was able to confirm that the bell clapper was indeed inside the child, wrapped in its colon and small intestine and snug against the spine. Judging from the size of the child's rectum – a mere finger's width – it seemed unthinkable that the clapper could have been pushed into it. But further examination revealed absolutely no indications of how it had found its way there.

Returning to the matter of the bell ringing, the most likely explanation seemed to be that the child's head had struck its side. Indeed, the bones of its skull appeared to be both stronger and heavier than generally occur in children and showed no visible fractures, which to the doctor's mind, both refuted his explanation and made the preceding chain of events all the more mysterious.

The rest of the child's remains seemed neither entirely unnatural nor precisely normal. Its brain seemed poorly developed – it was a darkish purple, around the size of a date, and floating in a turbid cerebral liquid. In light of this, the doctor suggested to the constable that the child had been abandoned by its parents, who had seen death in its eyes. But of what happened next, he could say nothing, and nothing came to mind but the most dubious of fantasies.

News of the child traveled fast, and the islanders immediately began speculating about what could have caused its death. Mountain spirits, avenging themselves for the mines, for the way the mountains had been hollowed out from within. God, punishing the islanders for the way they lived – they were gluttonous and lazy and some of them overindulged in drink. Then there were the more pragmatic explanations. The child was sleepwalking, had wandered into the bell tower, gotten tangled in the rope, and stuck the clapper up its bum. Basically, the kind of suppositions that all communities have to endure from the most simple-minded among them.

All theories posited seemed to take it as a given that they were dealing with a real baby, and more particularly one of the town's own tots, but the house-to-house inquiry conducted by the constable and numerous volunteers – both within the village and across the island – revealed that no one was missing a child. There wasn't even the faintest rumor about a pregnant woman whose child had vanished or was presumed dead. There was nothing suspicious, not a trace – except, of course, the faceless corpse of a child turning blue on the examination table in the doctor's house. For a time, the constable considered conducting an examination of the genitals of all the women on the island, to identify signs of childbearing, but ultimately found the prospect too repulsive. In the end, the child was buried in a brief but well-attended ceremony in the village cemetery – everything, that is, except its deformed brain, which the doctor retained for further analysis.

2

After this, very little of note happened, although it did feel as though there was a palpable malaise hanging over the village. Maybe it was nothing more than the creaking of the timber houses when the winter tightened its grip on the ill-used, beleaguered villagers. Maybe it was the gruesome memory of the child – the unending speculations about its beginning and its end shared amongst them, speculations that pursued some of them even into sleep before propelling them half-sobbing into their kitchens in the middle of the night to sip coffee, or trembling into the pub the next day.

No, nothing near as exciting had happened in the village for some years – decades, even. But less than two weeks after the child was buried, the horrors resumed, this time as a mystifying lice epidemic that struck down several old folks in the village, while younger residents descended into one or two days of seething madness, spewing incoherent words and ejaculations – many of which concerned children and clappers. The source of the vermin was never confirmed, but their bites clearly transmitted some kind of infection, possibly a result of contact with a rabid rat that had staggered and swayed along the main streets of the village until it was finally killed.

The latter was not but a spur-of-the-moment supposition of the doctor's, but over time, it became the explanation of record. In reality, the doctor knew nothing about such things, and after conducting an autopsy of the rat, he stuck it in a jar and poured formaldehyde over it, preserving it in the event that something should occur to him later; into another jar went a few of the lice, and liver samples from one of the old folks who'd been felled by the epidemic went into a third. Thus had the doctor acquired three new jars for his research in just a few short weeks.

The plague of lice didn't last long. The villagers collectively undertook to clean every nook and cranny of their homes and destroy all the rats. And soon life resumed its regular routines – that is, until one dark and stormy night when the church bell began to ring.

Just as before, the ringing started shortly after midnight and events played out much the way they did before: the sexton, the priest, and a few of the villagers who lived near the church gathered in the square and, even more terrified than before, gazed up at the bell tower. This time they dared not go inside, but rather waited for the constable to arrive.

When the constable got there, he accompanied the priest up into the tower, where the scene was all too familiar. A few stray dogs hovered ashamedly along the wall, yelping, and, much as last time, a babe hung from the bell, head-down, its face a mauled, blood-white wound. This time, however, the child's stomach had dropped from its casing and was lying in a steaming, blue-green heap on the floor under its head. The dogs had already invaded, scattering its intestines all over the room. And deep within the abdominal cavity, there in the matte-red darkness, glinted the clapper – the selfsame one that had been removed from the previous child and then rehung in the bell.

The priest crossed himself. By the time the doctor arrived, the priest and the constable and those assembled had moved into the stairwell, gagging at the sight and the powerful odor of charred intestines.

Thus did the doctor come to add another brain – and a fourth jar – to his collection. But neither the investigation nor the autopsy resulted in any concrete conclusions beyond what they already knew. This time around, they conducted a more concerted search of the church, since it seemed increasingly likely that this was a murder they were dealing with. Nothing of note was discovered, however, except a new crack in the church wall, which accounted for how the dogs got in. This aperture was on the other side of the altar from the first one, which had been repaired.

People were now much freer with their outlandish theories, and even the more useless proposals – that the rope from which the clapper and child had hung should be unraveled, for instance – seemed increasingly less obtuse. There might be something to such schemes, people agreed, although precisely *what*, no one could say. Upon analyzing the rope threads, the doctor determined that the end of the rope was made of some sort of organic material. Closer examination revealed that it actually looked a little like meat, and progressively so, the closer you got to the clapper. The doctor also showed the constable the bizarre sheath that enveloped the clapper; the innermost layer was tightly woven and snug, while the outer one was looser and softer. It made him think of a uterus turned inside-out, but he kept this latter observation to himself.

In the end, the length of rope that extended from the bell

to the clapper – not, in and of itself, the least bit nefarious – was removed from the church and burned. The priest took considerable pains with the consecration of a new rope, with many prayers and much wailing. For a time, there was even talk of changing out the bell itself – as if the bell had done anything! But of course, there was no money for something like that.

And so, the investigation came to a close. No culprit was found, and none was considered likely. Just as with the previous child, the incident induced all manner of foolishness, the unquestioned pinnacle of which being when a woman, within earshot of her husband and his friend, asked the obvious question concerning the rope and how the child came to dangle from it; she asked, that is, about an *umbilical cord*, but this line of inquiry was not widely taken up, nor was it discussed much further.

'Virgin birth' was far from the most imbecilic hypothesis that swirled in the minds of the villagers. It seemed evident that the children must have been born in the bell because no link to the village or elsewhere on the island was ever uncovered.

After much debate about whether the second child should be burned, buried, or even allowed anywhere near the church again, the villagers elected to inter it on a desolate spit in a brief, sparsely attended ceremony presided over by the priest.

Afterwards, various things of little to no consequence changed in the life of the village. The constable started carrying a gun on his patrols, not least to show people that there was nothing to be afraid of, and the priest decided that the bell would no longer be rung for mass – not, at least, until the memory of those grim events started to fade in the villagers' minds. In his best-attended, most inspiring sermon, he implored people to keep calm and enumerated the hazards of letting imaginations run wild. For some reason, he said, Good always had trouble taking root in people's minds, while Evil had a knack for inciting all kinds of ungovernable emotions – anger, sorrow – and before you knew it, everything was doom and gloom. That was just the way of it.

But what was this menace? What were the villagers afraid of and what was the Evil they spoke of? (Or, for that matter, the Good, if you followed that logic to its end.) Children had died and no culprit had been found, but why be afraid, why turn everything into something so onerous and sinister? Why conjure forth such things from the darkness? Did they think their number was up next, perhaps? Did they think that life wouldn't go on?

But, of course, life went on. Generally speaking, people's attitudes were fairly measured, and they understood that while maybe some things could be explained, others could not, and their fear was probably just a result of the uncertainty of the situation. And maybe some people were just *too* curious. Maybe there was only so long you could let your mind dwell on such events before they led you astray, before they pulled you – at least sometimes and much to the dismay of the priest – over to the dark side, to the side of those who said that you, too, would die one day and have to answer for the life you'd led, who said that day might come sooner than you expected and that it might even have something to do with the strange series of events in the bell tower.

All of this was speculation, but thoughts in this vein started running wild in people's minds; fear began to creep into their conversations. It was taken as a given that there was no end in sight for the chain of events that were now underway. Things were going to get really *bad*, that much was certain, but in reality, no one could make heads or tails of any of it. No one had seen anything like it before – not even the mayor's brainy son, who was always hanging around the pub.

'A chain of events,' people called it, but what was it leading up to? Where would it end? Where had it begun?

There was no end to the blathering and new theories, and all of it was tinged with despair, such that some people started to avoid any mention of 'the events', as they came to be known. Even silence became fraught. There was something in the air.

3

And then came the day when that something in the air came down to earth. Not long after the second child was buried, the grain in one of the fields not far from the burial site began to wither and die. Upon closer inspection, it appeared that black mold had settled over the crop and not only infested the surrounding fields, but also those some miles away. The farmers set fire to the infested fields to prevent the mold from spreading further, but by evening, those who'd taken part in the conflagration began to fall ill. They spent the night laid up in bed and were dead by morning.

The doctor, who had now been appointed an assistant by the mayor, sprang back into action, setting out around the island to gather the dead and prevent the infestation from spreading. The deceased were mostly farmers and their laborers. Some farms along the route were completely silent, while others were filled with the drawn-out squeaking of suppressed sobs behind closed doors. Island folk weren't big on showing their emotions.

Carefully concealed behind a mask, the doctor had the bodies gathered up in a covered wagon and took it with him back to the village, which had been barricaded and assigned a watchman to prevent infected persons from getting in. It was still largely free of the scourge.

The doctor's working hypothesis was that the black mold that had infested the fields had now started infecting people. In every instance, the chain of events was the same: after working out in the fields, the infected individual complained of nausea and a headache, then difficulty sleeping, then numbness in the lower back that spread down their legs and throughout their whole body. By morning – roughly twelve hours after having left the field – it was as though the infected person drowned in their own blood, silently. The doctor suspected that a plague – the first of his career – was on the verge of wiping out most of the island's inhabitants.

He moved all of the bodies save two into cold storage before proceeding into his autopsy room, and, filled with equal parts anticipation and disgust, began to slice into a middle-aged farmer who seemed to be a typical case. The doctor had also kept out the body of a teenage girl who'd died within an hour of her first symptoms.

For the first few hours, it seemed to the doctor as though the diagnosis, per his handbook, was a disease called *ergot of rye*, which produces a special kind of fungus that settles on stalks of grain and consumes the plant's carbon before releasing spores that are carried through the air. It was in this second phase that the fungus could infect people, although that wasn't common; when it did, however, it entered via their respiratory system and made a pulp of their lungs and organs in very short order.

He quickly brushed such musings aside, though, when he observed the awful beauty manifesting on one of the bodies. The doctor was bent over the girl's lungs, scooping out a strange, moldering growth, when he noticed that the face of the farmer on the adjacent slab appeared to be changing. The eyes became creased and then desiccated before sinking into the sockets; a low buzzing emanated from the nostrils and mouth, reminding him of the corrosive bubbling of acid. The skin at the farmer's crown, where the three bones of the skull met, started to bulge as though something was trying to force its way through a wafer-thin crack.

'*The soul, the soul . . .*' murmured the doctor in his agitation, retreating from the body while manically crossing himself and staring at the darkly hued, glistening knob – undeniably similar to the cap of a mushroom – that was growing out of the man's head, gingerly at first and then much faster and straight up into the air. The part of the doctor's hypothesis concerning fungus appeared to be correct, then, but what he was seeing before him wasn't in any handbook. Based on what he'd seen in the countryside, the girl's spine, and piecing together this and that detail, the doctor thought it fairly certain that a spore had entered through the man's respiratory system and from there the infection had spread through the bloodstream. What happened next, however, was unusual: the spore had entered the medulla oblongata and traveled down the spine, feeding on gray matter and spinal fluid – hence the numbness in the lower back that people complained of – and paralyzing the body from top to toe as the fungus wended its way along the spine and into the brain, where it mushroomed inside the skull. At the same time, it spread through the peripheral nervous system, stringing itself along each nerve into the hands and feet and thereby establishing some kind of root system that absorbed the water and nutrients it needed to make it the final stretch and finish the job: up out of the skull.

Seeing the writing on the wall, the doctor shook himself out of his stupor; he knew what would come next. Reproduction. Or hopefully, just its initial phases, if he could get out of there in time.

He rushed out of the room, fetched his tools, and hammered a peephole in the door before affixing a piece of glass over it. Then he shut the door to the lab, most likely for the last time. As he did so, the girl's face, just like the farmer's before, began to sink into itself. Soon, a mushroom burst through the top of her head as well.

The mushroom appeared to reach its full size – around three feet tall – within an hour of sprouting from the farmer's skull. The same thing happened to the girl, although for her, the process was much faster. The thickness of the mushroom at the base of the skull was barely an inch – around the diameter of the spinal canal – and it tapered as it moved away from the hole, which was gradually beginning to widen. In the end, the mushrooms on both bodies released spores which the doctor watched float around the room, illuminated in the last rays of sunlight like dust motes before the room grew dark.

In the days that followed, the plague descended over the island in full force. The villagers began to fall ill, and the watchman vanished into thin air. The doctor distributed face masks, but the supply was limited and it wasn't long before it was decided that he, along with the mayor, the shopkeeper, the priest, and their wives and children – the upper echelons of village society, that is – would remove themselves to an isolated cavern down on the beach and wait out the plague there.

The spores scattered quickly and efficiently. They were transmitted on the breeze, in sneezes and coughs, and by the people who gathered around the bodies of the dead, as they'd done from the start, the better to watch the bizarre blooms as they emerged from the skulls and stare, open-mouthed, at the steady stream of spores they emitted.

Once the village appeared to be devoid of all life, the ruling class returned, masks on, and surveyed their surroundings. There were people, animals, and even flies lying everywhere you looked; they were scattered through the streets and in the houses, their heads all adorned with slender-stalked mushrooms. The spores hung over the village like a silver mist.

A few days later, the wind blew the spores away. Those islanders who were still alive gathered together and discovered that around a hundred people had survived the plague, most of them by self-isolating and keeping their faces covered. Masks firmly in place, they began to clear away the carcasses under the direction of the mayor, dragging them into heaps: one for horses and cows; one for birds, dogs, blowflies, wasps, and bees; one for people. Then they set them on fire.

That evening, the priest was standing over yet another formless heap on the main street. Just as he lifted his hand and was clearing his voice to bid adieu to these unfortunate creatures, the church bell began to ring for the third time – rapidly and erratically, although, if possible, it now seemed to be ringing even faster than before.

This time, there was no sexton to lead the way and no constable, either – both were lying in the heap in front of the priest with fanned-out, three-foot mushrooms extending from their heads. And so, the priest, along with the doctor and several others, steeled himself for the church bell to fall silent and mounted the stairs first, death behind him and death before.

Everything was different, but it took the priest a moment to determine what precisely had changed. As before, something that looked like a baby was hanging from the bell. It was the size of a baby and dripping blood that was red like a baby's, but it was not a baby. Hanging from the bell was a *dog*, one of the strays that had straggled into the tower. A rope was wrapped around its neck and its back paws dangled over the floor, twitching in its death throes. The other dogs were in the corner, but something in their manner had changed – they were no longer running anxiously along the walls, but were sitting absolutely still, and instead of yelping, they were growling softly. And there was something else – something that the priest couldn't put his finger on. He scanned the dogs, scrutinizing each of their faces in turn. Finally he saw it: the child. There, in the middle of the pack, a child sat watching him, expressionless, or no – so utterly and profoundly *not there* that the priest forgot who he was; the world turned upside down and disappeared. The blank expression became a grimace and then suddenly it was as though a curtain was drawn; the child's eyes rolled back in its head and it lay down on its side on the floor, frothing at the mouth and convulsing.

The priest snapped back to attention, raised his crozier, waded into the middle of the pack of dogs with the doctor, and groped for the pallid child. Then they raced to the infirmary, the dogs following in a single-file line behind them, yelping and snapping as though frantic with a hunger that had yet to be sated.

4

Over the coming days, the child lay in the infirmary in a stupor. The doctor examined it and was struck by a number of observations, though almost certainly fewer of these than some may have feared. The child's rectum was torn, and badly so, undoubtedly because the clapper had been drawn out of it, and the end of the bowels bulged out from the gash. The clapper itself was hanging around the child's neck, secured there by a strange, organic rope that was looped around it many times. It looked not dissimilar to an umbilical cord, except perhaps that it was too tough for the doctor to cut through. In addition, the child had teeth – unusual in babies – light brown and sharp-edged, and its penis was, unlike the previous two children, hairy and about the size of a full-grown man's, or probably a good deal larger.

The examination was far from easy for the doctor. Every time he touched the child, a shock ran through him. This eventually gave him a headache and made him nauseous, but, on the other hand, seemed to arouse the child, as evidenced by its stiffening member, which rose up from its hairy, dark nest like a condor and drew so much blood into itself that the child's cheeks grew sallow, its body shaking with some sort of mild cramp.

At first, the child seemed to be only a few days old, but over time, it looked like it was aging more rapidly than might be considered normal; it fattened and filled out until it seemed to be at least three or four years old. One day, while the doctor was trying to puncture the umbilical cord with his knife so as to remove the clapper from the child's neck, he suddenly noticed that the child was awake. Its eyes were open, and it was staring at him. It was late at night and the doctor was alone; those preeminent plague survivors had gaped their fill at the child and more than one (more than two, even) had urged the doctor to 'take care of it' at the first opportunity. He'd always refused, but now, as he looked into its eyes, it occurred to him that he'd made a mistake, possibly his last.

The doctor and the child gazed at one another until it heaved itself to its feet and started to toddle around the bed as if limbering up, getting its blood flowing. This unsurprisingly came as a shock to the doctor, who fell back against the wall, open-mouthed. The room was silent, aside from the yelps and yips of the dogs that had gathered outside. Then the bed began to creak as the child started to alternately thrust its hips and head so that the clapper lifted and fell against its chest with heavy thunks – it was happy, from the looks of it, and seemed not to notice the doctor. Finally it got out of bed, waddling or shambling, like a monkey, in circles on the floor in front of the doctor, its body still ill-suited for movement, its little legs protuberant and bowed, its head grotesquely oversized, its prick far too large, and then the impossibly heavy clapper – though the child seemed not even to be aware of that.

Then it ran out of the room as the doctor watched from the doorway, making its way towards the storeroom where the doctor kept his jars and samples. He trailed behind it, saw the child heading toward the new jars that contained, among other things, lice, old folks' livers, the rabid rat, and the brains of the last two children. The child scrabbled up the shelves, squeaking: '*My brothers were not brainless for nothing,*' or that's what the doctor heard. Its voice was pinched and sharp, not unlike that of a cheery mouse, or so he imagined to himself. Then he watched the child open the jars and stick the purple prune-brains into its mouth, rolling them around and chewing reflectively, but with great determination.

'What . . .' began the doctor feebly, but then he fell silent, having finally collected himself enough to see the situation from the outside. He knew how grotesque the whole thing was, how deeply *evil*. He was still holding his surgical knife and now tightened his grip on it, sent a little emergency flare up to his god in the form of a prayer and then walked toward the child. He started to stab the knife in the direction of its head, tried to get its eye or slash it across its throat. But the next thing he knew, he'd lost his mask and he felt the child's breath on his face, a humid, silvery breath that smelled like an autumn morning atop a garbage dump in Pus, Kaohsiung, or Minsk, like a final fart of fetid air from the asshole of a worm-eaten draft horse. Death overcame the doctor's senses until the child released him, and he bent forward, gagging softly until he fell dead to the floor.

The child left the doctor's house, pausing on the front steps to stretch out its little arms as though just waking up from a nap. Then it inhaled the stench still hanging low over the village, took a long look around, and set off down the main street. Wherever the child passed, survivors drifted to their windows or doors, as if they could tell that their time had come. They stared at this creature, at the clapper hanging around its neck, at the dozens or even hundreds of stray dogs that now streamed into the village from the surrounding woods, from the fields and beaches, and besieged the child. The dogs were now fat, their teeth sharpened from gnawing on the carcasses that the plague had bestowed on them. They crowded around the child, growling continuously like pots left to simmer, before it scattered them throughout the village with a single flick of the wrist. In the blink of an eye, they'd surrounded all the houses that had anyone inside.

The child walked to the end of the street and then turned around and started back. A faint, pale light now shone from the clapper around its neck, a glow like the one on the faces of those on their deathbeds. The clapper also seemed to be quivering, emitting a tone that was too low for human ears to fully distinguish.

Wherever the child went, death followed. In some instances, dogs would crash through doors that opened of their own accord or leap through windows, smashing through any that were unopened. Many of the dogs went up in flames, though it wasn't clear how, and the fire spread, and the dogs seemed almost mad with fury. But regardless of how the blaze started, the houses now filled with screams and the surviving islanders were driven into the streets. Everything descended into chaos. Occasionally, the dogs would come flying back out the windows – in some instances from the upper stories – and some exploded in the air like fireballs. Occasionally, it was people who flew out the windows or doors; some alone and some locked in struggle with a dog, some on fire and some not. The houses and streets were painted with blood. Those who thought to flee the village suddenly discovered, when they made their attempt, that they no longer remembered which direction would be best – actually, it was increasingly difficult to think about anything whatsoever. Instead, it was as though they were being dragged towards that grotesque little child with its shining necklace, as if something was happening *right there* that they could not bear to miss.

One of these people was the mayor. Before he even realized what was happening, he found himself out in the street, right in front of the child. He knelt before the child, who clambered onto his shoulders and squeezed its legs around his throat. The child stuck some sort of bridle in the mayor's mouth, the wire slicing his mouth from ear to ear. Then it dug in its heels, yanking on the reins and pulling the mayor to his feet, nearly mad from pain as well as a deep feeling of frenzy that compelled him to obey the child.

And so did the child ride the mayor past the last houses on the street, exhaling something reminiscent of the plague spores. These weren't spores, however, but rather tiny, mote-sized flies that proceeded to spread throughout the town, homing in on the living, boring their way into eyes and nostrils and summarily ripping bodies from throat to groin like overripened fruit that will split open at the slightest touch. And so were the poor shopkeeper and his wife, the mayor's wife and their brainy, drunken son, and the priest and his wife all split open in just such a fashion. And all the while, the mayor – held fast between the child's legs – grinned broadly though in a blind panic, and though there was the occasional heroic glint in his eyes, his overall expression remained decidedly gauche and gutless.

By the time it reached the end of the street, the child had

had enough. It pulled in the wire it had been using as a bit and sliced off the mayor's head, leaving behind his bottom jaw. The carotid arteries spurted in a steady rhythm, and in a flash the child buried its face in the stump, bathing itself in blood. Then the carcass crumpled to the ground and the child dismounted.

The entire village was in flames. The sky was no longer visible for the smoke and when all the people were finally dead, the dogs turned on one another until none were left alive. The child's hair curled in the heat from the fire, coiling upwards, its member standing like a spear at the ready; its eyes were no longer distant but fathomlessly deep and filled with pure longing.

The child walked through the streets, looking at all it had made. Then it walked to the church and mounted the stairs in the bell tower. There it sat beneath the bell and as the floor grew hot and the smoke choked off its thoughts, it opened its mouth as wide as possible and forced down the clapper until it was lodged deep in its stomach. Then it leaned forward, clasped its hands around its knees, squeezed its head between its legs, and was swallowed in the inferno as the tower collapsed.

And in that very same moment, one dark and stormy night in a little village, on a little island, far, far away from these shores, the church bell began to ring.

*Translated from the Icelandic by Larissa Kyzer*

# Jayaprakash Satyamurthy

# Shelter from the Storm

JAYAPRAKASH SATYAMURTHY *burst onto the weird fiction scene in 2014 with his debut collection, a chapbook entitled* Weird Tales of a Bangalorean, *which has attracted wide acclaim from readers and critics. Christopher Slatsky called it 'reminiscent of Hearn and M. R. James' while also drawing parallels to 'the lingering dread of Ligotti, the haunting subtlety of Aickman'. Satyamurthy describes his own tales as being based on a sort of 'mythos which evokes the history, folklore and urban legends of the city where I live', namely Bangalore, a city of some eight million people in southern India. But though this author has his many admirers, his body of work is not yet a large one, so we're sure that readers will eagerly welcome 'Shelter from the Storm', his first new tale in some time.*

2003. YOU'RE AT WORK, at the second job you've ever had. You finish up around 8 p.m. as usual, head down, buy a cigarette at the corner shop, suck down three drags before it starts raining and you have to scuttle for shelter. You find an inch of space under an awning, the fumes of your cigarette mingling with strangers' breath, with the acrid reek from someone's beedi, with someone else's cigarette smoke. It's close quarters and little comfort. A gust of wind blows the droplets closer to you. Too close. You want to go home. You hail a passing autorickshaw. Two, three autos ignore you. The fourth stops. You run up to it, blurt your destination to the driver. He demands a fare you find unacceptable.

You curse him. He laughs, rides away. Getting wet, getting angry, feeling tired and hopeless, you return to the awning but your space has been taken. Shrugging, giving up the idea of getting home – home to your small flat, your cramped bachelor pad – you head back into the rain, head down, hands in pockets, cigarette long since discarded, your nice office-casual outfit drenched, you striding to the pub down the road. The one you'd planned not to spend another night in, but any port in a storm . . .

Half an hour later. A mug of Kingfisher Lager gripped in your fist, another cigarette burned three-fourths of the way down, you're starting to dry out, to feel better. Someone slides in beside you, sits down on the next stool. A slightly older guy, short hair, chin beard, big, watchful eyes, sweat-shirt, jeans. He orders a mug, pulls out his cigarette carton. Offers you a cigarette. You pull out one of your own instead, but accept a light from him, the flame from his blue plastic lighter starting up between you like a sudden shared secret.

Hours later, you're chatting, laughing. The music is good: Chicago blues. A few other drinkers, a few other refugees from the city scrum, have joined the two of you. Some you know, some you don't. You all work in more or less the same kinds of jobs – copywriters, graphic designers, a content writer for a dotcom, a freelance photographer. The music pulses. More Chicago blues. Muddy Waters is the mannish boy, is the man. The bartender, Senthil, is the man. You're the man. Your new friend, Ashok, is the man. More beers, popcorn, french fries, chilli beef fry.

Closing time. The gang decides to get more drinks at the bar next door – Fuel Up, it's called – and drive to Ashok's farmhouse. Just outside the city. You grab four bottles of Kingfisher and a quarter of McDowell's whisky at the bar. Pile into a car – Ashok's, as it happens, Ashok in front, next to his driver, you in the back with these weird software dudes, Onir, or Onny, and Amit – just Amit. A Bengali and a Jharkandi. Onny has to go pee, which he does, leaning on a lamppost, watering a patch of dead weeds. There's a plaque on the wall – Johnny Sait's Corner, it proclaims in black letters on pale stone. Ashok tells you Johnny Sait used to live on this street 20, 30 years ago. Used to come home from the bar drunk, late at night, pee here. His neighbors pooled in and put up this plaque, trying to shame him. It didn't work. Anyway, he's dead now. More or less.

More or less?

Onny yelps. Quickly finishes off, zips up, wipes his hands on his jeans, rushes back to the car. – What happened man? – I don't know. Could have sworn someone came and stood right next to me for a moment. Fucken creepy. – Ah, you're so wasted, Onny! Laughter. The car starts up, Ashok puts a tape on – Nirvana Unplugged. Cool. You forget about how Onny might just have met Johnny. You rage on into the night. Shelter from the storm.

The ride goes on and on. Somehow, so does your quart of whisky, you take neat swigs from it and occasionally swop with Amit, who is nursing a quart of rum. Ashok has many good tapes in the car, and lots of fascinating ideas about reality, the universe, religion, science . . . but his ideas keep looping around. He engages Amit in a discussion about string theory. Geeky Amit gets voluble. Then Ashok steers the discussion to the Bhagavad Gita. Amit is skeptical, shows it. Ashok gets quietly nasty. There's a jab and a jibe, a hidden snare in his words as he talks about quark, strangeness and charm, about vishvarupa, about anamnesis, gnosis, theophany. – Stop it, says Amit. – Stop what? – This . . . this Bugs Bunny logic. – It's not logic, pal, I'm trying to talk to you about truth. – No, I don't want to. I won't play the fool for you. – OK, pal. It's beautiful. It's all beautiful. Ashok detaches from the conversation, sifts through his tapes. Finds a Grateful Dead live tape. The regulars at that pub love the Dead, and so does Amit. A long, long rendition of 'Casey Jones' begins and the tension is broken, the only sound is the music, the low rumble of the engine, the rasp of Onny snoring.

It feels like days later, but it's still only night. The road has been climbing for a while, as if uphill. Is this the Nandi Hills? It's too dark to make out, and you're too drunk to really care anyway. Onny wakes up, needs to pee again. The car pulls over and you all troop out. There's a fire blazing somewhere in the slopes above. Ashok produces a hip flask, and it gets passed around. The astringent bite of single malt. Amit rolls a spliff, it gets passed around too. It goes out when it reaches you. – Need a light, pal? Ashok holds out his blue lighter. In a moment, you're lit, you're ablaze, a blaze like the hill above. Superstrings twirl in the sky, the beautiful night sky, so much darker than in the city, the stars so much brighter, the glow from the fires a golden-red root note, a backdrop to infinity. The sounds of Uncle John's Band, the aroma of weed.

Later that same night. You keep glancing at the corner where Ashok's driver sits, having joined you all for a couple of drinks, here in the farmhouse, before he heads to his own room elsewhere in the compound. He looks just like the auto driver who tried to rip you off. Or does he? You're too drunk to care. You think. The story about Johnny Sait's corner gets brought up. Nearly everyone here has peed there after last orders some night or other. Laughter, but Onny looks a bit uneasy. Amit passes him the latest joint. He takes a deep drag, like breathing in life. Exhales, like he can't hold on to life after all. There's something more spacey playing on the stereo, something with phaser effects and long, wah-laden guitar solos. Ashok's wife is there, a creative director at some agency you've heard of before, one of the big ones, but you can't remember the name, she's walking around with a camera, photography is her main deal, taking pictures of everyone. You smile for her and she steals a piece of your soul. You were too drunk to need it anyway.

Morning. A harsh, unasked-for morning. You're in the boondocks. You haven't slept, haven't eaten, you're unshaved, unwashed, stinking of last night's smoke, yesterday's clothes sticking to your skin as you sweat. Bright sun above. A hillside road. How far is this place from the city anyway? And when did you decide to take a little walk on your own and which way is Ashok's house? You stumble, twist an ankle, curse, limp on, not knowing which way to go. Rain clouds on the horizon, but no rain, now, when it would be a welcome relief. You pass through a place of charred ground and it seems more real than all the lush greenery elsewhere. Too lush, too green, or maybe your two-and-a-half decades in the city have made you think gray is normal. You hear an engine, turn around. It's an auto. You try to flag it down but the driver laughs at you — actually takes the time to laugh at you — and speeds away. You sit down by the side of the road, make a pillow of your backpack, lie down, try to rest a bit.

Later. You're in a little hilltop village. You're naked and the people are playing dice for your clothes. Your office-casual outfit from yesterday, your good boots. She's there too. Taking photographs. Ashok's there too, talking about the Rig Veda, about quasars. You think Onny and Amit are somewhere in the picture, momentarily embarrassed, like you. You think someone with a cockroach for a head is dancing to a 12-bar strut.

The rain drives down. The city breathes foul, fearful gasps. You're perched in a corner under an awning. Shelter from the storm.

Blue lighter. Ignition. The fires rise higher. The sky is so clear up here on the hilltop. Someone is wearing your khaki slacks, someone is walking in your boots. You're trying to bargain, to live. Each click and whirr of the camera leeches away more of your will. You see it all. You remember it all. Vishvarupa. Theophany, they call it in English. Like Oppenheimer, like Arjuna. You smile for her, hoping for the lethal dose, hoping she'll steal away all of your soul, all of you, hoping she'll crush you underfoot before you can feel the flames reaching for your feet.

# Roberto Causo

# Train of Consequences

*We had planned to include only one story from each country, but given that Brazil, with over 212 million people, is the world's sixth most populous land and has one of the world's longest horror writing traditions, at over 150 years, it didn't seem unreasonable to showcase two Brazilian tales. Like our other Brazilian entry, ROBERTO CAUSO's 'Train of Consequences' was chosen as one of Brazil's all-time best horror stories by the editors of a recent anthology. The story deals partly with a familiar horror trope, the Faustian bargain, but what we liked about Causo's tale is how it incorporates elements of Brazilian politics and history. The main character, we're told, was a military officer who engaged in terrible acts during Brazil's military dictatorship, which lasted from 1964 to 1985. With Brazil's sharp veer towards the extreme right and totalitarianism in recent years, Causo's story, originally published in 1999, is as timely as ever. The original Portuguese publication of this story included an epigraph from the Megadeth song of the same title; for reasons of copyright, those lyrics have been omitted here.*

THE DARKNESS SWALLOWED THE LIGHT, erasing it and leaving a trail of emptiness in its wake. The reality of the senses followed the same path – at one moment vivid and unquestionable, at the next, impossible to grasp. The light is always one second ahead, never reachable for the passenger traveling in the last second-class cars of a night train.

Sergio Lopes pulled his head inside and closed the

window. The cool mountain air had helped his motion sickness to pass. So there was that at least.

Lopes was going to Belo Horizonte, coming from somewhere... He couldn't remember where. He lived like a gypsy, hopping from place to place, not staying long enough to put down roots or form memories worth remembering. Maybe that's why the old memories prevailed, the ones he preferred to forget.

He remembered other dark nights, the reality of them uncertain, lived in other mountain ranges, in other jungles, but not in other lives. Sometimes he thought that he wasn't the protagonist of these memories, that they were someone else's remembrances which had seeped into him. Like an infection from some strange virus.

Lopes looked around, trying to find something to distract himself from his memories. The last second-class car was almost empty. A handful of people, only three of whom weren't asleep: him and two men who were smoking in the back. Several people were lying across the seats, sleeping soundly like they were at home. A couple with four children had turned their two benches to face each other and had set up a kind of tent around them, with blankets stretched to block out the sunlight that would come in through the windows later, and had lined the floor between the seats with their suitcases so the children could sleep on them. Sometimes trains were like moving, communal houses where it was impossible to avoid the presence of other people. Tenements running at thirty miles per hour through the middle of nowhere, crossing the mountains, making the animals' burrows tremble.

He looked back outside. He opened the window so that the reflection of the light from inside the train wouldn't be superimposed on the landscape of black humps, which looked like curly-haired heads in the darkness. It was bitterly cold, and despite the darkness Lopes could see a fine mist stretching out like a veil over the lower parts of the mountain range. A few stars were shining, but the sky was almost completely covered by rain clouds. A flash of lightning opened a rip of ephemeral light in the night. Seconds later, large drops started to form transparent pearls on the window glass and to strike warm against Lopes' face.

He resented the presence of the other people in the car. For a long time now he had always traveled on the last train of the day, in the last second-class car, hoping to have as little company as possible. Sometimes he couldn't help being bothered and feeling invaded by the mere sharing of the same space.

He poked his head out the window, not caring about the rain, and looked once more at the disconcerting image of the locomotive's headlight illuminating the way in front, with a trail of darkness following a second later. For some reason Lopes looked back. He saw that besides the car he was in, there was another, and that its windows were lit up, caressing the vegetation along the edge of the railway with ghostly reflections.

It was weird. Lopes was almost certain that there was no other car behind his. He was struck by the strange feeling that someone would have if they believed they were on the roof of a building and then discovered there was another floor above them.

He stood up, thinking of taking a look in the other car. He couldn't sleep; his nausea was returning. It occurred to him that maybe the other car was less full than his.

Walking down the aisle, he realized he had been mistaken; there was a girl awake too, curled up in a seat almost at the back. The dim light of the second-class carriage didn't reveal much, but the girl's body seemed to be out of this world, even if her face wasn't much to get excited about.

Without stopping, he opened the door at the back. The two men, still smoking, cast curious glances at him.

The air was cold in the passage between his carriage and the other one, and Lopes felt a slight easing of his motion sickness. The rain was coming down with redoubled force. He hurried to open the door in front of him and enter.

The carriage was dark. But he remembered seeing light pouring from the windows . . . Fatigue was messing with his head. Maybe someone had just switched out the lights, or who knows, maybe a power outage . . .

As his eyes grew used to the darkness, he saw a faint light coming from the back. A diffuse red light, as if someone was smoking inside a halo of fog. He walked towards it.

Gradually he noticed that several people were nestled in the seats at the back, smoking and producing strongly scented crimson clouds. Lopes couldn't make out any features; the faces were red blurs to his eyes. It was like being inside a submarine, but maybe it was some kind of smoking section inside the train. He never knew this line offered that type of service.

On the back wall there was a seat, or a chair, and in it sat a man who looked like a high-contrast drawing done in black and red – it was as if the light from all the cigarettes cast a crimson glow on him. Intrigued, Lopes went closer and saw that the seat had metal arms, decorated with embossed designs that he couldn't make out. Looking around as far as the smoky light reached, he saw that the carriage had curtains and pillars and carpets and metallic details on the windows. Like in one of those old-fashioned train cars you saw in Western films . . . Strange how his eyes were getting used to the red light, revealing more and more details to him.

'Come join us, Senhor Sergio Lopes,' he heard.

He turned towards the man occupying the seat in the center.

'You know me?' he asked, as he instinctively looked around for a place to sit. The voice expressed an order rather than a request, and Lopes felt compelled to obey it. He was a man trained to obey orders given in the right tone.

'Definitely,' the Other responded. His voice was husky, but clear and sonorous. It resonated with authority.

'From where?'

'You are the Sergio Lopes who participated in the crackdown on the guerillas in Araguaia, I know. Captain Lopes, I *know* you.'

Lopes sat up straight in his seat.

'That's all over now . . .' he said.

'Of course it's not. It's very much alive in you, isn't it? In your heart, so full of resentment. After all, many guerillas and even some of the soldiers you fought with are now politicians, well-placed officials, or intellectuals who made names for themselves with the insurgency. While you, at fifty-three, are a nobody. And it's not as though you didn't fight as hard as everyone else, we know.

'Those years of fighting brought you nothing, did they? Only memories you want to forget. And the end of the insurgency meant an end to your life. Not that I think your experiences justified the beatings you gave your wife and children. You turned into a loser, a little man who sees shadows and enemies everywhere . . .'

Lopes stood up. His view of the man sitting in the midst of the smoke seemed even blurrier and more indistinct to him. Anyway, he didn't have to stay and listen to all of this.

He thought of leaving, but he couldn't seem to move. He was having a hard time breathing. All that smoke . . .

'But we also know what methods you used,' continued the Other. 'Torture. Summary executions. That's not to say, however, that it was the insurgency that turned you into the mean-spirited thing that you are . . .'

'So you've come for me,' he managed to say.

He had expected this all along. During every waking moment, in his nightmares. He knew that one day someone connected with his victims would find him. He looked around in fear. He was surrounded. The dark, crimson faces of the others were turned towards him. Was this how the faces of his team of torturers had looked to his prisoners?

The Other gave a raucous laugh.

'You don't sleep well at night, do you, Lopes? There's no safe haven . . . It's your conscience eating away at you. Those memories you can't get rid of. And if you ask me, that's the worst thing of all. *Conscience*, Lopes. It's the greatest weakness, and it's what we can't tolerate.'

'What do you want?'

'You have no idea, do you?' The man paused to take a long drag from the cigar he was smoking. The ember glowed brightly and Lopes saw that his eyes were dull and black like two unpolished steel balls. 'All right, then. We have the solution to your problems. All of them.'

'Look here,' Lopes interrupted. 'I don't know who you are, nor how you know all these things about me, but if you think you can blackmail me, you might as well know I have nothing to give in exchange, you understand?'

'We know that you've been estranged from your family for a long time, that you no longer have any friends or possessions, and that you barely get by on a military pension that doesn't go very far. These are hard times for your class, my friend.

'We know *everything* about you. Even more than *you* know about yourself. That's why you have to trust me when I say that you do have something to give us in exchange. In exchange for a new life, for forgetting the past. It's not a question of blackmail, more like a business deal, all above board, where you and we each have something the other needs.'

Lopes ran his tongue along his lower lip. It was dry, like his throat. The smoke . . .

The man produced a bottle of beer out of thin air. Lopes reached out his hand without thinking and grabbed it. It was ice cold, and the smoke from all the burnt tobacco floated around it in threads, like spiderwebs around a trapped fly. He unscrewed the cap and took a drink before saying anything.

'What kind of deal?'

★

Leila Aparecida Ribeiro struggled to sleep, but couldn't. She was going back home after two years trying to make a life in São Paulo, and this return had the bitter taste of failure. The prodigal daughter . . . Her parents would be happy to have her back, of course. But she knew that once she went back to her folks, they would never pay for her to try pursuing a modeling career in the big city again.

Leila knew what her problem was, the reason her career had never taken off. She was plenty hot, but her face was plain and inexpressive. The body of a goddess and the face of a farm girl.

She had managed to find work doing ads for jeans and swimsuits, where her face didn't show up much or at all. There were a lot of companies in São Paulo using her ass and legs to sell their jeans and bikinis. But that didn't really count as success.

Leila had even won a round of the 'Wet Girls' competition, that embarrassing and ridiculous situation where she and other contestants would shower on live TV during a popular, nationally televised program wearing nothing but a T-shirt and panties. She remembered how the two country singers judging the contestants had stared at her body and at her T-shirt clinging to her breasts, their eyes bulging and mouths gaping. The host, on the other hand, must have been professional to the core – or else gay – because he hadn't deigned even to glance at her or the other women. The win, however, hadn't given Leila's career any brighter prospects.

She would give six inches of her firm 38-inch bust to have a face like Michelle Pfeiffer's or Luciana Vendramini's, instead of her own round face with its drooping cheeks. She couldn't stand her dark brown eyes either, or her flared nostrils – the pitfalls of genetics, since the same blood responsible for her curves was what had given her her coarse facial features. She had thought of plastic surgery, but to do the 'full overhaul' she had envisioned would cost her a sum she didn't have.

There had been other invitations along the way, which she had gone so far as to consider. High-end call girl. Porn actress. But deep down she knew those weren't just steps along an imaginary road to success; a decision like that would mean being trapped. Somehow she still had enough self-respect to say no.

Now, on the night train on her way back home – on her way to a public acknowledgment of her failure – the bitterness weighed so heavily on her that she thought maybe she should have accepted one of those invitations. Going back to the monotony and tackiness of her hometown seemed an unbearable prospect.

Someone sat down beside her.

It was a man of an indeterminate age with thinning but well-groomed hair, wearing a gray overcoat. He settled into his seat without ceremony, looked at her and smiled.

Leila turned towards him without really knowing why. Underneath his overcoat he was wearing a dark suit of a very fine cut. His silk tie showed an impeccable knot. From his shiny black shoes to his well-coiffed hair, there wasn't a single thing about him out of place, not even a drop of rain on the collar of his overcoat or a flaw in the crease of his trousers.

'Do you know what's on the other side of those hills?' he asked, stretching his arm in front of her.

Leila followed the movement and, squinting, saw only the dark outlines of three round and almost identical hills.

'Not the slightest idea,' she replied, turning back towards the man, wondering where he was going with this. She was used to being hit on, but this wasn't a pick-up line she was familiar with.

'There's an old still and a brickworks. The still is a remarkable building. It has an elevated track inside, with a little mine cart used to take sugarcane pulp to a place where it's thrown into a compost heap, which is then used as fertilizer for a vegetable garden maintained by the workers. Below the tracks, further on, at the end of the line, there's a kind of narrow cave and a spring that forms a pond. There's a stream that originates at the pond and leads from the still to a grove of trees and bamboo. It's a special place.'

Leila observed him carefully as he spoke. Only now did she notice that the man's lively brown eyes, the color of hazelnuts, seemed somehow familiar. And the image that he had painted in words – *a special place* – existed vividly in her memories.

When she was about fourteen, she used to run off that way with Miguel da Silva, her boyfriend. She had spent some of the best moments of her life in that secret spot. Many years later, she had come to think that Miguel might have been the only man in her life who ever really understood her. He too had left the city to pursue his dreams, which were far off and separate from hers.

But how could this stranger, whose eyes were the same soft color as Miguel's, know about the place? Not even she remembered its precise location.

'I know the place,' she said in a low voice. 'You live around here?'

'No. But I'm a frequent visitor.'

Leila couldn't imagine what would bring a man dressed this well, and apparently equally well off financially, to such an uninteresting part of Minas.

'I work in real estate,' he said, anticipating her question. 'My name is Sergio Lopes. I look for picturesque spots that could interest potential buyers from São Paulo and Rio. You know, wealthy people looking for nice rural properties where they can build country houses and exclusive clubs. The properties around here are fantastic . . .'

'And have you found much?' she asked in total disbelief, although Lopes' profession might explain how he knew about the secret place in the old still.

Lopes laughed. His face, laughing, struck her as especially charming.

'You have no idea! You must have been away from your hometown for a long time, my dear, otherwise you'd know about the VIPs who have been moving here the past few years. We've transformed this part of Minas Gerais into a fashionable spot.'

Leila thought it was strange. Her mother would have said something about it in her letters.

'What's your name?' he asked. 'Leila? A lovely name. Listen, Leila. Look out the window – can you see another car behind the one we're in?'

'Another car! Whatever gave you that idea?' But, looking, she did in fact see the lights from the windows of a car behind theirs, reflected in the ravine and the clumps of weeds the night train was cutting through.

'That's my private car, Leila.'

'*Private* car?'

She couldn't remember seeing that train car when she got on.

'Exactly. To give you an idea of my success. I normally

bring special clients in that car. It usually works, really impresses them. To tell the truth, business is going so well that I and my associates in the region can no longer keep up with the demand.

'You seem to be a clever girl, not to mention pretty. It occurred to me that maybe we could use you here, if you're thinking of coming back to stay. You know the area ... you're charming and elegant. I'm sure we could find a position that would be a good fit for you, one that would allow you a nice percentage of the profits and the chance to meet some really important people.'

Leila remained impassive, looking at him intently, wondering if she could trust those brown eyes and that solid appearance of confidence. She couldn't help but acknowledge that Lopes' flattery had caught her off guard.

'I'll tell you what I'll do,' Lopes said. 'I'll take you to my private car and show you all the publicity material and the sales data. I bet that'll get you really excited.'

Leila ignored the double entendre. Something about this man was attractive and dangerous at the same time. But she decided to call his bluff.

'All right.'

Lopes got up and offered her his hand. It was hot, almost feverish. And dry. Despite the humid atmosphere surrounding them, the hand was dry, hot, and rough.

His other hand, his free one, reached for the chrome handle that opened the door to the passage leading to the last car.

★

Lopes opened the door and was caught by the spray of the rain outside. That slowed him down for a moment, waking him up a little from the haziness he still felt from that reeking atmosphere of tobacco.

From his crimson cloud of cigarette and cigar smoke, the Other had said he would solve all his problems. That all his problems were caused by the weight of his conscience. That the weight would vanish with a simple 'leap'.

Sergio Lopes had tortured, mutilated, and murdered men and women in the communist insurgency in Central Brazil. He had been motivated to do these things – although he was reluctant to admit it – by a strange sense of superiority that came from inflicting pain and destruction on others. He wanted to believe he'd been doing his duty, that he'd fought the enemy with the weapons and tactics available to him, and nothing more. But he couldn't fool himself. A cold assessment of his feelings would show the filthy sadism deep inside him. Still he had insisted on hiding behind ideas of duty and military responsibility. But the Other was right. There was a weight on his conscience. An oppression that increased his resentment and made him a misfit in society.

But the Other – the dark-faced man seated in the ornate chair in the back of the train car – had made him see the truth: he didn't have to suffer from remorse. The pain and death he had caused had sometimes been carried out with quiet pleasure, at other times with furious enjoyment. Rarely had he identified with the victims and their fates. They were *things* that looked like human beings – and seeming to be human even though they weren't, they again became things that affirmed Lopes as *the* human. Maybe by killing others he killed the weakness that existed within himself – he couldn't be sure. He had thought about it a lot over the years, but he didn't have any answers. Sometimes everything seemed like a vain and meaningless psychoanalytic game. But he had no stories to tell, aiming for redemption at the end of the tunnel – only a series of deaths. In the end, he only longed to forget.

That was what the Other promised. And it all seemed so simple. He'd done it before and he didn't see why he couldn't do it again. For whatever reason, there was no moral impediment. No coercion – the fear of getting caught, of condemnation, of losing his freedom.

All he had to do was kill again. This time without the shield of duty and orders to hide behind. Just one more murder would be enough for the 'leap' that the Other had promised would set him free.

And it would, Lopes knew, tightening his hold on the woman's cold, damp hand.

★

In fact there was another car. A small dim porthole revealed a reddish glow, overcoming the gloom. The second Leila and Lopes stood in the narrow walkway, it occurred to her that going in there would be a bigger step than she had thought.

She saw him open the door, still holding on to her. He pulled her, but she hesitated, still puzzled by her intuition.

There was a faint haze coming from the last car. Leila felt that something was wrong, and the doors of fear opened up for her.

Lopes pulled her again, but now she struggled against him.

★

The poor woman was standing there at the end of his arm, her curvy body shaking with a fear that was visible in her eyes, her ugly little face in a terrified grimace. She radiated fragility, asking for some kind of mercy, for pity.

Lopes hated her weakness and wanted to destroy her, to make her bleed and scream and rob her of everything else. To destroy the weak, small, ugly thing that was this deluded girl, who expected too much from a world he knew all too well. There was nothing to hope for from the world except pain and oblivion. And Lopes wanted to be on the right side of the dividing line between those who suffer and those who administer that pain.

He looked inside the car. There in the back he saw the group of men seated in their red cell of smoke and vice, and he felt that they too were on the right side. He felt they were superior to him, that they had already made the 'leap' long ago. He wondered what they might represent.

What did it mean, making a deal with them?

How did they know so much about him and the woman?

He looked at her. A born victim. Sooner or later, the fate he had to inflict on her would have caught up with her anyway.

'But what about me?' he wondered. 'What's my destiny? To join those men there in the back?'

He looked at them more attentively. They seemed tense, sitting on the edge of their seats, watching him anxiously, they too wanting and pleading with their blurred faces, with their dark, metallic eyes. They *needed* him. They were asking him with a similar need and frailty, they needed more men to fortify the right side of the line. The side of the strong, the winners. Those who had called him petty, small, and scared.

They were so weak that Lopes wanted to spit on them.

He let the woman go.

'Go home.'

She turned and sprang towards the door of the other car, opening it and running inside. Lopes' face sketched a small and out-of-place smile.

He turned towards the men in the back of the wagon. He brushed a few drops of rain from his eyes, and, without blinking, he advanced towards them.

★

Leila ran to the first seat at the front of the car and sat down there, cowering and looking behind her. She went on staring at the entrance to the car at the far end, expecting the man to return, but he didn't come.

She still hadn't translated what she had felt into rational terms. Why the panic, such an intense impression of imminent death?

The ticket collector passed by, walking sleepily. He didn't go into Lopes' car. The attendant announced the next stop; Leila would get off there.

Still looking behind her, she wanted to get off the train and go home, as the man had ordered.

★

The men rose from their seats as Lopes walked towards them.

'Why did you throw away your last chance, Lopes?' the Other asked.

Standing, he seemed so tall that his head might hit the ceiling of the train car. Lopes continued to advance towards him and his companions.

'You people aren't worth the shit that comes out of your asses,' he said, at the exact same moment that he felt a sharp pain in his chest.

He felt like his rib cage was slowly imploding. He lost his breath and one of his arms started to tingle and go numb in a matter of seconds. He fell to his knees, groaning in pain. A sharp, unbearable pain.

'You're an idiot,' he heard. The harsh, authoritarian voice of the Other. Lopes could no longer see him, since everything was going black and hazy before his burning eyes. 'Your time has come, and if you think that your little act of mercy can save you, you're mistaken. There's enough destruction and hate inside you to keep you with us for a long time. And it won't be a pleasant time, I can assure you.'

What was he talking about? The pain and pressure in Lopes' chest was so great that he couldn't think.

'You lost your chance to become one of us,' he continued to hear. 'You spurned the leap and proved yourself to be a fool, the victim of the worst of weaknesses. How could you let your conscience get in the way? Why did you spare the woman?'

Something was happening to Lopes. The pain gradually diminished, and he regained full control over his thoughts. In fact, the pain subsided so quickly that Lopes suffered a strong dizziness, the sensation of falling headlong, and in that fall into himself his mind cleared all at once, and his thoughts formed at the speed of light.

Looking up, he saw the nebulous figures looming over him like smoking, human-shaped towers, looking at him with leaden eyes, angry and anxious.

Intoxicated by the strange euphoria filling him, Sergio Lopes was able to respond, even as he was struck by the certainty that he would not get out of there soon, that these beings would have hold of him for some time.

'It was totally arbitrary,' he said. 'I let the woman go purely on a *whim*, you bastards. Or do you think it would take more for me to spare her than it would for me to kill her for you?'

They never responded.

★

Leila jumped hurriedly off the train into the semi-darkness of the poorly lit arrival platform. Only one other person got off with her, from a car further ahead.

She started to rush inside the station but stopped for a second. Unable to restrain herself, she looked back at the train. Her eyes searched for the last car, Sergio Lopes' private car.

Where her eyes expected to find it, there was nothing. Only the second-class car she had come from.

She turned all the way around, straining her eyes, straining her mind. She couldn't have dreamt all that. She still felt the dry, rough touch of Lopes' hand on hers.

She stood there frozen on the boarding platform, looking silently at the train. Finally it began to move, ready to resume its journey.

The rain pursued the train as it moved away and picked up speed, advancing through the dark night. Curtains of water fell in a continuous rhythm, a single bombardment, a single wave.

And at a certain moment Leila Aparecida Ribeiro thought she saw red lights in the last wagon through the rain. Dark flames spreading out in wet reflections and going on as far as the eye could see.

*Translated from the Portuguese by James D. Jenkins*

Mélanie Fazi

# Dreams of Ash

*Horror in French dates back almost as far as it does in English. In the 19th century, it could be found in one form or another almost every-where: short stories by Gautier, Nodier, and Maupassant; poetry by Baudelaire and Lautréamont; novels by popular writers like Paul Féval and Eugène Sue; and tales of Satanism and torture by fin de siècle 'Decadent' authors like Huysmans and Octave Mirbeau. But in the late 19th century the Naturalism movement associated with authors like Flaubert and Zola seems to have dealt a major blow to French speculative fiction from which it has never fully recovered. In the 20th century, horror writing in France became much scarcer, although a handful of authors, like Claude Seignolle and Serge Brus-solo, helped the genre avoid extinction. One contemporary writer helping to put France back on the horror map is MÉLANIE FAZI, one of today's premier French authors of* fantastique *(the French term usually applied to horror; it's also used more generally to include speculative and weird fiction). The following tale originally appeared in her first collection,* Serpentine, *in 2004 and makes its first English appearance here. A handful of Fazi's other stories have appeared over the years in English in various magazines and anthologies and are also well worth seeking out.*

C ANDLES EVERYWHERE, FROM FLOOR TO CEILING. On my bedroom bookshelves, on the floorboards. On the desk, amongst the notebooks. In front of the switched-off television. As many candles as I've been able to gather and hide here. If Mom saw this – her and her fear of matches. All mothers have the same fears. You would think they get over them when their little ones grow up. It never left her. But my parents won't wake up at three a.m., and Gabriel is snoring like a piglet in the bedroom across from mine. I was careful to stuff a T-shirt in the gap under the door so that no light would show through. I turned down the volume of the music so only I could hear it. The bass notes, heavy and throbbing, organic, fill the room like incense. The voice floats, barely a murmur, encouraging me and telling me what I'm doing is right.

And there are all these candles around me. As many as I could collect without anyone noticing. There are all kinds. Tapers and tealights, birthday candles shaped like numbers, grandmother's old candlestick that I found in the attic. Straight candles, twisted ones, ones shaped like animals. Santa Claus and snowmen. And those scented candles you can buy at flea markets for next to nothing. The air is permeated with them: nauseating fragrances of jasmine, strawberry, honeysuckle, and citronella, all mixed together, the smell of birthday cake. I feel good in the middle of the flames, their calming eyes resting on me, silent witnesses. The membrane seems to answer their call. I feel it awakening, softly palpitating, barely a tingle. The mark of the bird on my forearm.

I was seven years old, the first time. Gabriel had beaten me at video games and I had taken refuge in front of the fireplace to plot my revenge. One of the countless fights between us two little brats, completely in bad faith. He won at every game, and it was humiliating. I accused him of cheating and he responded, unfazed: 'It's not a game for girls, anyway.' Tired of having his little sister around all the time, I imagine. So I let him finish the game alone.

In the winter, our parents would light a fire in the hearth

every night, more for atmosphere than heat. A Christmas tree and a big wood fire, that was their idea of the height of domestic comfort. Halfway between a furniture store catalog and a Norman Rockwell painting. They had taken lots of photos of me and Gabriel in front of that burning fireplace, with our forced smiles and absent expressions. Especially on Christmas Eve. Bérénice in her doll's dress, Gabriel in a white shirt, a whole ritual.

I got up on the rocking chair and the world started to glide around me. As disorienting as the pitching of a boat, minus the seasickness. Closing my eyes, I could almost hear the waves. I pressed with my whole body to make the chair rock faster. The voyage was underway. Back, forth, back, forth, the room swayed; I was like a pendulum marking the passage of time. I heard spaceships exploding at the other end of the room, and Gabriel urging his pilot on in a very loud voice to taunt me. He would only lower his voice when calling the aliens bad names, in case Mom was listening. Let him have his fun with his silly games, for all I cared.

In the fireplace, the flames came closer and retreated, again and again. I heard them crackle, distracted, busy swinging my legs in space. I was still too little to touch the floor. I felt so good there in the heat of the flames. A little numb, like in the minutes just before sleep, the ones that erase the contours of things and abolish time. The light of the flames filled me, permeated through to my bones. I settled all the way back in the chair, my arms on the armrests. That's when I saw it.

I didn't understand right away that it was a bird. It moved too quickly for my eyes. A miniature comet that turned, whirled, fluttered, a crackling vision. A spray of feathers and sparks dancing before my eyes. The details were still too blurry. Here the curve of a wing, there the outline of a crest and a beak, disappearing as soon as they formed. An apparition that changed, like a cloud changes as soon as you make out its contours, yet much more quickly. But just slow enough to make sure I would see.

The flames sketched a bird, dancing among them. A bird with brilliant plumage and a supple and shifting body, like a Chinese dragon. A disembodied spirit, kept prisoner by the flames like ectoplasm by its cord.

I leaned forward to look and the chair rocked backwards again deviously. When you're seven you don't stand a chance against the laws of gravity. Nor against a chair that's been broken in by my father's 180 pounds. I leaned farther forward, my mount continuing to rear up until I gave up the fight and let myself slide to the floor. I opened the glass of the fireplace, without worrying about scorching my fingers, and brought my face closer to the flames.

The vision was clearer now. What I saw was definitely a bird. Still half hidden by the flames, half held back by them. It was struggling to regain its shape, it was whirling more than ever. Its endless tail traced arabesques, its wide-open beak spat whorls of smoke. Its entire body crackled and shot out sparks. The flying sparks became feathers that changed colors. Even their texture was no longer quite the same. They looked soft enough to touch.

I reached out to stroke the feathers. As long as it didn't defend itself with its beak . . .

Behind me, I heard Mom scream.

'Béréniiiiiiice!'

I was yanked back abruptly, like a rag doll. My sleeve had caught fire.

I felt Mom busily trying to put out the flames with a blanket or a coat. And I was squirming to get free because she was between me and the fireplace. Her whole body was blocking my view of the fire. I kicked and pawed at the ground like a wild colt; she held me even tighter. Once the flames on my sleeve were put out, I got a couple of huge slaps. But Mom was the one crying.

I heard, without listening, the same old tune she'd been giving me since I was old enough to string two words together. Never do that again, do you see what you almost did, what on earth got into your head, and so on.

As soon as I could break free, I turned towards the fireplace. Behind the half-open glass the flames crackled quietly, in all innocence. See nothing, hear nothing, say nothing: even the fire knew that. The most important thing, in all circumstances, is to act like nothing happened.

On the way to the hospital, I screamed and cried every tear in my body. But not because of the pain; I'd hardly felt anything. It was barely a bite, dozens of tiny teeth planted in my arm, scarcely sharp enough to hurt me. Maybe I'd have a tough time later, but at the moment I felt almost nothing.

I was crying because the bird was gone. Because Mom had made him flee, and he might not come back.

Because if she hadn't scared him off, I could have touched him.

When I came home from the hospital a few days later, Gabriel gave me a funny look. He shut himself in his room without saying a word to me, only coming out at mealtimes, if even then. Because a brother or sister who's sick is by definition suspicious: they're trying to get attention. And meanwhile we're alone with Dad eating lukewarm ravioli because Mom hasn't come home to cook.

But I couldn't tell him either. That it hadn't hurt, or only a little. That I would have gladly traded all the visits and presents for a little bit of peace and quiet. I dreamed of finally being left alone so I could tear off my bandages and look underneath. See what the bird had done to me. It tingled under there, it itched, like a living thing, something in the process of changing. But it didn't hurt very bad.

When I was younger, one day when my parents had stopped for coffee while Christmas shopping, I spilled a cup of hot chocolate on my lap. I couldn't have been more than three or four. I had shouted with surprise, and a little from anticipation, because I expected to feel pain. There was embarrassment too, the sight of my stained tights, completely ruined, the looks of the other customers fixed on me, all those adults who didn't even have the decency to look away. I had cried from humiliation, not from pain.

This time it was the same. A sensation of burning, still present but bearable. The constant urge to scratch the affected area, like the dead skin under a plaster cast. Nothing worse than that. Just a phantom pain running down the length of my skin.

For a long time I regretted not having watched more attentively while my sleeve burned. But I was so busy trying to see the bird. If only I had looked, really looked, I would have had some stories to tell on the playground. I had caught fire and was still around to tell about it. The kids my age were fond of horrid details, and all I had to offer them was a scar.

But I couldn't show it to them. The bird wouldn't have wanted me to. And how much would they really have understood? Sometimes it doesn't take much to drive a wedge between you and other kids. All it takes is to have seen things that they can barely imagine. How do you reestablish the dialogue after that?

The scar changed with time, sheltered by my clothing. I spent summers wearing long sleeves to camouflage it. Mom thought I was ashamed, when all I wanted was to safeguard it from looks and questions. There are some things too precious to share, even with those you're close to. Especially with them.

I watched it change in private, alone in the bathroom,

under the covers, in the restroom during recess. The area was larger than I had thought before seeing it. In places it was like the skin was dead: the skin of a grilled chicken – you would think I had escaped from a giant barbecue. That had fascinated me at first. But it got old very quickly. I won't claim I never played at frightening Gabriel by showing him the extent of the damage. There were even a few occasions when I rolled up my sleeve in front of my classmates. It's funny how the little tough guys lost their desire to look up my skirt once they knew what was hidden under my sweater.

Long practice at spying behind doors had taught me no shortage of awful words that sounded like they were spoken in code. I couldn't help it: as soon as I heard someone say my name (I had a sort of sixth sense), Bérénice the mouse would sneak to the nearest keyhole. 'Cosmetic surgery,' that was their latest thing; I would hear it ten times a day when I listened in. The phrase itself was a nightmare, nothing cosmetic about it. They talked about it a lot at the time and still do today. I would have killed them if they had tried. I will kill them if they ever do try. Are they embarrassed of me, their ugly duckling with grilled skin? Did they ever wonder if it bothered me? That spot has never embarrassed me. It's part of the whole.

Besides, a new membrane had formed. Brand new skin, very pale pink, almost see-through. Fragile like a baby's skin, all smooth, with no hair growth. At first glance, I would have thought I could break the surface just by touching it. Like an egg on a plate that's destroyed by the first poke of a fork. But I was thick-skinned, literally. I explored the whole surface of it with my fingertips, shyly at first, then more confidently. I had never touched scar tissue. It was like if you scratched underneath the dead skin there was something else to discover, a new texture. The map of a strange land on my own arm. No, more like the fire had transformed it. The contact with the flames, the contact with the bird, had changed me. But it was too early to say how.

It was around this time that I started to look for him. I was about nine and I watched out for signs. Since he had come to me one time, there was destined to be a second. And then others. So he could finish what he started. He had left me alone with that, the mark on my arm, my newborn skin, my eyes filled with a spray of sparks. He had to come back and finish.

It was because of Mom that he had fled. If she hadn't snatched me away from him, no doubt he would have gone all the way. In the meantime I looked stupid, with my half-human arm and my little secret hidden from view. The bird had wanted to change me, he had come to me, and no one could take him away from me. But I had sworn that no one would know anything about him. Only nine years of age, I had kept my word, and I keep it still.

I only hoped that he had understood. And what if it hadn't just been Mom's barging in – what if he thought that it was really me who had been scared? That I wasn't ready to receive him? If he had fled with the image of me giving up, he would never come back to me. My phoenix, my totem. The one who was going to offer me the chance to be reborn from my ashes. So I looked for him.

I watched for him in the flames of Dad's barbecue grill, in the odor of grilled sausages and burning alcohol, behind the smokescreen that irritated my eyes.

In the little blue flames of the gas stove when Mom was busy cooking. I would sit beside her, my chin resting on my folded arms, and I would watch it burn.

In the smoke from the cigarettes the adults would light at family meals.

In birthday candles, Gabriel's as well as mine. In the sparks from Dad's lighter.

Everywhere I could, in fact. Wherever a flame burned. My parents hadn't lit the fireplace in two years.

Like every kid, I had often amused myself by passing my finger through a flame, as fast as possible, so I wouldn't get burned. Except that I didn't really try to avoid the burn. I knew how to slow down just in time, one clumsy second, and the sharp little teeth would come to tease my fingertips. A paltry promise, but a reassuring one. During the second that I offered half an inch of myself to the flame, I regained a little bit of him. His burning breath on my skin. And I remembered like it was yesterday.

If only my body held on to the memory of the pain. At least I'd have that to fall back on, to play with a little. Instead of finding myself empty again as soon as the flame went out.

But the phoenix didn't return. I waited, then I lost patience. Now and then I would still play with fire, alone in my room with some matches, just in case. But I had come to believe that there were other ways. He had come to me, he had shown me some clever tricks, all right. Now I had to figure it out on my own, forge ahead my own way. There were things to be discovered by scratching a little below the surface. Just enough to reveal something a little less human. There are some days – the ones when you stay away from mirrors – when you even get tired of your own humanity.

The cigarette burns started during the summer break between middle school and high school. Summer goes on forever when you don't have anyone your own age to talk to, and not much in common with those you share a roof with. Nothing to do with your days except wander the streets and go rewatch the same bad movies that have already been playing for two months. So you shut yourself up in your room, close all the blinds, and entertain yourself as best you can.

I quickly gave up that little game. Other than leaving

marks on my arms, ridiculous marks that weren't even pretty to look at, it didn't go very far. Even the pain was sterile. Just an instant, a tiny point, like getting an ear piercing, stronger but less attractive. I have about twenty marks in all, on my arms and thighs, where no one would venture to look. I had always been a fan of long sleeves, and even the doctors would have to resort to rhinoceros tranquilizer if they wanted to get a look at my altered skin.

My sophomore year I took it up a notch. Nothing really bad: I wanted to feel the razor, just a little, because I hadn't tried it yet. Just to see if I was capable, and to study the matter more in depth. Because there had to be something down there, under the bark, beneath the surface. I had the proof of it on my right arm, the phoenix's mark. What if, in the end, the skin was only there to conceal? To be pulled back, strip by strip, like you peel a banana?

I could have explored the question fully if they had left me alone. If I had gone straight to the point from the start instead of beating around the bush. I started with incisions, just to tease the epidermis, to see a few pearls of blood from the secret area where the bird had changed me. I did it again several times. The coppery taste of the blood on the tip of my tongue, the pain, as brief and precise as a flash of lightning, the waves spreading down the length of my arm, it was a ritual. And behind it all, the promise of seeing things clearly if I dared to go further.

I learned things about human skin during those weeks. Its texture, its resistance, the ease with which a blade can cut through it like a piece of cloth. The pain that woke me up inside, reminded me I was alive and destined to change soon, that made my ideas so much clearer. Once or twice I tried to scratch the surface a little to see what was hiding underneath. In little areas barely wider than my cigarette burns.

The night when I wanted to look deeper, of course I

screwed up. It wasn't midnight yet; I had forgotten to close the door, and Gabriel came in. He saw my sleeves rolled up, the cuts on my good arm, the razor blade between my reddened fingers. He saw the straight line traced on my skin and the blood escaping from it, onto my clothes, my face, my hair. I have to say, I hadn't gone about my work properly. I looked like a painter so absorbed in his creation that he's spilled paint from the palette all over himself. Or an escaped extra from one of those low-budget horror films Gabriel and his friends watch on repeat.

At least he wasn't laughing for once. Without a word he closed the door. I stayed seated, licking the last drops of blood from my lips and my fingers. I knew I wouldn't taste their bitterness again for a long time. And also that I wouldn't have time to clean up the mess. The damage was already done.

Twenty seconds later, a fury burst into the room in the hysterical form of Mom. Dad felt obliged to tear the razor blade away from me by force. Maybe he thought I was too stupid to give it to him politely. Gabriel watched the scene from the doorway, his face completely drained of blood. Dad shook me until he almost dislocated my shoulder, Mom poured out a flood of tears to wash away the sight of the blood. Hadn't it ever crossed their minds that to open your veins, you have to slice *inside* your forearm? Did I really seem like a candidate for suicide?

Apparently so, because they kept me away from home for quite a while. With the crazies and the doctors in white coats. The school year ended for me the night before Easter break. The following months passed like a dreamless sleep, fed on a diet of colored pills. The place probably had no shortage of desperate cases, a carnival of suicidals, psychotics, and schizos, but I don't remember. Instead of a blank page, it's more like a handwritten page on which someone has spilled a glass of water. The words are still there, but distant, erased. I dreamed those few months behind a screen of drugs.

Occasionally I would emerge from the fog to undergo the Inquisition. All those doctors who fancied themselves apprentice Champollions, trying to decipher my scars like the Rosetta Stone. Who tried to rip words out of me with their forceps and sift them through their scholarly theories. My whole story unfolded. And I let them imagine whatever they wanted. I couldn't tell them about the bird and all the rest of it, the promise he had made me. Tell them that all I wanted was to expose the other body, under the surface, under the membrane, the one the phoenix had helped me glimpse.

When they let me leave, with prescriptions for enough antidepressants to stun an elephant, the school year was over and the fog in my head refused to dissipate. I returned to a new sophomore class, a year behind. The night before my great return into the land of the living, I cut my hair very short in front of the bathroom mirror. I chopped off my ponytail with a single stroke of the scissors and trimmed anything that stuck out. I felt good, so light. Then I dyed it with henna, the color of scorched grass. I must have looked like someone the day after a fire. Gabriel made a face when he saw me come out. Maybe because of the circles of eyeliner under my eyes. Or my soot-colored clothes. He called me a goth and I laughed in his face.

Back to school. The same tired teachers' faces, the same mind-numbing classes, word-for-word the same as last year. All that had changed were the students' names and the looks the teachers gave me. Word got around quickly. You don't join the class in the middle of October without attracting attention. I sat all the way in back, by the heaters, next to some sleepyheads who snored all through class. There I could watch the world at my own pace behind a wall of fog. Some of them avoided looking at me, out of modesty I imagine; the others watched me out of the corner of their eye.

Hiding in the back row, the ones Gabriel calls the 'losers' (or even more scornfully, the 'freaks') cast envious looks at me. I'd earned their admiration before I even met them, since at least I had dared to go all the way. I wasn't going to undeceive them. Even they would have had a hard time swallowing the story of the phoenix. I let them think what they wanted. I saw that more than one of them would have liked to lift my sleeve to gaze at the scars from my little accident.

The boy I sat next to, Simon, was the first to ask the question openly. During the break he offered me coffee and cigarettes to get me to talk. Not the kind of guy you'd want to run into in a dark alley after midnight, Simon, who was built like a caveman brought up on beer and red meat. But his tough guy exterior hid a softer side. His questions were frank and direct; he wanted to know everything. Why I'd done it, what I'd felt, and if I'd been scared. My life with the crazies, the doctors' questions, and if I was thinking about trying again one day. I avoided the embarrassing questions rather than lie to him. I kept the fabrications for the other curious people.

Even to Simon I didn't say anything about the phoenix. The cigarette burns, the cuts on my arms, I could mention those, and he listened to me smiling and nodding. I was sure he was convinced he understood. He must have tried the knife himself once or twice, just for fun. The rest of the story is mine alone.

Simon's the one who got me started smoking when we skipped class. I've never liked the smell of tobacco, the bitter smoke that makes your eyes water. I can't say I take pleasure in it. But I felt the bird so close to me every time, in the glowing end of my cigarette. He was there, somewhere. It was an Indian ritual: inhale the last breath of a dying animal to take a little bit of him, my totem, my protector. He who had wanted to change me. I watched the smoke rise, so light, a whirlwind of feathers. I inhaled a little of the phoenix and I felt his heat spread through my insides.

Go all the way: that was Simon's phrase when he talked about my accident. I never dared to set him straight because there are some things you don't talk about, even with friends. But he had been right from the beginning. You should always take things all the way. I had beaten around the bush all these years, while my bird was perhaps just waiting for a sign. The cigarettes, the burns and razor marks on my arms, all that was just a start. A foretaste of what he expected of me.

I have to say I believed, for a while, that Mom had chased him away for good. Or that he had abandoned me because I had failed the first time. He was always there, lurking even in the rays of the sun. He was waiting for me. I was seven years old the first time. Ten years had passed.

It's true, Simon's right: you have to go all the way. I started collecting candles, little by little. Ones I found in the attic, in drawers, bought at the flea market or swiped from shops. I stashed my treasure in several hiding places that Mom wouldn't find. Like the cheap lighter Simon gave me, a promotional item for one of those crappy movies you forget as soon as it's over. It's bad enough that Mom gets hysterical if she sees a match within a ten-yard radius of me ... She never quite got over the fireplace incident.

But it's three a.m. and I've collected as many candles as I could hoard without getting caught. I remind myself of a schoolgirl playing voodoo priestess. It's magnificent, all these little flames around me, their breath gently caressing my face. They know I'm one of them, my little sisters. They know he's going to help me, take me to where I'm not Bérénice anymore. They know the mark on my arm, his signature. He's hiding in each one of them and waiting.

Just now I burnt some old photos over the flames, images of me as a little girl, the Bérénice from before. I watched her shrivel and wither, losing all human appearance. I burnt some strips of clothes too, and the lock of hair that Mom had treasured since my first visit to the hairdresser. Hairs of a girlish blond color that hasn't been mine for a long time.

Soon, in a moment, I'll set the room on fire. I'll start with the bed; the comforter will catch fire easily. I'll wait until the beast, once unleashed, consumes the whole room, and the rest will follow. When the fire really gets going, he will return to me in all his glory, a flood of feathers and sparks. He'll blow his burning breath in my face like a homecoming kiss. And he'll rise above this room, this house. They won't prevent him: the door is locked.

He'll take me into him like he promised that day, and he'll change me. He'll return to give me another body, more beautiful and more fragile. Like the scar tissue on the back of my arm. A body that will look like me at last, that I'll be able to recognize as mine.

I'll become a phoenix, a spirit of fire, I'll melt into the smoke, I'll be dispersed to the four winds. Since he'll allow me to.

The hour of liberation, at last. The first candle is calling me.

*Translated from the French by James D. Jenkins*

Luciano Lamberti

# The Nature of Love

*American publishers have been releasing Argentinian horror and weird fiction at a record clip the past couple of years, with books by writers like Mariana Enríquez, Samanta Schweblin, and Agustina Bazterrica among the best and most successful works of horror and weird fiction in translation of recent years. In several interviews, Enríquez has championed the work of a fellow Argentinian author, Luciano Lamberti, who is still largely undiscovered outside his home country, and called for it to be translated and published in English. Although some of Lamberti's stories do feature the supernatural, the horror in 'The Nature of Love' is entirely human and originates in our own heart of darkness. The tale concerns shocking events captured on video, but the lingering question is whether the true horror consists in the events described, or in the narrator's reaction to them — or our own.*

Two A.M. They appear on the screen.

They can't be more than twenty-three. They're beautiful, pristine, almost angelic. The boy is smooth-faced, with fine, straight, blond hair that covers his right eye; every so often he brushes it away with a motion of his hand. She's dressed like a schoolgirl (white blouse, pleated skirt, tie) and still has the round cheeks, the smooth skin, the lively eyes, the cruelty, the impertinence, the anger, the self-confidence, the savageness, the barely contained madness that you find in children.

They're sitting on the edge of the bed, looking at the camera.

Details of the room can be seen on both sides. One might think it actually is the girl's room, or else that it's been decorated deliberately to give it the look of a teenager's room, with those teddy bears at the head of the bed, one pink and one white, the latter with a big heart inscribed I LOVE YOU. The walls, also pink, have a similarly intentional 'teen' look. On a shelf off to the side, almost out of the camera frame, there's a photo of the girl when she was eight or nine. In the video that will circulate on the web months later, it will be possible to zoom in and see it up close: the girl has braces on her teeth and is holding a rolled-up certificate. No way of knowing if she put the photo there on purpose, if she forgot it was there, or if all of this has just been set up to satisfy her clients' pedophile tendencies.

The kids call themselves Christian and Bibi. That's how you could find them online, before, when none of this had happened: christianandbibi.com. Fake names, as it turns out, but the ones their clients know them by. They charge twenty-five dollars an hour for a public show, where they kiss, show a little skin, chat, and fifty for a private show, where they engage in oral sex, anal and vaginal penetration. Their clients are numerous and, according to the site statistics, come from all over the world, especially Germany, the United States, Australia, Belgium, Brazil. Most of them have a simple desire: they want to see them in action. For others, it's a little more complex.

During the three years they did their shows, the requests were sometimes ridiculous. One time they were asked to have a threesome with an animal. They declined. Once the girl was asked to defecate on the boy. They declined. One time they were asked to poke each other with needles. They accepted. The girl agreed to masturbate with a cross. The boy penetrated her with his big toe, with the heel of a shoe, with the severed hand of a mannequin, with a cucumber wrapped in a condom. The boy pissed in the girl's face. He made a little cut on her arm with a scalpel and sucked her blood. He pretended to rape her while wearing a ski mask.

All of this had a special price.

Unlike many in this line of work, the boy and the girl work for themselves. They don't have bosses, nor a website that advertises and exploits them. They're independent and always have been, and in the next few hours, when their case makes it to the news sites and even a couple of TV programs, in the days that would follow that night, this fact will be commented on and discussed: there will be talk about the responsibilities of the government to impose limits on the web, about the scope of the laws, about ethics, voyeurism, mental illness. There will also be talk about satanic sects, schizophrenia, feminism. All the explanations will be partial, unsatisfactory.

It will be discovered, too, that the girl's real name is Ashley, and the boy's is Luke. That they're nineteen. That they met in high school and recorded the videos at the home of the girl, whose mother was quadriplegic and never found out what was going on. That they lived in Wisconsin, in a comfortable middle-class suburb. That – according to their neighbors and acquaintances – they were very much in love. That they belonged (*might* have belonged) to a satanic cult popular with the city's young people. That they made a pretty good living from their videos, which even allowed them to cover the cost of the girl's mother's treatments, the nurse who came some nights to care for her, the drugs she took for her various conditions. It was learned, too, that Luke had been jailed twice for possession and use of marijuana, that he had dropped out of high school, that his father was an alcoholic. All of that will be found out in the months to come.

Now, at this moment when they're sitting on the bed, naked, no one knows anything about them.

Watch the first few minutes of that video again: there's something in the way the boy and girl act, a kind of look or aura that foretells what's coming. It's there, floating in the air. Tonight there's something else. We still don't know why, what to call it, but it's there.

The girl types on her laptop.

Tonight is special, my little bunnies.

Why, asks user XSO127. What's special about it?

Tonight we're going to go beyond all limits, the girl writes.

Ooh, fantastic, says LOVE2077.

GIOGADULL: Brilliant.

NACHO1092 sends them a row of hearts.

GEORGICOST: Why is it a special night?

It's going to be a surprise, the girl writes. You all like surprises?

I love surprises and I love both of you, writes GUL266.

MACAROON94 requests a private room.

No private rooms tonight, the girl writes. Tonight we're all going to be together. It's the night of the offering.

Offering? asks DONALD132.

The girl waves at the camera with a chilling smile.

(A lot will be written about that wave, especially in relation to the couple's recent mental state. There will be talk of infidelity, a possible breakup, an end to the website; but they'll only be hypotheses. What they were going through, what they talked about and planned, the reason why they did it, is something that will never be fully known.)

The boy, who until that moment had his hand in his pants, touching himself, now pulls out his penis, described as 'practically perfect' by online users in terms of appearance, length, girth. The girl strokes it and then brings it to her mouth. Comments follow one after the other like a waterfall. They're desperate, nervous, crazed. We'll see them afterwards, in the replays, once the video first goes viral and is then pointlessly banned by the authorities.

The boy, like every night, looks at himself in the camera and fixes the girl's hair to improve the shot. Then he takes off his T-shirt.

What's on his skin? asks MIKY008.

Indeed: the boy's white skin that everyone loved so much shows some rather serious cuts, messy cuts that haven't had time to heal. There's one in particular, below his left nipple, that really catches the eye. Now we understand why the boy moves as though he's recovering from a surgical procedure. That's what the girl performed on him, according to the police investigation: a 'prior surgical procedure'.

Now the girl has climbed on top of him and is mounting him. There's a flood of comments.

Faster! requests HOWLL321.

Like that! Like that! writes VANESSABURT.

I'm going to marry you, I think I love you! writes YXHDM02.

He looks at the camera, he gifts to us the pleasure in his eyes. But before the climax, she stops and gets off him.

The boy is still lying on his back, breathing heavily.

The girl approaches the camera.

Now comes the good part, she writes.

Now she heads towards one side of the room and turns a crank. We don't see her, but we hear her. We see the metallic structure descending from the ceiling, a structure they set up a couple of weeks earlier. We see the platinum-plated chains hanging from that structure, each one ending in a load hook which the girl attaches to the grommets protruding from the boy's skin. We hear them talking, but we can't make out what they're saying. The boy is lying down, with the hooks in place, looking at the ceiling. The girl approaches the crank again and begins turning it in the opposite direction.

The chains tense at first, and then the boy is lifted by the hooks until he's about ten inches above the mattress, with his skin stretched as though made of plastic.

The comments stop for a moment.

My username, MARMO981, appears at that moment off to the side. Everyone can see it.

Yes, I write. Don't stop.

The boy appears almost relaxed. Days later, a meme will make the rounds, comparing him with Michelangelo's *Piety*. His face points upwards. His hair falls to his sides. The girl keeps turning the crank and the boy's body now hangs three feet above the mattress.

A scalpel has appeared in the girl's hands, its blade sharp and gleaming. Do I keep going? she asks with a gesture.

To the end, writes JULKCA.

Don't stop, writes MARIANE9.

Take it all off, I write.

Those comments will be shown on television later. My own username will be there.

The girl goes to work.

On this side of the screen I experience – I don't know why – a huge erection. I hear the sound of my own breathing. I'm sitting in the dark. My wife and children are asleep in their rooms. The boy screams for the first time. I hear him in my headphones. At first I can bear it. At first I can't distinguish whether what I'm seeing is real or not. I masturbate like crazy, come in the palm of my hand, wipe myself with a tissue.

After a while I have to take off the headphones. The screams are too much for me.

Five more minutes go by.

I run to the bathroom and vomit. It's not much, a kind of

yellowish paste, because it's been hours since I last ate any-thing.

I drag myself back to the desk. I look at the screen, where the boy doesn't look like a human being anymore, but rather a skinned rabbit hanging from the meat hooks in a butcher shop. His skin dangles in the air, dripping blood on the mattress.

The girl waves again, with the same insane smile. She's naked, covered in blood. Then the screen goes black (some-one reported it, we will find out later).

I switch off the computer. I go out to the yard to smoke a cigarette. The images, the boy's screams, flash through my head. I take a piss and brush my teeth. I lie down beside my wife, and I hug her.

I love you, I tell her.

And I sleep like a baby.

*Translated from the Spanish by James D. Jenkins*

Indrek Hargla

# The Grain Dryer of Tammõküla

*Though* INDREK HARGLA *is best known internationally for his series of crime novels featuring the 15th-century apothecary Melchior of Tallinn and considers himself primarily an author of science fiction (for which he has won many awards in his native Estonia), he has also written a number of fine horror stories over the past twenty-odd years. The following tale is taken from his collection* Kolmevaimukivi [The Three-Spirit Stone], *released in 2018. One Estonian critic grouped the book's tales under the term* ulme, *a uniquely Estonian word that incorporates elements of science fiction, fantasy, and horror. Hargla's collection contains several tales — including this one — which the author calls 'ethno-horror', a concept he considers distinctly Estonian. The same critic singled out 'The Grain Dryer of Tammõküla' in particular, calling it 'a hair-raising tale that skillfully weaves Estonian history, storytelling traditions, and the art of tension-building'. This is the first of Hargla's horror stories to appear in English.*

M Y GRANDMOTHER TOLD ME THE STORY of how an evil spirit had once infested the grain dryer of Kärojaagu farm. Back then, my grandmother had been working at Kärojaagu as a farm girl during the summertime. She said she saw and heard everything herself, so I believe the story to be true.

The grain dryer had been built back in the manor times when the Mõniste Manor landlord put up some of the money and had logs hauled in. The rest of the money was cobbled together by the farmers from Tammõküla and Saruküla villages who had bought out their homesteads, and the bricks were made right there in Tammõküla village where there was a small factory. After the War of Independence, when plots of land were being distributed, the dryer went to the owner of Kärojaagu, as his farm was the nearest. He used to have two farmhands who took turns keeping the fire in the kiln going and mixing the grain day and night during the harvest season. It was a big kiln, big enough for a grown man to fit in. The foundations of the dryer were made of granite rocks that had been brought in from nearby forests and fields, the walls and chimney were made of bricks and the dryer had a gabled shake roof. The house itself was about twenty yards long and was used for drying the grain of all the nearby farms. Mehka, the owner of Kärojaagu farm, did not charge money – instead, people brought him smoked meat, eggs, potatoes, and vodka, as these were things a farm could do with more than money in the autumn and winter.

And so, my grandmother was working as a farm girl at Kärojaagu when an evil spirit infested the grain dryer. There were two other farm girls there at that time and their names were Anni and Tiina.

The way it worked back then during harvest time was that there was a steam-powered machine in the field where the grain was threshed, put into sacks, and taken to the dryer on horse carts. There was a wooden ramp at the north end of the dryer, horses went up the ramp to the hatch, and the grain was then laid out on wicker beds in the kiln bowl above the flues of the kiln. Even when the weather stays dry for harvest time, the grain is never dry enough to be ground right away, and damp grain is prone to rot. The grain must dry in the kiln bowl for a good few days, with a farmhand keeping the fire going and feeding the big kiln with dry stumps that burn for a long time with a slow flame and do not spit sparks. Feeding the kiln and mixing the grain in the grain dryer all night long is exhausting, tedious, and sooty work. The farmhands usually got a day off as well as a big leg of smoked pork and a bottle of home brew on top of their wages for doing that.

These events took place around the end of August, when the nights were starting to draw longer and darker. The summer had been very drab that year, and the spring chilly, with winds howling and rain pouring all summer long. The barley fields of Tammõküla had not wanted to take at all at first and it was feared all through the summer that the rain would destroy the crop. So the farmhands had to keep the fire burning for longer than usual and mix the grain more diligently, crouching and stooping in the smoke, fumes, and soot.

Naan was the name of the farmhand who worked in the dryer at Kärojaagu back then. He was a boy of sinewy strength who talked little but worked hard, and when he did talk at all he talked of wanting to go to Tartu to study. He was from Mõniste, from a poor family, and Mehka, the owner of Kärojaagu, promised him an extra five silver pieces if he could make sure the grain would dry just right.

One still night when only a cold moon was hanging in the sky, grasshoppers were chirping, and stags were bellowing farther away at the edge of the forest, Naan suddenly burst out of the dryer and ran up to the house, banging on the door and yelling in a bewildered manner. My grandmother, whose name was Lagle, opened the door for him, and Mehka rushed out from his chamber, holding a hunting rifle. His son Ao also shot up from the bed of his young wife, as everyone was scared that some accident had happened in the dryer, the fire had got loose, the grain had got burnt or the chimney had collapsed.

No one had ever seen Naan in such a state of primal fear, for he was truly a serious and hard-working boy and did not believe old wives' tales or any other such things. Besides, no one had ever seen him afraid of anything.

But now he was shaking all over and his hands were cold as ice. At first, he could not utter a single word, he only howled and flailed his arms about. Mehka and Ao went to check the dryer and saw that all was quiet there, no fire or any other trouble. Naan was then given a swig of home brew and my grandmother held his one hand and Ao's young wife Ebel his other; they spoke to him in a kind voice until Naan calmed a little.

When Naan regained his ability to speak, he blurted: 'Banging and scratching! And flinging things! Then grabbed my hair and yanked!'

Everyone then asked who was throwing and who was pulling and yanking. Naan said he didn't know, but he thought it was an evil spirit.

'The boy has taken in too many fumes,' old Mehka then reckoned. 'There's no evil spirit in my dryer.'

'Didn't let me make a fire,' Naan carried on. 'The fiend didn't even let me near the kiln. When I got the fire going, some sort of scraping started right inside the kiln, and the fire was blown out. I went to start it again, but then a rusty barrel hoop flew at me . . .'

'This is crazy talk!' Mehka barked.

But Naan took another swig of home brew and then said that the spook or evil spirit had first clogged the fire hole and blown smoke in, and when he kept trying to light the fire, it started flinging things and raking his back as if with claws. Things had flown from the corners of the dryer, a tankard had been smashed to bits against a wall, and then the sounds had come, as if someone was breathing heavily and whispering in the dark. 'I picked up a big hammer,' Naan said. 'And I stood in front of the kiln and told it to go away. But then . . . Then it came at me.'

'What do you mean, it came at you?' Ao's young wife Ebel asked.

'It was as if eyes filled with pure malice were looking right at me and the air around me started choking me. I suddenly felt like I was in some vile fog that was about to rip out my soul. It was as if it wanted to tear out my hair and get inside my head.'

That was the longest anyone had ever heard Naan talk. Everyone at Kärojaagu remained silent for a while, not knowing what to say.

'It must be the fumes,' old Mehka finally surmised. 'A putrid rotten stump most probably got into the fire, with toadstools on it, and the fumes of that poison made you see all kinds of things.'

'Fumes do not throw barrel hoops about,' said Naan.

'Must have fallen off a rusty nail,' Mehka said. 'What we'll do now is get you back to work, and I'll add another two silver pieces to your pay.'

'No, chief,' Naan said resolutely. 'You can threaten me with a beating, offer money, or promise your daughter in marriage, but there's no way I'm going back into that dryer until the evil is gone.'

They were all astounded at such talk, because Naan very much needed the job and the pay and he had always been a smart, earnest, and brave boy.

'I will not give you a beating and you will certainly not get my daughter,' Mehka then said. 'But I can let you go. And where will you find new work before the autumn?'

'Let me go then if you will,' said Naan. 'But I'm telling you I'm not going back in there. Neither man nor bear fazes me, but evil spirits are another thing.'

The talk continued at Kärojaagu for some time that night, but the fact was that the grain was spread out on the wicker lattice and the fire needed to be lit. They couldn't let the grain rot, what with new sacks coming in from the field for the next few days to come. Finally, young Ao stood up and said he was not afraid and would go in and light the fire, spook or no spook.

Ao was twenty years old at the time, with coal black hair, and he had been training at a wrestling club in Võru for several winters and had also shot two wolves on a hunt the winter before. No one tried to talk him out of it. Mehka decided that if Ao saw an evil spirit in the dryer, Naan would keep his job as a farmhand, but if all was quiet and peaceful, Naan would be sacked in the morning.

They all went up to the dryer. It was a calm night, with a full moon hanging in the sky and stags bellowing far away in the forest. Ao put on a sooty threshing jacket, picked up a lantern, slipped a bottle of home brew into his pocket just in case and told the others to go to sleep, for there was no point in staying up. He also said that there was no need for anyone else to enter the dryer, he'd manage on his own. Then off he went through the door. The others didn't go to sleep because they couldn't – they stayed up, and my grandmother Lagle was among them.

A faint wisp of smoke started trailing out of the chimney of the grain dryer, then stopped, started again, and then stopped again. Ao did not come out, the door was closed and the light of the lantern could be seen through cracks in the door. Mehka then went to bed, as did his wife and the others, but Ao's young wife Ebel stayed awake with my grandmother and they waited till dawn began to break. They didn't hear a sound from the dryer, but they waited, as Ebel did not want to go to bed. They both felt immense fear and anxiety, they saw it in each other's eyes, but they did not dare say it.

A dim early autumn light then grew in the sky – the hour in which stags fall silent and grasshoppers no longer chirp, the wind is still, and a faint light spreads across the land. It is the hour in which day replaces night, dark gives in to light and time stands still for a moment. It suddenly felt as if the air around the grain dryer had changed, carrying the sickly-sweet stench of death, the putrid stink of rot.

The door of the grain dryer slowly opened and a dark figure stood on the threshold. He panted and staggered, stumbled and held out his hands, then fell to his knees and let out a piteous squeak, unable to utter anything else. He crawled onwards along the ground, as if feeling for a way forward. It was Kärojaagu Ao, but then again it was not.

Ebel screamed with terror when she saw the man, for she had not recognized him at all at first. Ao's coal black hair had become light gray in the night, his body was frail, he stank of rot, and he was feeling around with his feeble hands as if blind. He had, indeed, gone blind.

He still had eyes, but those eyes could no longer see. And just like his vision was gone, so too were his wits and strength. It was as if the strapping young man who had enjoyed wolf hunting and wrestling had been rendered a hundred years older in a single night. No one heard another coherent word from his lips ever again, he only wailed, whimpered, and cried. And even when he did talk, his words were so deranged that no one could understand him.

There was no fire in the dryer and the grain had rotted away in the night. It stank of corpses, and ice-cold air emanated from the kiln.

Several educated doctors came to Kärojaagu in the days following, but none of them knew how to cure young Ao. He had seen or heard or felt something so terrifying that his hair had turned gray in one night, he had lost his vision, and insanity had torn out his soul. Ebel sat by him day and night and tried to make him better in any way she could, talking to him gently, hugging him close and crying, but Ao only whimpered and foamed at the mouth.

Kärojaagu Mehka was downright gloomy for a few days, at times flying into a rage when he went to the dryer, yelling at it and throwing stones at its walls. The thresher kept working in the field, as it was the busy harvest season and the grain of several farms wanted drying. Unfortunately there was no one in Tammõküla village, or even farther away where the stories had spread, who would dare come to Kärojaagu to feed the kiln and mix the grain.

It was Ebel who then reckoned that they had no other choice but to appeal to a seer from Süvahavva farm. Ebel was from Põlva County and she knew that since olden times, Süvahavva farm had been home to a family that always bore an *arbuja* or seer who was able to communicate with the netherworld, see ghosts and spirits and drive them away, and cast spells and enchantments. At first, Mehka refused to entertain the idea, but ultimately he had little choice – his son was deranged, blind, and decrepit, the dryer stank of rot, the air in the kiln remained as cold as ice, and none of the farmhands dared go in there, while more and more grain was being brought in from the fields.

They found a man from Taheva who had a lorry and he drove Ebel from Tammõküla to the town of Võru and from there to Süvahavva, where the seer was said to live.

Ebel returned the following day, bringing with her an older man with curly white hair, dressed in jackboots, a white shirt and a coat, and carrying an old-fashioned birch bark satchel across his shoulder. His eyes were very sad and his voice was very deep. The man was called Pääru Kivioja – the owner of Süvahavva farm and a reputed seer.

He first went to see Ao in his chamber and no one else was allowed in. He stayed with Ao for nearly two hours and when he came out his eyes were even sadder.

'I know of no way to help that man,' he then told Kärojaagu Mehka. 'He has brushed against the netherworld and that kind of thing tends to rob a man of his wits and strength.'

'Then sort out my grain dryer,' Mehka asked. 'And I will give you a bagful of silver coins, a big bottle of home brew, and half a pig.'

'Yes, I could use some silver,' Pääru the seer replied. 'But I want it right away and it must be soaked in enchanted water. Then give me some fresh black bread and milk and have the women quickly bake a curd cake.'

He did not want these things for himself to eat, he explained, they had to be given to the dryer as an offering. A little while later, when Pääru was brought the bread, the milk, and the cake and given some silver coins, he said he would need a maiden or child to help him in the dryer. There were no small children at Kärojaagu and none of the neighbors would have dared send a child of theirs to that chamber of dread. The only maiden there was my grandma Lagle. She was afraid, of course, and refused at first, saying she did not want to lose her eyesight and wits, but Ebel begged her desperately and Pääru the seer promised that nothing would happen to her.

They then went into the dryer, my grandmother and Pääru. It truly was cold in there and the air heavy with a terrible stench, as if an animal carcass was rotting away. The grain in the kiln bowl had decayed into a thick mouldy sludge, which is something that simply cannot happen in just a couple of days without witchcraft or evil.

The putrid stench of a corpse was so powerful that they both had to hold a scarf to their mouths to keep from retching. Various tools and items lay strewn all across the dryer floor and it did, indeed, look like someone had been throwing things about.

Pääru asked my grandma to stand by the door and then started to walk around in the dryer. He muttered some words to himself while breaking off bits of bread and dropping them onto the floor. He then sprinkled milk around, still muttering some sort of incantation, and drew crosses on the walls with his fingers. The cold air shifted slightly in the dryer, and the rank stench of rot became stronger. When Pääru had paced around the dryer several times, he stopped in front of the kiln, took a big bottle from his satchel, poured water from it into a bowl and placed the coins there to soak. He asked my grandma to come closer and then very slowly opened the kiln door.

'You're a pure and untouched maiden, you give it some cake,' Pääru whispered.

'Give the cake to whom?' my grandma asked in a shaky voice.

'I do not yet know who or what the fiend is,' Pääru said. 'But we are seeking to appease it.'

My grandma wondered what was there to appease, since the evil spirit had rendered the young master feeble-minded and blind and rotted the grain. She was terribly scared, but she did as Pääru asked. Cold wind blew up at her from the kiln as she gingerly placed a piece of cake on the ash and coals.

'Is it in there?' my grandma asked.

'I guess so, but not like other things in this world, things we can see and touch,' Pääru replied. He then took the silver coins and used these to draw crosses on the kiln bricks. He gave one to my grandma and told her that they had to hold the coins in their hands, pass these into the kiln, and recite some magic words. My grandma did as he asked. She was forbidden ever to repeat those magic words and so never has.

She was terribly frightened while she held the coin in her hand in front of the kiln because she could not see what else was in the kiln and the stench of rot around her was stifling.

'Can you hear that?' Pääru suddenly asked.

My grandma could not hear anything. Pääru told her to listen more keenly and then she did truly hear as if an infant was whimpering very faintly. Although it could have been a bird screeching outside, or just a figment of her imagination.

'I have to light a fire in the kiln,' Pääru then said. 'You, my child, must leave now, I no longer need your help.'

'Did it accept our offerings?' my grandma asked.

Pääru very slightly shook his head, his face was now as if of stone and those sad eyes of his were shot with blood. He dug some matches out of his satchel as well as a dry waxy stick and told my grandma to go outside.

And there they waited for Pääru for quite some time with Ebel and old Mehka and his wife and Naan, farm girls Anni and Tiina, all the other household folk, and even some neighbors. It could have been an hour or perhaps even longer because evening was beginning to set in when Pääru finally emerged.

And again, some of the women cried out with fear and the men swore out loud, for the man who came out was not the same man who had gone in.

Pääru staggered and swayed and his clothes were torn, but the most horrible thing was that his beautiful blond curly hair had been ripped from his scalp, with only a few bloody clumps left, his face was all covered in blood, and the skin on his head had been torn open in places. Pääru did not say anything, but he had his wits and his mind remained lucid, for the evil spirit had not been able to claim him. The women wailed and sobbed and rushed to treat his wounds. The blood was gently washed from his head and chamomile salve was smeared on it. Throughout it all Pääru still did not utter a thing. It was as if he was deep in thought and contemplation. He must have been in terrible pain, for he chewed some seeds to soothe it.

Later, when his wounds had been tended to, old Mehka

came demanding to know what fiend was living in his grain dryer and whether Pääru knew how to get rid of it.

'I do not know who it is,' Pääru then told him. 'That soul has clearly not been christened and given up to God. It is filled with a terrible rage and hatred, but as to why it is like that, I do not know.'

'In that case, you are of no use to me and you have lost your hair for nothing,' Mehka concluded.

'I have only just started,' Pääru replied.

He then just sat there, looking at the grain dryer and studying it from afar. After a while, he started asking about when it had been built and who had built it and whether the man who built it was still alive. He was told that it had been over thirty years and a Latvian man called Alfreds had been the main builder, but no one had seen him around for a long while and he had probably since died. Pääru started walking around the grain dryer, studying its walls. The foundations were made of granite rocks and the walls were made of red bricks. He kept walking round and round the dryer and muttering to himself and examining the walls, when he suddenly stopped at a corner. He knelt down, looking closely and then reached to touch a rock in the foundations, as if he had found something of import. He requested a hammer and a crowbar and started to chip away at the mortar around the rock until he finally managed to get one edge clear.

No one could see anything special about the rock. But it did seem to somehow perk Pääru up and he told them that things were perhaps beginning to make sense.

'What's starting to make sense?' Mehka asked.

'What or who has infested the dryer,' Pääru muttered, explaining that an evil spirit like this does not come from nothing and it has to have something to do with the building. For it is obvious that the evil spirit is somehow connected to the kiln, and the kiln is a part of the building. And now he had found the first trail to follow that might lead to some answers.

Still no one could understand what relevance the cornerstone bore. It was an entirely ordinary large, rough, gray lump of granite with small holes in it. But Pääru was very excited about the rock and told them to bring him warm quilts, for he was going to sleep right there beside the rock that night. He also asked them to bring him some more black bread and curd cake as well as a few shots of home brew. He told them to find someone in the morning who had worked there when the dryer was built, as some of the builders were surely still alive and would remember that time.

My grandma sneaked out at night and saw in the moonlight how Pääru poured home brew on the cornerstone and stuffed bread in its holes.

By morning, a man had been brought in from beyond Pala forest, a man by the name of Tõnnis who had worked on building the grain dryer during the manor times. Pääru then gathered everyone up, took Tõnnis to the cornerstone of the grain dryer and asked him if he remembered where the rock had been brought from.

Tõnnis proceeded to study the rock more closely. Suddenly his face dropped and he said: 'I think it's that very same pocked rock from the old sacrificial pine.'

'It must be the one,' Pääru said. 'For only sacrificial rocks had holes carved into them in the olden days, and offerings were made on such rocks.'

The story of that sacrificial rock, as Tõnnis then explained, was that the manor landlord had had all the big rocks from the neighborhood hauled in, and one such rock had stood right by the big road, beside a thick and gnarly pine tree. In olden times, people used to hold the pine and the rock sacred, for snow never fell on the rock and it always stayed clear of snow as if it was hot. Back then, it had been a sacred grove, with the rock in the middle and the pines around it, but now only one pine remained. When the grain dryer was being built, there had still been a few pines, but those had also been cut down. Tõnnis recalled that when the rocks were being hauled in and the pines felled, some old women had come bidding them not to do it, saying that the rock must not be taken away or else a terrible curse would be born and a great evil would be unleashed, especially on children. In olden times, people used to go to the rock to make offerings, for they believed that the underground spirits who protected children from misery and misfortune lived underneath the rock. But the dryer had to be built and rocks were needed, and the overseer had the rock taken away for the foundations of the dryer. And a few years later, bad things, indeed, began to happen. One boy from the village hanged himself from the pine one night, and no such thing had ever happened before.

'Should I have the rock broken out now and taken back to the pine?' Mehka then asked. 'Would that help?'

'The forces that the rock was keeping dormant have been released,' Pääru replied. 'I tried to appease them, but they didn't want that – they want something else. It is a terrible malice and evil that has now infested the dryer and it has a horrible secret. It lay idle for an eternity, until it attacked Naan. And then Ao. And it would have also attacked Lagle, if she hadn't kept it at bay with her incantations.'

'Well, teach us those words then,' Mehka asked.

'This I cannot do. And it wouldn't help either, for the fiend would still not let you light the fire in the dryer. There is no other way but for me to find out the secret of the evil spirit. Tell me, is it true that Ebel is with child?'

Ebel turned red in the face at the question and admitted that she had started feeling a bit odd a few weeks back. And then she burst into tears, for she realized that the child's father now would only be half a man.

Pääru then took my grandma Lagle aside and talked to her so no one could overhear. Pääru asked her whether it was true that she and Naan had secretly lain together and my grandma Lagle now carried Naan's child.

My grandma became terribly frightened, for it was true, but no one knew about it. It had, indeed, once happened that she had stayed on the pasture with Naan. They had found shelter from the rain under an old linden tree and began to embrace. My grandma actually liked Naan very much and had not resisted when Naan lifted up her skirt and lay down with her. So now there truly was a new life growing inside her, although it was not yet showing. And that was a very bad thing, for no one wants to marry a girl with a child and she would be disgraced in the village if it became known. Naan was poor and wanted to go to university, and he definitely did not want to marry yet. They had then secretly agreed that after the harvest Naan would find an old hag from a faraway village who would instruct her how to get rid of the child.

Pääru promised that he would not tell anyone about it so that my grandma would not fall into disrepute, and then he left Kärojaagu farm to walk around the parish. He said he was looking for the secret of the grain dryer and would return when he found it.

Pääru was away for two days before he returned. A strange woman came with him. She was old, about fifty, and did not have an ounce of wit in her head.

The woman was called Mad Maarja and she lived in Laanõmõtsa village in a sauna where some farm girls took care of her. The woman was so deranged that for decades she had not done anything other than sit in that sauna and stare far into the distance. Sometimes she would pick up a stone from the sauna heater and cuddle it as if it were an infant. At other times, she would start screaming and thrashing and rolling on the floor, but then the fit would pass and she would again just sit at the sauna window, stare outside and do nothing other than cuddle a heater stone. The farm girls would come to feed her gruel with a spoon and wash her and help her defecate between potato furrows, for otherwise she would have soiled herself and starved to death.

On Pääru's orders, this woman had now been put on a cart and brought to Kärojaagu. She probably thought – if she even had any thoughts in her head – that she had been brought outside to defecate again, for as soon as she was lifted off the cart, she went to lift up her skirt to start defecating in front of everyone. But then she looked more closely at where she had been brought to, saw the grain dryer, and started screeching in a terrible voice. The voice was so awful that the others covered their ears with their hands, unable to listen.

Pääru put his arms around her and soothed her until she calmed. Mad Maarja did not want to walk, but again Pääru forced her and the two of them then went into the grain dryer. No one could understand what was happening and why Pääru had brought the demented woman to Kärojaagu.

They stayed in the grain dryer for a very long time and no one ever learnt what happened in there. When they finally emerged, Mad Maarja was as quiet and subdued as she usually was. Pääru ordered for her to be taken to the sauna and fed gruel. As he said that, everyone saw that there was a tear at the corner of his sad eyes and his face was as pale as that of a corpse.

Mehka then angrily demanded to know what in God's name was going on and what kind of crazies Pääru was inviting to his sauna.

Pääru took a sip of home brew, then took Mehka and my grandma aside and told them everything.

It was an ugly and atrocious tale.

It had happened decades before, right after the kiln of the new grain dryer had first been lit and the threshed grain had been put on the wickerwork to dry. The farmhand who was tasked with keeping the fire going and mixing the grain at night was a lecherous boy who used to seduce and disgrace the village girls. Mad Maarja had been a pretty girl when she was young, and she had also been lured by the sweet promises of the farmhand and had ended up becoming pregnant by him. She was even silly enough to fall in love with the farmhand and think that he would marry her. But when Maarja's belly started to grow, the farmhand began to stay away from her and had not wanted to have anything to do with her. To keep her indiscretion from being known, she ran away to Latvia where her relatives lived, and hid there until it was time.

It was harvest time when Maarja's child was due to be born.

She got a lift from her relatives and came to Kärojaagu, as she knew that her sweetheart was working there as the grain dryer. She hoped that the birth of the child would soften the farmhand's heart and he would marry her.

The child was born in the grain dryer.

The farmhand, however, was by then engaged to a girl from a rich family in Koobassaare, and he was hoping to get a good dowry. He did not want the family of his bride to know that he had had a child with another girl.

When Maarja was half-unconscious and weak and exhausted after the labor, the farmhand spoke some pretty words to her and coaxed and cajoled her into agreeing that the child had to disappear from the face of the earth, until a right and better time would arrive and the farmhand and Maarja could marry.

The farmhand then picked up the newborn babe, a girl, and took her to the kiln of the grain dryer, threw her into the fire and tossed sappy logs of a sacred pine on top to make sure the child would fully burn and nothing of her would be left.

When the flames from the sacrificial pine touched the newborn child, she shrieked in terrible pain and these were the last sounds Maarja heard before she lost consciousness. Her daughter was burnt alive in the kiln of the grain dryer until nothing but ash remained. And the sacrificial rock that had been placed in the foundations of the dryer and was supposed to keep evil spirits at bay remembered her death.

Naan, the Kärojaagu farmhand, had probably got someone pregnant in the village, Pääru continued. The witchcraft that had been conjured upon the kiln and the dryer had sensed that Naan had wanted to get rid of the child, thus the curse did not let him light the fire and fought Naan to prevent a new murder. When Ao went to the dryer, the curse sensed that he also had an unborn child growing in someone's belly. Ao stayed in the dryer for longer and the curse took his bodily strength and wits. And now the evil curse sits in the dryer and won't let anyone light a fire in the kiln where an innocent baby girl had once been burnt alive.

Maarja had lost her wits because her child had been burnt. The farmhand had also been cursed, so much so that he had gone to the old sacred grove and hanged himself from a sacrificial pine.

My grandma was speechless with fear. Kärojaagu Mehka said that he would have the grain dryer pulled down and the rocks buried in the ground. Pääru shook his head, however, and told him that this would not help. Only Mad Maarja herself could do something to alleviate the curse.

At that point, neither my grandma Lagle nor old Mehka had yet understood what Pääru meant. But the same night, Mad Maarja had come out of the sauna and gone to the grain dryer. She had taken dry pine stumps and sappy twigs, stuffed them in the kiln and then climbed in herself.

When those at Kärojaagu awoke in the morning, the entire garden was filled with the rancid stink of burnt meat and bones.

My grandma Lagle told me that the curse of the evil spirit then left the grain dryer, the stench of rot was gone and the kiln was no longer filled with ice-cold air. From then on, the fire burned and the grain was dried every summer.

The Tammõküla grain dryer still stands today and the pock-holed sacrificial rock is clearly visible in its foundations. Nowadays, the house is used as a barn and no grain has been dried there for a long time.

If the evil spirit had not infested the Tammõküla grain dryer, I would never have been born. My grandma Lagle would then not have given birth to my father. I only exist because of that curse. Every year on my birthday, I go to the Kärojaagu grain dryer in Tammõküla village and place some bread and curd cake on that cornerstone.

And I know I am not there alone.

*Translated from the Estonian by Kati Metsaots & Dan O'Connell*

# Viola Cadruvi

# The Runner

*In the foreword to Volume One, we said we were working on a book
of horror stories in endangered languages. Consider this a teaser for
that book. Most readers will know that Switzerland has German-,
French-, and Italian-speaking regions, but many probably don't
know that Swiss law recognizes a fourth official language, Romansh.
As the name suggests, it's a descendant of Latin, though not mutually
intelligible with French or Italian. UNESCO classifies it as 'definitely endangered'; as of the 2000 Swiss census, only about 60,000
people said they still spoke it regularly. Over the past century, a language has gone extinct, on average, about once every three months,
and linguists estimate that of the 6,500 or so languages in use today,
at least half will be gone by the end of the century. Will Romansh
be one of these? Not if* VIOLA CADRUVI *has anything to say about
it. Cadruvi (b. 1992) published her first book – and perhaps the first
horror collection in Romansh –* La feglia dal fraissen [The Ash
Leaf], *from which this story is taken, in October 2020. Switzerland
is known for its natural beauty – mountains, valleys, lakes, forests.
But in Cadruvi's tales Nature can be a threatening force. In 'The
Runner' the natural world seems to be flashing warning signs at a
young woman out for a jog, but will she heed them?*

I T'S QUIET IN THE FOREST. Only the sound of her footfalls
breaks the silence. The blood flows through her veins.
She puts one foot in front of the other at a regular pace, her
heart beating to the rhythm of her steps. A rabbit near the

path perks up its ears and vanishes into the bushes when the runner approaches. She perceives all the life in the forest. The rabbit, which hides itself deeper in the brush. The three deer grazing in a little clearing. The fox that digs around at a mole's hole and ignores the runner's footsteps. And a whole lot more. She hears the last drops of the previous night's rain dripping off the leaves. She hears the treetops as they whisper, telling of the sun that's squeezing through the clouds. She savors the moss that creeps over the rocks and the lichen that spreads on the tree trunks. She smells the water that the plants suck from the ground and draw up to their very tops, as if it were their own blood. She feels how the leaves inhale the carbon dioxide, as they help to turn it into the oxygen she takes in with every breath. Sometimes, between the pines, she glimpses a few of the big city's buildings extending out behind the woods.

She knows her route well. In the beginning she always used to bring her cell phone with her to check the numerous hiking and jogging trails that branch out over the hill, but she doesn't need to do that anymore. The road gets steeper and becomes a path. She follows the tracks left in the dirt by some mountain bikes. All at once she stops. There's a deer on the path, only twenty yards ahead of her. It's looking straight at her. Carefully, so she doesn't startle the animal, she reaches into her bag to get her phone out and take a photo. Then she realizes she's left it at home. The deer stands still, watching her. Hello, she says. The deer looks at her. She takes a couple of steps. The deer shakes its head. What? Should I not keep going? The deer shakes its head again, as if it's trying to scare off a fly. She laughs. Sorry, but I have the right to be here too, and I'd like to finish my run now. Her pleas don't seem to persuade it. I'll just keep going, she thinks, the deer will go on its way then. She starts jogging slowly. Another ten yards. The deer doesn't move. I'm not stopping. Another five yards. The deer doesn't run away. Anytime now, go! Two more yards. Shoo! she says and waves her arm. At the last moment, the deer makes a jump and vanishes into the brush. Her heart's pounding. Her pace is uneven. She tries to breathe calmly.

I don't believe it, she thinks. There's something not right about that animal. Maybe it has rabies? No way. She goes on, following the trail of the mountain bikers. She looks up towards the sky. The sun seems to have disappeared behind the clouds, but it will be disappearing behind the hill soon anyway. She's already been running for an hour. At the next crossing, she'll take the turn towards home. The crossing would be coming up in a quarter of a mile.

Her bright yellow shoes sink into the soft ground. The impact breaks the peaceful silence. Her arms swing back and forth to propel her body further. The orange stripe on the back of her shirt drowns out the mild colors of the woods. The leaves rustle angrily in the wind. The rustling becomes a crackling. Again she looks around. The treetops are no longer green. They're black. Covered in black feathers that flutter in the wind. Crows. All filled with crows. She knows these birds. In the park across from her house there are a lot of crows. But she's never seen this many before.

She runs faster. Maybe a storm's coming. Animals can sense that. She's concentrating on the path when she realizes that something's pinching at the bun in her hair. She immediately starts waving her arms – and feels feathers. She screams. The crow has sunk its claws into her hair. She shakes her head and runs even faster. Leave me alone! Go away! The crow cackles and calls to its companions. She doesn't dare look back. Fortunately the crossing should be coming up soon.

But it doesn't come. Still the plants whisper and still the material of life pulsates through nature. The runner is no longer a part of this life around her. Larger and larger roots stretch out across the path. More and more nettles shoot out their foliage and try to whip her legs. The woods become thicker. The branches hang in her face. The sweat flows down her neck and onto her breasts. She constantly has to leap over roots and duck her head to avoid boughs and branches. They couldn't possibly have done such a bad job clearing this path. We're here in civilization, not a wild jungle, dammit!

Something tears the orange stripes from her shirt. She keeps going. She can't run any faster. The plants crowd in even closer, seem to want to grab her. They snatch at her legs and her bare arms like greedy lovers. A root stretches out across the road. She stumbles. Lies on her stomach on the ground. Tastes the flavor of the woods. Moss, resin, sour, sweet, earthy. It grows over her legs. The green covers her like a blanket, over her yellow shoes and her calves. She tastes the woods on her tongue. Ivy covers her face and entwines with her hair, which has come out of its bun. The root that tripped her twists around her arms. Leaves fall from the sky and cover her bright-colored clothes. The forest swallows her. Her blood runs through the roots and up the trees. She reaches the top. Somewhere a crow caws and a rabbit comes along and nibbles a dandelion. She drinks in the sun and inhales carbon dioxide. A runner jogging through the woods below her breathes the oxygen that she exhales.

*Translated from the Romansh by James D. Jenkins*

# Konstantinos Kellis

# Firstborn

*Greeks have been doing horror longer than just about anyone. Flip through almost any book of ancient Greek myths and you'll find snake-headed women who'll turn you to stone, people trapped in labyrinths with vicious monsters, three-headed hell hounds, beautiful but deadly sirens who lure men to their doom, and plenty more. Three millennia later, Greeks are still writing horror, though the scene today isn't a large one. Among Greek horror authors, we might single out Abraham Kawa, a prolific writer of paranormal mysteries and horror novels, Chrysostomos Tsaprailis, author of an excellent collection of folk horror, and the writing duo of Marios Dimitriadis and George Damtsios, whose horror collections inspired by heavy metal songs have won acclaim. But the most popular and best-selling horror writer in Greece today is* KONSTANTINOS KELLIS, *who has published three novels and a short story collection in Greek and has also had several stories published in English. The following folk horror tale, the author tells us, is loosely inspired by stories his father told him about strange practices in some mountain villages in Crete.*

'WE ARE NOT GIVING THEM THE BABY.'
Anna's forehead is leaning against the window glass. Scant drops of rain hit the Land Rover's windshield, a passing cloud in an otherwise beautiful Saturday. She doesn't see the beauty. The vastness of the countryside as it sprawls beyond the highway barriers just makes her eyes mist over.

Despite Nikos' efforts to spark a conversation, she's been

silent for hours. Now, her husband's knuckles have turned white on the steering wheel, his lips crushed in a thin line as they put more and more distance between themselves and Athens.

The 'invitation' from her family village had come barely a few hours after they'd returned home from the maternity clinic. Half a year unfurled in one instant, a gray spool in her mind, empty of actions or even thoughts save one.

*See you in six months, Anna. The family will be waiting for you with open arms.*

She knows what those open arms mean: to grab, to pull, to take away. In the back, the little one is asleep in the car seat. Anna closes her eyes, the glass pane cool against her forehead, and listens for the infant over the noise of the car, trying to find some calm in that soft breath.

'We are not going to let this happen, Anna. We are not giving him away.'

Nikos had always wanted children. It started more like a joke between them, him talking about a big family, her turning it down. Not yet. Not yet. That joke quickly turned sour, it morphed into their go-to reason for a fight. All the money of her family's dowry, all their travels, and the luxurious life so distanced from what Nikos knew before he met Anna hadn't proved enough to fully quench that need. They did love each other, and got married despite that disagreement, but it only grew harsher with the years. Not yet. When? Later. She trembled at the very idea of having to explain *why* they had to wait for another woman of her generation to bear a little boy. Why their son couldn't be the family's firstborn.

Then, five years into their marriage, it happened. Despite all the protection, and her meticulous care, Anna got pregnant. She tried to hide it from Nikos, from her relatives, from her entire circle. When, a few weeks later, a big basket filled with presents and baby stuff was delivered to their apartment door, Anna finally realized how futile her efforts to keep such a secret had been.

The card on the lavish basket simply read 'Stavropoulos Family'.

Her waking hours overflowed with dark thoughts. Her sleep brimmed with nightmares. Worst of all was that little speck of hope amid those nightmares, the chance that it wasn't a boy and that all her worries had been for naught. The chance for a normal family.

She'd had to endure this torture for four long months, until the second ultrasound. She'd never cried so hard with relief as when her doctor pointed at the image on the sonogram's screen.

*It's a girl, Anna. You're having a little girl.*

★

The clinic's floor resembles that of a slaughterhouse. Red footprint stains on white tiles run in every direction.

'You told me it was a girl, you bastard!'

Nurses struggle to keep Anna down. The bleeding won't stop. She's badly torn and no matter how many hasty stitches they manage to apply, they break and come undone as she kicks and flails. But Anna shows no pain; it has been smothered by her wrath.

'How much did they give you to lie to me? How much, tell me!'

The doctor stands speechless a couple of steps away from her. The little boy in his arms remains silent, still caught in the dream of the womb. A lump protrudes over his left eyelid, soiled with amniotic fluids and bare of skin.

It takes the midwife violently pulling on his scrubs

for him to snap out of the sudden languor. He hastily pats the newborn and soon the room fills with a high-pitched cry, ridden with agony. It's not enough to smother Anna's screams and curses.

'You bastard! You bastard!'

★

'We're getting close, love.'

Nikos' whisper draws her back to the present. She sits up on the leather seat and looks outside. The empty edges of the highway have been replaced by trees and shacks. Has it been five hours already?

The road continues uphill, its turns winding more and more. They come across a few vehicles, mainly pickup trucks and tractors going the opposite direction. She lowers the window just a crack and the wind carries the smell of dry grass, smoke, and animal dung. A bell echoes in the distance, out of tune. She's not sure whether it's joyous or mournful.

Sooner rather than later, the road sign appears.

The village has been called Stavros – the Cross – for more than two hundred years. One of her ancestors built the first church here and named himself Stavropoulos, 'Son of the Cross'. It's her father's surname, her grandfather's; the surname of a line of patriarchal figures lost in the mist of centuries past. The entire area belongs to them. She remembers her late father saying that her forebears hunted boars on the surrounding mountains, going for days without having to set foot outside their own land. Anna took Nikos' surname when they got married, in an effort to put as much distance as possible between her and them. But, there she is now, going up the familiar hill of her childhood, passing by derelict, weedy walls. The village is almost entirely abandoned; everyone has taken refuge in the cities.

Her older brother is the only one still living here. The firstborn son of her generation. His name is never mentioned. He has no place in family celebrations, receives no wedding invitations. He never got married, or studied, or traveled. His only aim in life, for almost forty years now, has been to take care of the house and the graves out in the garden, until the next generation's firstborn arrives.

All his life he's been preparing for this moment, for tonight, when Anna will meet him with her little boy, in the presence of the entire family. The mere thought of it traces cold fingers down her spine. Her stomach has been empty since yesterday, but even now she can feel the retching of nonexistent vomit.

The baby stirs and coos as the broken road puts the Land Rover's tires to the test. Music reaches her ears, violins and clarinets lead a circle dance yet unseen. The house now looms at the top of the uphill road.

'Everyone else is already here,' Nikos mutters. A dozen cars, give or take, are parked on the street. People climb the stairs to the house; relatives kiss twice before proceeding inside. Men in suits and ties, women in furs and heels, unused to the gravel and the dirt roads.

Her gaze falls on a girl kissing one of the attendants, a big smile on her face. Her swollen belly stretches the red, tight-fitting dress.

Nikos has stopped thirty yards away from the closest car. She studies his expression in the mirror, his wet eyes gazing at the gathering ahead. He hadn't believed her when she explained it to him. It took time for him to realize the price of her family's wealth. Only a few minutes ago, his denial to accept what was happening had kept him cool, but this defensive mechanism had now shattered and tears were finding their way through the cracks.

'We are not giving him away,' he says and his voice,

unused for hours, trembles. 'They can have their houses back, their money, this fucking car. They are not taking our boy.'

Upon seeing him, she realizes she's been crying herself. She leans over to him and hugs him. She wants to believe him, she can't do it alone. Anxiety courses through their veins, breaking out in spasms. The baby is the only one remaining calm, and when Anna turns to check on him she sees he's awake. With every day that passes the lump above his little brow seems to be a touch more swollen. Now it's turned black, a hard piece of bruised meat.

At the hospital they had told her that it could be removed with a simple procedure. How stupid they were. As if they understood what they were dealing with.

'Let's go,' Nikos says, wiping his tears. 'We'll tell them tonight. We'll tell them together.' He straightens his blazer and steps out of the car first. The bystanders have realized who the jeep belongs to. Those who were already in the yard rush out to meet them.

Outside the car, the cold mountain air whips her face. She neither looks at her relatives nor answers their calls, she just turns and opens the rear door. Her movements mechanical, as if dressing a wound, Anna unfastens the car seat, places the baby in the basket, tucks him carefully under his blanket and takes him outside.

She walks towards the spot where the entire family awaits them. Siblings, cousins, daughters, and brothers-in-law. Almost thirty people, most of them couples. They look happy, but behind their plastered smiles she traces nervousness, expectation, well-hidden relief sprinkled here and there, like servants waiting on their dying master. Insatiable eyes fix on the basket as it comes closer. They all crave for a glance at the baby.

Even from afar, the women's bellies reveal several stages of pregnancy. Most of them seem happy to show it. The news that she's had a boy has spread like wildfire. Their clothes are expensive, their jewelry dazzling, their hair done up perfectly. They've come to celebrate. Anna wears no makeup, her hair is a mess, her clothes still faintly smell of baby food and vomit.

She's a few steps away now when a man breaks away from the crowd and approaches her. Sotiris, the second-born man of their generation. She hasn't met him since their father's funeral years ago. *He's put on a lot of weight,* she thinks, even though she often sees him on TV giving heated speeches and offering elaborate arguments up on the podiums of parliament. He hugs her tight and she feels as if she's made of cracking ice. He smells of tobacco and expensive perfume.

'Welcome, little sister,' he says, and seconds after the kiss he turns to the basket. Before she has time to answer or complain, Sotiris has pushed the blanket aside. His eyes gleam just like his rings as he studies the infant. Fat fingers caress his little face, trace his baby gums, close around the meaty lump on his forehead.

'*Yasan*, Anna,' he says and laughs. '*Yasan*, well done! Here is the firstborn!'

He yells again back towards the rest and they rush to hug her, to kiss her. Someone grabs the basket and Anna wants to scream, but the various perfumes and the unfamiliar arms choke her. She tries to find Nikos with her eyes, listens for his voice, but then a double gunshot tears the air and Anna jerks. Sparrows shoot out from the nearby roof tiles and fly over her head towards the trees. As the family leaves her behind, she sees two strangers loading their shotguns. Another one walks to their side, with a cigarette hanging from his lips, raises his gun and shoots in the air as if it's Easter Sunday. That one smiles at her through his unkempt stubble – some third cousin she barely remembers – but his eyes are cold.

The shot echoes off the stone walls of the house as the cartridges hit the ground.

She has seen them before and that realization numbs her even further. In the past six months, she's seen them outside her house, during her walks with the baby, or at the supermarket. Never as close as now, but they've always been around.

The baby is crying. The bangs scared him. The family cheers upon hearing his cries, some of them clap. Some of the women cry along with him, with their arms placed tight around their bellies. Anna knows the burden that's been lifted off them: the same one that has sat on her chest like a marble gravestone and has her paralyzed.

She watches them, her gaze unfocused, as they cross the threshold of the yard. Nikos is nowhere to be seen, perhaps he has already entered the house, trying to explain. She can still hear her boy crying as the sun sets behind the house. She's left all alone in the middle of the dirt road.

★

Three gas lamps burn in the vast living room of the house, struggling to illuminate every corner. Few pieces of furniture have remained in the space. The doors that lead to the interior of the house are shut. The walls stand empty. Anna sits alone in a corner, lulling the baby, watching the congregation in the half-light. Outside, the feast has reached a crescendo: family acquaintances and hangers-on have gathered to suck on any bone her siblings throw them. The coals burn red under the turnspit, the smell of soot and slaughtered animals filling her nostrils, but the need for food has transformed into an unfamiliar, disgusting tugging. Her innards are a tangled ball of yarn.

It's been awhile since the pseudo-compliments stopped.

No one approaches her, no one talks to her. Some of her relatives remain in the living room, half hidden in the smoke of their cigars and cigarettes. They huddle up together in small groups as they wait for their turn. Unlike those outside, they don't dare raise their voices, and the reason for their reverential behavior is seated on a low chair at the other end of the room.

Leaning forward, with his elbows resting on his long legs, her oldest brother seems to be at ease, with Sotiris, the second-born, kneeling beside him. An old pelt covers his shoulders. Tufts of greasy hair fall in front of his face, barely covering the lumps that sprout from his skull, making him look as if he's wearing a wooden crown. Anna sees his hands, which seem leprous from afar, sown with warts and hard edges, the crooked fingers ending in dirt-filled nails, his fat lips whispering secrets in Sotiris' ears. A bulging eye gleams every now and then behind the tufts, looking here and there like a feeding crow.

Sotiris just nods. Sometimes he looks surprised, at other times he bites his lips trying to keep his mouth shut. His eyes well up, teary; then they light up. When the firstborn leans back in the chair and stomps his heel on the floor to mark the end of their talk, Sotiris, on all fours, kisses his feet. Anna feels bile climbing up her throat, she looks away.

Sotiris stands up and stumbles outside, and the hangers-on in the yard scramble around him, to steal whatever tidbit of information he might spare, anything that might provide them with a pinch of the happiness and the heavenly riches of the Stavropoulos clan. None of them care *how* it is possible for the firstborn of each generation to know all that he knows, and his siblings never breathe a word of what he tells them. It's enough that whatever these lips confide comes true within the next years, and it's up to them to use those omens to fatten their pockets and bellies.

Time passes. With every stomp of the heel yet another brother comes and kneels beside him. No women of the family are allowed to listen to him. Their job is to give birth to the firstborn. Then it's the brothers-in-law's turn. Nikos' turn.

Her husband's fists open and close as he walks towards her brother. She can see his lips tremble and thinks she can hear the words, a mantra that will grant him strength. We are not giving them the baby.

Outside, the relatives dance and sing. More shots in the air. The baby mumbles in his sleep and Anna holds him tighter in her arms. Every slight cooing makes that bulging eye from the other side of the room fix on him, turning her skin to ice. Despite her efforts the baby is restless as if her heartbeat doesn't let him calm down.

Nikos has kneeled by her brother's side. She tries to hear his voice but the music outside is deafening. The talk with her husband seems to be the shortest. Her brother stomps his heel once more and falls silent.

Anna stands up and walks over to Nikos as he shambles towards the exit. His gaze is unfocused. He barely seems to recognize her.

'What did you – ' she starts to say, but his expression scares her. A blood vessel on the surface of his eye has burst, a red drop wets his lashes.

'Give him away, love,' he says in a broken voice and grabs her shoulders, perhaps to steady himself.

Another gunshot outside, more felt than heard. It might as well have hit her in the heart.

'No, Niko, we said – '

'You *have* to give him away,' he stops her. 'Do it. We'll have other children.'

'What are you saying . . .' she whispers, trying to break free. Tears run freely down her cheeks. It's not possible, her

Nikos uttering such stuff. No way he's talking about their baby like that.

Without another word, her husband walks toward the yard. The music and dancing have ceased. Everyone has turned toward her, watching her stand in silence under the threshold in the twilight.

No, it's not her they are looking at, she realizes. The song hasn't stopped for her.

Behind her, her brother has stood up and stretches himself, *no*, he unfolds, the pelt dropping from around his shoulders. He's nearly seven feet tall, a human scarecrow, bound with rags. Horns and bones protrude from his leprous body like sick branches. His eye, swollen, robbed of an eyelid, dominates his crooked face as it turns to face her.

As he approaches, he looks aged, crushed under the curse that's burdening him. Now that he's close enough, Anna realizes that his normal eyes are shut and that his swollen one is jutting out of his thick brow.

He stands beside her holding a gas lamp and points his black nail outside. Goatlike teeth shine behind his lips, but his whisperings make no sense.

They step out together. Some of the people in the yard raise their wine glasses towards her and the infant, but she doesn't go near them. As if caught in a dream, she moves towards where the black nail is pointing. The other garden, the one behind the house.

★

Night has fallen for good now. The wind swoops down from the nearby trees, Anna feels the cold breath on her wet cheeks. The family house is the last building in the village, and the area surrounding it spreads green in every direction. Despite the darkness, she can make out the graves in between the garden's weeds. Vigil oil lamps burn like eyes of beasts on the marbles.

Her brother opens a door in the back of the house and motions her to get inside.

She doesn't move. The darkness ahead seems solid.

'Please,' she tells him. The baby stirs in her arms. 'Take pity on my child, I'm begging you.'

His wild eye shines yellow in the light of the gas lamp. The same nod. With a sob, Anna crosses the dark threshold.

It feels like entering a fridge. The low-ceilinged room smells of ash and spices. Piles of undefined stuff are lined up against the walls, the light being too weak to reveal them to her: sacks or old clothes, perhaps. Anna's hoarse breath echoes against the stone walls. Prayers escape her lips, mixed with lullabies. No mother has ever revealed what she saw in the back of the house. Not all of them returned either.

The firstborn follows behind her, whispering. He brings the lamp along, the gas turned down, a sickly blue flame behind the glass. He sets it on the floor and slowly increases its light, revealing the secret of the room to Anna.

They're not sacks, they're not piles of clothes. They're gaunt figures, sitting on thrones, hunched, with their backs against the walls. Glistening bones catch the scant light. Skulls covered in lumps. Nothing stirs; the limbs of some of them are bound in shrouds, keeping them from falling apart. The more her eyes become accustomed, the more details reveal themselves. There must be around ten of them, her mind refuses to count them. Their mouths gape half-open as they lean forward, revealing dry gums and blackened teeth.

The sight paralyzes her. With a fluid movement her brother takes the baby from her arms. Despite her reflexive effort to resist, fear has wrung the strength out of her arms, and the only thing she manages to hold on to is his blanket. Anna lets out a sob and the baby starts imitating her.

At the sound of the infant's cry a new rustling fills the space.

The basket slips from her fingers and drops to the floor. Anna covers her mouth, trying to smother the horror that's being born inside her. One of the blind skeletons has just raised its ossified skull towards them. From all around them come sounds of bones grinding, the rustling of the shrouds, and whispers, endless whispers that fill her head. The figures stir.

The firstborn offers the baby to the figure before him. Anna sees its bony arms taking it into its lap. The shrouded figure lets out a sigh, a breath that rolls from its throat after decades of silence. From nearby she can hear high-pitched moaning, like a sign of admiration for the baby's presence.

The distorted skull has a third empty socket where its brow should be. The same goes for the rest.

One by one, the skeletal figures of her ancestors leave their thrones and huddle up around the youngest member of the family as his cries begin to flood the air. Anna knows these cries, she feels them tear her in half. It only stops just long enough for him to take the next deep breath, then the crying pours out again louder. More whispers, more sounds of approval from the figures while the baby screams.

Anna stands gaping, frozen, unable even to move. Only what's left of her heart is racing, a prisoner banging against the bars, fighting to break free.

And then, one of the figures touches the lump in the middle of the baby's forehead, and the crying abruptly stops. This sudden, unexpected silence is the catalyst, as the frayed fabric keeping her sanity together stretches and breaks.

'No, no, no!'

Her long howl ends in a kick that shatters the gas lamp. A flash instantly fills the room and the whispers turn into asthmatic screeches. She lunges towards the baby, indifferent to anything that stands in the way. A taste of ash and spice coats her mouth, sharp edges cut her hands. She can't see, but soon she feels his warmth in her hands, his little heart beating crazily like hers. She pulls him, and the sound of bones breaking like dry twigs echoes through the room.

Weak fingers close around her, toothless mouths. As she turns towards the exit, a strong hand rips through the darkness to grab her. He catches her loose hair, just enough to tear off a couple of tufts. He can't hold her back.

Anna runs. She crosses the garden in seconds, towards the forest beyond the back yard. The vigil lamps on the graves – on the empty, empty graves – flicker as she passes them by. The wild eye is fixed on her back, she can feel its gaze like drops of dripping melted wax.

Bare trees surround her. The ground has become hard, uneven. She doesn't stop. Not a minute has passed since she took him in her arms, but she already hears voices at her heels. A shot reverberates among the bare tree trunks and the baby in her arms starts screaming. They call her name. She's certain that one of the voices belongs to Nikos. He calls, he pleads. It no longer matters to her.

A ray of light illuminates the dirt at her feet. Another one. The lights continue their crazy dancing as those bearing them run behind her.

There is no path for her to follow. Branches and thick bushes slash her like knives. Once in a while, her pursuers lose track of her, but soon the cries betray her, the cries of the creature she's trying to save. She pauses for just a moment to take a breath and a shot explodes on a trunk not five steps away.

She remembers the look of her distant cousin earlier on, when he shot in the air. They are not interested in her, they only want the infant. There has always been a firstborn at the family house.

The way she's leaning forward to protect the baby from the thorns, she can hardly see where she's heading. The forest's darkness swallows her up, but the flashlight beams never fall too far behind.

Suddenly, her foot steps onto nothing and the world loses its solidness. Anna tumbles down the edge of a steep slope until she ends up with her back against a thorny bush.

She can't breathe. She has to get up, she knows it, but it seems impossible. Pain and terror have overwhelmed her.

Anna's crying dies away to a murmur, as she holds her baby tighter in her arms. She tells him how much she loves him, she asks him for forgiveness. She feels his little lips against her earlobe, as if looking to breastfeed. They're still warm despite the cold she forced upon the both of them.

She closes her eyes, trying not to cry. They'll catch her. Most likely they'll kill her and abandon her in the middle of the forest. She can imagine her body lifeless, lying dead between the thick bushes, shrouded in the night dew, a cold meal for the mountain beasts. She can imagine her baby, doomed to lead this semblance of life; up here, forgotten by the world, with nothing but that cold room as his final destination.

The mumbling dies down. The spreading silence is broken only by the rattling of her teeth. The baby's breath still caresses her ear.

Seconds pass, and their pursuers get closer. Flashlight beams illuminate the tree branches above their heads.

And then, the baby starts whispering to her.

Upon hearing him, Anna's eyes open wide. An otherworldly light floods the place and every whisper makes it stronger: it turns every tree silver, every unknown path, every beating heart in the ground and in the bushes miles away. It shows her a way that leads far from her pursuers, the road to their salvation, far from the family. As if the baby's whispers have broken the future into paths and that's the only one without blood and darkness at its end. In a matter of seconds, fear and pain have left her body, replaced by a feeling of pure, instinctual love. It's a feeling so real that she feels it flowing into the pores of her skin, filling her veins and breath.

Anna stands up and brings the baby in front of her face.

He's smiling. The peaceful light of his whispering showers down on him, a light only the two of them can see. The lump on his little forehead where he was touched is open. A lidless eye has bloomed there, studying her. And the whispers – not exactly human, but now finally comprehensible – keep flowing from the baby's lips as the mother turns towards the silver path and runs.

*Translated from the Greek by Dimitra Nikolaidou & Victor Pseftakis*

# Dare Segun Falowo

# Owolabi Olowolagba

*Nigerian literature has a long tradition of the strange and ghostly. Among early examples we might cite D. O. Fagunwa's* Forest of a Thousand Daemons (1939) *and Amos Tutuola's* My Life in the Bush of Ghosts (1954), *both adapting Yoruba folklore into tales involving the weird and fantastic, while more recent examples include Ben Okri's* The Famished Road (1991) *and works by the British-Nigerian writers Helen Oyeyemi and Nuzo Onoh.* DARE SEGUN FALOWO *has been steadily building a reputation as one of the best of the younger generation of 'Nigerian Weird' writers. This story involving an impoverished young Nigerian man who is willing to do almost anything in exchange for wealth (the title plays on the character's name: 'owo' is Yoruba for 'money') is loosely inspired by urban legends the author heard as a child.*

I

COME DAWN ON THE DAY HE WAS BETROTHED, Owolabi Olowolagba sat at the edge of his bed and wept. He sobbed in ways that would have made Pelumi, his ex-wife, find more reasons to laugh at him, pack her bags and leave even quicker. She would have said something like, 'Not only have you lost everything and become this poor, you have also turned yourself into a woman.' She might have spat, disgusted by his uselessness.

He didn't sob when she left, only looked very timid and

pale beneath his hard black skin as she reduced him with the look in her eyes, hissed loud enough to give him an earache and slammed the netted door to the one-room she had managed with him for six years hard enough to pop the spring.

Owolabi Olowolagba hadn't cried once during all his life living in the underbelly of Lagos, in the slums of Idumagbo. From his birth which had resulted in the death of his mother, to when he was eleven and his father had died driving a truck delivering iron tubes to a construction site on the Lagos-Ibadan expressway, to his youth as a fare collector in downtown Lagos, spent harassing danfos, okadas and taxis for N50 notes from morning to night – he couldn't remember himself ever feeling the need to cry.

Even when he and Pelumi's only baby had died within its first year of life, he had remained rock solid, a place for her to rest her head on as she drained herself of sorrow and a surface to be screamed at when she lost her grip on understanding why.

He continued to sob now, snot slipping to smear the fingers he held up to his face. The night before had been grisly and he had washed and washed his hands after he did the deed Baba Fresh had asked him to do, after which he went to lie like a log on the bare mattress, not sleeping, but waiting.

Dawn came and Owolabi Olowolagba sat up. He looked at the package he was to take to Ibafo. It was wrapped in red cloth, spots on the bundle were darkened by seeping, bloodied things within. He was alone. No Pelumi. No father or mother. The friend who had lured him to Baba Fresh was gone too, his phone number a dead tone now.

His weeping began when he remembered what Baba Fresh had said to him three days before, when they had agreed on the stipulations for the ritual.

'On the day you bring them to me, imagine you are about to marry in one of you people's churches. There will be no turning back, no divorce. No returning to the life you live in now. You will be leaving everything behind. If you can, when you leave where you are currently living don't look back. Forget poverty. You are leaving everything behind.'

## II

How he ended up in Baba Fresh's shrine had seemed like fate.

He had been at the Idumagbo Bus Park that had been built shortly after the Fare Collectors unionized under the government. Owolabi had stopped standing beside the roads fighting okadamen and danfo conductors for money once he passed the age of thirty. He hated seeing men like him pass in their shiny cars, surrounded by beautiful wives and sharp talkative children.

When he hailed them and the windows rolled down, the alcohol scent of wealth would make his stomach turn even as he screamed 'Baba o!' and made other spirit-rousing noises just to get these men to slip some new naira notes into his palm. And when they complied, saw in him something deserving of their earnings, he still had to pretend to his co-workers like he didn't get anything.

They usually knew though, because he would order extra goat meat and Gulder with his amala during lunch. After a few grudges and scuffles, he respected his age and stopped standing there. He instead began to call people to buses traveling both intra- and inter-state. The drivers gave him a percentage of the collective fares and that was enough to feed him, and get more liquor and cigarettes.

There was never enough money left for Pelumi, who roasted corn and plantains on the streets when they were in season and did freelance housekeeping when they were not.

She had grown bitter towards him once Gbolahan died in his sleep.

Owolabi, whose surname and its reference to money mocked and haunted him in his penury, continued into deepening unhappiness, rigidity growing under his skin like armor, until the mere sight of his face was enough to deter any rowdy behavior at the parks (even though he never, ever got into fights).

On the afternoon of the day Pelumi left him, he was hungry for something extra at lunch, because he would get home and be met with the nothing she had left behind as dinner.

He walked out to stand again in the middle of the road and the area boys parted for him, murmuring things under their breath. He wasn't sure if he was sad because his wife had just left him or simply hungry. After a few minutes, a black Hummer slid into view and rumbled towards him. Usually, they would leave the very big cars alone and try only the smaller fine cars, but Owolabi Olowolagba put up his hand. He was a man of the streets and had a nose for these things. The Hummer stopped. The boys behind him went into a frenzy, but he stared at them one by one until they quieted and returned to stand behind him.

The black pane of the driver's side slid down. There was a girl dressed in red, her lips and eyes dusted a burnt orange. She was the driver, apparently. 'Get in. Oga wants to see you,' she said, her voice like sugarcane.

### III

Inside the Hummer, Owolabi watched the area boys gape as it drove away with him inside. *Baba ti ri connect!* A man in a red agbada sat opposite from him. His cap and the chest of his cape were overwrought with gold embroidery and his wrists and sunglasses flashed with diamonds. Olamide played at a low volume from all angles of the car.

When he finally smiled and said, 'Champagne?', more than half of his dentition shone golden in the cool white light of the interior. Owolabi shifted, uneasy in his butter-like seat but he didn't, couldn't say anything in response. He strained to imagine why he would be allowed into the presence of someone so filthy rich, just because he had tried to somehow beg in the middle of traffic.

The man took off his glasses and Owolabi Olowolagba almost turned to dust. His eyes were deceiving him now, he was sure.

'It can't be?! Seye. Seye? Is this really you?'

'Yes, Olowolagba. It's really me you're looking at. It has been a while. Champagne?' Seye said again, a coy smile lifting his thick lips. Owolabi and Seye had started out collecting fares together and smoking weed with their cuts afterwards under trees that were eventually cut down to build the Bus Park.

Owolabi sipped champagne, which wasn't as wonderful as they made you think, as the Hummer cruised out of downtown Lagos into the flash of Lekki. He still felt the urge to be silent but his mind was whirring. How did his friend get to be here swimming in wealth, in the things they had dreamed of all those years ago as stoned boys hoping to escape the place life had given them as birthright? Seye didn't press him to speak until the car stopped, then turned to him and said,

'I know you're wondering how I got here.' Owolabi dropped the untouched drink into a hole in the arm of his car seat and looked into his friend's face. Seye took off his sunglasses. His eyes were clear and intense as ever. 'You know, I don't even live in Nigeria. I just came around to do some business.'

'Ye – yes. How did you come to be here, ore?' then he

heard himself say as a footnote, 'Pelumi left me this morning.'

Seye chuckled, 'So you ended up with the daughter of the pepper woman? Did she tie you down with a baby?'

'No. I actually loved her, but there was nothing to build on. We could barely feed ourselves. And our child died.'

'I am so sorry to hear that.'

The two friends gazed at each other; Owolabi's sadness and Seye's bated breath hung in the air. The music continued to play. The driver was unseen behind a screen.

'I can take you to a place. To the one who saved me.'

'A pastor?'

Seye chuckled again, no longer laughing in his old stormy way.

'No oh. Churches take money. You'll never find someone to make you rich in there. I'm talking about the old way, the way of our origins, our land.'

'Ah.' Owolabi put his hand to his mouth. Of course, such excess could only come from something as sinister as that. 'Babalawo?'

'This one is more than that. He doesn't belong to any sect. He is a solitary priest. The guardian of an ancient wealth-giver.'

'I don't know about that oh, Seye.'

'Okay. Will you think about it?' He reached into a leather purse that had lain between them all the while and pulled out a dense wad of thousand-naira notes. He handed it to Owolabi, who started to count it. Seye called the driver's name, Janet, and told her to take them back to the Bus Park.

Owolabi Olowolagba's mind changed halfway into counting the fresh money. Janet took them away instead – over the Third Mainland Bridge, down, out of Lagos towards the expressway where Baba Olowolagba had died.

## IV

Baba Fresh lived off the expressway. Seye's Hummer rocked down an untarred path dense with weeds and climbers, mud-rutted. Owolabi held his own hands as they approached the shrine. He felt lost, yet found. It was time for him to take a leap, to try to change his own situation.

The only other option he often considered to find change was drinking raw insecticide and jumping off a bridge, but then the thought of Pelumi alone was what had stopped him from going through with the thought. Now she was gone. What difference did consulting with someone with the power to solve his problems make? Even if what they demanded was something he could not afford, at least it wouldn't be the cost of his own life.

The shrine was a small unpainted cement bungalow, dwarfed by plantain trees. Seye climbed down from his side of the car, full of joviality like he was about to enter a party and eat some hot jollof.

Janet remained seated, unmoving like a robot. 'Come now,' Seye said as the door to Owolabi Olowolagba's side remained open without any exiting body. 'He's waiting. He'll even know you're coming.' Owolabi shuddered and placed his feet onto the flat mud of the area around the bungalow.

They walked. Before they stepped into the living room, where a brightness pushed against a curtained doorway and window, they took off their shoes. As they parted the thin curtains, Owolabi realized they were made of crisp money. Inside, their feet rested against cool clean five hundred and one thousand naira notes. Lingering in the air was the chemical scent of more money, like an air freshener that could never have been bought.

There was no television. There was a couch (made of what Owolabi slowly came to realize were bales of more money), three low stools were scattered across the small room, made out of pale pink cubes of . . . money. Owo. Ego. Kudi.

The brightness that filled the place came from a clear wall of glass that faced an open field of low green grass, through which streamed rays of the setting sun. A man was walking towards the glass. He wore a long buba ruined by use and age. A beard of cream hair reached his chest and his bones shook as he moved closer and closer to them, looking straight into Owolabi's eyes from behind the glass as he leaned on a black cane.

When he got to the glass, it rose up in reflex to his presence and he stepped in, smearing mud over the new notes that carpeted his home. 'You've brought him?'

'Yes. Baba Fresh. Just as you asked.' Seye said, his smile almost splitting his jaw.

Owolabi turned his head very slowly to look at his friend. He was aware now that he had been lured into this den. He felt even more uneasy when he realized he felt no urge to exit. He looked at the bare unpainted walls as Baba Fresh sat beneath an enormous gold coin that was engraved with the visage of a reptile head. A lizard, it seemed. The heavy wooden chair he sat on was the only thing not made of money in the room.

'Calm down. You will face no harm. Do you want water?' Owolabi realized the bald old man was talking to him. His eyes pierced so deep, they seemed to reach into his brain and make him nod yes. He whistled and said, 'Iyawo, bring cold water for my guest and my Chinwe for me.'

After a while, someone filled the doorway beside where Baba Fresh sat. She wore a white wedding gown and carried a thick clear mug of water with ice floating on top. Her face was covered by a veil. She set the water down on one of the money stools and turned around to go back into the doorway.

Owolabi drank the water because he had become so thirsty at the sight of it. He gulped the chill sweetness, but began to choke violently when the bride returned, holding a gold chain with a large crocodile at the end. She handed the chain to Baba Fresh and turned around to float away, drifting into the house again.

The crocodile waddled over to Baba Fresh, kicking notes under its claws in its rush to put its jaw on his knee. 'Chinwe baby. How are you?' He rubbed the cream scales under the reptile's jaw with his knobbed fingers and its long mouth opened like a trap.

## V

Seye left after talking to Baba Fresh in hushed whispers, on his knees beside the chair for a while. He barely looked Owolabi in the face as he waved his parting. His Hummer grumbled to life moments later and was gone.

Baba Fresh, his feet moving back and forth to scratch against the corrugated back of his pet, looked at Owolabi and Owolabi looked back. He looked. Owolabi looked back. This went on for a long time. The only sound was of the wind in the trees around the house, like the arriving waves of some unreal ocean.

'Are you thirsty?'

'Yes. Baba. Yes.'

'For money.'

'No. What did Seye say to you about me?'

'Nothing new. He remembered you from his youth and wished his miracle for you. He told me. I told him to go and find you. You've been drinking moneywater. It lets me know how much you really want this.'

'Agh!' Owolabi tried to spit. 'Where is he now?'

'Stop worrying about that. He's gone, you can't ever see

him again. Stop acting so naive. You'll bring one hundred heads' – Owolabi's heart leaped and began to beat too fast. He put his hand to his mouth – 'of the male agama lizard.'

Baba Fresh smiled white as starch. His feet continued to scrub against Chinwe's back. 'The bodies too. But you must separate the heads neatly. That's what we need for a seed.'

Owolabi wondered where he would get one hundred lizards. The thing now seemed so simple. He could do this and be stinking rich! He began to laugh at himself without moving his face.

'How will I find one hundred lizards to remove their heads, Baba?'

'It's "Baba Fresh", all together. I don't know. I've been told they like cockroaches drowned in gin.' The priest seemed bored. His voice was a flat monotone and he kept staring out of the glass into the distance where nothing but low fields, speckled with some odd-looking trees, rolled out to the horizon.

'Okay. I'll figure it out. I will. I promise. How do I find this place again?'

'When you're ready, Iyawo will come and bring you back. She'll smell the blood.'

'Thank you, Baba Fresh.'

'Don't thank me yet. Wait to see what the Lord will do with the works of your hands and on the day you bring them to me – ' Baba Fresh looked into his eyes and spoke the words hard. 'No looking back.'

## VI

Owolabi Olowolagba still had the money Seye had given him and he found his way back home easily. He spent the night thinking of how to find and catch one hundred male agama lizards. He didn't have Seye's number to ask for help.

In the morning he stood up and searched for a cockroach to no avail. They used to love climbing over him and Pelumi in the nights before then. Finally, he found one hiding under his Bible. He caught it with an old receipt and placed it upside down inside a cup that he filled with gin. When it drowned, he went outside to the empty yard of the house and placed it on the ground.

As he stood before it, he watched them begin to gather along the hot walls of the house. The lizards, dark-blue bodies scurrying in bursts, their scarlet heads nodding from a distance. All gazing at the dead insect before him. They continued to cluster on the walls until it seemed like they were one being, alive, writhing on the rough brick.

Owolabi went inside (with the dead cockroach in his palm) and came back out with an empty water drum. He placed the cockroach inside and went back inside to watch.

They moved like a wave as soon as he settled down under the window, rushing to fill the drum with their short hungry bodies. Owolabi didn't know whether to cheer or scream in horror.

He covered the rumbling drum and carried it inside before his nosy neighbors returned from their thankless jobs and went to work with Pelumi's old knife that was sharp enough to cut air.

Blood spurted across his face and down the narrow sink, but he did not stop.

## VII

Come dawn after a hundred little executions, he waited for Iyawo and mourned the death of his old life.

He was afraid because he had no idea what would happen next. All his life he had been sure of how his life would go, how he would never get above a certain amount of money working on the street, how his life would never become better than it was because he could never dream of being anything more, due to the lack that was like a second skin to him and the emptiness that he had long embraced as wealth, and now, like a new dream, he was going to become someone else. Afford all he desired. A new Pelumi, children, happiness, peace, cars, space, food as he wished. He would have people begging him too. Working under him. Someone knocked on the door and he pulled his wrapper off the bed and wiped his face hard. 'Come in.'

Iyawo entered the narrow room, all tulle and lace. She looked around from under her veil at the mattress, a table, a chair. Under the table there were old clothes, shoes, and paperwork from the Bus Park. The kitchen door was shut, scrubbed too clean with detergent. The heads were wrapped in a red cloth and the bodies were a heavy mass in a large polythene bag. Owolabi picked up the bundle and the nylon bag and nodded at her. He was sure he never wanted to see what was under that veil.

'Follow me,' she rasped, her voice the residue of a million small fires.

## VIII

Iyawo drove a white Maserati with a 'Just Married' license plate. It rode low on the road and rumbled with its own quiet thunder, oblivious to potholes and policemen and hold-ups, dashing above and past them like wind. They went from Idumagbo to Baba Fresh's shrine in less than twenty minutes. Owolabi Olowolagba felt his scalp wrinkle with the rush. Iyawo's arms were thinner than normal and her fingernails were long as small knives, painted bubblegum pink.

Iyawo drove them past the shrine, around and under the plantain trees, over the green fields that Owolabi saw through the glass wall when he and Seye first came to visit. She stopped the car mere inches from Baba Fresh's knees. Today he was dressed in a black velvet robe, his fingers gleaming with rings of gold.

'Give her the bodies and bring the heads for me,' he said, as soon as Owolabi stepped out from behind the wings of the white sports car. Owolabi handed her the dead bodies of the lizards and stepped towards Baba Fresh. The Maserati shot off, back to the house.

There was a hole already dug, fresh like a wound in the green. Baba Fresh began incantations under his breath as he hefted the bundle of red cloth and nodded to Owolabi. He threw the heads into the hole in the ground. 'Piss,' he said. Owolabi did as he was asked.

Baba Fresh and Owolabi pushed the soil back over the buried heads. 'Come and get some sleep. We'll come back at midnight.'

## IX

In Owolabi's dreams, Iyawo removed her veil and he screamed and screamed at what he saw, and also because he was covered entirely in the bodies of dead, headless lizards, cold and sticky-wet with thickening blood. He screamed for what seemed like an eternity, until he woke. When he opened his eyes, he found her standing there, veiled. The money couch was surprisingly soft on his spine, and he rose.

'No clothes,' Iyawo rasped in that voice. Owolabi stripped till he had only his hands as covering. She led him out through the parting glass wall, and they walked through the cold midnight until they reached where they had buried the heads of the lizards.

Baba Fresh was standing before a strange tree that had risen out of the burying of the heads. Chinwe lurked between his legs, immobile as a log. There were other trees like this in the near distance, when Owolabi squinted. They looked like inverted nooses. The tree's branches grew up and entwined in a spiral, a circle upright like a door. There was only the light of a new moon to see by.

Iyawo held Owolabi Olowolagba's hand, exposing him to the eyes of those he could not see.

Baba Fresh shook a rattle and began to make a continuous guttural sound that sounded like he was about to turn inside out. Owolabi realized he was no longer there, his eyes were pale orbs and he grasped onto Chinwe's chain like a lifeline.

Baba Fresh made the sound again and again until the tree began to shake.

X

The Lord Alangba stepped out of the moneytree into this world. Its head was on a gold coin inside the hut of its Priest. A muscled body, half man and half lizard, gleamed. It stood seven feet tall – the exact height of the tree. The flat triangular head, red as a slit throat, overflowed with long spikes. Its tiny gleaming eyes blinked and its entire blue-black body shivered. It moved forward and Baba Fresh collapsed to the ground, on top of Chinwe.

Iyawo spoke, 'My Lord. A new offering, to be returned after his service, filled with all the wealth he can swim in.' Owolabi Olowolagba trembled, wetting the grass beneath him. He was so sure he would throw up his intestines. He shut his eyes tight, praying to go back to his narrow room and the naked bed that bit him when he lay on it.

The Lord Alangba walked up to him, too heavy for this world.

It leaned down and licked his face. It made a smacking

sound at his taste and took Owolabi's hand from Iyawo's, its hard claws digging into his forearm.

Owolabi felt his breath leave him and he went slack, leaning into the wet scaly side of the demon.

The Lord Alangba lifted and cradled Owolabi Olowo-lagba's limp body in its arms like a new bride, then it walked back into the eye of the moneytree, a groom over a threshold.

Stephan Friedman

# The Pallid Eidolon

*Though our focus for this book was on stories that had not previously been published in English, we made an exception for Stephan Friedman's tale, which originally appeared in an anthology in Brazil that was limited to fifty copies, figuring it would be new to most or all of our readers. Born in Russia's Ural Mountains, Friedman moved to Israel at age 18 and has lived there since, where he is known as one of the most prominent figures on the Israeli underground music scene. His macabre and esoteric fiction has appeared in several anthologies, chiefly from publishers of small limited editions, such as Raphus Press in Brazil and Mount Abraxus Press in Romania. We're very pleased to help bring the following weird and atmospheric tale to a wider audience.*

THIS STORY SEEMS to have originated in an appalling nightmare or, perhaps, in a warped parallel dimension. Yet, it is completely real. As real as you are; as real as your left hand; as your thoughts of detestation and iniquity. This is a story of detestation and iniquity, of anguish and sacrilege, of adversity and ruin.

*

In 1946, I was in Wrocław on a mission with the Red Cross. These were turbulent times. The city, once a glorious Silesian capital, a bastion of art and architecture with grandiose halls and statuesque cathedrals, was reduced to a pile of smoldering ruins. An invalid of war, desperately gasping for a breath of fresh air. Although small, frantic hopes for a new beginning were arising here and there, like tiny embers kindling anew, and many areas were starting to be rebuilt, the air was still filled with destruction, misery, and turmoil. Chaos ruled the streets. Getting from place to place often meant climbing over heaps of rubble. Looting, pillaging, and rape were commonplace. The grayness of the sky above merged with the grayness of the streets and the demolished structures below, creating an uneasy feeling of anxiety, uncertainty, and creeping fear. In the evening, I could manage to numb it down a bit with beer and żubrówka, but the following morning it would be back gnawing at me again.

Among other tasks, our team took care of shelters and orphanages, providing all the aid we could. After all the horrors the war left behind, the worst was seeing the children affected by it. Like poor little creatures, helpless and abused, they huddled together seeking food and comfort. We could not possibly imagine what they had to go through. Hearing their accounts left us horrified and speechless.

In a renovated orphanage on Ostrów Tumski, I spent most of my days. It was a large orange building with spacious rooms that could suitably house the ever-increasing number of children. They were all hanging together, except one boy who kept on his own. He did not communicate much with the other kids and always sat at a distance, staring at something afar. I started paying extra attention to him and noticed that there were times when he would disappear for a while and then come back. Obviously, he was visiting someplace. On one of these occasions, I decided to follow him.

I saw him crawl through a hole in the fence surrounding the orphanage, cross the street, and proceed towards the bridge over the Oder to the old town. He was moving very fast, so I had to hurry to keep up with him and not lose him from my sight. Like a trained acrobat, he bounced over piles of rubble, dilapidated fences, and along crooked pathways. He surely knew where he was going.

At last, he arrived at a house on the southern side of town. It was mostly unharmed and stood erect like a black fang among scattered decay. I saw the boy disappear inside and felt I should go after him. Upon entering the dark interior, I was overwhelmed by a moldy, putrid smell. I stumbled around, aided by whatever light came in through the windows, trying to find the boy. At last, through the cracks in the floorboards of the living room, I could see something moving. I crouched on the floor and peeped through the hole. I saw the basement underneath, in the middle of which the boy was standing still. He was surrounded by what at first glance looked like thick clouds of white smoke. The more I looked, the more these clouds took the shape of a vast transparent entity coiling around the boy like an enormous worm. As I was trying to figure out what to do, suddenly, with a loud snap, the rotten floorboards under me broke, and I fell crashing down to the house's murky underbelly.

*

I see the boy. He is walking through the streets of a vibrant city, among bright Christmas lights and enticing market stalls. 'Breslau,' read the signposts. 'Fresh dumplings! Kielbasas! Mulled wine!' scream the eager vendors. The wintry air is crisp and resonant, filled with ringing bells and joyous singing. Crowds are moving to and fro, jovial and dressed for the holidays; families with children, dazed by the festivities and the attractions. The boy walks past them, out of the city center towards the south side. He passes a long building with an arch leading to a large courtyard. As he glances inside, he sees a horde of rabble dressed in black uniforms and reeking of booze. He keeps walking. A minute goes by, and he hears: 'Hey, you, Yid worm, where do you think you're going?' Next, a kick in the back sends him flying to the snowy pavement. A kick in the head and he passes out. He does not feel how they brutally beat him with their clubs and urinate on him, leaving him lying half-dead. He does not feel how someone picks him up and carries him away.

★

He woke up in a strange house. A tall, blond woman in a long white sheer gown was standing next to his bed with a cigarette holder in her hand. Curls of pale smoke floated around the room.

'Stand up. Let me see you,' she said.

He slowly removed the blanket, stood up, and saw that he was stark naked. The woman motioned him towards the bath in the middle of the room.

'Step in. Let me wash you.'

Soaking a sponge in the soapy water from the bath, she began washing him thoroughly while humming a soft motherly tune. When she finished, she took a towel and dried him off. Then, she threw the towel on the floor and started touching him between his legs. First, with her cigarette holder, then with her hand. She aroused him, pushed him down on the floor, and eased herself on top of him. An obnoxious, musky smell of lilac overwhelmed him.

'Don't you dare finish!' she hissed while moving up and down. 'You only do so when I tell you.'

After a while, she shuddered all over her body and stopped moving. She stood up, towering over him.

'Now you can do it,' she commanded.

He stroked himself and ejaculated quickly.

'You, little worm!' the woman screamed, slapped his face, and spat on him. 'Go to your bed at once!'

Blackness. Hopelessness. Fear. Shame. Months or years passed, he could not tell. He was completely under her control, being played with, used and abused, ravished each day, and then discarded.

'You are not leaving. Not ever,' she would whisper, encircling him with coils of pallid smoke from her cigarette.

Sometimes she would cuddle him in her bed, stroking his hair and humming her tune. She would cry a little, and he saw the tears sparkle on her eyelashes like tiny diamonds. Then, all of a sudden, she would push him away, shrieking: 'You, filthy worm! Who do you think you are?'

One day, a huge explosion sounded outside the house, shaking it to its foundations. The woman became very scared and ran to the bomb shelter. The boy used this opportunity to escape. He roamed through the barraged streets, trying to recognize the area, to find his way home, only running deeper into the night, into the horrors of war. He had been hiding in the ruins for several months when Red Army soldiers found him and placed him in the orphanage. There he lay in bed for weeks. Numb, violated, damned. Until finally, he felt a pull from the old house. A low, rumbling noise started nagging at his brain like the sound one hears when sitting inside a flying aircraft. He stood up and left, led like a somnambulist to his impending doom. He entered, stopped in the middle of the room where the bath used to stand, and felt the rustling white gown encompass him.

★

I lose track of time. I feel that the shifting, squirming phantom has mesmerized me too. All of a sudden, I am reminded of how our Professor of Assyriology, Sigismund

Bernstein, told the story of the serpent Lotan, an embodiment of the chthonic Goddess who reigned supreme in times primordial. In the myth, the Goddess went to the great ocean where the serpent dwelt, displayed herself naked in his presence, and recited the incantation:

> 'Lotan, the twisting serpent,
> Lotan, the coiling serpent;
> Thou, who crossest the abyss,
> Thou, who causest the oceans to boil;
> Thy maw is that of a lion in the wilderness,
> And the gullet of the tempest of the seas;
> It craveth the flows as the wild buffalo,
> The streams as the crowds of antelopes;
> Thy throat consumeth loads,
> Thou devourest volumes;
> Thy seven portions are in a dish,
> And into thy cup they pour rivers;
> Rise thou from the watery depths
> And feast thine eyes upon my fearsome beauty.'

The serpent coiled around her, engulfing her inside him, but she diffused and permeated him, thus binding him to her will and making him forever her avatar.

The writhing vapor becomes so thick that I can hardly see the boy. I hear a hollow whisper, like a gust of a distant wind: 'Little worm! You're my little worm now!'

What can I do? How can I save him? If I provoke or attack her, she might hurt him or even kill him. I cannot put his life in more danger.

I decide that the best thing would be if I wait for the boy to come back to the orphanage and then talk to him. After all, he has always returned. I start carefully crawling back to the farthest corner of the basement. Slowly, so as not to disturb the hideous apparition, I climb up the stairs. When I am back on the ground floor, I cast a final glance at the horrid spectacle below, open the door, and leave the darkened abode.

★

A day passed. The boy did not return. Then, several days. A week. I waited. He never came back. Finally, one particularly gray and dismal morning, I went out looking for him. Clouds of grizzled fog hovered over the streets like a dusty veil, as I walked randomly, trying to remember the way to the house. I asked strangers about it. They just shrugged their shoulders and lifted their hands in dismay. At last, I found a spot that looked familiar, but the building was not there. Instead, there was a massive shell crater, at the bottom of which a turbid white liquid bobbed and shimmered under the dull light of the pale sun.

Ana María Fuster Lavín

# The Footsteps of Hunger

*Our next story is paradoxically both foreign and domestic. Located 1150 miles southeast of Florida, Puerto Rico has been a U.S. territory since 1898 and its residents are American citizens, though that's sometimes easy to forget. After all, Puerto Rico has no representation in Congress, doesn't get to vote for president, and when it was leveled by Hurricane Maria in 2017 the federal government largely left the island in the lurch. Maria's devastating aftermath plays a role in the following story, in which a dilapidated home in a part of San Juan still plagued by hurricane-related power outages serves as the backdrop for a series of horrifying events. 'The Footsteps of Hunger' was chosen for a recent anthology of the best horror by Spanish-language women writers and makes its English debut here. Those who enjoy this tale and wish to explore more of the horror being produced in Puerto Rico should check out the two volumes of* No Cierres los Ojos [Don't Close Your Eyes], *edited by Ángel Isián and Melvin Rodríguez-Rodríguez.*

THE FLAVOR OF THOSE EYES still danced in her mouth as she savored the aftertaste, making little smacking sounds. She looked up, discerning the blue, almost amber, light of dawn. For her, time is measured in relation to food. We have all been hungry. We are hunger. But she was just a little girl and she was alone. Especially since the morning of that awful hurricane that left her house in shambles and snatched away the lives of three of her kittens, her only companions. She stayed in the ruined mansion. It was the only way to hold on to her mother's scent and, with it, to remember the moment when she picked her up off that trash heap and held her in her arms. Where she had been dumped, or had been reborn; she was too young to understand it. Better to focus on that fragrance, until she finds her next mother. Think of her, smell her, savor her death. Because memories are the key between the two worlds: silence and life.

In the early morning hours she would wander, looking for food. Hunger was a constant companion, along with the ghosts of loneliness. In particular, the ghost of her *mamá*. She called the memory of that first woman *mamá*; her scent carried her through the nearby alleys in search of cats, to hunt them and devour their eyes. Besides cats, she also fed on human blood and eyes, but that was trickier since she was so little.

The eyes prolonged her eternal childhood in a city where everyone ends up saying goodbye, whether to die or to move to some other city or country. No one knows how many disappeared, died, or emigrated after the great storm. And she was alone there and had to eat.

Early one morning she fell asleep in a little corner inside the house, close to the door. She was so tired that she forgot to bar the door, and the wind blew it ajar. The owner of the neighboring salon noticed her little body and approached. Since acquiring the premises a decade ago she had never seen anyone in that house. She had heard all kinds of stories, urban legends of people vanishing, of curses on anyone who crossed that threshold. The hairdresser had always laughed at such superstitions. Now, climbing the three steps to the entrance, she caught a scent of flowers and of something she couldn't recognize, mixed with the smells of moisture and rotting wood. When she pushed the door open and took one step onto the threshold, that aroma transformed into a horrible stench. She decided to go back to the salon, but something grabbed her foot and she fell inside.

*Mamá! Mamá!*

The door closed.

The girl knew that if she stayed outside very long during the daytime, the sun would turn her to ash. That's why she had spent two decades shipwrecked in the world of silences, those intervals without defined units of time between the living and the undead, like the eye of the hurricane or the fine thread between voices and nothingness. The girl's wings had been broken just when they had started to emerge, like those of her foster mother, or the immense wings of her mother, the Lady in Gray, the immortal one. She just has to stay on the move, looking for eyes, bits of living flesh and blood to ease her hunger. Small sounds guide her, step by step, to the outside world. Sometimes time forgets those who aren't counted in the social statistics, those who aren't part of the so-called normal.

It was five a.m. when one of the youngest employees of the nearby parking lot decided to head home. He was stumbling because he'd lost a bet and had drunk a whole flask of *chichaíto* almost in a single gulp. *Mam-má! mam-má!* he heard. Turning around, he didn't see anyone. 'Shit, I drank too much,' he thought. He got to his car. 'Fuck, the lights in this street have been out since the hurricane.' *Mam-má!* He looked behind him while trying to get his car door open. 'How old are you? You're way too young to be out here!' The girl pounced on his leg. The young man lost his balance and fell onto the sidewalk, knocking himself unconscious. *Mam-mmá!* The smiling girl groped at his face. The smell of blood tickled her nose and made her howl with laughter. She heard some footsteps and, with a rapid movement, crawled under the car and started pulling the young man by the foot. Whoever it was, they took a piss nearby and kept on walking. The little girl bit the young man's neck and began to suck his blood. After drinking her fill, she gave him a kiss on the cheek and with a quick movement of her index finger plucked out his right eye, devoured the veins and flesh that dangled like noodles until the squishy globe was clean, and repeated the same procedure with the left. Then she put them in the back pocket of her tattered little dress and went off, clambering quickly and exhilarated back home.

Twenty years had passed since her first mother, who, she remembered, had given her dying breath to her. She died nourishing her with her own body. With that *mamá* she had been able to grow from baby to infant, but with her death, her development stopped once more. The girl sat on the edge of the bed where that *mamá* lay, observing her mummified remains, caressing her forehead and hair while sucking her thumb until she fell asleep, hugging a dead little cat like a stuffed animal.

That mother was also the person who raised her for five years, after finding her in the trash where, just as she was starting to die of hunger, the Lady in Gray had granted her new life but condemned her to eternity. There, that mother had picked her up among cats and the corpses of three vagrants and had brought her home with her to her mansion in the Santurce neighborhood. They were five lovely years, during which she never had to worry about looking for her own food or getting hold of toys.

When she woke up, she gave the maternal cadaver a kiss. A rain of black butterflies zigzagged through a crack in the house's high ceiling. '*The black butterflies flyyyyy, fly with mmmy hands.*' She sang softly to herself, waving her little hand at them as she played hopscotch, the smallest of the kittens circling between her legs. 'Skip, my girl / skip, my love / You came into my life / and stole my heart . . .' Laughing, she hummed one of the songs her third *mamá* used to sing to her. Her body was lying in another bedroom.

When she got tired of that game, she went back to the living room, in front of an old and cracked mirror. She started to make faces, watching herself. Those eyes looking for me, is that me? she thought, while she made the little cooing sounds that she used to communicate with the little girl who lived on the other side of the glass. *Pway with me. Your eyes, they're me.* She grabbed a little box and put it between her legs as she sat down. She picked up a little ball off the floor and rolled it to the other girl in the mirror, who smiled like her and rolled it back to her. When the girl went to get up, she heard the one in the mirror saying to her: 'Stay with me, always.' *I hungry.* 'With me no hunger, never again.' She smiled, showing five eyeballs on the fingertips of her right hand as she reached out with her left. The girl wiped her little hand across her mouth and headed towards the door, picked up a paper bag and, opening it, found a pigeon. Smiling, she wrung its neck and drank its blood. Then she put it back in the bag, threw it into the secret bedroom and went back in front of the mirror. *I hungry, but today I no eat dreams that watch. Pway outside in the night. Come onnnn.* 'With me, you can dream until the end of eternity. And without eyes you will find the way.' *No, you bad. I no pway with you anymore. I hungry. I sleep now.*

Officer Pérez had just handed the report off to District Attorney Castillo, assigned to be there for the removal of the corpse: a young man, twenty-one years of age, apparently under the influence of alcohol at the time of the assault, an employee of the private parking lot adjacent to the market square. Although the lawyer wrote down that it must have been a mugging, and when the victim resisted they cruelly slaughtered him, that didn't make sense to the police, as it wouldn't to any sane person. The killer had drained the dead man's blood and removed his eyes, but they didn't take his car, his cell phone, or his money.

Pérez had been investigating the area around the little square for over fifteen years. The percentage of people who disappeared in the nearby blocks was much higher than in the rest of the island. Two weeks ago, the owner of a beauty salon in the square was reported missing by one of her employees, though the neighbors pointed out that after the hurricane she had said she would be returning to the Dominican Republic soon. A little over two years ago, someone had also kidnapped the Ortiz Gutiérrez triplets, who weren't even eight months old at the time of their disappearance. The unbelievable part is that the boy was snatched early one morning and the two girls a week later. They were never seen again, just like Laura, the girl who had gone to school with Pérez's daughters and had vanished almost five years ago. A week later she was seen in the square with some friends; she told them she was going to the bathroom and never came back. Many pets had also disappeared in the area, according to what he'd read on a Facebook group about lost animals.

'Come on, López, let's do the rounds in Alto del Cabro. You drive today,' he said to his partner. They got in the squad car.

Officer Pérez looked closely at the posts, the sidewalks, the houses and shops, whether inhabited or not.

'It's weird, there used to be much more life here during the day; there were even stray dogs pissing on your tires, pigeons shitting on you, or . . .'

'Oh, cut it out,' his partner laughed.

'Park here,' he said, as he saw a young woman fastening a padlock on the entrance to the hair salon and hanging up a '*For Sale*' sign.

'You're not giving up?'

'No, we're going to solve this one soon. I have a feeling. Stay in the car.'

Pérez got out, and as he smoked a cigarette in front of the hair salon he stared off into space towards the city skyline. An old cat quickened its steps to enter an abandoned house, and Pérez followed it. At that moment he noticed a strange smell of flowers and, without thinking first, climbed the steps of the little balcony in front of the entrance. 'It's open! Of course, that's where the cat went in,' the officer said to himself, thus helping to convince himself to enter without a warrant. The floor creaked. That mix of smells aroused his instincts. There was a closed door with some cushions on the floor in front of it; the smell coming from there, though muffled, was that of decomposition. His pistol and flashlight in his hands, he made his way through the house. At the end of the living room there was an enormous but somewhat worn-out couch, some boxes, and a blurry old mirror with a crack in it. Despite the low light, he glimpsed a silhouette reflected in it.

'Stand up and identify yourself,' Pérez said in a booming voice.

No one answered, but he knew he wasn't alone. A movement on the couch, when he was on the verge of firing, revealed that it was a little girl, not older than four or five, extremely pale, who was sleeping almost embedded in the cushionless couch, wrapped in an old bedspread. She was hugging a little cat, which hid at the sight of Pérez. He noticed the girl was weak; he looked around and, besides the mix of odors, sensed only an immense loneliness. As is the protocol in cases involving minors, he proceeded to carry the girl to the squad car. Cradling her like a baby, he checked to see if she was breathing; she was, but very faintly. Just before crossing the threshold, the girl opened her eyes with difficulty and sighed a *Mam-má?* Pérez trembled, so moved by her tears that he almost broke down, but he kept his composure. *Mam-má?* He figured the sunlight would hurt her pale eyes, so pale that they almost seemed to lack pupils; he put his sunglasses on her and a handkerchief, in addition to wrapping her up well in the bedspread.

'López, ask headquarters for reinforcements and call Family Services.'

'But . . .'

'Do it. Take care of the girl while I go back and look around. It's getting dark and there's no light in the building. Call, I said, *now* – ' he said, as he headed back into the wooden structure.

'*Mmmamá!*'

The female officer hugged the girl, kissed her forehead, and cradled her in her lap. A *mamá* or a new friend always made the girl feel stronger. If this was the right one, at least she'd have new company, protection, and food for a while. She took deep breaths, huddled in the warmth of that new *mamá*, as she convinced herself the woman would be. She waited a few minutes, wanted to be a normal girl. A normal girl who was perhaps twenty or thirty years old, maybe more, but whose body was condemned to remain like this until the next change. To go on adopting new mothers, new friends, so she could continue on the path of hunger, so she wouldn't be captured by people who didn't understand. At least until she could find others like her, or else find the Lady in Gray again. She liked this woman in the car snuggling with her, who smelled of green tea and fresh herbs and stroked her hair.

'*Mmamá!*'

'Everything's going to be all right, little one,' López said to her as she hummed a lullaby, after calling headquarters.

'*Mamá!* Pretty eyes, mama's eyes. You pway with me,' the girl said, as she stroked the officer's hands.

'I'm not your *mamá*, but we'll find good people to take care of you. What's your name?'

How can you blame a seagull for flying across oceans? How do you condemn a snake for swallowing eggs from a nest that might have hatched into seagulls? Nature is irrepressible. That woman's embrace and her tender words had brought the girl a moment's happiness. But she said they would take her away. The girl in the mirror said never to allow that, that they would draw her blood to find out who she was, that they would torture her to death.

She nestled her head between the woman's thighs to hide her face and cry, thinking of how to escape without more problems, and with her. That scent, the woman's crotch, whetted her appetite. She inhaled deeply: it was a buffet of clotted blood, and the blood awakened her hunger. Her nails grew as she recharged. She tried to bite the officer's pubic area, but the woman lifted her up and asked her what she was doing. The girl made a feline leap and hugged her.

'*Mamá!* Don't leave me,' she said in her ear, her voice sounding somewhat more adult now. The girl was so hungry that she ran her nose along the woman's neck and was on the verge of nourishing herself.

'Don't worry, little one. They'll help you. I'll help you.'

After the girl had fed, they hugged each other tightly, crying with tenderness, fear, and despair.

Pérez continued his tour of the old wooden house. He took photos with his cell phone of the mirror, the furniture, two small wooden boxes, some old toys. At the end of the hall there was a bedroom. Entering, he saw a body on the bed. It was a woman who must have been dead a long time. The forensic examiner would quickly figure out exactly how long, if he ever showed up. Could it be her mother? What kind of terrifying madness is this, he thought, as he snapped photos. Why are the goddamned reinforcements taking so long? He looked at his phone, but there was no signal. At least López doesn't have to see this. And we rescued the poor little wretch.

'I don't believe it!' Pérez almost shouted, picking up and reading the first page of a small diary he had stepped on as he emerged from the bedroom. 'It's Laura Suárez's, but if she . . .' He realized night was falling, but he couldn't help flipping through the pages. 'This is crazy, the things she writes here are like something out of a horror movie. That girl can't be a monster. How could Laura have been here over a year? And what happened to her?' Pérez had a hunch and ran towards the closed-up bedroom. He removed the cushions blocking the door, broke the padlock. Inside it stank of death, garbage, damp. There was trash, women's clothes, some old cell phones, toys, a box containing empty bags with a few drops of what might be blood, like the ones they use for serum or blood donations. He opened a suitcase and found two small bundles inside that corresponded to the bodies of two babies. Could they be two of the triplets? He went on looking in search of the third. There were hundreds of dead cats and other small animals, too much death.

A loud slam of a door. 'The front door, the reinforcements are here,' he thought. A sweet scent once more pervaded the building, so strong that Pérez sneezed. He heard footsteps behind him, those of more than one person. He turned around, didn't see anyone. Could it be the other officers? He heard a woman's laughter, but saw nothing. It was coming from where the mirror was. He looked at his watch and realized it was almost midnight. How had he lost track of time? 'López!' He rushed out of the building at full speed. 'The backup we called for never came, neither did the district attorney or Family Services . . .' His cruiser was there. Approaching, he didn't see anyone. He opened the door and there was nobody. Only the empty blanket the girl had been wrapped in and a strong floral scent.

*Translated from the Spanish by James D. Jenkins*

Teddy Vork

# The Wonders of the Invisible World

*We hadn't planned to repeat any countries from the first volume in this one, but then something odd happened. Submissions started to pour in from Denmark. Lots and lots of them. In the end, we had around 25 submissions from Denmark, a country of fewer than six million people. To put it in perspective, Thailand (67 million), Turkey (84 million), and Indonesia (274 million) sent in a combined zero stories. Given Danes' enthusiasm for horror – and for this book – we made an exception for the following story. One of Denmark's leading horror authors, TEDDY VORK (b. 1977) is the only writer to win the Danish Horror Award twice – in 2014 for his story collection* Spræk-ker [Cracks]*, from which this story is taken, and again in 2020 for his novel* Mulm [Penumbra]*. Though it unfolds in modern-day Copenhagen, 'The Wonders of the Invisible World' takes as its point of departure a 17th-century text by the American witch hunter Cotton Mather. We enjoyed the twists and turns the tale takes – just when you think you've figured out the disturbing direction it's heading, it takes a seriously weird detour and becomes even more unsettling.*

IT WASN'T THE FIRST INVISIBILITY FORMULA Asger Schmidt had seen, but there was no question it was the simplest. The words were written in red ink on the frontispiece of the copy of Cotton Mather's *The Wonders of the Invisible World* he had just acquired for a client.

Asger brushed off some dust with his white-gloved hand and tried not to breathe on the yellowed paper. The book, a first edition from 1693, was the American minister and witch-hunter's best-known work. The leather spine creaked as Asger carefully closed the book and wrapped the cover in its protective velvet cloth. A moment later he opened it to the frontispiece again:

> *Quoth the Wordes then Thou art rendered invisible to Friend and Foe.*
> *Va-Orsagi Balata Gnang*
> *Zookare in Umbere Gang*
> *Ak Heed Obskura Male*
> *Od Naj Hark Daj Tale*
> *Goodwife Brown tolde me under the Red Oak.*

The copy had belonged to one Hannah Ashbery from Salem, Massachusetts. The name was printed at the top of the frontispiece in the same handwriting in which the spell was written. Ashbery had added formulas on several of the book's pages – they ran down the margins and in several places completely encircled the text. In so doing, Ashbery had turned Mather's masterpiece into her own personal cyprianus – a type of book that had been rumored to exist in every medieval European culture and according to popular belief was written in red ink and impossible to burn. In French they were called *grimoires*, in German *Faustbücher*. A year earlier, Asger had unearthed a splendid example of the latter for a client, a parchment manuscript, *Julius Ciprianus der XII*, from 1734, with mystical symbols and spells for summoning demons.

Ashbery's handwritten spells were a provenance that only increased the book's desirability, especially when Asger found out from his research that Ashbery had been one of the women acquitted at the witch trials in Salem in 1692-93, in which around twenty women were executed, mainly by hanging.

The spells indicated that Ashbery considered herself a witch – or else had a deliciously black sense of humor, since she had written the spells down in Mather's book. Mather hadn't just been one of the principal figures behind the prosecution of the accused witches; his theory about 'spectral evidence' had also served as the cornerstone in proving the cases. Because the crimes belonged to the unseen world and therefore couldn't be proved in other ways, spectral evidence meant that the accused could be convicted solely based on the testimony of the people who claimed to have been attacked in invisible, spiritual form.

The witnesses could give testimony like: 'Goody Proctor bit, pinched, and almost choked me,' and the judges took it as proof that the accused was responsible for the assaults, even though no one had seen her.

Asger took a sip of red wine, set the glass on the sofa table, and took the book with him over to the window. His steps echoed in the high-ceilinged apartment. As carefully as though it were a Fabergé egg, he laid *The Wonders of the Invisible World* down on the windowsill.

Lately that had been his favorite spot in the apartment. When he turned his back to the window, he had a stunning view of the built-in bookshelves around the French doors. The books' brown and gilt bindings shone, looking just as smooth as he knew they were to the touch. Their spines were brown like old bones and bumpy like vertebrae.

Some evenings he could almost hear voices resonating from the books, as if he were surrounded by a tremendous choir. A choir chanting knowledge, beauty, truth. And the scent: books had their own unique smell. Not just of aged paper, but of trees, chestnuts, honey, sun-warmed skin, autumn. The feel of them in your hands. The heavy leather binding, embossed gold inlaid like veins. The titles, so suggestive. And then, finally, that moment when you opened the book and it was a trapdoor to another world. Books offered many gifts. One of them was knowledge. Another was escape.

Strangely complex things, books. The binding, paper, and ink were matter, but at the same time spirit; they conjured up worlds and people from nothing. Magic.

He *knew* Madame Bovary and Don Quixote, understood their anguish more than that of 'real' people. He suffered with Anna Karenina and Raskolnikov. Felt a closer connection with them than with any flesh-and-blood person he'd come across in his life. They existed. Without trivialities and awkward situations. People were only themselves in literature, or when they were alone.

Asger turned away from the books and looked out the window. On the opposite side of the street the windows were dark in the fifth apartment on the third floor. She wasn't home.

Asger looked at the invisibility formula. The intricate writing resembled blood vessels branching out across the paper. He read the words aloud.

Waited.

He didn't notice anything unusual.

He looked down at himself. Still visible. Obviously. He snorted and trundled over towards the bathroom. Stubbed his foot on the hallway threshold, stumbled. He grabbed the door frame and held tight until the dizziness passed. The light bulb in the kitchen shone with a woolly glow and seemed weaker than the 40 watts it usually emitted. It was like looking through sunglasses on a cloudy day. Asger pinched the bridge of his nose with his index finger and thumb. Too much wine on an empty stomach, it happened now and then. A little food would help. But first to the toilet.

The bathroom too seemed dimmer than usual. Still it failed to hide the bald spot on the crown of his head, which he involuntarily inspected every time he was near a mirror. Definitely not invisible. No more than usual.

She wouldn't notice him, even if he were standing right beside her. And so why was he even speculating about it? Things were all right as they were. He just didn't function well around other people. Everything closed up in him. It was so easy for other people to be together, and they could instinctively tell that he didn't fit in. That's just how he was. His nature. A pariah. Perhaps a natural shyness had grown to unhealthy proportions and become a social phobia, one that dozens of sessions with psychologists and therapists, and different combinations of antidepressants, couldn't conquer.

Asger bent down to take a sip from the faucet. Suddenly dark spots flashed before his eyes, and vomit rose up in his throat. He swallowed hard and managed to keep it down.

The dizziness passed, he brushed his teeth, and left the apartment. A late dinner at Yammi Sushi would help temper his slight buzz and relieve the feeling of being wrapped in a sound-absorbing, veiling material.

He slammed the front door shut behind him and stepped out onto Møntergade. There were only a few people around. The February cold had been intensified by a stinging wind that whistled through the streets. People with the lower part of their faces wrapped in scarves passed by him with determined looks, their gaze directed at the sidewalk in front of them.

Yammi Sushi was half empty. Asger stood by the counter, where the hostess usually took the orders. He checked his bald spot in the mirror, which was visible in the gaps between bottles of sake and Kirin and Asahi beer. The hostess was busy sending a text on her iPhone. He cleared his throat.

'Excuse me, do you have a table for one?'

She looked up and smiled effusively in a characteristically Japanese manner.

Asger unzipped his jacket.

The hostess nodded again. 'Yes, I'll bring it right over.' She took a bottle of sake from a shelf and went over to a table.

Asger grabbed the edge of the marble countertop. It was smooth and hard and cold. He had stood twelve inches away from the woman and she hadn't seen him.

The hostess came back. Asger reached an arm out and waved his hand back and forth under her nose. She didn't react.

He spun around and stormed out.

Once home, he went straight for the fridge and opened it. It had a sour smell of white wine and hummed with a murmuring sound. There were pearls of ice on the back wall.

The hostess hadn't even reacted to his voice. Asger slammed the door shut, hurried over to the book on the windowsill and paged through it. He didn't find anything, not the slightest thing, not one single goddamned word that could be interpreted as a formula for removing invisibility.

The windows of the fifth apartment on the third floor caught his eye. They were lit.

Down in the street, Asger once again noticed how much darker the evening was than normal. The moon hung bone-white and pockmarked, what the Aztec priests had called a demon moon. He crossed the street.

The entrance was locked. Asger pressed all the door buzzers around hers. A few seconds later someone buzzed him in. He crept noiselessly up the stairs.

One day when he was walking past the building, he had seen the name Aya Fohl on the door buzzer.

He had read her two books. The first a collection of short stories, the most recent a novel, *Modu*: a chamber play about a woman's single-minded obsession with an older, refined upstairs neighbor.

Asger's enthusiasm was on par with that of the critics, who lauded Aya's highly realistic portrayal of her characters. He also agreed with their claim that with that novel, Aya Fohl had taken her place alongside Kirstin Hammann and Helle Helle at the top of Danish literature's Parnassus. Yet Asger found Aya even better than Hammann and Helle Helle. In contrast to their ironically funny, tongue-in-cheek way of writing about their characters' behavior, Aya wrote without the slightest tendency towards a 'meta' tone. She gave the reader access to her characters' inner thoughts to a degree Asger had never come across before. The portrayal of the main character, Iben, even revealed the smallest, most profoundly unique details to such a degree that Asger was convinced Aya had been writing about herself. A person couldn't have such a thorough knowledge of anyone except themself.

Aya's jacket photo had captivated him just as much as the contents of her book. She had dark hair, black in the black-and-white photo, which was slightly overexposed. A long pageboy cut with sharply clipped bangs. Light-colored eyes, dark eyebrows. She was one of those people you instinctively envied, because their beauty matched their talent. If there was any complaint he could make about Aya's appearance, it was that she was a trifle too thin, even taking conventional ideas of beauty into account. According to the caption, she turned thirty-eight in March.

Since he had discovered that Aya Fohl lived in the apartment opposite his, he had kept an eye on her windows. He had reread her books and studied articles about her. He seldom saw her behind the windows, but she was in his thoughts every day. It was easy to imagine a life with her, the conversations they would have – about art, literature, the human condition, and everything in between. He would be her first reader and her comforter; she had known loneliness too, it was clear from her works. They would be one of those couples with a deep intimacy. Sex more than just two bodies bumping together.

Asger reached the third-floor landing. What was he doing? Sneaking into the home of a woman he didn't know in order to spy on her was as far outside his character as anything could be. Icky. Something done by pathetic, sexually frustrated men. Asger turned around. Besides, her door was no doubt locked. He turned around again and closed his hand around the door handle. Pressed down carefully, pushed. Locked.

He put his ear to the door. Before he had time to think about it, he reached out his hand and pressed the doorbell.

Footsteps approached the door, he cleared his throat, heard a woman's voice say, 'Wait just a second.' The lock clicked and the door opened.

Aya looked straight into his eyes, her eyebrows raised questioningly. She was holding a cell phone up to her ear.

He was wrong, he wasn't invisible, how could he be, what had he been thinking? His armpits were getting sticky with sweat.

'Sorry, I . . .' he was going to say, but without removing the phone from her ear, Aya stepped out onto the landing, and he had to move back to avoid her running into him. She went to the banister and looked down to the floor below. Then she walked backwards towards her door, while saying 'Probably five or six months' into the telephone.

Asger managed to sneak into the apartment behind her with a couple of inches to spare. He pressed up against the jackets that were hanging on a hook in the entryway. Aya relocked the door, walked past him, and disappeared through a half-open door at the end of the hall.

Asger remained standing there. A woolen shawl tickled at his neck. The entryway was in darkness. Ahead of him there was a beam of light coming from a room off to the right. Here too the light had that strangely dampened appearance. He listened at the half-open door that Aya had gone through. The apartment smelled musty.

Aya had looked like her author photo, but even thinner. Even in the baggy navy blue sweater that went down to her knees, she looked skinny.

'I haven't quite got the main character down just yet,' he heard Aya's voice behind the half-open door.

Asger kept close to the wall, so the wood floor wouldn't creak. He walked by the kitchen on his right-hand side and went through the double doors into the spacious living room on the left. The TV was tuned to the news, with the sound muted. He was pleased with Aya's taste in decor. It reminded him of his. Sparsely furnished and with few decorative objects – mostly tall porcelain candlesticks – everything in black and white. The only exception was a still life of a bowl of rotten fruit above the television.

'I just need a couple of good days, get in the zone, and then I'll have her,' Aya was saying.

Asger stopped outside the door. The sound of bare feet on the wood floor reached him.

'Yes,' Aya gave a short, dismissive laugh. 'Flow. Then I need to write a bit more before you can see it.'

A faucet was turned on. Asger sidled between the door and the frame.

An oversized rice paper lamp hung like a full moon over the double bed, casting a vague glow over the bedroom.

The water was turned off. Aya stuck her upper body through a door opening that must lead to a bathroom. With an underhand toss, she threw the cell phone onto the bed and disappeared again.

Asger heard the characteristic clacking sound a toilet seat makes when someone sits on it.

He went on standing in the middle of the bedroom. On the wall behind him hung a flat-screen TV – not what he'd imagined he'd find in a writer's bedroom – to the right a wardrobe closet, to the left a balcony door and windows. He could see himself as a silhouette in the dark pane of the balcony door. To the right of the bed was a nightstand with a stack of books. A handful of Virginia Woolf, a couple by Philip Roth. Over the bed hung an atmospheric painting of a mist-shrouded Faroese landscape. Aya cleared her throat. A stench of feces spread. Urine trickled. Asger looked around, was on the verge of sitting on the bed, but maybe she'd see his weight pressing the mattress down.

A clang of metal. The toilet paper roll turning? A crackling of plastic. Water from the faucet. Aya came out holding a transparent plastic bag, knotted shut. A brownish mass splashed in yellow liquid. With quick steps she went through the bedroom and out into the hall.

Asger followed her in disbelief. The plastic bag had contained feces and urine.

In the kitchen Aya switched on a digital kitchen scale, put the bag on it and held her hands against its sides so it wouldn't slide off. She moved one hand to open up a notebook and write something before throwing the bag in the trash can. She washed her hands.

Asger stepped aside when she headed towards him in the doorway. When she had passed by, he slipped over to the notebook.

On each page there was a date above two columns, the left one headed *In*, the right *Out*. Under *In* there were various types of foods and drinks, as well as headache tablets and something called Movicol, which Asger thought was a laxative, all listed along with their weight in grams. Under *Out*: the weight of feces and urine.

Asger closed the notebook. Anorexia or close to it. In any

case, a desire for control, a way of balancing the world. Such a grotesque ritual to agonize over every day, no, every trip to the toilet. He felt sorry for her, but also felt a little less inferior in relation to her now.

He slipped back to the bedroom and saw that Aya had switched off all the other lights in the apartment.

She sat cross-legged at the foot of the bed, busy smearing lotion on her legs. As Asger stepped over the threshold, a floorboard creaked underneath him. Aya looked up with a start. Asger stood completely still. His heart pounded with hollow beats that reverberated all the way up to his cheeks.

Aya leaned to the side, probably so she could see out the door and into the hallway. She rubbed at the indentation below her throat.

Asger was careful to exhale slowly and softly through his mouth.

Aya's shoulders slumped. Then she went on rubbing in the lotion. Her legs gleamed; her fingers pressed the skin and left wet tracks up her inner thighs.

When she was finished with her legs, she pulled her sweater over her head. Her hair crackled with static electricity. A bordeaux-red bra with cups made of a satin-like material supported her small breasts. Her underwear was of black cotton with a wide waistband. Despite her slender figure, the elastic bit into the flesh at her hips.

Asger lifted one foot and stepped – slowly, gently – down on the floor a step closer to Aya.

She was smearing lotion on her arms. Thin. Exquisite, elegant. Her head was at an angle, her face thoughtful, her eyes staring blankly out into space. Asger knew she was pondering over her new book. Aya went on rubbing cream on her shoulders, then her throat, where the tendons stood out beneath the skin. Asger's member pressed against his trousers. He pushed his thumb against the bulge in his pants and enjoyed the exciting sensation that ran through his member and down his inner thighs.

Aya unstrapped the bra and slipped it off one arm. Asger took a step closer, so close that he could touch her if he reached out. Two light-red nipples stared at him. They were large in relation to the small, pointy breasts.

Asger lifted his right arm. His hand trembled. At the same second that Aya's hand slid from her left breast to the right, he reached out for the soft roundness. Hesitated with his fingertips half an inch from her breast. Small, blond hairs sparkled on her skin. He pulled his hand back.

Finished with her breasts, Aya smeared lotion on her belly, her motions faster now, and she frowned a little. She finished quickly, screwed the lid on the cream and set it on the stack of books. Then she crawled under the covers, fumbled for something on the nightstand. Someone laughed, Asger gave a start. A laugh track. Aya switched off the nightlight. A small glow flickered over the bedroom. Asger turned towards the TV. *Two and a Half Men* was on, and a timer on the menu bar was counting down from thirty minutes.

Aya turned down the sound until it was just a low murmur. Her face was hidden by the blanket.

Asger stood frozen. His erection drooped and left behind a cold, wet spot in his groin. He should leave. She was so vulnerable . . . so exposed. All her defenses were down; he was surely the only one who knew about her bathroom ritual. He couldn't get any closer to her than that.

Except when she slept. He remained standing there.

Aya shifted position several times.

Asger's shoulders began to hurt from standing in the same position.

After the first commercial break, Aya lay there more calmly. When the laugh track died away now and then, he listened for her breathing. It sounded heavy and regular.

Asger dared a couple more steps along the bed, so that he could see her face.

She lay on her side, one arm over the edge of the bed. Her mouth was open halfway. Her lips pouted and gave her a silly-sweet expression. Then her arm jerked, causing her nails to scratch against the nightstand. Asger slipped over to the other side of the bed, and with infinite care he sat down on the edge. Leaned back at an angle, until his upper body was lying down. Then he lifted his legs into the bed as well. With clenched teeth – the mattress yielded – he turned towards her.

And Aya turned too! As if she had been waiting for him. As if she instinctively accepted his presence. Her breath smelled of toothpaste, mixed with something sour.

Asger pulled her blanket back a little and stuck one hand in. The back of his hand brushed one of her breasts as he sought Aya's hand – his member swelled again – then he found what he was after and let his index and middle fingers slide into her half-open hand.

Then he lay there for a long time.

Enjoying the closeness.

The bedclothes smelled musty and needed to be changed. But that didn't matter. It smelled of her.

The light from the TV flowed over them in waves. And then the most fantastic thing happened: Aya squeezed his fingers. Tears welled in his eyes.

He could fall asleep here, wake up beside her. Watch over her. Be her muse. Whisper to her while she slept. She would come to know him unconsciously and miss him when he wasn't near.

Aya twitched and gripped his fingers harder. Her eyes rolled around beneath her eyelids. She was whimpering.

Asger stroked her bangs. Was he responsible for her nightmare? That creaking floorboard could have activated her subconscious, which was now drawing its own conclusions as to the cause behind the sound. People were impressionable just before going to sleep. Or maybe she sensed him, maybe his presence needed getting used to?

Aya's whole body suddenly tensed; she gripped his fingers even harder. And rolled on to her back. The blanket rose in a bulge at her crotch. Her other hand? Asger pulled his fingers out of Aya's grasp so he could lift the blanket. Suddenly the bulge changed to an elongated shape and slithered its way towards Aya's face. What was she doing?

The edge of the blanket quivered. Asger leapt out onto the floor as the gleaming, bald back of a head squeezed out onto Aya's chest. The blanket slid all the way off her.

The creature crawled up between Aya's breasts. It was about the size of a small child, skinny, nothing but skin and bones. It had arms, but no legs; instead there was a long fleshy stump, which gradually grew narrower until it disappeared into Aya's crotch or anus, Asger couldn't see which, because of her panties.

The creature grabbed Aya's throat, rocked back and forth in slow movements, as though it were copulating with her. It bent its face all the way down to hers and licked up her tears. Then it lifted its head with a jerk. Held it at an angle. Turned towards Asger.

Only the elongated, dangling breasts revealed that it was a female, for its face had no eyes, no nose, only a mouth. A thick tongue played obscenely in the air. And the creature saw him, sensed he was there, smiled at him.

A gurgling noise forced its way out of Asger, and he backed away, leaned against the wall. Vomit burned in his throat and splashed out onto the floor. Some of it got stuck, pressing against his windpipe. He gasped, couldn't get enough air. He fell on all fours and tried to force out more vomit, but produced only dry, barking noises. A dark heaviness pressed against the backs of his eyes. And finally the obstruction in his throat broke free.

The vomit felt firm and slid out slowly. Hung out of him. If he could have pushed sound past the obstruction, he would have screamed when he saw what was dangling from his mouth.

A tapeworm – white and articulated and slimy – was his first impression, but then he glimpsed fingers at the end.

With a retching sound, more of it slid free from his throat and mouth. Asger's jaws gaped, his tendons creaked. The pressure in his throat became unbearable; in a few seconds something would break. Asger grabbed the cold, flabby arm and pulled, tugged, ripped, out, away.

A hard and round shape scraped against his front teeth and rammed against the floor with a crash. Asger let out a half-stifled, gurgling shriek and leapt to his feet.

An ape-like creature, pale and hairless, lay in a fetal position on the floor. It was trying to get up, but its neck was so thin that it couldn't lift its head.

Asger ran – sensed out of the corner of his eye that Aya's . . . monster, incubus, parasite, leech . . . whatever it was, was riding her again, still with its face turned towards him. He fled the bedroom, out into the hall. He ran down the steps, out onto the sidewalk, across the street.

The asphalt felt soft, rocking. He got up on the opposite sidewalk, made it a couple of steps down the street before his legs gave way beneath him. He propped himself up against a wall. Threw up. This time it was just digested food that hit the cobblestones.

There was no doubt, no sense that he was going out of his mind, no belief that he was hallucinating or in a nightmare fugue.

He wasn't invisible, he was . . . Well, he *was*, but invisible to the eyes of others, because he had stepped into another world. Ashbery's spell had brought him to another world. The invisible world that Cotton Mather had written about. The world where spirits lived, and which some people – clairvoyants and madmen – claimed to perceive.

A front door slammed shut. Asger looked up. There was the clatter of steps. A shape was coming towards him. It was impossible to make out details; the light from the streetlamps didn't reach the street but hung hazily around the lamps.

The shape came nearer, looking back every two or three steps.

Fragments of words floated ahead of it.

'. . . you know . . . walk alone . . .'

The shape became a woman with curly hair and a cell phone pressed to her ear. 'I'm almost there, can you stay on the line until I've locked myself in the car?' The woman passed by Asger.

He hurried in the opposite direction, towards his apartment, had already grabbed the keys in his pocket. Stopped when he stepped on something. It moved underneath his foot. Long and thin. At first he thought it was a hose or a cable, but the material was too soft, could only be organic, an intestine or . . . Asger turned back towards the woman. The snake seemed about to disappear under her coattail. Metallic creaking. Asger stepped off the snake.

Something short was coming closer in a gliding movement accompanied by a metallic whine. A boy on a three-wheeled cycle. He was upright on the seat with his head bent over the handlebars and his body tensed with the exertion of pushing the sluggish pedals around. The boy was naked. The snake Asger had stepped on was attached to his body at the navel. It tightened to a taut line when the boy didn't press hard enough on the pedals; at other times it hung limply. Asger pressed his back against the wall.

*Creak.*

*Creak.*

The boy turned his head when he was right next to Asger. No face, just a round hole that contracted and expanded like a convulsing sphincter. Asger forced himself to look at the obscured streetlight and managed to restrain himself from crying out or screaming or losing his mind. The boy cycled past him.

Slowly both the woman and the boy disappeared into the darkness, and the metallic whine died away.

Asger pulled himself away from the wall and ran on stiff, sluggish legs towards his front door. He had to find a formula in the book, he had to find a way out of this place, the boy, Aya's incubus, his own ape-like creature, which reminded him of something . . .

Le Fanu's story 'Green Tea'.

Dr. Hesselius, the paranormal expert, had taken the case of a priest who was haunted by an ape-like demon because his inner eye – which could perceive the supernatural – had been opened by his drinking green tea. But Hesselius hadn't been able to help. The priest couldn't stand being persecuted by the creature and committed suicide by slitting his wrists with his straight razor.

Asger reached the entrance door, opened it, and ran up the stairs. In his closing commentary to the case, Dr. Hesselius had cited the philosopher Swedenborg, who argued that 'Every person is followed by at least two evil spirits', and they manifested themselves through 'images' in the form of the being – called the *fera* – that represented their nature. The feras' world was in the midst of the human one, and behind it, the invisible world.

When he finally reached his apartment, he checked the door handle three or four times to make sure it was locked before continuing his reading of *The Wonders of the Invisible World* on the windowsill. He paged through it, forcing himself to read at a slow pace, skimmed formulas for extending life, curses, love spells – if a woman baked bread and moistened the dough with her sweat and the juices from her lap, according to Ashbery she could gain power over whomever she chose.

Not a word about lifting an invisibility spell.

Why hadn't he checked first?

Because you couldn't turn invisible!

Asger leafed through it again, ran his eyes down a spell dealing with how to change a fetus into a parasite that sucked the life out of its mother ... *and that Child will be a veritale Tiger in the Wombe.*

The creatures. Feras. Did they manifest in the human world as mental illness, but in the invisible world as spirits or demons?

The shrill howl brought Asger to himself. The door buzzer. He craned his neck to look down in the street. Impossible from his vantage point. He wasn't expecting anyone; his only visitor the past few years had been his father. And no one at all recently.

A weaker ringing. From the buzzer belonging to the apartment below his. Asger kept paging through the book. He looked up when he heard the entrance door slam. Listened intently for steps on the stairs. Didn't hear any. He slipped out to the hall and put his ear to the door.

A slight creak. A weak, whispering sound like bare feet on stairs. Fast. Running. Asger looked out the peephole.

A click. The light was shining on the landing. The lacquered handrails gleamed. A hand grabbed the banister, pale and flabby like cooked pasta. The creature swung itself up on the landing. There was definitely something primate-like about it, not just its movements but also its thin arms, too long for that underdeveloped body. The creature's eyes were white like the rest of it, like the eyes on Roman statues.

Asger stepped back from the peephole as the creature – the fera – looked up. It felt as though it had made eye contact. But surely it couldn't see that he was in there? How had it found him?

If it had lived inside him, then it knew everything he knew.

The door handle was pressed down. Pulled up with a click. Asger held his breath. Backed away silently.

The letter slot clapped. And then the hand slid through it. The back of its hand was elongated, like a chimpanzee's, human-like fingers, but far too wrinkled. The forearm. The elbow. The arm waved back and forth like a snake about to strike. To the right, left, down – the hand brushed the floor – up. It groped at the inner side of the door. Then moved towards the lock.

Asger darted for the book, ran back to the entryway – heard the fingers fumbling with the lock – continued into the kitchen and rushed down the back stairs. He knocked over a couple of bottles outside a door two floors down, jumped over them, reached the bottom, threw the back door open and ran across the yard, through the gate and out to the street.

He turned at the first corner, continued towards Gothersgade. There were only a few cars on the road – their headlights as weak as all the other light sources. The asphalt was as black as swampwater at nighttime. His hands felt clammy with sweat and were no doubt damaging the leather binding of *The Wonders of the Invisible World*, but he didn't care now. He looked over his shoulder. The sidewalk was empty behind him.

Asger caught up to a middle-aged couple, both dressed in beige trenchcoats, the woman with matching, high-laced boots. And something on her back, a hump, but it was moving. Asger looked away and thought of another text about an ape-like, parasitic being. An English writer ... Chetwynd-Hayes? *Unnatural Entities*, or was that a work cited in the story about the creature, which dug under the skin of a woman's back and made her hunchbacked? It had a Latin name, Asger couldn't remember it, but its name among everyday people was the silly, fairly undisturbing *Jumpity-Jim*. The description had said: *looking like a cross between a deformed monkey and a monstrous spider and of low intelligence.*

Jumpity-Jim was a spirit from the lower plane and needed life essence and warm blood. If it sensed an opening in a potential host, it leapt on their back, dug into their skin and became as integrated a part of the unfortunate victim as his or her leg.

He had been host to a creature not unlike a Jumpity-Jim.

*Removing the lie shall reveal a demon in disguise.* King James Bible?

How long had he lived with it? Always? Since childhood? When had he become what he was?

A stitch in his side gnawed at him, too intense for him to maintain his tempo. Asger slowed down, he was almost to Kongens Nytorv.

He stopped when he reached the square. Bent over with his hands on his knees. Gasped for breath.

When he had caught his breath again, he continued to the right. The subway station was that way. He could be at the airport in no time and put thousands of miles between himself and the fera; the boarding pass was still in his inner pocket from the trip to Concord, where he had found that damned book. Then he remembered that he was invisible, they wouldn't need to see his boarding pass. He could sneak on board.

He reached the staircase leading down to the subway. The steps felt slippery, despite the salt crunching beneath his soles. On the escalator he passed a couple of people standing to the left.

Finally reaching the bottom, he saw on the noticeboard

that the train would arrive in one minute. The only other people waiting were an elderly couple. Asger kept his distance from them, even if neither of them appeared to have a fera spliced to them. How many people had a fera? Not everyone, the hostess at Yammi Sushi hadn't had one . . . as far as he'd been able to see.

The glass platform doors, which prevented suicidal people from throwing themselves in front of the train, reflected the station hall. Steel and glass and gray stone. Smooth. Cold. Architecture like an enormous mausoleum . . . like a hall in the icy Nordic underworld, where the disfigured goddess Hel ruled over the spirits of the dead. Asger looked at the grayish version of himself in the glass of the platform doors. His eyes and mouth were black holes in the sunken face. For a moment he doubted. Was he the reflection, or the one casting it? Which side of the mirror was he on?

Asger looked up the escalator. No one on the steps. The underside of the next landing of the escalator blocked his view of the floor above.

The subway train rolled in. The glass doors opened at the same time as the train's. He rushed in.

The train was deserted. He chose a seat in the middle of the car and sat down. The doors slid shut.

The U.S.? The Far East? South America? Asger laid *The Wonders of the Invisible World* on the seat next to his, on top of a folded newspaper. His legs hurt, and his toes ached from running in leather shoes. At the far end of his field of vision he glimpsed movement.

The fera was scrabbling down the escalator steps at a crazy speed. Asger got up, ran five or six steps. Stopped. There were doors everywhere, it could choose any one of them.

He heard the thump when the fera leapt from the railing and landed on the stone floor. It disappeared from sight under the windows.

He had hoped that it had only found him in the apartment because it was familiar with the place. That it was able to find him here meant that they were bound to one another. However far away he fled, he would be found.

The seats blocked his view of the doors. The world had changed. He had lived in unconsciousness. He knew the truth now.

Asger sat down on a seat.

How awful had it been to be possessed? He hadn't even suspected it, hadn't seriously suffered from it, life had been bearable.

He heard the doors slide open.

In his invisible form he had gotten access to Aya, an access he never would have had when visible. There was no such thing as complete intimacy. People were only themselves when they thought they were alone. The things he would experience!

The fera leapt into the aisle. It banged its fists against the floor and hopped manically up and down in uncontrollable joy. Asger looked into its white eyes and opened his mouth. Opened as wide as he could.

*Translated from the Danish by James D. Jenkins*

# About the Authors

VIOLA CADRUVI sometimes works as a teacher, sometimes as a research assistant in Romance Literature and Culture at the University of Zurich, sometimes as a columnist or on her dissertation – but almost always she writes. She writes short stories and novels, columns, anecdotes, funny, sad and scary, for herself and for others. In 2014 she won the Premi Term Bel at the Rhaeto-Romanic Literature Days for her short story 'La dunna da Benedetg Albin', and in 2018 the Audience Award for 'La curridra'. Her first book, *La feglia dal fraissen*, was published in 2020.

ROBERTO CAUSO is the author of more than 90 stories published in eleven countries in addition to his native Brazil and is also the author of five novels, two of them dark fantasy works: *Anjo de Dor* (2009) and *Mistério de Deus* (2017). His first story collection, *A Dança das Sombras*, published in Portugal in 1999, gathers stories of horror, contemporary fantasy, and borderline science fiction. Causo has been the Brazilian correspondent for *Locus Magazine* since 1987. He was born in 1965 and lives in São Paulo with his wife and one son, both also speculative fiction authors. (Photo credit: Beatriz Takeshita)

BORA CHUNG is a writer of science fiction and generally unrealistic stories. Chung currently teaches Russian language and literature at Yonsei University in Seoul, South Korea and translates modern literary works from Russian and Polish into Korean. She has published three novels and three books of collected short stories in Korean.

DARE SEGUN FALOWO is a writer of the Nigerian Weird. Their work draws on cinema, pulp fiction, and the surreal. Dare is queer and neurodivergent. Their work is published in *The Magazine of Fantasy & Science Fiction*, *The Dark Magazine* and others. Their novella, 'Convergence in Chorus Architecture', which appeared in *Dominion: An Anthology of Speculative Fiction from Africa and the African Diaspora*, was longlisted for the 2020 BSFA for Short Fiction. They haunt Ibadan, Nigeria where they are learning to express more of their truth in words, watercolor and Spirit.

MÉLANIE FAZI has gained recognition since her first publication in 2000, primarily for her fantastic short stories, which have long been her favorite format. She has published three collections (*Serpentine*, *Notre-Dame-aux-Écailles*, *Le Jardin des silences*), two novels (*Trois pépins du fruit des morts*, *Arlis des forains*) and more recently two autobiographical works, one of which is about the strangeness of discovering one's autism in adulthood, echoing the themes dealt with in her fictional texts. She also has a parallel career as a translator (including Brandon Sanderson, Lisa Tuttle, and Graham Joyce). Several of her short stories have been translated into English, in *The World's Best Fantasy and Horror*, *The Magazine of Fantasy & Science Fiction* and *World Literature Today*. (Photo credit: Vinciane Lebrun)

STEPHAN FRIEDMAN was born in 1976 in the gloomy and enigmatic Ural Mountain region, where he was raised on eerie folktales and stories about his grandfather, a renowned anarchist who perished in the Russian Revolution. When he was 18, he moved to Israel, where he resides with his wife, two children, and three cats. For years, Stephan has been productive as a musician on the Tel Aviv underground scene, composing and performing in the industrial, darkwave, and dark folk genres. He is a connoisseur of bizarre horror movies and bourbon whiskey. His short stories have appeared in several anthologies. In 2019, his debut collection of short stories and poems, *Serpentine Supplications*, was published by Mount Abraxas Press.

ANA MARÍA FUSTER LAVÍN was born in San Juan, Puerto Rico in 1967. A graduate of the Humanities Department at the University of Puerto Rico–Río Piedras, she is a writer, publisher, editor of scholarly texts, and newspaper columnist, and she has also been a teacher of Spanish and music. She has received a number of awards for her essays, stories, flash fiction, and poetry. Her YouTube book channel is Mariposas Negras and her blog is http://bocetosdeselene.blogspot.com/. Her work has been published in various magazines and anthologies in Puerto Rico and internationally, with translations to French, Portuguese, Italian, and English.

ANTON GRASSO was born in Paola, Malta in 1952. His first book, *Iljieli Bla Qamar* (*Moonless Nights*), which is also the earliest volume of horror stories in Maltese, was published in 1974 and was reissued in 1997. Grasso's works include novels, translations, essays, poems, studies, twenty-seven volumes of short stories, and an autobiography. His book *Enigma,* a study of the paranormal (published in 1987 and twice in 1994), was the basis of a successful television series. Grasso's favorite genre is horror, a genre in which he has written over one thousand stories that have proven extremely popular with Maltese readers and radio listeners. Starting in 1978, he read his horror stories on Maltese national radio on a program that ran for over twenty years; he has also read his stories on Maltese television. Grasso's championing of the horror story has kindled a particular interest and following for the genre in Malta, and he remains the best-known horror writer in Malta.

WOJCIECH GUNIA (b. 1983) is a Polish writer and translator considered to be one of the most important and influential contemporary horror/weird fiction writers in Poland. His debut collection, *Powrót* (*The Return*), was published in 2014. His second book, the novel *Nie ma wędrowca* (*There Is No Wanderer,* 2016), won the Stefan Grabiński Award for best Polish horror book of 2016. His third book, *Miasto i rzeka* (*The Town and the River*), was released in 2018. Gunia's fourth book, an enormous omnibus *Dom wszystkich snów* (*The House*

*of All Dreams*), released in 2020, was nominated for several literary awards in Poland. His latest book, *Złe wszechświaty (Evil Universes)* was published in 2021. As a translator, he mainly translates into Polish the works of Thomas Ligotti, whom he considers as one of his literary masters, next to Bruno Schulz, Franz Kafka, and Stanisław Lem.

INDREK HARGLA is the best-known Estonian science fiction and crime author. He has won 21 Estonian SF awards, several other Estonian mainstream literary awards, and he has received the Honorary Award from the Finnish Society of Crime Fiction. While he mostly writes science fiction, he is best known domestically and internationally as a writer of medieval crime novels. The books from the ongoing series featuring 15th-century apothecary Melchior of Tallinn have been translated into into French, Finnish, Hungarian, Latvian, English, and German. The books are now being made into movies. He has also written stage plays and TV series, one of which, the political thriller *Alpine House*, has aired in several European countries.

KONSTANTINOS KELLIS is a best-selling horror author from Greece. He has published three novels and a short story collection in his home country, while several of his short stories have been translated to English and have appeared in international dark fiction magazines and anthologies. He lives in Sweden with his wife and their twin boys.

LUCIANO LAMBERTI has a degree in modern literature from the Universidad Nacional de Córdoba (Argentina). He has published the story collections *El asesino de chanchos (The Pig Killer)* and *El loro que podía adivinar el futuro (The Parrot Who Could Predict the Future)*, the novels *Los campos magnéticos (The Magnetic Fields)* and *La maestra rural (The Schoolteacher)*, and the poetry collection *San Francisco*. He currently lives in Buenos Aires, where he holds creative writing workshops.

JAYAPRAKASH SATYAMURTHY is a writer and musician who lives in Bangalore, India. His publications include the chapbook *Weird Tales of a Bangalorean*, the novella *Strength of Water*, and the poetry collection *Broken Cup*. He's on Twitter: @flightofsand. (Photo credit: Vivek Mathew)

STEINAR BRAGI (b. 1975), of Reykjavík, Iceland, is the author of several books of poetry and prose. Debuting as a 23-year-old with the critically acclaimed poetry collection *Black Hole* (1998), he later turned to prose with the novel *Women*, a claustrophobic abstraction of the price of being a woman under the male-driven capitalist society and misogynistic power structures that threaten to break the nation's economy. *Women* was later nominated for the Nordic Council Literature Prize. In the modern Icelandic saga *The Ice Lands*, Steinar's international breakthrough, Iceland's economic demise is revisited, with four victims of the financial crisis hurdling towards an unthinkable end during a nightmarish trip across the nation's volcanic hinterlands. A nascent master of contemporary horror, Steinar illuminates the darkest corners of our collective psyche with Lovecraftian detail while in the vein of Stephen King.

BRAULIO TAVARES (b. 1950) is a writer, songwriter and translator, based in Rio de Janeiro. He won a science fiction award in Portugal in 1989, graduated from Clarion Workshop in 1991, and has been an active figure in the SF/F/H Brazilian fandom in the last decades. He has published two mainstream novels, five collections of short stories, and organized many anthologies of the fantastic. He translated books by Tim Powers, Jeff VanderMeer, Ted Chiang, Connie Willis, Raymond Chandler, Philip K. Dick, Dean R. Koontz, F. Paul Wilson and many others. His latest publications in Brazil are *Fanfic* (a collection of short stories, 2019) and *Crimes Impossíveis* (*Impossible Crimes*, an anthology of classic locked-room mysteries, 2021).

YAVOR TSANEV is a Bulgarian writer and publisher. He lives in the city of Ruse and writes science fiction, fantasy, horror, magic realism, contemporary short stories and children's books. He is editor-in-chief and publisher of *Dracus* magazine. He has organized several national literary competitions in Bulgaria. Tsanev has won a number of Bulgarian national literary awards and was nominated for both Best Author and Best Promoter in the European Science Fiction Society (ESFS) Hall of Fame Awards during the 39th Eurocon, 2017, in Dortmund, Germany.

YASUMI TSUHARA was born in Hiroshima in 1964. He began publishing *shōjo shōsetsu* (girls' fiction) in 1989. In 1997, he made his debut in the horror genre with the acclaimed novel *Yōto*. Since then, he has worked in multiple genres, including horror, fantasy, and mystery. His 2011 story collection *11* won the second Twitter Literary Award. In 2014, the manga adaptation of his story 'Goshiki no fune' won the Bureau for Cultural Affairs' Media Arts Festival Grand Prize. His most recent book is the best-selling novel *Hikky Hikky Shake* (2019). His work has been translated into several languages, including Chinese, English, Italian, and Korean.

GARY VICTOR (b. 1958) was born in Port-au-Prince, Haiti, where he lives today. He is a novelist, playwright, and journalist, and his work has won a number of literary awards. His works have been published in France, Canada, Haiti, and other countries. (Photo credit: Pedro Ruiz)

TEDDY VORK (b. 1977) is a Danish writer of horror fiction. His debut collection *Hvor skyggen falder* (*Where Shadows Fall*) was published in 2008. He has since published six other works, most notably the short story collection *Sprækker* (*Cracks*) and *Mulm* (*Penumbra*). Both books won the Danish Best Horror Work of the Year Award, in 2014 and

2020 respectively. He has an MA in English, Comparative Literature and Creative Writing and makes a living teaching Danish and English to nursing students. He lives in Esbjerg, a town on the west coast of Denmark, with his son August. Vork received the mail notifying him of his short story's acceptance to this anthology on his birthday, and he considers this one of the best birthday gifts ever, and a great honor. He grew up reading American and English paperbacks of horror and suspense which became a formative love affair not just with the genre but also the English language. To be published in English is a dream come true.

VAL VOTRIN is a Belgian speculative fiction writer writing in Russian and English. He was born in 1974 in Tashkent, Soviet Union, where he graduated from Tashkent State University. In 2000, he moved to Belgium, where he received a master's degree in Human Ecology and a Ph.D. in Environmental Science from Free University of Brussels. He was a finalist for the Andrei Bely Prize, the oldest independent literary prize in Russia, for his 2009 novel *The Last Magog*. His 2012 novel, *The Speech Therapist*, was nominated for several main literary awards, including the Russian Booker Prize. His story 'Alkonost' in English translation was included in the anthology *21: Russian Short Prose from an Odd Century* (Academic Studies Press), and another translated story, 'Compiler of Bestiaries', is forthcoming in 2022 in the anthology *Investigation of Horror: 200 Years of Scary Russian Fiction* from Columbia University Press. His English prose has appeared in *The Quail Bell Magazine*, *Trafika Europe* and *Eunoia Review*. He currently lives in Amsterdam.

ZHANG YUERAN (b. 1982) is one of China's most influential young writers. Her books have been translated into English, French, Dutch, and Korean. The French translation of her novel *Cocoon* won the Best Asian Novel of the Prix Transfuge 2019 in France. She has been the chief editor of *Newriting* since 2008, and teaches literature and creative writing at Renmin University.

CPSIA information can be obtained
at www.ICGtesting.com
Printed in the USA
LVHW091332030222
709357LV00001BA/1

9 781954 321076